Bone

....

Idle

Books by Susannah Stacey

Goodbye, Nanny Gray
A Knife at the Opera
Body of Opinion
Grave Responsibility
The Late Lady
Bone Idle

Published by POCKET BOOKS

Bone
....
Idle

Susannah Stacey

POCKET BOOKS
New York   London   Toronto   Sydney   Tokyo   Singapore

This book is a work of fiction. Names, characters (except Nicholas Buchanan), places, and incidents are products of the author's imagination or are used fictitiously. Any resemblance to actual events or locales or persons, living or dead, is entirely coincidental.

POCKET BOOKS, a division of Simon & Schuster Inc.
1230 Avenue of the Americas, New York, NY 10020

Copyright © 1993 by Jill Staynes and Margaret Storey

Originally published in Great Britain in 1993 by Random House UK

Library of Congress Cataloging-in-Publication Data

Stacey, Susannah.
    Bone idle / Susannah Stacey.
        p.   cm.
    ISBN 0-671-73531-4
    I. Title.
    PR6069.T177B66   1995
    823'.914—dc20   94-48227
                                                                   CIP

First Pocket Books hardcover printing September 1995

10 9 8 7 6 5 4 3 2 1

To David Brown,
who was kind enough
to lend his countenance

Bone

· · · · · · · · · · · · · · · · · · ·

Idle

Chapter

. . . .

1

THEY CONTEMPLATED THE CREATURE, WHO LOOKED BACK WITH bright, intelligent eyes.

"Why did your uncle get him in the first place?"

The larger man patted his companion on the shoulder, causing him to edge back from the water. "Conservation! They're becoming rare, you know."

"Why didn't you get rid of it? I would have."

"So you would. But, you see, *I* think it's charming."

Its mouth was a little open, giving it an unwholesomely eager appearance.

"It's expecting to be fed. I suppose it's near feeding time." He picked up a plastic box from the crumbling terrazzo floor and pulled out something, which he flung into the water. A violent thresh splashed them both, but it was over at once

1

and the creature was back, hopeful, attentive, the mouth wider.

"He's expensive, naughty boy, but then decorative creatures like him, and you, always are, I find."

"You're not classing me with that thing!"

The older man smiled widely, and groped in the box again. "Oh, you're *prettier* than Dundee, I grant you, but I don't think you'd make nearly such a nice handbag."

Another lump of meat reached Dundee's jaws, which clashed and, after a short pause, parted once more in a grin that Adrian thought a fair imitation of the reptile's owner. Nothing, come think of it, was more likely to amuse Lord Roke than keeping an alligator in his swimming pool.

Robert Bone, working under the apple trees on this unexpectedly warm September day, looked up as the garden door slammed, and saw his wife advance across the garden with a tray.

"There's some post," she said, "and I've talked to Jane about half term."

He watched her approach with a warm sensation of happiness. She was in a green, heavy cotton sweater and trousers, and he was comfortably aware that she wore green more often since he had remarked that he liked it on her. She put down the tray as he moved his briefcase along the wooden table, and she sat leaning on him briefly and pinching his knee in a painful gesture of affection.

"What did Jane say?"

"Just what I said she would. I explained to her all about my new husband and she said, 'Bring Robert too.' I was instructed to warn you about Roke's jokes."

"And you told her you'd done that already." Bone reached for his mug of tea.

Grizel sat back with her coffee. Sunlight through the apple branches glinted in her short blond hair, and turned her eyes a more brilliant green. "I think Jane has quite a difficult marriage. Benet's the type of genial bully I find very tricky indeed."

"Don't worry about me." Bone began to open the envelopes on the tray. "I'm not genial."

Grizel made an indeterminate sound that might have been agreement, but he had turned to her with a rueful "Damn!" holding a leaflet.

"What?" She put her head on his shoulder to see.

"One of Buchanan's stately house tours. You remember? He's going to Pattens on that very Saturday. It's got that ceiling . . . Never mind." He turned the page.

"That's a shame. Isn't there—"

"Incredible! Look! Look there!"

She read aloud: *"Sunday morning: Roke Castle, home of Lord and Lady Roke . . ."* She raised her eyes to his. "Jane *said* a party was coming. I don't believe it. Well, you'll get to see Roke, but I'm sorry about Pattens."

"Life's little ironies."

Grizel read the page intently; she said nothing, and Bone settled to the rest of his letters with a complicated thought that in missing Buchanan's tour to go with Grizel on her promised visit, he was making up to a very small degree for all the times his job was likely to interfere with their arrangements in the future. Even this little holiday might yet be interrupted or, on his part, canceled; even though he had made all possible arrangements to see that it happened, he could only hope.

She leaned to kiss his ear, and took the tray away indoors. Bone, by not instantly phoning Nicholas Buchanan and booking for the tour, tacitly gave it up—all Buchanan's gang of regulars knew the tours were too popular to wait.

When the advent of a heavy-shouldered bunch of cumulus drove him indoors, he found Grizel ringing off from a phone call and looking preternaturally smug.

"All is arranged," she announced, and came to hug him. Bone, with alacrity and hands clutching papers, hugged her back. A folder slipped to the floor.

"What's arranged?" he asked with husbandly apprehension.

"Half term. Your nice Nicholas Buchanan says we can go with them to Pattens on Saturday, and my nice Jane says of course she doesn't mind—she says she's rather pleased to have fewer guests on the day before the tour comes, because of getting ready."

"I hope that's a joke too."

"Jane's joke."

"And—*fewer* guests? How many are there?"

"Oh, long-term house guests. Nobody important."

He kissed her.

Angela North, with the contents of her purse and wallet spread on the breakfast table before her, tried to work out the total in Australian dollars. She needed to know if she must go to the bank today. Her hostess, soignée and tall, moved about the little kitchen behind the living room, and took the coffeepot out to Angela's son, Baz, on the garden steps. He found Melissa's house dangerous, as he was big and by nature exuberant. He had taken to keeping his hands pocketed, but still made abortive efforts at large gestures. He had knocked over a pottery jar containing an extravagant sheaf of seed-scattering dried flowers; and had knocked a painting from the wall, pulling away the nail it hung on. Angela felt a profound gratitude that the Bridget Riley print which had been strobing at her behind Melissa's head every mealtime could not immediately be rehung.

"Rather a shame," Melissa said, pausing to finish her coffee and flipping a sheet of paper toward Angela. "Nicholas Buchanan's got one of his weekends at half term; I have to have the grandchildren because Emma's working, so I

4

can't go." She took her cup to the kitchen and added, "Look at it, Angie. I rather think it might interest you."

"Do you get landed with Emma's kids a lot?" Angela obediently picked up the long sheet. "You as a grandmother are quite un—"

She stopped, reading.

Melissa, coming back, smiled. *'Thought* you'd be interested. Well, my sweet, quite a coincidence, no?" She bent her dark head near Angela's fair one.

"Yes."

"Wouldn't this just be the chance to show Baz something of historic England?" Her finger touched a name among the house owners.

"An ideal chance," Angela said slowly.

"If you want to go, I'll ring Nicholas and propose you."

"Oh, I'm not sure. This might not be the way to do it. Give me time and I'll decide."

"Then you don't go. By this evening all the places will be taken. Nicholas only runs small groups."

Baz came into the kitchen, put his coffee mug carefully down, and smiled amiably from the doorway.

"So like Michelangelo's *David,"* Melissa remarked. Baz began to pose elegantly, knocked his elbow on the door jamb, and rammed his hands into his pockets. His grin widened.

"The statue in question has one hand at its side and the other at its shoulder," Angela said. "Quite safe."

"You want to bet?" Baz spoke with a stronger accent than his mother had picked up, but it was the Melbourne private school variety, lacking the hearty gutturals believed in England to be universally Australian.

"Yes," Angela said. "Yes. I think it would be a very good way for my son to become acquainted with his English heritage."

"What would, Ma?"

5

"A private tour of some country houses."

"Including a castle," Melissa put in.

"You mean I get to see dungeons? Sounds right to me. But look, how many houses? How long's this tour?"

Angela looked at his corn-colored curls brushing the lintel. "Only a weekend."

"Oh well."

Melissa said, "I'll phone Nicholas?"

"Yes," Angela said. "It's an opportunity. It seems actually providential. I think it's exactly what we need."

Baz bent to peer at her. "Something up?"

Angela raised a guileless and still pretty face. "No. Should there be?"

Joshua Lawson was making tea when he heard the flip of the letter box and the tumble of letters to the mat. He fitted a badly stained cozy, embroidered with a pair of green wool parrots, over the teapot and went to pick up the post. His basement flat had been only partly converted from the servants' quarters of a more leisurely age, and the hallway was at the far side of a vast room which had a kitchen at the end, and a bed, with a warped folding screen partly concealing its rumpled sheets, at one side of the cavernous fireplace.

He came back across the floor, shuffling the letters, his dressing-gown cord trailing obediently behind him. One of the envelopes he opened at once, with a satisfied grunt, and settling into his chair he began to read the single sheet of paper while he discarded the cozy and poured tea. The paper had, centered at the top, an oval lithograph of a small Georgian house picturesquely embowered in trees. Below this came a description of the hotel where Nicholas Buchanan had arranged to lodge his group, followed by a list of the places to be visited, in chronological order, with the names of owners. Josh put two pieces of bread in the battered

toaster that sat on the table beside a pile of papers, picked a
biro from the crammed plastic penholder, and circled two
names, putting a question mark next to one.

This, for some reason, inspired him to get up and go to
look at himself in the mirror hanging above the kitchen sink,
where, it was clear from the film of ginger hairs over last
night's dishes soaking below, he was in the habit of shaving.
A large face made truculent by a slab of chin, with a spare
waiting underneath it, met his gaze. Small pale eyes
scanned this image speculatively. He felt his scalp, where
some of the ginger hair still clung in a losing battle;
advanced the large face to the glass and, inexplicably
pleased with what he saw, grinned. Behind him the toaster
clunked, and he returned to his breakfast.

Benjamin Maitland kissed the top of his wife's head in
passing to the window seat, where he sat down to breakfast.
He had been married to Catherine for so long that he could
remember when bouffant hairstyles of the sixties meant a
kiss on the top was considered a crushing assault rather than
a caress. She smiled at him now without attempting to
rearrange the pretty gray waves so saluted, and indicated
one of the letters by his plate.

"Don't miss that one, dearest. Nicholas Buchanan. Lucky
we didn't go away. I hope it's at a time when you can make
it." She poured the coffee, and handed his cup across. On
the window seat beside Benjamin, a large orange cat, paws
tucked under its chest, throbbed quietly in approval of the
morning sunshine. The sheet of paper with an oval lithograph shook in Benjamin's hand as he read it, and was put
down abruptly. Catherine glanced up from her croissant.

"What's wrong, darling? Have you seen them already?"

"No." Benjamin took a croissant from its napkined cradle
in the basket, and left it to cool on his plate while he drank
coffee. The faint engine of the cat's purr changed gear and

then sank into silence. "No. I don't think I shall have the time."

"When is it?" She reversed the paper and studied it. "Surely you said you had nothing till the middle of November? This is only the last week in October. And look, there are some lovely places to see: Pattens on the Saturday, Roke Castle on Sunday morning. Remember that *Country Life* article about Roke? It must be an amazing place, and this is the only way we'd have a chance to see it." She pushed the paper back at him. "Go on. You need a break, you've been working so hard. And your favorite thing, looking at houses; even ones you haven't designed yourself."

Benjamin put down his coffee cup and seemed to come to a decision. His thin, ascetic face took on a determination that contradicted the narrow chin, the melancholy of the brown eyes.

"Very well, we'll go. I'll make the time. You'd better arrange with Anna fairly soon about taking Wilbur for the long weekend. He won't like it." He extended a finger to tickle Wilbur under the jaw. Wilbur, innocent of this planned treachery, started up the engine again.

Chapter

·····················

2

FINALLY, EVERYTHING WAS SETTLED. GRIZEL HAD EVEN REMEM-
bered to give her brother the Roke Castle phone number, as
he was expecting to become a father at any moment, and
now she, who had the Friday afternoon free as part of half
term, brusquely stacked all the biology folders to be marked
into a cupboard and crammed the door shut as they began
to fall out. Charlotte, who had said her passionate farewells
to Ziggy and The Bruce the day before when they were
taken to the cattery, was noticeably more philosophical
when it came to saying goodbye to her father and stepmother.

"Don't forget one of those folders you haven't marked is
mine, will you? I'm expecting an A."

"That would look far too like favoritism. I've already
decided on a B minus."

Charlotte gave an indignant yelp. "You give minus for lack of effort!"

"You forget I watched you do your homework listening to The Cure."

" 'Hand in hand is the only way to land . . .' There's you two going off on honeymoon and I'll be shopping in supermarkets in French and trying to work out francs and being bullied by Mrs. Garland and Madame Lefeuvre. I do think it's unfair. Don't expect me to come back speaking perfect Frog."

"I know you too well," Bone said. He was helping Grizel into her coat, and she was failing to get her arm into the sleeve. Charlotte hugged the muddle of Grizel half in the coat and part of her father behind that.

"Have a lovely time, both of you."

Winterford was reached in the golden late afternoon, an October sun gilding the great beeches, now more rose yellow than green, at the top of the wide main street. Few people were about; the summer tourists had gone. Bone drove slowly up the street, past the market cross where two children sat kicking their heels on a bench and sucking lollies, past Georgian houses, some with shops on the ground floor, and on up the steeper part with railed-off grass on either side, to a pair of lichened stone gateposts that bore haughty but weatherworn eagles. The wrought iron gates were open, showing a long graveled drive winding out of sight under trees.

"Doesn't it look romantic?"

"You mean we'll find Heathcliff waiting?"

"More like Bluebeard, if you can believe Jane. I've met *her* often enough since she married, but never happened to meet *him*. We've met in town mostly, and she's stayed in Adlingsden with me. I'm not sure I'm looking forward to it; she's made him seem a bit daunting somehow."

"Why did she marry him?"

"He's terribly amusing, she said. Oh look, a blasted oak. I mean, it really is one."

Bone observed the twisted skeleton tree. "It's quite a handsome object in an eerie way . . . Amusing? Bluebeard's idea of a joke was to hang his wives up by their hair, I seem to remember."

"Jane can look after herself. Her hair is *very* short. Oh look!"

As they crested a small rise, the battlements of a Gothic castle were before them, glowing in the evening sun as though radiating light themselves. One end of the castle seemed genuinely old, and a theatrical drape of ivy fell from one turret toward the ground; the rest of the façade's wide extent was eighteenth century, perfectly melded with the original part. A slightly raised paved terrace went all along the front, its balustrading interrupted where a few shallow steps led up to the porch. Two people stood in the shadows of the porch, arms entwined, and one broke free to run toward them as the car stopped.

"Grizel, how lovely to see you! Benet said, 'I can hear a car,' and he's simply psychic about things like that, so we came out; and here you actually are."

Grizel was out of the car by this time, enfolded in an embrace. Bone had an impression of the large man in the porch rocking on his heels and grinning widely while the greeting, and Grizel's introducing Bone to Jane, went on, as though he watched from the wings and waited for the moment to make his entrance. This he now chose to do, and thin dark Jane turned to put a hand on his arm as he came forward.

"And here's Benet. He's been longing to meet you both."

There were too many teeth in Roke's smile to suggest benevolence, and Bone would have substituted "inquisitive" for "longing," but he did seem pleased to see them and made welcoming noises in an almost absentminded way. His hand was broad and warm, his grip confident without being fierce as Bone had half expected from such an overwhelming presence. He was surprised that Roke's hair, although still thick, was gray, and he appeared to be perhaps ten years older than Jane, with deep lines round eyes and mouth as though the jokes he was said to enjoy had taken their physical toll. Bone wondered what they had done to those on whom the jokes had been played.

"How *nice!* You married a policeman, and Jane tells me he specializes in murder. We'll have to see what we can do." The voice had a double helping of charm that failed to disguise the harshness. Lord Roke took Grizel's arm and, putting his free arm, heavy as a bear's, over Bone's shoulder, ushered them into his castle.

Drinks before dinner provided the opportunity to meet Roke's eldest son and his fiancée, and two more residents. Roke, the son and heir, and the fiancée were already in the comfortable formal drawing room when Bone and Grizel came down. Guy was about nineteen, and ready to display his boredom with social occasions, especially those involving his mother's friends. Bone, however, noticed the boy's eyes widen at the sight of Grizel in satin—black trousers, bronze jacket—and one could see, in the person of the fiancée, that he appreciated good looks: her dark hair was braided into a thick plait twined with gold ribbon; she had ivory skin and lively dark eyes; earrings of elaborate delicacy in gold wire with transparent green stones brushed her shoulders; she wore a skirt of orange and fuchsia sari silk glinting with gold thread, and a rib-skimming short bodice of sequined brocade. This exoticism went with the name of Keziah Barclay-Mayhew, and county vowel sounds. She had none of Guy's awkwardness, but studied Bone and Grizel from her armchair with alert interest. Guy put a tumbler of orange juice into her hand, and brought himself to ask what the guests would like to drink. Before they could reply, the soft explosion of a cork, from the sideboard where the drinks stood, announced that their host had already decided.

"Champagne, everyone." More a genial command than invitation. Roke had dexterously spilt none and was now offering Grizel a brimming flute, a long pale green glass that Bone was sure had first been touched to a lip in the seventeenth century. "We celebrate. My wife's dearest friend in girlhood and she hasn't seen you in *aeons* she tells me"—Roke's tone seemed to imply that Jane might well be deceiving him—"nor have you visited us; all the fault of your last husband, I understand. So glad you got rid of him and acquired this one; he looks *such a nice chap*."

Bone, taking the offered glass, was aware that he was being laughed at; he assumed a pleasant smile. Then the door opened and the man who came in collected everyone's attention.

It was difficult to tell how young he was. He looked perhaps twenty-five; Bone suspected he was older. The effect was of some Dorian Gray, imperishably beautiful. He remembered a letter of Oscar Wilde's, read out in the trial scene in the film on TV, apostrophizing rose-leaf lips and silver-gilt hair. This young man had both, by what means Bone could not say; and, in addition, a tip-tilted nose, petulant mouth, and an impatient frown, as though Life was never quick enough at producing what he required. He surveyed them as if he had opened the door on a zoo, and not a salubrious zoo at that.

"Adrian! Come and be introduced, my dear boy. This is Adrian Nash, our expert on hedonism. He has an honors degree in Nothing, and does it better than anyone I know." Bone, remembering the film, recognized the style. "This is

Jane's friend delicious Grizel, and her husband, Robert Bone, who knows more about sudden death than you do about sleeping late. Champagne?"

Adrian Nash almost visibly assembled his charm as he advanced to shake hands; it was as if he had donned a magic cloak. The rose-leaf lips smiled, the silver-gilt hair was tossed from his brow.

He took a glass from Roke. "Health and all that." He sipped, wrinkling the frivolous nose, and eyed Bone. "Sudden death? You a crime novelist?"

"A policeman, Adrian. He's a policeman. So don't do anything too naughty in front of him if you don't want to leave in a *van*." Roke's emphasized words were drawn out a little, as if they amused him. Another champagne cork, less skillfully drawn, scored a shot against one of the ceiling bosses.

"A policeman." Keziah Barclay-Mayhew's tone had an underlying hint of the word "pig," suppressed in the interests of politeness. Bone had a vision of her, in tee shirt and jeans, waving a placard and expecting to be painfully arrested. He wondered if she ever had been. Miss Muffet, on realizing the spider was a tarantula, could not have registered dislike more plainly, but a Barclay-Mayhew was not to be frightened away.

"Keziah's saved more whales than you've caught murderers, Superintendent." Roke confirmed Bone's guess, and came to throw his bulk on the sofa beside Grizel, drinking his wine deeply and viewing his guests with hearty enjoyment. "But the rate of clear-up for murders is *far* better than that for burglary, isn't it?"

The tone of malice was explained by Guy. "Father's never forgiven the fuzz for not collaring the blokes who lifted his jade collection all of ten years ago." He was perched sideways on the arm of Keziah's chair, his sleeve brushing her magnificent plait. Adrian stood, his back to the log fire, staring at Bone, who had become principal exhibit in the zoo.

"The police get used to being treated as scapegoats." Grizel spoke before Bone could, and he was touched by her speed in his defense. "Robert's having a holiday from it all this week." Her tone indicated that they had better allow it to him, or else. Roke laughed, and coughed on champagne.

"Jane *said* you hadn't been married long. Bless you, we shan't tease your Robert any more. Ah, Jane, right on cue—and here's Marcus! We can tease him instead."

A thin man, whom Bone had noticed sliding into the room behind Jane a moment ago, now came forward. Roke had surged to his feet, and drew him into the circle. He had mouse-brown hair, flecked with silver, and a scholarly, humorous face which, as Roke steered him forward, wore a nervous smile. "Marcus Weatherby, my librarian."

Marcus bowed to left and right. Bone was not wholly amused to see Roke's glance rove over Grizel as he presented Marcus to her; her effect on other men was still new to Bone, and normally gave him great pleasure.

"Marcus is collating the records here, an *unbelievable* muddle left by my uncle, who invented entropy. By the little boy scout of Etna! Decay did not so much *set* in as *race* in. Bookworms—and I don't mean Marcus here"—Roke laid a broad hand on the librarian's shoulder—"bookworms held banquets in the best books. Marcus is putting all to rights." He patted the shoulder. "Ah, and here's Knebworth to tell us dinner is ready."

Bone, who had not in the past liked champagne, was realizing that perhaps he just hadn't come across the right make, and was happy to see Roke pick up another bottle to take in.

He had imagined a dining room paneled in oak with

perhaps crimson brocade paper above. He found something marvelously otherwise. Roke ushered them in with his treacherous benign smile, watching their faces. Grizel's gave him a vivid answer.

A long mahogany table, lit by several candelabra, was traditional enough. The upper walls, far from being dark, were the brilliant turquoise of a Mediterranean sky. This was wholly appropriate, because beneath it on all sides spread an Italian landscape. A balustrade, realistically crusted with lichen and seeming to throw its shadow toward the room, was painted up to elbow height. Marble vases spilled ivy and scarlet flowers, cypresses dwindling in height beyond suggested steps sloping toward a sea only a little more turquoise than the sky. That was on one long wall. On the other, the balustrade seemed to separate the room, across an apparent hundred yards or so, from a villa, white in the sun, almost purple in shadow, partly veiled from view by an ancient pine whose gnarled branches brushed the balustrade and threatened the dishes on the marble sideboard. Only sea and distant mountains floating in a silky haze occupied the third wall, the sea interrupted by a single glittering sail. The inside of the door was painted and there were no windows. On the fourth wall, a hound lay sprawled on a semicircular terrace before the balustrade, and a man in a white suit, leaning on the stone, turned his head to survey the room. The face was unmistakably Roke's.

"What a perfect room!" At Grizel's exclamation, Roke's smile extended to include some more teeth. He waved at the chairs.

"So glad you like it. Jane will tell you where to sit . . . A young friend of mine called Cosmo painted it before he went on to become rich and famous. He doesn't paint rooms any more, only portraits, portraits of mayors and army commanders, far more in demand I'm told, so I was lucky to catch him in his Rex Whistler phase. He offered to paint all the family along the balustrade but I said no—the only person I can be sure of is me. Children hate to be frozen in time when their only ambition is to grow up."

He did not mention his wife, as though he could not be sure of her either; as though, even as the mother of his children, she couldn't be trusted to last. Grizel had told Bone that Jane was his second wife, so perhaps the first had inspired him with uncertainty.

By now they were all seated, had unfurled the coral napkins, and the tall, white-haired butler, Knebworth, was ladling soup at the sideboard. A tiny elderly woman, obviously Mrs. Knebworth, carried round the plates. Tentative conversation came temporarily to an end because of the excellence of the soup, so subtly flavored that Bone took almost a minute to identify it as artichoke. Glancing up, he saw Jane anxiously surveying the table and, not for the first time, rejoiced that he now had a hostess, in the delightful shape of Grizel, to cope with the meager entertaining he indulged in; perhaps she would even change that . . . Being married to Roke, he thought, was not the best formula for worry-free convivial evenings.

"Do you *like* being a policeman?" Adrian had evidently recognized the subject as unwelcome, and returned to it as promising a fine yield of embarrassment. At once he had the satisfaction of seeing Grizel's eyes flash, and of drawing Jane's reply faster than Bone's.

"Of course he does. People generally like what they're good at." Apart from the compliment, the unspoken corollary was that Adrian, good at Nothing, needed telling this. "The tour that's coming on Sunday: Grizel tells me you've been with them several times. Can you tell us about them? Nicholas Buchanan sounded a nice man when we talked on the phone."

"And he writes a coaxing letter." Roke had finished his soup before anyone, possibly from having a wider mouth to spoon it into. "Charmed *me* out of my tree. I don't show Roke to anyone."

"Yes, he's a nice man. Knowledgeable, tactful—"

"Does that go for the whole group? Or is it them he has to be tactful about?"

Bone, leaning slightly aside to allow Mrs. Knebworth to reach his soup plate, thought that although Roke seemed amused at the thought of a tour invasion on Sunday, Jane feared he wouldn't be nearly as amused when it arrived. He tried to reassure.

"The people vary. Some come along almost every time but I don't know who's to be on this particular tour. I've certainly found those I've been with before to be very"—he hesitated, rejecting "well behaved" with its suggestions that normal tours were made up of vandals with hammers for the Meissen—"very amiable."

Roke's laugh was remarkably like a saw catching on a snag of log before it broke through. "I'm looking forward to this bunch of *amiable* gawpers. Must put up a good show for them."

"I think it's going to be absolutely boring and I don't intend to have anything to do with it." Adrian tossed his hair, looking around as if to warn of the blight his absence would create. Jane, helping herself to potatoes from Knebworth's proffered tureen, commented almost sotto voce, "That's all right, then," and Adrian gave her a sharp glance, visibly wondering whether to react or to pretend not to have heard. Roke was in no such quandary.

"Excellent. We want as little *boredom* as possible." His drawl and glance gave the remark ambiguity: was it Adrian's presence or his absence that would increase the likelihood of boredom? "Though I had been thinking, my dear boy, of stripping you and setting you up in some niche to amuse the party by, say, cocking a snook at them when they admired your classic lines. *October*, though! I wouldn't dream of asking."

Bone, watching Adrian's expression, between flattered and annoyed, was sure that this decorative young man must in part owe his position as permanent guest to his inability to be sure when he was being teased. Jane's dislike might spring from jealousy, but she was surely too intelligent to believe that Adrian had any influence over Roke; more probably, Roke retained him as a goad to provoke others, and reserved the pleasure of provoking Adrian to himself.

Guy was speaking. "A moving statue! God, I hope you're not going to embarrass everyone on Sunday by playing tricks. *That* would be the real bore." He pushed away his plate and, ignoring his mother's warning eyes, stared at Roke, who ate away with unabashed enjoyment. "Like that ghastly time you drenched the Wrigleys—"

"Underground pipes." Roke turned to Grizel. "Put in by some eighteenth-century Roke—Marcus will know who—to give the guests a pretty shock on the pleached avenue. Unfortunately, *far* less interesting in this century with skirts worn shorter—all those bell shapes were ideal. Besides," he added with regret, "they're out of order again, so no luck on Sunday, Guy." He grimaced at his son, commiserating, then turned again to Grizel. "My son, you must understand, thinks differently from me. I dare say when he inherits he'll turn the place into another Beaulieu and install a *motor museum*. Have the underground pipes mended, Guy, you can use them for the carwash." He rose, shedding his napkin into his chair, and picked up the wine bottle to go around the table. After attending to Grizel's glass and Adrian's, he met polite refusal from Marcus, with hand over glass and a defensive murmur. Bone, opposite, felt that

Marcus was ill at ease, nervous of his employer and of his neighbor—Adrian had dumped his napkin on the table and, perhaps carelessly, partly across Marcus' plate.

"My dear, you'll have more, I *know*." As Roke leaned over Jane to pour, he ran a hand down her back caressingly and glanced, Bone saw, at Adrian. *What a setup*, he thought, soberly eating. *Here I am married, for the second time, to Grizel, also for a second time; yet, thank God, what innocents we are in this sly warfare—unless Grizel went through it with Lewis; she doesn't talk about him—innocent of the whole strategy which a man like Roke can weave out of his relationships for his entertainment.*

Bone, brushing his teeth over the bathroom basin, remarked, "That was an excellent dinner." He rinsed his mouth circumspectly because Grizel, early in their relationship, had idly remarked on the vigor of his spitting. He wondered if in the years ahead, he would become trained to quiet spitting or would forget. The prospect of years ahead with Grizel distracted him euphorically from her reply. "M'm?"

"I said, was that all you could enjoy?" Grizel appeared in the doorway in a kimono of cream and tawny silk, and came to sit on the woven cane lavatory lid beside him. "Poor Robert. Frustrating to be in a house you've wanted to see, and not seeing it."

"That dining room was worth seeing. Wonder where the windows are."

"Jane suggested we join the tour on Sunday morning and let Roke show it properly. That way we'd not miss anything."

Bone watched the water swirl away. "Ideally I'd like to see his castle without his intervention, but nothing's perfect, I suppose." He looked down at her upturned face, the dark-lashed green eyes and generous mouth. He said, "Present company excepted." Her cropped hair had that silken electricity under his lips. "I'm lucky to be here."

She stood up into his arms and they stayed a moment content, before she wandered off to look at one of the prints on the bathroom walls. Bone, toweling his hands and mouth, glanced around at the tobacco-brown walls, the small white Gothic alcove that framed a pot of ivy with a rich fountain of tendrils. Only a square of plain white tiles above the basin and a double line along the wall over the bath acknowledged that water might occasionally be splashed. He, who disliked all-tiled bathrooms for their suggestions of mayhem, of gargantuan tidal waves caused by violent bathers—not to mention their reminder of the pathology department—approved of this décor. He was hanging up the towel, also tobacco brown, when Grizel gave a cry of disgust and recoiled towards him.

"Eugh!" As he fielded her, not loath, she explained, "I was just going to say, come and look at this, isn't it nice to have a medieval picture in the bathroom, look at that gorgeous scarlet color. And then I saw what it's all about."

Bone, unhelpfully resting his chin on her shoulder, looked. The picture showed nothing bad at first glance but some gracefully contorted figures, dressed in blue and gold against an indigo sky diapered in gold. They were engaged in something he could at first not make out. The scarlet Grizel had mentioned was certainly very beautiful, glowing amongst the blue and gold.

"What *is* it all about?"

Grizel's pointing finger shrank from touching. "They're flaying him, that's what. Some wretched saint and those two are peeling his skin off. That red is his raw body."

Bone could now see that this was true. He kept still, but revulsion tightened his stomach. The victim of the flaying looked down at the process in critical distaste. The tormentors, wielding their pincers with professional skill, were clearly doing a task they were used to. Bone, queasy, laughed; which he recognized as a defense mechanism.

"One way of getting undressed. I imagine even the electric chair's an improvement on *that*."

"And he puts it in the bathroom! You'll not tell me that is Jane's choice!" Grizel, kimono whirling, went into the bedroom and dumped herself on the bed. Bone followed, sat beside her, and took her hand in both his.

"Jane has put up with him for how long?"

"Guy's nineteen, I think. Yes, we can put up with him for a week—him and his *my dear boy*."

"It sounds a very affected *fin-de-siècle* Wildery."

"Eugh," she repeated. "Just don't ask me to like him."

"Ah but," and Bone quoted, " 'Jane says he's terribly amusing!' "

Grizel snorted. "He's the sort who'd go to an execution for a good laugh."

Bone had not her aversion to Roke, whom he did find a source of amusement. "No one's going to be executed this week, so he'll have to get his fun some other way." He pulled back the bedclothes and got in, patting the place beside him. "Nothing's going to spoil my honeymoon."

Fate, listening, made a note.

Chapter

. . . .

3

BONE HAD FAILED TO REMEMBER THAT GRIZEL, ALREADY AND delectably part of his life, was a stranger to Buchanan's group; but on joining them in the cozy gloom of the hotel foyer she had endeared herself by announcing, "I'm Grizel Bone," with sparkling pleasure in the name's morbid quality. The tall Simpson-Bates sisters gave her their antiphonal greeting. They had been occupied with introducing another newcomer to the thin wary architect Maitland and his wife, who smiled and shook hands. The sisters were pleased to see him talking, for they had thought Mr. Spencer might feel out of things—he would not be here if Mrs. Cheadle, a Buchananite of many years, had not succumbed to an attack of severe arthritis and had to cancel at the last minute; and the nice woman on Reception had naturally heard this, and had proposed her brother. He was interested in old houses, and had recently suffered bereavement and truly needed a break. Nicholas Buchanan had been, though hesitant, glad to accept him. The sisters knew that this meant he could make it an excuse to refund Mrs. Cheadle's money, saved all year, as the regulars of the tours knew, for this one treat.

Now Nicholas Buchanan himself darted through the crowd, trim and alert as a robin in his red pullover, took Grizel's hand, and said, "You're exactly like your voice. I'd envisaged someone just like you. How clever of you to convey it and give us a hint of the treat we were going to get . . ."

Bone, too, was greeted and congratulated and, the coach arriving at this moment, habitués, newcomers, acquaintances and strangers clustered toward it, and were momentarily held up as the first to reach it were an ancient gray couple who required the driver's strong arm to hoist them up the steep steps. They then wavered toward a seat, changed their minds while a logjam of the group formed behind, and eventually sat down. The man wore a gray checked flat cap, the woman a squashed black tam-o'-shanter, and they sat, extinguished beneath their headgear, silently watching the others board the coach. Bone, identifying the Webbs from previous tours, had once again the impression that they had wandered in from some graveyard and were now in search of a little stimulus after some years below ground.

Apart from them, the party had something of the air of a school expedition. Bone wondered how Cha was faring in France, and only knew he was worrying when Grizel pinched his arm and said, "She'll be all right."

He emerged from gloom, made a face at her briefly, and watched the last few waiting to come aboard. A slender woman with delicate features, only lightly touched by middle age, her fair hair still in girlish waves, looked up at the coach windows as she moved to the door, as if she feared no place would be left. Her tweed suit of softly blended mauve, green, gold, and rust, like heather and bracken on moorland, soothed the eye and showed, Bone thought, possibly money and certainly a trim figure. She was followed, so closely that he was obviously with her, by a tall young man whose hair improved on hers by having more gold in it and curling enthusiastically over his head and down the strong neck. His build suggested that Michelangelo's *David* had jumped from his pedestal, pulled on a navy sweater and jeans, and wandered off in search of some fun, perhaps a reward for all those years of being respectfully stared at. His progress along the side of the coach was accompanied by waves from the Simpson-Bateses and Catherine Maitland. Even Mrs. Webb dipped her hat, a decayed mushroom, in welcome. The short time that the group had been together already had been enough to forward fellowship. He smiled at all of them with a lack of shyness unusual in an English boy of what Bone guessed to be his late teens.

This was explained by the Australian accent when he came on board saying, "I'm easy, Ma. Sit anywhere." They moved down the aisle to sit near the back, the young man including Bone and Grizel in his friendly grin. Bone was sure that the young man would be popular with Nicholas Buchanan, who, with his dry humor and charm, created the atmosphere which brought people back again and again. This made the few newcomers both conspicuous and objects of curiosity. Bone, half turning as if to see who was still to climb aboard, caught the eye of the newcomer behind him, a small balding man with eyes like pale marbles behind his glasses, who gave him a tentative smile before going back to reading his tour leaflet.

"Do you know everyone here?" Grizel's murmur warmed his ear and he turned back to her.

"Most, by sight; but I haven't managed to get to many of these tours. Once I made the first day and was called away on the second."

"People are wholly inconsiderate when they get murdered."

Buchanan was taking a roll call now, standing with his back to the driver. He said, "Robert and, I'm glad to say, *Grizel* Bone are joining us for at least part of the tour. I really think we should provide a *haunting* for you two, but as you're staying at Roke Castle I dare say you'll have all you can handle on the premises." Bone grinned and said, "Not so far, but we can hope," and Buchanan moved on down the list.

"Lawson? Josh Lawson?" He peered about, the high backs of the coach seats making it difficult for him to see who was there.

"Here he comes," called the soprano Simpson-Bates, closely seconded by the contralto. A tall square man clambered aboard, Buchanan's making way for him unacknowledged; his chest supported camera and light meter, his large pale face, a meaningless smile. As he came up the aisle he stared hard, briefly, at each person. The smile remained. It gave Bone a sense of unease. The roll call continued. The mother and son were identified as Mrs. North, "and I hear I must call you Baz"; the little man Bone had noticed with eyes like pale blue marbles was Donald Spencer. Then Buchanan turned to the driver with his map and the coach buzzed with quiet, anticipatory conversation. Bone was conscious of a lift of joy, like a boy on the first day of the holidays; the coach swung onto the road, with a cheer from somewhere at the back. Bone, still possessed of Grizel's hand, gave it a tap on her knee.

"So far so good," she said. "They've not called you back to work yet."

* * *

26

Pattens' herringbone brick and blond oak basked in October sun. It nestled among beech and ilex, its lichened tiles golden, and a copse of tall chimneys, barley sugar twisted, fluted, trefoil, or hexagonal, rose above. The small panes of the windows reflected variously, not flush with each other. Bone felt welcomed. The group approached the house over mossy cobbles, and most of them had to duck under the porch's Tudor lintel. Flagstones, scoured down into wavelike contours, were underfoot. People spoke in low, polite, visitors' voices. An oak table bore several oriental dishes and a big Chinese bowl of potpourri. One of the tour regulars, Arnold Mabey, preceding Bone, swung up his stick to point this out.

"Handsome object," he remarked as the splayed rubber tip grazed the rim, and he moved on after the others into the big hall, while Bone breathed again.

"That's a dangerous old party," Grizel murmured.

They had assembled, under a splendid hammer beam roof whose ridge lay some forty feet above, in a smell of woodsmoke that emanated from a sizeable hearth at the far end where half a tree smoldered on a bank of wood ash. Buchanan was talking to the owners, a bluff man in a hacking jacket that had seen a lot of hacking, and a slender woman with dark hair, wearing blue.

Buchanan turned to his flock and announced, "Sir William and Lady Gedd are very kindly going to tell us about the house first, and then we are allowed to wander. Because of security, no photography indoors, please. The avid camera fiends will restrain ourselves."

This raised a small laugh. Buchanan had also given a mock-severe stare at someone in the back of the group; as Sir William began to speak, the "mock" in the stare switched off. Buchanan was giving someone a clear warning. Bone suppressed his instinct, and his training, to turn and see who.

He missed a good deal of the information Sir William gave, lost in examining the roof and its structure. The beams, pickled by smoke, stood out in their intricate geometry against creamy plaster. By the time he picked up, the party was being told it could wander. Buchanan was saying to Lady Gedd what was, as always, a reminder to the group: "Any door that is shut stays shut, so we only go into rooms whose doors are open; and we touch *nothing*."

Baz North stuffed both hands into his pockets, and grinned. Perhaps he was an inveterate toucher. He did not seem a likely member of this party; perhaps he had some unsuspected interest in Tanagra figures or stumpwork. The young man followed his mother toward the stairs.

Bone wandered off with Grizel, content in her company, enjoying the house. The Gedds, either these or their forebears, had filled it with comfort. There were window seats with tapestry squabs, deep sofas, small prim Victorian chairs, and tables full of little displays—of quartz here, of little boxes there. Grizel said, "Oh!" and pointed at a glass-fronted hanging cupboard. Bone went closer to look. A jade rat was dragging another by its tail, and this other, lying on its back, clasped an egg. Another object, in jade of three colors, was a lily leaf, a duck's back, and a frog. The shelf beneath was of mirror and showed the verso—the lily stem, and the duck's head and underside, and a small hiding fish. Bone wondered if Roke's lost collection had contained things like these. There were little ivories: a badger at a washtub, a fat baby, two men with a game board, both wrapped in a printed quilt. The mirror showed their feet and the underside of the firebox they were huddling over.

"No wonder they're smiling. What coziness." Grizel leaned on his arm a moment. "Let's steal this house and live here."

"Right. Will Monday do?"

They strolled on. Bone noticed the red "eye" of the alarm system up in one corner.

The stairs were stone, and steep. More portraits and a gray tapestry of some unknown battle adorned the walls. The warriors in this were eighteenth-century Romans, with a curious pantomime look, so plumed were their helmets and so wide their metal kilts.

In a bedroom, a boy of fifteen or so, Sir William shrunk down, was explaining the repair of bed hangings by the Royal School of Needlework. His confident tones were echoed by his father's from downstairs. A Labrador panted at his side. A well-dressed couple—were they called Rose? Bone did not know them—stood listening hand in hand. She was dark, rounded, slightly Mediterranean, tall. He was dark, heavyset, with horn-rimmed spectacles and hair combed forward as if to conceal its recession. Were they too honeymooning? A step at the door heralded Mabey entering heavily with his stick. The Labrador burst out in a barking objurgation and young Gedd, hardly stopping, reached for *Horse and Hound* from the bedside table and flapped the dog's rump, producing silence.

The end bedroom had an oriel. Grizel stepped into it and sat on the window seat, turning to look out over the formal gardens and the fields beyond. Bone sat too, relaxed, aware of happiness.

There was a click, as of a door shutting, and then the soft whirr of a camera shutter. Bone stepped from the oriel to find Josh Lawson lowering a camera from his face.

"You ought not to be doing that." He heard his tone, authoritative, condemning.

Lawson was disconcerted. He giggled, a curiously girlish sound from that great slab of a face.

"Oh yes?"

"House owners don't say *No photography* for nothing. It will be part of their insurance. And it's Buchanan's rule."

"Naughty, naughty, breaking rules. What are you going to do? Take down my trousers and smack my bottom?" His eyes looked past Bone; Grizel must have come into sight. "Oh *yes*, trying to impress the little woman."

"Buchanan would bar you from these tours—"

"Your lot always like to throw your weight around. I'd have thought *you* would know anyone can make a mistake."

In reply to this baffling remark, Bone could only say, "You'd do well not to make this particular one again." He went on looking at the man. After a moment Lawson, once more with that oddly unpleasant giggle, opened the door and went out.

Bone turned to Grizel.

"Sorry. The policeman inveterate."

"Don't worry. I knew when I married you." She smiled, her eyes luminous. He noticed that the shadow of the frayed curtain lay on her cheek like the shadow of her long lashes, and it moved him inexplicably. She shifted, and the shadow shifted, and she spoke.

"What did you say?" He hoped he had not heard.

"I said, my hubby the bobby."

"My God, is this the creature that I endowed with all my worldly goods?"

She slid an arm around him. "I fear it . . . Will you tell Nicholas Buchanan of that man?"

"I suppose I have to, though I think he knows what he's like. It's a matter of security." He looked up at the room's electronic eye. It was in a corner over the door, registering their presence with a red stare.

AT LUNCHTIME IN THE PUB, BONE HAD A WORD WITH NICHOLAS Buchanan, as soon as the tour leader was able to attend for a moment after organizing lunches, ordered by phone and mostly sandwiches, to their rightful recipients. Lawson, not to be satisfied with sandwiches, had ordered steak and chips; he was known to Buchanan as Hot Lunch Lawson. Bone returned to Grizel with their drinks, his beer and her cider, and said to her in a voice pitched below the pub's cheerful racket, "Nicholas didn't want Lawson on this tour at all; he's on a sort of blacklist, for persistent photography among other things. A new secretary slipped up."

The afternoon's house was a satisfactory contrast to Pattens. Bone would have been content to see Pattens alone, but Haxley Manor too was a notable place, a classical

eighteenth-century gentleman's residence, pleasing the eye
with that exact ratio of wall to windows, of height to
breadth, that its century was master of. Mr. Kealey, the
owner, who came out on the gravel, had not an appropriate
air. He was in carpet slippers, gray flannels that sagged, an
open-necked shirt, and a navy cardigan, respectable until a
wave of his arm showed it as through at the elbow. Silky
gray hair stood at various angles from his head, and more
discreetly from his ears. Bone thought from his manner of
greeting the party that he now regretted allowing them to
come, but Buchanan, chatting assiduously, made him suddenly laugh; and he relaxed a little, beckoned them into the
house with a small gesture one might make for a hurrying
dog, and shambled into the hall.

The structure of the place was beautiful, but the furniture invited comparison with the owner's clothes—great
brocade sofas, frayed and with dead cushions wilting in
their embrace, a Queen Anne dining table and chairs unpol-
ished and kicked about the legs, an Adam chimney piece
with postcards and invitations stuck round the glass and
a great stain of smoke rising across it, a Matthew Boulton
hearth with cinders and burned paper in the fire basket and
ash scattered below. A sheaf of flowers had been rammed
into a jug on the sideboard, in a ring of water drops and
shed leaves and petals, as if Mr. Kealey retained memories of "flowers brighten a place" and the need to please
visitors.

Donald Spencer, who usually sidled in the rear of the
party, had come to rest by the sideboard and was looking at
the flowers as though they were the most remarkable thing
in the room. Bone wondered what had brought him on the
tour; he seemed to know nobody and to care little about
what they saw. With his round eyes, and his round glasses
glinting as he moved his head, and his transparent gray

mac, he looked so like a caricature of an inoffensive little man that he was almost sinister. Bone was reminded of a little man he had once arrested, who had looked just as dreary and drab but had stashed bits of his wife in plastic bags in the freezer.

Someone had been over the place with a duster, and shabbiness was not universal. There was a small cozy study, where a dark shape in an armchair resolved itself into an old dog who took little notice of people coming through, even of Arnold Mabey taking a book from a shelf. Susan Simpson-Bates took it from him, tutting, and put it back, and Mabey said, unabashed, "Ruling passion, you know," and lingered to admire the snug wing chair and reading lamp. Josh Lawson wondered how many books there were, and Maitland the architect, running an eye over the shelves, guessed "about three thousand." Mr. Kealey, following them in, said, "Two thousand eight hundred and four," and there was general congratulation of Maitland. The dog raised its head and a tremor went through its tail. Bone saw that it was nearly blind.

Grizel murmured, as they left Kealey talking to Buchanan and the Maitlands, "Do you detect a confirmed old bachelor?"

"My guess is, a widower; though I couldn't say why. You realize that this pastime—this tour—is merely an extension of my professional nosiness?"

"Vice versa. You're by nature inquisitive, like Mr. Mabey, so you chose a profession that would legitimize it."

"Well, thank you." Bone was visited by the picture of Mabey as a detective. He would do very well as the amateur who in fiction so continually stumbles over corpses.

Mr. Kealey seemed content to let them stray over his property. Some owners, in Bone's experience, tended to hover or to herd, as though anticipating damage or theft.

Others either didn't care or couldn't bear to watch; Kealey was perhaps one of the latter. He allowed photography.

At the moment, though, Lawson seemed satisfied to shuffle along with the rest of the party making their way upstairs. Donald Spencer, aware suddenly that people were on the move, took his eyes from the flowers on the big room's sideboard and trotted obediently to catch up with the flow. Bone reproved himself for having thought of him as anything other than an innocent, decent little fellow. Perhaps he was a flower fancier and had come on the tour for the sake of the gardens rather than the houses. One must not indulge in fantasy about people simply on the grounds that they looked harmless and because harmless-looking people had, in Bone's experience, committed some quite startling harm.

"Look at this." Grizel was pointing through a lancet window in the hall, set low enough to allow sight of a very small chapel, with room for little more than some kneelers on a worn carpet and an altar covered with an embroidered, gold-sewn cloth and carrying two tall candlesticks with large candles. A vase of carnations had been put in front of the altar cross and the smell of them wafted to Bone as he stood behind Grizel peering in. Sheila Simpson-Bates, passing them on her way to the stairs, said in a low voice, "It's where he's going to be buried. He's just been telling Nicholas. His wife's there already, with one of the children. Touching, isn't it?"

She moved on. Bone and Grizel continued to look in at the chapel in silence. He was conscious that she could not easily make any comment to a man who had lost his own wife and child only four years ago. It was up to him to lighten the atmosphere. "Cozy having them under one's roof. Would you like me to pop you under the flagstones in the cottage? The flat doesn't offer the same scope."

Grizel squeezed his arm. "When we move, we'll have to bear in mind that we're looking for a walk-in cemetery. And it'll be the last move. I'm not having you digging me up every time you want to shift."

They started up the stairs together, leaving Buchanan and Mr. Kealey laughing, deep in conversation by the fireplace. A confused sound of shouting came from upstairs, and Bone glanced to see if Buchanan had heard. Certainly the noise could not be caused by his catching Josh Lawson at work with his camera, though Lawson's voice was audible. Bone's professional reaction took him racing up the stairs and across the landing toward the voices; he found Josh Lawson looking down amazed, his jacket fronts in the grasp of Donald Spencer, who was shaking him with all his force and barely succeeding in rocking Lawson's heavy frame. Spencer was incoherent, and Sheila Simpson-Bates had got him by the wrist and was trying to stop him, while her sister hovered anxiously.

As Bone and Grizel came in, Spencer seemed to sense the futility of his attack, and he let go. He'd had more effect on himself than on Lawson, for his spectacles had fallen off and he was flushed and in tears.

Susan Simpson-Bates picked up the spectacles and put them in his hands. Lawson said indulgently, "You shouldn't get so het up. You'll do yourself an injury."

Spencer put on his spectacles, hooking them behind his ears, and looked at Lawson. Then he turned and marched out, Bone making way. The sisters hurried after with intention to comfort and calm him.

"What *was* that about?" Grizel inquired. Bone, who had no wish to talk to Lawson, blessed her curiosity.

"Just a remark. I only passed a remark."

"It must have been quite a remark," she said. Lawson gave his odd, rather glutinous laugh, and walked out past them. Grizel looked around the pleasant bedroom with its chintz curtains and pastel family portraits on the wall. Bone agreed with her unspoken wonder at what could have caused that explosion. Lawson could laugh, but Spencer's face as he marched out had been no laughing matter.

Chapter

....

5

"When are these ghastly people turning up this morn-ing?"

Adrian's challenging inquiry was directed at Jane; Grizel felt that it was also intended to make Bone and herself conscious that they by association were among the ghastly people. Jane may have felt this too. Her reply was curt.

"Benet asked Mr. Buchanan to get them here promptly by ten-fifteen. There is no need for you to be there at all." Her tone carried the implication that everyone would be grateful for Adrian's absence. Guy set down his coffee cup and muttered in a disobliging tone something about Adrian figuring in the Roke Collection, though not, one felt, as an *objet de vertu.*

"I can't think why you allowed it." Adrian thrust back his

chair, whose creak of protest sounded as if it felt old enough to be respected.

Roke, at the top of the table, the *Sunday Times* by his plate, consumed kedgeree with gusto. Whether Adrian meant that he should keep touring parties out of the castle, or not allow his son to be rude about his guest, was unclear; Roke chose the former meaning.

"Charity, my slim gilt youth, charity, I do it for charity."

"I thought Buchanan was going to make out a check for the tower restoration." Guy was, as usual, indignant.

"Absolutely. Charity begins at *home*."

Jane said to Grizel, "This place costs a fortune to keep up. Bits continually crumble and fall off. Currently it's the tower." She evidently did not want her guests to see her husband as grasping. Grizel remembered the checks yesterday, at Haxley Manor for a cancer hospice, at Pattens for a local church. "Benet, you're not going to take them up there today?"

"It's perfectly safe, my dear." He said it like "Medea." "You wouldn't want them to miss the view from up there."

"The workmen have left their stuff all over the roof."

"Good Mary Christmas! *No one* expects battlements to be dusted."

Grizel had a hazy memory of an episode in Scottish history when the chatelaine of some castle under siege had, to demonstrate nonchalance, strolled the battlements with her waiting-women, poor souls, flicking away the dust raised by the siege engine's gun stones. Jane, meeting her husband's gaze of affable malice, was demonstrating nonchalance now.

"Oh, very true. Then I'll have coffee ready for them all in the small morning room at—eleven-thirty? Does that give you time enough for everything you have in mind for the first leg of the tour?"

Roke smiled blandly and looked round the breakfast table till his gaze came to linger on two of his guests in particular.

"Yes. I do *so hope* you'll enjoy everything I have in store today."

Grizel, making a social face and hearing Robert meet the challenge with a dry, "I'm sure we shall," was aware of Jane's movement of unease, as if she would signal a warning of some kind.

It was odd, Bone thought, to be watching the tour coach arrive, instead of sitting in it and watching Roke Castle's outline grow larger. He could see, past Benet Roke's bulky shoulder, the familiar faces: the scarlet wool cape of Sheila Simpson-Bates (her turn today for the window seat), the lugubrious black tam-o'-shanter of Mary Webb, other faces he knew but could not put names to, and Angela North pointing out something to Baz, who leaned over to see. Buchanan was first off the coach as always, neat in dark jersey and lovat trousers, advancing with cheerful smile and outstretched hand.

"Lord Roke—it's enormously kind of you to suffer this invasion. I hope we're not late. Our driver had a spot of difficulty getting through the gates."

Roke was consulting a fob watch, a half-hunter of some antiquity, which he put back to bed in a pocket of his tweed waistcoat. "But exactly on time, my dear fellow. I ought to have told you to allow for the gates, though. They take their toll of quite a few visitors."

Bone would not have put it beyond Roke to have his gateposts moved closer together, had they been too easy to pass. He was watching the group descend from the coach, and his face expressed a terribly benign anticipation. Even without Jane's warnings, and several remarks of Roke's, he would have suspected him of a warped sense of humor. The drawl, the glance through half-closed eyes, the sudden brief wide smile, made Bone wary. Roke chatted to Buchanan. Josh Lawson was for once last off, and remained at the back of the group as they assembled before Roke in obedience to his expansive gesture; Lawson's uncouth corduroy hat was pulled well down, and he was examining the two cameras slung on his chest, with obsessive concern. Bone wondered if Buchanan had spoken to Lawson yesterday, and if Roke was going to allow photography and, if not, whether Lawson would still try it on.

"Welcome! I'm very sorry to start with restrictions but, for obvious security reasons, I can't allow photography inside the castle. All you like in the grounds—and now, here outside if you wish . . ." Several cameras accordingly registered Roke's wide gesture of permission. "Now, I'm not going to bore you with a history of the place. I'm sure you'll read it up if you're interested, it's in plenty of the relevant books; but when we go in, I'll simply take you round a few things that may *amuse* you and then we'll go up the tower and have a look at the grounds from there—and you can see the various periods of the house clearly from above. Then my wife will provide coffee"—the group gave forth an indistinct sound of appreciation—"and you can tour the gardens. There's an alternative schedule: those who would prudently look at the grounds before it rains"—they all looked up, as he did, at the bright blue of a fine late October morning, and at the ominous buildup of thunder clouds beyond the castle—"are, of course, at liberty to do so and to see the house afterward, though without the ineffable benefit of my guidance."

Their smiles at this expected him to smile. He did not, and their smiles died.

Watching this, he said, "It's enough history to remark that various Rokes built bits onto the place when they had the money . . ." His gaze halted, a classic moment of the disconcerter disconcerted. He said, "Hallo, there." As the visitors, turning, identified Angela North as the recipient of this greeting, he said to them all, "We've met. It's been a long time." Angela nodded gently in response, and colored.

Bone was beginning to build a story on this when a vast shock of noise, battering at them, hideous, sudden and dreadful, passed into the apparition of a receding black aircraft above the trees. Everyone had reacted. Some ducked, most grimaced, some put belated hands to their ears, many cried out in distress. Grizel had seized Bone's arm with violent speed. He had happened to be looking at Mary Webb when it happened, and had detected no reaction at all.

As heartbeats dropped back to normal, Roke said, "So we'll start indoors," and turned to lead the way into the house. Bone gave him full marks for cool. *That* was a surprise he could not have planned.

Someone stumbled on the porch as they were coming in, perhaps in delayed shock. Bone was reflecting that the toleration people had accorded to low-flying aircraft after the Gulf War had certainly eroded.

Most of the group trooped into the hall, stared up at the great convolutions of the chandeliers, down at the marble slabs, round at the dark portraits viewing them from gilded frames. Arthur and Mary Webb tottered with determination to an ancient oak settle, flanked by vast brass bowls of parlor palms. They sat, and fixed on Roke their clouded gaze. Bone thought they meant to postpone dwindling to a pair of little piles of dust until they had obtained their money's worth.

Roke's voice echoed in the considerable expanse of the hall. Behind him the staircase rose to a half landing, parted, and swept in twin curves to the upper floor. Light filtered down from a glass dome high above.

"This is the eighteenth-century part. Portraits! You see

41

there Lady Sophia Battel, who was an heiress of quite stunning fortune and is *vastly* flattered by Reynolds here, but that was his job. Some ancestor of mine astutely married her, doing the family a very good turn. Over there is her husband, understandably morose; nevertheless they had eleven children. Over that door is an astonishingly bad picture of the castle in the seventeenth century. Next to the window is the eldest son of these two, also out of the Reynolds workshop—they tell me Reynolds probably did the face."

Susan Simpson-Bates said, "He's rather like Baz." It was true. Baz, standing below the portrait, had been looking out of the window. His strong chin, corn-colored hair and level eyebrows did resemble those above. When he heard his name he turned, caught on, glanced up, and took an exaggerated pose, spoiling the likeness with his wide smile. Roke's harsh laughter joined the others a little late. He said genially, "Welcome to the family.

"Well then, forward," he went on, and led them all to the left, past the stairs, into the dark domains of the old castle.

In the dim corridor, with people exclaiming and warning each other about uneven flagstones and the fractionally more dangerous matting laid over them, Bone kept hold of Grizel's hand. This part of the castle, which they had not yet seen or even guessed at—a realm of limbo opening so abruptly from the ordered classicism of the hall—was in some way more sinister than even its natural gloom gave it a right to be.

They trailed after Roke into an enormous kitchen, flagged and matted like the passage, with a table down the middle big enough for the dismemberment of two dead stags at once. Keziah smiled from across the room where she was busy with trays on a sideboard. The walls were lined with dressers, where hung copper pans.

A telephone had been ringing somewhere, and

Knebworth now came into the kitchen peering at the tour group; his air of anxiety dissipated when he saw Grizel.

"There is a telephone call for you, Mrs. Bone."

"It'll be the one I'm expecting. No, go on, Robert. I'll catch up when I've talked to Sandy."

Roke had opened a small door at the far end of the kitchen, ducked through, and led them down another brick-walled passage. Bone thought of a psychic friend of his, Emily Playfair, and wondered if she would have had visions from another time in this place. Had Roke, instead of opening another low door to one side, simply stepped through the wall, it would have been in keeping with this curious atmosphere. Gray light came from unseen windows some way ahead and the air struck chill.

Roke was waiting for them in a room whose brick vaulting could hardly be seen in the shadows above. A high, barred window let indirect light find its way in but was too deep in the wall's thickness to allow a view, and the light had a sickly, thunderous quality, as if it came from the wrong quarter. This room was empty and the brick floor sloped.

As Roke stepped aside, he displayed the reason he had brought them here. In the center of the floor, and of the slight but definite slope all round it, lay a large grating. As they stood there, each fighting the slight pull of the downward slope, Arnold Mabey straining to see over Bone's shoulder and pressing him forward, Bone could feel the tomblike cold air rising through the grating, and smell a fungal rot it carried on its breath. Roke's eyes and teeth gleamed in the shadow as he flourished a hand.

"Ladies and gentlemen: the castle oubliette. Please take great care—the grating is not quite secure." He grinned more widely as Sheila Simpson-Bates, finding herself edged down the slope by the press behind, emitted a tiny shriek and battled her way back, clutching Maitland's sleeve.

Buchanan could be heard to murmur what an amenity to a family was such a place.

"Yes, indeed. The idea was, of course, that, once down there, the victim should be *forgotten;* but do you know, I have a feeling that the Lord Roke of the day would lie on his bed three stories up, and *remember.*"

Bone was positive that at this moment every one of the group visualized Roke himself lying in some medieval bed and smiling from ear to ear.

"If you will gather round, and I recommend great care, you will be able to look down and examine the victim's dying conditions." Roke produced a torch from his pocket and shone it down. It had a quite powerful but narrowly focused light. Bone braced his feet on the brick as everyone edged cautiously forward. He did not entirely put it past Roke to allow a member of the party to demonstrate while pretending it was an accident. Logic informed him that Roke's insurance was not likely to cover such indulgence, but it was not logic that made him cautious as they peered down.

The torchlight glinted on something about twelve feet or more below. There was a murmur and much craning of necks as the light steadied on the object.

"It's a bowl. What's a bowl doing there?" Unexpectedly it was Donald Spencer who brought this out. His glasses glinted in reflection of the bowl as he bent to look closer. The rubber tip of Mabey's stick squealed on sweating brick as he buttressed himself against the pull of the incline, and he gripped Baz by the shoulder as he collided with him.

Baz set him upright with ease and hunkered down beside Donald Spencer, Mr. Universe beside Mr. Magoo. He pointed.

"What's there—past the bowl?"

The torch swung obligingly. People gasped.

What they saw was the remains of a hand, stretched

toward the bowl but not quite reaching it. Each delicate bone shone in the torchlight.

"Oh, poor chap—I must have forgotten him." Roke let the beam travel slowly up the radius and ulna, along the humerus to the shoulder and then the skull, jaw sunk on the bare earth, eye sockets fixed with hollow longing on the bowl.

The general reaction, the recoiling, the clustering to see, the exclamations of shock and disbelief, must be gratifying to Roke. Bone admired the showmanship with which the skeleton had been gradually revealed. Roke should take to directing horror movies. Bone doubted if the skeleton was real, though it was of a proper size. The last joke one he had seen had been too small.

One of the party did not react like the rest. Baz, still crouched over the grating, was clapping hands and grinning with deep enjoyment. Roke slid the torchlight onto his face and let it dwell there for a couple of blinding seconds. Baz half rose, dazzled, and his foot tipped the grating, which gave a hoarse groan as if a voice below had spoken. Angela North screamed and Roke with startling speed seized Baz and, stamping on the grill with all his weight, stabilized it. After a second, he pushed Baz clear and said, "Everyone's safe so long as I stand on this end, so perhaps you will all make your way out by the far door and I'll join you." His flat tone negated drama, the lazy smile answered the disapproval, belittled the shock. A showman indeed.

Angela was disposed to fuss a little. Baz propelled her toward the door saying, "She's apples, Ma. Come on." It was the first Australianism Bone had heard him utter.

The party, recovering from the impact of the "joke," began to chatter, to laugh; Donald Spencer was polishing his spectacles vigorously as though what he had seen through them might be their fault. The Simpson-Bateses were deep in discussion over the human or plastic provenance of the skeleton, but not quite able to ask Roke about it, and Mabey was telling Angela North that Josh Lawson could have taken a splendid flash photo of the scene in the oubliette had it been permitted. She, however, was watching her son's fine head above the little crowd as though she feared there might still be some hungry hole in the floor.

Baz, completely recovered from the shock of "nearly joining Old Bones," swung on ahead down a well-lit whitewashed passage as Roke directed. Arthur and Mary Webb shuffled forward without comment, giving Bone the thought that, in their home town, the bloke with the bones could have been a neighbor; though not, to judge from their faces, a friend.

Bone, profoundly aware of Grizel's absence from his side, drifted with the crowd.

No surprises manifested themselves in the sitting rooms Roke led them through when they left the brick passages. These rooms, with which Bone was already familiar, lay on either side of the hall and roused admiring comment among the party. Some asked questions about the china in the cabinet, and Roke showed himself knowledgeable as well as courteous. One of the women whose name Bone could not remember asked about the tapestry cushions on the yellow sofa, showing various animals astounded by wildflowers on a navy wool background. "My wife's work," he said, his smile suggesting unexpectedly that this pleased him. "Her design, too. Based on the *Dame à la Licorne*."

A seventeenth-century Roke followed them with dark disdainful eyes from the chimneypiece, hand fingering his sword as though he could willingly have used it on these gawking strangers. A dog, just visible in the shadows round his feet, gazed up at him with a devotion it was hard to believe he could deserve. Bone had remarked to Grizel, on the night they arrived here, that he was surprised there were no animals about. It was not his idea of what one might expect in a country house. Grizel distinctly remembered that Jane had been fond of dogs and had owned several, so it must be that Roke did not care for them. Bone, speculating on the pet that might suit Roke, was fitting up a scorpion with a collar and was wishing Grizel was there to tell, when her hand slid into his. The green eyes with their long lashes were smiling.

She whispered, "I'm an aunt, Robert; to a nephew. Name not decided."

"Congratulations—"

"Ah, move along, we're away upstairs."

Indeed, the Simpson-Bates sisters were urging Arnold Mabey from the room, following their usual instructions— in the form of a begged favor—from Nicholas Buchanan to see that Mabey never lingered alone anywhere. On the way upstairs, with Bone and Grizel on their heels, they were however too late to prevent him from leaning over the banister, and plucking with curiosity at the wrought-iron links that held the elaborate chandelier in place. "Very strong," he remarked with satisfaction when they had managed to hustle him on up the stairs. Bone half expected to hear a crash behind them when they reached the wide landing.

Roke opened one half of the double doors, allowing them a brief glimpse of a long room set up like a museum with display cases, before he shut the door just as one of the party moved forward to look in. Roke having, it seemed, deliberately just missed catching his visitor's nose in the door, now affected to recognize him and started back, hand to bosom in theatrical surprise.

"Why, isn't it *Maitland*? Benjamin Maitland? My dear fellow, what a pleasure to see you again—and so unchanged by all your good fortune since your *striking* work for me." He pulled the obviously reluctant Maitland to him, an arm round his shoulders, and addressed the party.

"Designed such a splendid house for me—Oh, many years ago! Made his *reputation*, I believe, which he *well* deserved. No, no!" as Maitland attempted to protest, "I won't hear a word of modesty!" He released Maitland, and surveyed the group jovially. "If you want proof, you can look in there," he tapped the panels of the door he had just shut, "and see for yourselves. The muniment room contains a record of my life. Plans, pictures, documents, a record of all the houses I've lived in before I inherited this place—a *checkered* past! Maitland's work is there, for you to see, but," he wagged a large finger at them, "not yet. We must reach the roof in time."

In time? thought Bone.

Chapter

· · · · · · · · · · · · · · · · · ·

6

ROKE SET OFF AT SPEED, AND WAS MAKING FOR THE BACKSTAIRS
when he paused, looked at his watch, and said, "A glimpse
of the library!" He surged back among them and pointed to
doors corresponding to the muniment room across the
landing. "The Japanese armor. After coffee!" He flung open,
with a flourish, the door beside this and marched in,
followed by the group.

Marcus Weatherby, surprised unwrapping a Mars bar,
rose from behind his desk, holding the bar awkwardly and
looking at them over his demilune glasses. His navy bow tie,
white spotted as if with mold from the books, was crooked
as usual, and he was quite at a loss what to do with the Mars
bar. His desk lamp under its green shade shone down on a
pile of books waiting his attention, to be catalogued perhaps
or, as a jar of glue suggested, mended.

On all sides of the room rank upon rank of books stretched. There was even a small gallery reached by spiral stairs. The air breathed deliciously of musty paper and leather bindings. Roke surveyed the scene.

"My librarian, *hard at work* as ever. We have an extensive collection of erotica, which Marcus is busy cataloging and which needs his detailed examination. Mustn't disturb you, dear fellow," and he led the party out by a farther door. The library seemed well supplied with doors, as if access to it was a necessity of existence; unless, of course, they were for escape. The backstairs climbed from a small landing here. As the party trailed after him, Bone remembered his remark to Grizel about Bluebeard, and wondered when Roke would open a door, with a flourish, on the figures of past wives hanging by their hair from ceiling hooks, the floor covered in blood that could never be washed away from anything that touched it. Now *that* would be extremely useful to the CID.

They followed Roke along an attic corridor whose windows gave a view of parkland, then up a flight of stone stairs which brought them out on leads between two slate slopes. At the end, a turn, and they were at the front of the house on a long stretch of leads behind the battlements. It was littered with sand, and there were stacks of cut stone and cement bags, a large four-by-four board for mixing mortar, a pile of loose stones of all sizes which Bone took for infill, and a pulley shedding a coil of rope which Roke kicked aside.

"Watch your step, *messieurs, mesdames . . .*" Roke waited until all the party had arrived and disposed themselves. Although they stood in sunlight, the slate-blue clouds with their internal yellow light were high behind him.

"This end of the battlements is genuine; the rest, along there, all Gothic pastiche. The level underfoot is higher than when this part was built. The merlons," and he laid a hand on the nearest upward-jutting block of the parapet, "should be high enough to shield an archer, and the embrasures would have to be waist high, at least."

Baz promptly stood behind a merlon and drew an imaginary longbow at the horizon.

"That's right," Roke said, and stepping up to him arranged his hands, the right arm around him. "Thumb to the mouth, elbow out, And then *ztt!* Have you done any archery?"

"No, just Robin Hood on the box."

"You've quite an idea of it. Over there, past that nasty little holly hedge, is where we put up targets."

"How far," Mabey asked, "can you see from here?"

"D'you know, I've no idea. At night you can see Blastock."

Mabey, as if inspired to see whether he could spot Blastock by daylight, leant perilously over an embrasure, hand shading his eyes, and Bone was amused to see Roke unobtrusively take hold of the slack of Mabey's jacket. Fond of spectacle he might be, but he was evidently not keen on allowing guests to land on the terrace unannounced. A few seconds later, Bone understood the precaution better.

A vast metallic clang made everyone start and some cry out. It continued, a noise like a monster saucepan hit by a metal spoon, over their heads, enclosing them. Bone felt his heart speed up. He saw the clock turret now, and Roke's demonic grin. The sound continued, remorselessly, eleven strokes. In the deafened silence came a nervous laugh or two, an expostulation. Arnold Mabey was executing some sort of dance, supported by Roke, before he calmed down and stood still. Grizel murmured, "He's a naughty man," and something of the same kind was being very smoothly said by Nicholas Buchanan.

"So far it doesn't look as if any of us has a weak heart," Bone observed. "No wonder Roke got us up here by eleven, though."

Grizel moved to the corner of the tower, where she and Bone leant on the warm stone and looked out. The woods were a brilliant livid green and gold below the threatening sky.

"Look, there's the other lovebirds."

Bone leant close to her in the embrasure to follow her gaze. Far below, in the shelter of a yew-hedged sunken garden, the Roses stood, embracing each other, looking each into the other's face. Josh Lawson, camera at the ready as ever, was approaching the stone steps to the terrace that went round the house, and if he turned left along the side of the tower below, he would certainly see the pair.

"Let's hope he heads for the front door. I wouldn't like to be interrupted by that man in a spot of canoodling."

"A lovely term, that: canoodling."

"Can 'oo canoodle in a canoe?" Her face, with that alert liveliness, seemed to daze him. He suffered a brief wish to vaporize the whole party so that he could be alone with her.

"If the canoe had a canopy."

"Both quick and modest." She looked past his shoulder. "I think we're all to go down again."

He gave a last glance at the parkland below. Guy had appeared, kicking leaves as he walked, hands in pockets, toward the house. Bone wondered what, apart from late adolescence and a difficult father, made him so morose. Perhaps being nineteen and having a difficult father were enough.

They came down through the house. Roke waved an arm at bedroom doors and said, "After coffee this floor is open, but before that I am sure you would like to see one of the domestic animals." Bone looked at Grizel and raised his eyebrows. More than one scorpion, then? He communicated this idea to her as they went.

Roke turned abruptly in at a door off the backstairs opposite the library. As the party filtered through after him,

Arnold Mabey stopped to examine the heavy curtain, caught back with a thick silk cord, that could close off the arch onto the landing. Before he could unhook the cord, the sisters had turned him round and crowded him through the door.

This room was a drawing room, on the first floor as was once the general fashion. It gave an impression of gold. Sunlight scarcely entered it at this time of day, and moreover the world outside had darkened now with storm clouds. Carpet and curtains, the soft cream of the walls, the gilt of the picture frames, of looking glasses, and of a delicate pattern on the ceiling, made it glow. There was a quiet little fire in the hearth, newly fed with wood.

"This is the gold drawing room, so-called for reasons I will not state. The door there"—he pointed with an orator's gesture—"is out of bounds even to my family without invitation. It's my study. Next to it, the muniment room, which will"—he glanced maliciously round—"be open later," and he smiled suddenly, briefly, at Maitland.

Catherine Maitland, by the fire, asked where the pale golden marble of the chimneypiece came from, a wifely distraction that clearly amused Roke even more. He told her, and went on, "But now: this way."

It seemed at first glance like a conservatory opening from the drawing room, glass roofed and full of lively green in tubs, urns, wall sconces, and troughs. The likeness was borne out by Keziah, watering plants carefully. From this area, however, a flight of wide steps led down toward a curving pool, and Roke descended. Mrs. Webb lowered herself onto a white iron chair, her expression saying *j'y suis, j'y reste,* but the others trooped after Roke. A glass wall to the right showed parkland.

The far end of the "conservatory" held plants as well, and a curiously tropical smell, dank and faintly decaying, gave Bone the thought that carnivorous plants would be quite

Roke's style. The pool swept in its curve, lapping quietly and giving its touch of chlorine to the air. Their voices echoed. The roof was held up by complicated ironwork not unlike fan vaulting. The far end of the pool could now be seen, walled off with rocks and above that, oddly, a metal fence. When they had all passed this and stood on the damp terrazzo beyond, they found a low grill fenced them off from the water. A little rocky bay had been constructed from this end of the pool. Something moved on the slope of rocks beneath an overhang, there was a *schloop!* and an ugly head came across the water. It was smallish, square, and rugged. Among the group there was a tendency to step back. Some of the party had definitely started to appreciate Roke by now, and someone applauded, but this could not be counted as a universal view.

"Dundee was my uncle's pet. I find it very sympathetic of him to build this and to keep so charming an animal."

"What kind is he?" Buchanan asked, rather as though, thought Bone, everyone would want to hurry back and order one.

"A cayman. They're not pretty alligators and far less lovely than crocodiles—"

Arnold Mabey had gone up to the grill and suddenly extended his stick toward the creature's head. Whether he meant an experimental prod or a caress was not clear, but with a quick tumultuous flail and plunge, Dundee snapped the end off the stick and backwatered to gaze enigmatically at everyone.

One of the sisters had hauled Mabey from the brink. The party on the whole evinced a touch of exasperation with Mabey; this was one of the few houses where his urge to experiment might be called suicidal. Roke's face was all at once as inscrutable as Dundee's, but he was at Mabey's side, examining the stick and promising one of his own—"At least, my uncle's. I'm indeed sorry, my dear fellow, not to have given a *specific* warning . . ."

Bone was wondering if a warning specific enough for Arnold Mabey could be got, short of the Last Trump, when a ringing splash from the main pool sent spray over the partition and onto the visitors. There was a sound of someone trudgening. Roke smiled again; one could believe in his sympathy with an uncle who liked caymans. It was family feeling. Dundee in the water gaped enticingly.

"We have another exhibit, in the swimming pool. Shall we move round?"

They shuffled and trod round, wary on wet terrazzo. Adrian stood poised on the springboard. He paid no attention to his audience but, after a moment, raised his arms— having, Bone thought, given the world a chance to admire. In blue very-briefs, slender and long legged, he certainly stripped well. He took off in a good shallow dive, came up, turned over, and lay on the water with his hair haloing his head; turned again and appeared to see his audience for the first time. He raised a graceful arm and began to speak.

Roke had stooped. Now he roared, "Out! Get out! Dundee's loose."

A dark shape underwater shot along the depth, obscure, predatory.

"OUT! GET OUT, MAN!"

Adrian flailed across the pool, reached the side, hauled himself up, gasping, slipped back, and, helped by Baz and Buchanan, scrambled out. He stood up, hair plastered flat and dripping, chest heaving, and looked back. A formless shape surfaced. Black plastic drifted away from a midget radio-controlled submarine that bobbed on the disturbed water. Roke held up the control box.

Baz broke into laughter first. "Near thing there! He'd have had your leg for lunch!" The idea almost incapacitated him, and Arnold Mabey was thwacking the remaining length of his stick on his palm to express his own enjoyment. The others were tittering, perhaps as much from relief as in genuine amusement. The sympathy was quite likely to be with the victim of the joke, but he was not really able to appreciate it.

"You *bastard!*" His voice cracked, almost out of control. "You *bastard!*" He whirled, and thrust his way out past the onlookers, who hastily drew back from his wet arms. He stumbled up the stairs, grabbed a towel, kicked his feet into sandals, and was gone, to Baz's echoing laughter.

Comments varied between Catherine's "poor boy" and Mabey's "rather a poor sport, I fear."

Bone said to Grizel in an undertone, "If Roke works that sort of joke often, young Adrian must pay dearly for his keep. I wonder he thinks it's worth it."

Roke brought the submarine to his feet and picked it from the water.

"Time for coffee," he said, "almost. Wander toward the small morning room, to the right of the front door as you go down the main stairs, and look at anything you like on the way." He took Angela North by the arm as everyone moved off, and bent to speak to her. She went with him, and as Bone and Grizel paused in the gold drawing room, Roke and Angela disappeared into his study.

Grizel said in an undertone, "Going to ask her about Baz, wouldn't you say? It can't be a coincidence."

"He's far more Roke's style than Guy is."

She rubbed her head against Bone's shoulder and looked up at him. "You mean Roke is one kind of bastard and Baz is another; the literal sort."

"I wonder what Jane will think of it."

"Oh dear. Yes, I wonder. I don't think Baz knows, do you? Though it may be we're jumping to a false conclusion on the strength of a likeness and circumstantial evidence."

They made their way toward the coffee room. The Webbs, by a dedicated trudge, were ahead of them descending the last step to the front hall.

Grizel, still *sotto voce*, went on, "How on earth will Jane feel? An ex-lover of her husband's turning up like this? Should I warn her?"

Bone thought about it. "As a professional interferer, I'd be on the side of saying nothing and keeping out of it. But Jane's your friend and you'd know best."

Keziah came from the kitchen quarters, crossed the hall, and shut the front door on the darkening garden. She was carrying a coffeepot, and under her arm held an assortment of walking sticks for Arnold Mabey to choose from. Bone and Grizel followed her.

The Webbs had already drawn chairs up to one of the tables, where biscuits, currant buns, and small iced cakes were displayed, and Keziah supplied them with coffee. She turned warmly to Grizel, hefting the coffeepot.

More of the party came in—Mabey and the shepherding sisters, others whom Bone felt he really ought to have got sorted by now. Baz ranged in, handing coffee cups at once, depriving the Webbs' table of a plate of cakes to offer it round and, when he reached Bone, being unable to speak by reason of mouth being crammed, and icing on his top lip.

Buchanan came in, talking to Jane and carrying a tray for her, a silver tray with piecrust edges which held another coffeepot and milk jug. Lynda Rose followed them.

"Who isn't here?" Buchanan asked, putting the tray down. He scanned the room's inhabitants in a rapid silent roll call. He said to Bone, "Ah. M'm. Lawson's missing. Still, he was in the garden, wasn't he? He'll have to miss coffee. Let's hope he's still safely outdoors. And the Maitlands I saw, lingering upstairs. And no Donald Spencer. We'll have to find where he's sleepwalking." He turned to Jane and plunged into conversation, leaving Bone wondering if he ought to find Spencer. He abandoned the idea. He was on holiday and not accountable; he got into a conversation with one of the sisters, Sheila, and an unknown sturdy woman, about crocodiles. He heard Jane, talking to Buchanan of the stolen jade collection of Roke's, break off as Guy came hurriedly in and spoke in her ear. She excused herself, frowning, and went out with him.

"I'm *beginning* to think of Josh Lawson at large, indoors, with a camera," Buchanan said to Sheila Simpson-Bates.

"I'll go and have a look for him," Bone said. "No, it's all right, I don't mind and I know the place a bit." He stopped to tell Grizel, who in Jane's place was pouring coffee, and Lynda Rose, standing with a coffee cup, said, "He went into the house by the turret stairs. He was heading for the roof."

"If he's up there he's out of harm's way, but I'll go and check. He'll want his coffee." Hot Lunch Lawson would not want to miss any prerogative he could enjoy.

"If he's on the roof he won't stay. It's going to rain."

"All the same." Bone touched her arm and went.

"Rain?" Lynda raised her penciled eyebrows. "It's going to *piss* down at any moment. I'm glad we saw the grounds first."

Knebworth entered bearing hot milk, and after him came pink-cheeked Angela North, who was patting her hair and looking so self-conscious that Grizel at once suspected that she had been brushing up her relationship with Roke. She looked, in fact, very pleased with herself, and went to talk to her son.

Grizel heard the general talk, as she leaned against the sideboard with her cup . . . "bit of a show-off, that swimmer . . . got his comeuppance! . . . exquisite room . . . very much the joker . . ."

A brilliant flash of lightning caught the party in a second's freeze, cups poised at lips, mouths open to receive cake. A low ominous rumble succeeded, a celestial Rottweiler getting its hackles up, and the last vestige of daylight was suddenly gone.

"Knebworth, would you put the lights on, please?" Keziah, in Jane's absence, showed a touch of the future Lady Roke. Knebworth started for the door, but Arnold Mabey had a better idea. Before anyone knew what he was doing he reached out and hauled on the cords hanging by the nearest window. The ruched cream silk of the Austrian blind folded up on itself with a discreet hiss. The amount of light was not, however, much increased. The top panes of window were still obscured by something not at once remotely recognizable; or to which everyone instinctively refused recognition.

Because some stopped dumb, those not looking turned and their talk too died away. Baz, hands on knees, bent to peer up sideways. His mother seized him incongruously by the jutting back pocket of his jeans. "It's not real, is it? It's a joke. It's a joke."

Others contorted, bending over like Baz, as though, Grizel thought with sick disbelief, they had all started up some silly game. Keziah put her hands over her eyes after one glance as if to blot out what she saw.

Beyond the glass, Josh Lawson continued to swing gently to and fro, upside down. His blackened face stared in with suffused eyes, tongue protruding as if greedy for the cakes and coffee he would not now enjoy.

At last somebody began to scream.

Chapter

....

7

THEY CROWDED OUT, IRRESISTIBLY. GRIZEL RAN WITH THE REST, wishing Robert were here, her strongest feeling disbelief. *If this is something Roke's cooked up . . . Oh, let it be something Roke's cooked up.* Arnold Mabey quite shoved her in his effort to see. For a moment, there in the chill lowering air, no one approached the swinging figure, which the vagrant wind caught of a sudden and turned as if he swung to look at them. There was calling out, shouting. "Get him down . . . Frightful . . . Someone go up and . . . Oh, God . . . a doctor . . ."

Lawson was swinging by one ankle caught in a loop of rope. His jacket's skirt fell behind his neck like a Tudor ruff, his arms preventing it from sliding off. His free leg wagged. Grizel went forward, automatically a teacher taking responsibility. She reached him just as Buchanan did and they stopped him swinging. She looked around, thinking someone must get help. People do odd things in moments of stress. Mabey, finding he was still holding a bun, put it in his pocket. Lynda Rose strode to pick up Lawson's camera from a tussock of thyme on the flagstones. She fumbled with it and said, "It's broken."

Baz tried to reach Lawson's roped ankle. He put a foot on the windowsill and precariously reached up. Grizel saw Lawson's appalling face close to. Her feelings brought down a portcullis, her mind said, *Asphyxiation.* Someone nearby retched, and footsteps ran stumbling away.

A voice hailed. She looked up at the heavy sky and saw her husband leaning between merlons overhead. "I'll lower him," he called.

"Right oh," Baz returned, and he jumped down and helped to steady the dreadful thing as it descended. They had put him on the flagstones when John Rose appeared around the corner of the house, paused, and came running.

"Someone ill? I'm a doctor."

"A doctor?" someone said. Grizel, trying to undo Lawson's shirt without touching the engorged face, felt surprise; he'd hidden it well, she thought.

Lynda tiresomely repeated, "His camera's broken," as though Lawson were likely to care, or as if it could make a difference to the diagnosis.

John Rose felt for a pulse, and tried to tilt Lawson's head back to clear his air passages, but the neck was too swollen to be flexible. She thought of mouth-to-mouth resuscitation, and mentally recoiled.

"He shouldn't have gone on the roof," one Simpson-Bates said tearfully.

"He told us he gets vertigo," chimed the other.

Baz said, "We thought it was a joke. A Roke joke, you

know." Dr. Rose's face showed no comprehension. Of course he knew nothing of Roke's sense of humor. He had missed it all.

"He shouldn't have gone on the roof alone if he had—"

"Lord Roke ought not to let people go on the roof with all that builders' stuff there—"

"Of course, Mr. Lawson didn't hear Lord Roke warning us—"

Lightning took the scene in and out of focus. An instantaneous crack of thunder and huge drops of rain followed. Some people, with cries, fled to the porch.

"Get him onto that lounger."

Buchanan, Baz, and Rose lifted Lawson and, tripping on the plants that tufted the flagstones, put him on the rusty canvas.

"An ambulance must be called."

"I'll find Lord Roke," Buchanan said. He was white, anxious.

"We'd better carry him indoors." So far there was no sustained downpour, but the sky was black. Grizel looked toward the roof. No Robert. She hoped he was coming down. Surely he could throw some light on all this. Perhaps he had even seen Lawson fall. Buchanan, who had hesitated over whether to find Roke or help with the carrying, saw Grizel about to pick up a corner of the lounger, with Rose and Baz, and he hastily superseded her; and she, feeling suddenly incapable, let him.

"Do get under cover, Mrs. Bone. Go indoors." Now the rain was smacking down on her head, and through her shirt. It fell on Lawson's helpless form. His arms were splayed out still. She thought of the reason, the dammed-up blood vessels, tissues already stiffened. A touch of nausea made her desperately turn her mind away. *Robert.*

A rift in the driving cloud let sunlight fall on the castle as if singling it out. She came into the hall, which was full of shocked voices and people brushing rain from shoulders and hair.

"Where's Lord Roke?" Buchanan asked from the porch, where they had put down the lounger.

Grizel willed her husband to arrive. If anyone knew how to cope in this horrible time, he would. She saw for a second his lifetime of experiences like this one. She also was shocked at wondering how this would affect the tour and whether it would be canceled.

A noise, footsteps slowly dragging on marble, made her look up. Someone was coming down the left-hand flight of the great divided staircase, taking each tread with ominous deliberation. Those in the hall, their minds still occupied with the shock of Lawson's death, raised their heads as she did, to see who it was.

Roke, at last. But what kind of trick was he playing now? Grizel had seen enough Japanese films to recognize the samurai armor he was wearing, the shoulder guards like *Dallas* power-dressing, the skirt of shiny metallic ribbing, the steel platelets laced on with thongs, the helmet with its iron sweep. What riveted her attention was the face under its curve, a face as grotesque as the one outside, with eyes fixed, staring, the mouth drawn in a rictus like a samurai war mask.

Through his neck, clearly seen under the outward curve of the helmet, was an arrow, the fletched end standing out a good few inches one side, the point on the other.

Grizel had seen Kurosawa's film of *Macbeth*, in which his own soldiers send into him flight after flight of arrows until he bristles with them; but he will not die until one transfixes him through the neck. She remembered the joke shops that sell hatchets that stick in your head, knives to pierce a hand, no doubt arrows for your neck. She thought, Roke doesn't know about Lawson; he's staging this, his promised view of the Japanese armor after coffee. He doesn't know what's happened, and the ghastly bad taste of what he's doing; someone should tell him.

Roke stood on the half landing, facing the last wide flight down to the hall. His hands were raised as though to claw at his neck, and he made some guttural sound, and then he lurched, groped at the banister and, missing it by yards, tumbled down the stairs to land with an echoing crash sprawled on the floor at the foot of them. The only thing that moved in that long moment was the dark stain that spread along the marble beneath Roke's head.

Chapter

8

HE LAY THERE. BAZ, WHO HAD MADE A NOISE OF APPLAUSE, AT once stopped. Bone, followed by Jane, came running from the back of the house, Angela too, along the other side. The spell broke, synapses unjammed, people moved.

Angela and Jane, both crying, "Benet!" ran to Roke. Bone had already reached him and crouched at his head. Grizel, relieved at his coming, had a sense that he was immediately lost to her in his professional role.

She saw people staring down along the balustrade of the top landing: the Maitlands, Marcus the librarian, Adrian; and Guy rounding the newel to run down the stairs. Dr. Rose had joined the group around Roke. She heard him say, "I'm sorry. He's dead."

Angela, who had one of Roke's hands in hers, now broke into whooping hysteria. Jane, leaning across, gave her a swinging slap and she fell sidelong. Baz, instantly beside her, helped her up, drew her away. They happened to stand below the portrait that he resembled and Guy suddenly halted on the bottom step, looking at Baz.

Bone said in a low voice to Jane, "You must call the police. This isn't an accident."

Nicholas Buchanan had come forward, used to responsibility, and it was he who stopped Mabey and the Webbs from approaching Roke's body. They resisted him, clearly eager to avail themselves of all the tour could offer. Bone stood up and said, "Everyone must keep away from here. Would you please all go into the coffee room and wait for the police?"

Knebworth could be heard somewhere in the depths and stone-arched passages of the house, saying "Police!" at the volume used on the telephone by those older people who feel the voice itself must carry all the way to the other end of the wire.

Buchanan shepherded his group back to the coffee room. Grizel hesitated, thinking she should go with them, wondering if she should go to Jane. She looked at Robert's back, and crossed to the coffee room. Only Sheila Simpson-Bates was coming the other way, and, meeting Grizel, she whispered, "I'll just go out and stay with Mr. Lawson. I don't think the poor man ought to lie there alone." She slipped out to the porch. Grizel, hardly registering this, paused by the coffee room door. Baz had led his mother in, and the Maitlands, who must have come down by the backstairs, were tiptoeing along the hall to join the group. In the center, dark against the dim light coming from above, Bone and Marcus Weatherby stood, Jane and Keziah now knelt or crouched at one side, Guy at the other, of Roke's body. It looked disconcertingly like a huge insect with the carapace of ribbed armor askew. Adrian Nash leaned on the curve of the banister a pace or two away, an expression on his face of shock and incredulity. A murmur from Keziah seemed to multiply itself in the roof.

Grizel shut the door.

The coffee room, officially the small morning room, was large enough for Baz to have been able to find an almost private corner for his mother. She still wept convulsively and he sat shielding her and holding her hands in both his. Others were talking in low voices with awkward pauses. The Webbs had gone back to their place and had drawn a plate of buns closer.

Grizel found Buchanan at her side. Low voiced, like the rest, he said, "You don't, I suppose, have any idea what happens now?"

"I think we all hang about until the police arrive and want everyone to give an account of events."

"I rather feel I had better telephone to Colonel Makepeace to say we shan't be there this afternoon." There were practical obligations he had to attend to.

Grizel looked at the Webbs. "That won't be popular with some of the party."

Buchanan followed her gaze, and turned abruptly toward the door. She could see he wanted desperately to laugh; she herself felt the danger of light relief, that it could escalate into hysteria.

Keziah came in, slipping around the door. She said to Buchanan, "The police are coming. They ask that everyone should stay put. I'll get more coffee; you could all probably do with it."

"I ought to telephone this afternoon's host."

Keziah told him where the telephone was, and he went out. She turned to Grizel. "Jane asked me to take over here. Could you go to her? I think she needs—"

"Of course."

Keziah reached to pour the last of the pot for Mrs. Webb, who, if she looked up, could have seen that the girl had been crying. She only reached for the milk jug that she and her husband had lodged between their elbows, but she nearly spilled it when Baz said loudly, "My *what?*"

Angela drew him closer and went on talking.

Bone stood waiting. The random sunlight had gone and the hall had become dark. He felt useless, without his proper function yet unable to abdicate responsibility and retire. Knebworth moved with his slow tread to turn on the lights in the wall sconces. Jane, sitting on the lower stairs between Guy and Grizel, was silent.

Although he was without occupation, Bone had already begun a professional appraisal of events. Instead of having to establish afterward who had the opportunity to commit the murder under investigation, he had already filed away those absent—at least at the time when he had volunteered to fetch Lawson. He would not yet consider his personal reactions to what he had seen from the roof.

Whoever came to take up the case of Roke's murder would have plenty to do in sorting out a richness of motives: almost anyone who had been in Roke's vicinity for long must have suffered the impulse, however temporary, to go for him with anything handy. That it should have turned out to be a Japanese arrow went well with Roke's own taste for the bizarre. The irony for Bone himself lay in that, being for once at the scene of the murder, he had no authority to explore it.

Adrian still leaned decoratively against the banisters, as though audience at a play. A telephone rang upstairs and Marcus Weatherby said, "I'd better answer it. I'll be in the library, Jane, if I'm wanted. If there's anything I can—"

"Thank you," she said. Her voice was flat. "Yes, do answer it." The ringing might be an irritant to her nerves. He ran up the stairs; the noise swelled as he opened the library door, and then stopped.

A familiar warbling sounded in the distance. Bone automatically stirred, and then did nothing. It was Dr. Rose, who went out saying, "That will be the ambulance."

"Well! I was going to say, thank God for that," Adrian remarked, "but I dare say the next few hours will be just as tedious."

Jane raised her head and replied, precise and calm, "Since there's no longer any excuse for your being here, as soon as possible I should like you out of this house."

Chapter

....

9

CHIEF INSPECTOR PRIOR ARRIVED IN A CHEERFUL MOOD. IF HE had politics, they were socialist. For a single family to own and live in a place like Roke Castle was a privilege no one should be able to afford. Now that Lord Roke appeared to have paid for the privilege with his life, it would be a pleasure to deal with the consequences. He whistled through his teeth all the way across the rolling parkland (his sergeant as usual longing for earplugs) and commented on the waste of good land that could be used for development. There were enough people needing homes. The rich had for too long owned too much; hardly a surprise that someone had been inspired to kill Lord Roke. *Lord*—what did "Lord" mean anyway except that he'd had grabbing, conniving ancestors. You got made a lord only by some kind of arse-licking. From time to time there'd been gossip about this one: that girl in some bizarre get-up in the grounds; and there'd been a row in some club in London—Prior recalled the photoflash of a big man coming out of a door, the face of a grinning bully. Death could only improve men like Lord Roke.

Sheila Simpson-Bates, sitting uncomfortably on a still-damp bench in the drafty porch beside the shrouded figure of Mr. Lawson, was the first to see the Chief Inspector emerge from his car and stride toward her across the terrace, followed by his sergeant. Another car and a van drew up on the gravel by the tour bus. She saw, as he approached, a short, frowning man in a not-too-clean mac over a dark suit, a man whose light eyes fixed on her and then on the shape beside her as though its condition were her fault. A gutter above now maliciously discharged a wad of leaves and a pint of rain, that hit the porch and spattered the badly cut graying brown hair. He shook it off impatiently. She rose. His square jaw gave him an air of permanent truculence, which helped to make her feel once more accused as he bent to twitch off the anorak covering Lawson's face and, staring, turn to her.

"This isn't Lord Roke!" He was indignant, as though she had been trying to deceive him.

"No, it's Joshua Lawson. He had an accident. Lord Roke is in the hall." She pointed.

Lady Roke had come out of the front door, and was speaking to a man in jeans, cluttered with a metal carrying box and tripod. He called, "Sir, Sir!" and Prior strode off, giving orders, toward the door.

Bone watched him stride in. Prior took a comprehensive look around as he entered and his mouth's corners turned down, condemning the lot. He came to stand over Roke, stared at the armor, the arrow, and said, "What the hell's going on? Is this a hoax?"

Roke's reputation was evidently known, but Bone gave

this unknown officer ten out of ten for a crass beginning. He said, "No. He's been shot through the neck."

The man crouched briefly and, convinced, stood back and called his team. A sudden noise broke out from the incarcerated group in the small morning room, and he said irritably, "What's going on in there?"

Jane said, "We've got a tour seeing the house." She was contained and tense.

"And you are?"

Guy said, "It's Lady Roke." He was, understandably, curt.

"And *you* are?"

"My son, Guy Paisley. This is his fiancée, Keziah Barclay-Mayhew."

Bone felt that the sneer this time was for the double-barrel. Swinging farther around, the man looked up the stairs.

"And you?" he called to Marcus, who had come out on the landing, probably at the sound of sirens.

"Marcus Weatherby. The librarian."

"Librarian? What are you doing here?"

"I've just come from the library."

A snort of exasperation, and he clarified his demand. "What are you doing *in this house?*"

Oddly enough, it was Adrian who saved the police blood pressure, putting in petulantly, "How much longer is this crosstalk act going on? Marcus is Lord Roke's librarian. He *works* here."

"And *you* are?"

"Adrian Nash. A friend of the family."

"A friend of my husband," said Jane, with ice.

The Inspector gave Adrian a particularly hard stare, before he turned on Bone.

"And you?"

For answer, Bone pulled out his card. He had thought, that morning as he dressed, how absurd was his automatic transfer of it to the jacket he was going to wear. He had transferred it all the same. Prior took it and, after a moment's frowning examination, shifted his stare to Bone's face, not apparently liking that any better. He handed back the card, and remarked abruptly, "Didn't you have enough trouble where you came from? What's your position here? Sir?"

Jane said, "Superintendent Bone and his wife are my guests." She added, and Bone could have cheered, "And *you* are?"

"Chief Inspector Prior, Blastock police."

Prior thought he could probably avoid having to call her by title. Because she'd hooked a lord didn't make her anything. The boy wasn't Roke's, he supposed, with the different name. He wanted the place cleared, and particularly he wanted the extraneous Super out of the way; he could be trouble if he chose to interfere.

Perhaps the man was psychic. He looked at Prior down his toffee nose—a washed-out, po-faced type—and said, "You'll want to get on here. I'll join the tour group in the coffee room."

"I think that'd be a very good idea," said Prior. "Sir."

The Super took himself off. Prior was relieved. Courtesy of the Force was all very well, but when rank got loaded on, and that one was the sort to let Prior know it, then, thanks very much.

They had put up a screen. The police doctor came out and said, "From close to, I'd say, that arrow. I'd think an arrow, even a light bamboo thing like this, fired from any distance, might have stuck without going clear through. That's theory, though. It will need testing. I'm not up in toxophily."

Although the doctor had spoken in a confidential tone, the family had heard. He saw them stirring.

"You mean it's poisoned?" Then he could have kicked himself. *Toxicology!* This toxo—was something different;

and the pretty poove on the stairs was laughing. At this point the ambulance arrived.

"Who sent for that?" Prior asked as it backed up to the door.

Roke's widow said, "I did. For the man who fell off the roof."

"Fell off the *roof?*" Nash all but squawked. "Who fell off the roof?"

"Man named Joshua Lawson," Prior told him. "Let's keep to the point. Who shot this arrow?"

There was silence. He'd expected nothing else.

"Isn't that what you're going to tell us?" asked the poove.

With enormous patience Prior said, "Who was here when he was shot?"

The librarian remarked, "Adrian Nash and I were in the library."

Lady Roke said, "I was coming back from phoning for the ambulance when Benet came down the stairs."

"Did you see it happen? The shooting?"

"The arrow was there. Already. He came down the stairs . . ."

She was beginning to show the strain. Prior said, "Where's there a room, eh?—a room we can talk in."

Not, after all, difficult to get Lady Roke moved without saying her name.

A man and a woman had hovered into sight along the wall. Lady Roke spoke to them across Prior. "I'd like coffee, please. Black coffee."

"Right oh," Prior said. "I'll have a cup. Black. Two sugars."

The man said, "M'lady. Very good, sir."

Lady Roke was being helped into a room off the hall by her son and the girl. The poove—Nash, wasn't it?—whom she'd as good as called her husband's boyfriend, dawdled after, and the librarian followed. The WPC with the good legs went in after them, and Sergeant Williams came with a question about taking Lawson's body away.

"Carry on. If there's a connection I'll link it up all right. I'll have the PM report."

Prior was again making for the room the family had gone into when a neat man in a navy jersey and twill trousers appeared as if from nowhere and said, "Chief Inspector," and Prior had to halt again. The man said pleasantly, "My coach driver's here. I'm the organizer of this tour, you see, and we are supposed to be at Norton Crawley for lunch . . ."

"Is your bloody tour really more important than a murder?"

The face closed down. *That's put him in his place*, Prior thought.

"As you're in charge," said the man crisply, "I am informing you that I have telephoned Colonel and Lady Elizabeth Makepeace to put off this afternoon's visit, and I'm about to phone the Lion in Norton Crawley about lunch."

He went smartly off. Colonel Makepeace was the Lord Lieutenant. Prior stared after him with a knowledge that he'd been trumped.

The family, in a large posh room, had grouped themselves on a dark blue settee, with the librarian behind. Nash perched on a chair arm. The butler was serving coffee and brought Prior's cup with the sugar bowl on a tray.

"Now. Who was there when Lord Roke was shot?"

Silence. They looked at him.

Lady Roke finally said, "He came down the stairs with the arrow. I was here in the hall." Her voice was very strained.

"I only came out on the landing," Guy Paisley said, "when I heard screaming."

"Same with us," Nash said. "Marcus and I were in the library."

"What did you see then?" Prior ignored Nash. "Where was your dad when you came onto the landing?" Was it his dad or his stepfather? No matter; he probably called him dad.

"My father was on the floor. Where you saw him."

"What was the fancy dress for?"

"My father liked practical jokes. He was going to stand in the gallery in armor and when my mother took the party up there he would move. He was going to startle them."

Nash remarked, "I'd say he pulled it off, wouldn't you?" and the young man swung around and said savagely, "Shut up."

Prior had been watching them as he drank his coffee. Now he pushed the cup among the china ornaments on the mantelpiece and said, "None of you saw this arrow shot at him, but anyone in the hall could have done it?"

"He must have been shot upstairs," Lady Roke said. She spoke with more calm now. A cool customer.

"And you three were upstairs?" he said to the men.

"I don't know how often I have to tell you," Nash said, rolling his eyes upward, "I was in the library. So was Marcus. We didn't hear or see a thing till there was all the screaming."

Weatherby concurred, "And I last saw Lord Roke in the gallery starting to put the armor on. I helped him to lace up the leg armor and then the library phone rang, so I went to answer it."

"And I came in after Marcus. I mean I heard the phone from the landing and I went into the library and I said, 'Where's Benet?' and Marcus said, 'Do give him a hand with that armor.' But I knew what he could be like if you tried to help him with anything so I stayed to chat with Marcus."

"And you?" Prior said to Guy Paisley.

"I was looking for my father because of this accident—"

"Oh, yes. The accident. It's been a busy day here."

They were none of them giving him anything in the way of body language except hostility and reserve. Guy Paisley had stopped when Prior interrupted, and said nothing.

"Go on, go on."

Lady Roke said, with even more chill, "I had asked my son to find his father."

"Where'd you look, then?"

"In the gallery, but he wasn't there, so I went into the library because I heard them talking. They said my father was in the gallery, but he wasn't, so I tried the muniment room—"

"The how much?" Prior demanded. The poove was turning up his eyes again.

"The muniment room. Where all the records and so on are kept."

"Oh, right." It has to be the music room, he thought. God, these poncy words.

"Two of the visitors, the tour party, were in there, but he wasn't, so I went to his bedroom . . . Then the screaming—"

"Who were they, these two visitors?"

"I've no idea. Man and a woman. Grayish."

"That covers most of them," Nash said with a laugh like a snort. Paisley started to say something angry and was stopped by his mother's hand on his.

"And where were you, miss?" Prior asked the hippie-looking girlfriend. Funny to see that Indian floaty gear and plait in a house like this.

"Helping with coffee in the small morning room."

"Well, I'll want statements from you all. For the moment, though . . ."

Sergeant Williams came in. Prior, with a nod at the family, went to meet him and came out into the hall.

"There's a whole lot of bows and arrows upstairs, sir, in a big room with oriental armor; and there's quite a bit of blood on one of the chairs. And they've finished here." He indicated the screened body. "All right to remove him?"

"Right. Set the team onto this big oriental room. I'll be there when I've had a word with that tour group."

The small morning room turned out to be a sizeable place full of chairs and sofas and small tables, very crowded at the moment. The tour leader came toward him at once. Everyone looked at him, a score of faces. PC Unwin rose from behind the door.

"Well, you lot next. Got the names, Unwin?"

"I've given him a list," the tour leader said, "one of mine."

Unwin handed it over, and Prior began a roll call, looking at the faces as each of them answered. When he came to "Bone," it turned out that the Super had a striking, blond wife, slender, with large eyes and short hair. Most of the rest did seem to be "grayish," as Paisley had said.

"Joshua Law—Unwin, why didn't you delete that?"

"Sorry, sir."

"Arnold Mabey?"

A tall angular vague gent examining the underside of a biscuit plate was tapped on the arm by the woman next to him. There was a cascade of biscuits, which the people around him fielded without surprise, and the woman said, "This is Mr. Mabey."

"Benjamin Maitland?"

A gray, precise, pale man who gazed mistrustfully and half raised a hand. His wife, Catherine, was a gray-haired anxious woman; looked spry.

"Dr. Rose?"

Dark with spectacles, square-faced; tricky eyes turned

aside. His wife, Lynda, was ten years younger at least; among the younger lot here, a looker with frank gaze.

"Mrs. Angela North?"

"Yes," said the fair, still pretty woman in the corner by the fireplace, pulling forward a big young man, tough but with girlish curls. "And this is my son, Lord Roke."

Chapter

10

BONE WAS AWARE OF A MENTAL *CLICK,* AS THOUGH A CROSS-
word answer that he'd been niggling over had suddenly
arrived. Baz, however, gave a protesting sound regrettably
like a hoot.

"Ma, really!"

"I'm sorry, Baz," she said, and to Prior, "Benet Paisley,
the late Lord Roke, was my first husband and Baz is his
son."

It was like a scene from a comedy. Bone's swift glance saw
everyone fixed, attentive, even the Webbs frozen, biscuits in
hand.

Prior, with sudden interest, demanded, "Why were you
on this tour, then?" Baz, stunned to silence, listened with
gaze fixed on his mother.

"I wanted his father to see Basil."

"You mean"—Prior was incredulous—"they hadn't met?"

"They'd never met." She seemed to have got over the hysteria with which she had greeted Roke's death, and to have tidied and composed herself, even to be enjoying this center stage drama. Excitement made her pretty. "When I divorced Benet, I went to Australia and married again."

Baz said hoarsely, "But just because Lord Roke you say was my father . . ."

Prior demanded what everyone longed to know: "Why haven't you mentioned this before?"

"It was—it was a kind of joke." Angela fluttered her hands vaguely. "Benet always liked jokes. He liked this one very much."

Bone could believe this. He had noticed Roke watching Baz from the moment when he had stood under the portrait, and was sure Roke had cottoned on well before he was told.

"When did you tell him?"

"We were allowed to wander for a little before coffee. He took me into his study. He was delighted with Baz. About Baz, I mean. Then he said it would be charming for Guy, giving him a chance to get out of Roke, and I didn't like that. I didn't come here to get anything."

Prior's tone was cynical. "Then whatever did you come for?"

"Why, for my son. It was time he knew his father."

Bone heard the touch of drama in the statement. If keeping her son's existence from Roke all these years had been a joke of Angela's, then introducing him on this chance tour was a refinement Roke might well appreciate.

Arthur Webb now carried the biscuit up to his mouth, and his wife a second later copied him. Neither moved from a fixed regard of Angela.

"Where were you when the deceased came down the stairs?"

"I was in the hall. I was just coming back from being sick."

"Being *sick?*"

"Well, yes. It may be nothing to you, but when we saw Mr. Lawson hanging . . ."

As she could say no more, the pretty pale face twisted up, the memory overcoming her even in her absorption in her own drama, Sheila Simpson-Bates took up.

"It really was appalling. He looked dreadful."

Bone saw clearly that Prior hadn't known about Lawson hanging at the window. Roke's death had taken all his attention when he should have had time for the "accident." He rallied fast, however. "We'll go into that later. Who else was out of the room, this room, when Roke fell on the stairs?"

The group looked at one another. Buchanan said, "In fact most of us were. We'd gone out on the terrace to—to do what we could about Lawson."

"Most of you. What about the others?"

Dr. Rose said, "I for one wasn't there. I'd been out with Lynda in the garden."

"We were in the muniment room," Benjamin Maitland said, "Catherine and I." He took her hand.

"Who else wasn't here?"

Bone said, "I went to look for Lawson; he hadn't come for coffee and Nicholas"—he indicated Buchanan—"asked me to look for him."

"Why for him? Why not for the others?"

"I wasn't sure he might not be taking photographs," Buchanan said. "We've been asked not to in this house."

Prior waited for the family to leave Lady Roke by herself with him. It would be odd if she hadn't been enraged with Roke over this arrival of another son. Perhaps she thought it was a put-up job between the ex-wife and Roke; and perhaps it was, too. That washed-out prettiness of Mrs. North could well disguise a very smart cookie, and the idea of coming on a tour to introduce her son was more than a bit far-fetched.

He had also noticed that Lord Roke had been Benet Paisley, so the Paisley boy, Guy, was his son after all, and both he and his mother could be out of their minds about the young Aussie's arrival.

"So," he said to her as the door shut, "who's the new Lord Roke?"

She looked up, annoyed. "My son Guy, of course."

Prior watched her fiddle with one earring, as if exasperated with it. He thought, *Yeah? I bet she knows!* "What about the first wife's son?"

"They didn't have children," she said curtly.

"You didn't know the first wife's on this tour—with her son?"

"Certainly I saw *her.* I was very surprised that she should turn up in that manner. Trying to force her way back into Roke's life, I suppose. If she has a son with her, he can't be Roke's."

"You sound very sure of that."

"I am. He left her *because* they had no children. Guy was born the year we were married."

Ah, was he then! "That why you married?"

"I didn't suppose it needed underlining," she said contemptuously, perfectly cool about it. "Is the woman pretending she had Benet's son after the divorce and never said a word about it until now? After all these years she turns up on a coach trip, with this ridiculous story! Perhaps she did tell Benet and he laughed at her. She must be unhinged, cooking all this up. Perhaps she's mad enough to have killed him for seeing through her. I dare say he wasn't kind about it. He never bothered to spare people's feelings."

"Oh? Did he hurt yours a lot?"

She looked at him, as if faintly surprised. "We understood each other."

"Did he?"

"Chief Inspector: he hurt *everybody's* feelings. That was his life."

"What terms were you on with him?"

"Terms? I've lived with him for nineteen years. He needed an audience and he knew I appreciated him. I was—hostess for him. *And* the mother of his sons."

"You have other boys?"

"Two. They're spending half term with some friends."

"How did he get on with this eldest one?"

There was a slight pause while she considered. "How did he . . . ? In fact, very well. It might not appear so because Benet was always acerbic"—she glanced at Prior and elaborated—"sarcastic, critical. All the same he was very proud of him. Guy was devoted to Roke but he's too shy to show it much."

"A shy lad and a sharp father. Doesn't sound ideal."

"On the surface, it might not show how well they got on. Guy is very upset indeed."

"Is he due to inherit a lot?"

"The estate, naturally."

"In actual money, I mean?"

"I really couldn't tell you." A little shrug. She looked out of the window. "It will all be taxed, of course. The lawyers would know. Roke didn't discuss money." From her tone he gathered that money just wasn't talked about. *In a pig's eye*, he thought.

"How about the librarian and the other piece of fancy work? Roke on good terms with that lot?"

"Lord Roke"—her emphasis on the title was of the slightest—"found Marcus invaluable. He's become a dear friend of the family. He's worked for some time on the archives here, and cataloging the library. Everything was in perfect chaos when we came here." She paused, then added, "Adrian Nash is one of those people with whom Benet amused himself from time to time."

"Was Roke homosexual?" He refused to pick up her hint about the title.

"He wasn't above flirting. What more he did was his affair."

"Never discussed that either?"

"It was his affair." Her hands lay quite still, fingers linked, on her blue skirt. No rings but the wedding ring. A cufflink of plain gold gleamed. "When I married Benet I knew he was a man who would live his own life, however anyone felt."

"Did you mind?"

"It had nothing to do with our marriage."

"Worth putting up with a faggot or two to be Lady Roke, eh?"

"I do not have to put up with impertinence from you," she said, without any anger, only the confidence that it was true. "He was not Lord Roke when we married, nor was he likely to be."

"Is that so?"

She put her lips very firmly together and stood up. Prior had finally got through that upper-class varnish. He grinned.

"Thank you, Lady Roke. Now I'll talk to your son."

The WPC only just got the door open in time for Lady Roke to sweep out. She followed her and came back with the young man. He seemed thoroughly ill at ease, peering past a swathe of dark, rather greasy hair that looked odd with the short back and sides of the rest of his head. His clothes were no class at all: brown check shirt, brown sweater, jeans, trainers; unless the sweater, leaf patterned, was more pricey than it looked at first.

"So you think you're the new Lord Roke?"

He glowered. "I think it's bloody bad taste to mention it. But of course I am."

Prior picked up the tour list. "How about this Mr. Basil North, then?"

"*What* about him? Who is he?"

"According to his mother, he's your father's eldest son."

"Absolute balls. Who is she, anyway?"

"The first Mrs. Benet Paisley, she says."

"Father's first wife didn't have any children. I don't know whose her son is but he's not my father's."

"What did your father think of her claim?"

The young man didn't waver. "How do I know? How could he know anything about it? When did she say all this? Was *she* the woman being hysterical over my father in the hall?"

"So you know nothing about this?"

"Nothing at all."

"To coin a phrase, when did you last see your father?"

"It'd be when I told him about the photographer." He flung himself back in his chair. He frowned still, and his hands were in his pockets. For a young man trying to behave as if he were in charge of the situation, he was very defensive.

"Photographer?"

"He was the same man that had photographed all the things that got stolen from our old house. He had a beard then and a lot of ginger hair, but I knew him all right. I thought he might be up to the same trick again. We didn't let these people take photographs this time just because of that. My father never got over losing his jade collection. I saw a flash go, and I thought"—he shrugged—"here he goes again."

"What did your father say when you told him? Wasn't he taking the party around?"

"They didn't all go around with him. I saw some of them

in the grounds. Three, including this bloke, but he went into the house by the tower door."

"What did your father say?"

"He was pretty damn annoyed. We've a good security system, but if this man was a professional scout for house-breakers he might be taking that in too."

"What did your father do when you told him?"

"I've no idea. And we'd no *proof* connecting this bloke with the break-in, so calling the police would've been no use."

"Yet here we are!" Prior grinned, less than engagingly. "Suppose your father had decided to take matters into his own hands?"

"What d'you mean?" He glowered up under the lank hair.

"Found Lawson on the roof and helped him over." Prior made a scooping gesture with his blunt hands.

He sat upright. "My God! I thought you were here because my father's been killed, not to make out he's a murderer. That's the end of enough. That's revolting."

"What terms were you on with your father?" Prior, having ruffled young Paisley, pressed on with relish.

"What *terms*? He was my father! One doesn't analyze what *terms* one is on with one's father."

"Analyze it now. You got on with him?"

"Of course I got on with him!"

"No 'of course' about it." Prior rocked on his heels. "By all accounts Lord Roke was a difficult man. Your mother says he hurt everybody's feelings. How did he hurt yours?"

"He knew how to get people on the raw, I suppose. But that was just his style."

"And did it hurt?"

"Look, he's been doing it ever since I can remember. D'you think I—he's *dead!* I mean, he teased, he sent people up, he made fun, but one doesn't kill people—d'you think I'd kill my father for *teasing* me?"

"Did he tease you about not being the next Lord Roke?"

"I tell you the first that I heard of this story came from you just now."

"What time was it when you told him about the photographer?"

"I don't know. After eleven. I'd heard the tower clock when I was in the garden."

"Where was he when you told him?"

"In the gallery. Putting the armor on."

"And if I told you he'd already talked to his first wife and heard about the claim, what would you say to that?"

Paisley took a breath. "I'd be surprised. I mean he didn't say anything."

"Your father," Prior said casually, "was disappointed in you, wasn't he?"

"Who told you that? I've told you he was always getting at people. Good God, don't you realize he's—it's my father you're talking about, and he's dead. I've just lost my father and you're talking about whether he cared for me. It's inhuman!"

"*Murder* is inhuman," Prior said. "Thanks. That's all for now."

Chapter

....

11

WHEN GUY HAD GONE, DISCONCERTED AT BEING DISMISSED from his own sitting room, Prior stretched out his legs and fished in a pocket for his pack of cheroots. He did not as a rule smoke on duty but he felt, now, like rewarding himself. These interviews were going well. He hadn't looked forward to dealing with the toffee-nosed set but it was simple really. He was getting somewhere. Lady Roke and her son didn't care for him—because he was getting somewhere.

He lit up, leaned back, and sent a thin stream of smoke at the ceiling, noticing without interest that a ring of plaster cherubs seemed to resent this. He was aware of Sergeant Williams' eyes upon him and put out a hand, clicking his fingers.

"Anything you can see for an ashtray? Lady Roke"—he used the name like a swearword, with emphasis—"won't want her carpet to get ash trodden in." He sat up and looked around. "Place is crammed with ornaments. You'd think they'd have something useful."

He watched Williams cautiously examine first an occasional table full of small boxes, then the mantelpiece where there were various pieces of china among the figurines, mostly deer and huntsmen, probably valuable but all white, very boring. "There, that cup and saucer. The saucer'll do fine."

Williams brought it, but without enthusiasm. "Mayn't it spoil, sir? I mean, it'll be an antique."

"Nah." Prior tapped ash into the center, turning it to look at the forget-me-nots around the edge. He looked up sharply at Williams. "Well? Who's next?"

"You didn't say, sir." Williams sounded uncertain as to whether he had or hadn't.

Prior groaned and pointed the cheroot at him. "Think, Bill. You're supposed to *think*. We've heard the wife, we've heard the son. Well?"

They both knew that if Williams got it wrong, Prior would be damningly sarcastic, but Prior could never make out why Williams was so slow to have an opinion.

After a moment, Williams said, "The other wife and son? The first wife?"

"And the son she says owns all this." Prior's expansive gesture distributed smoke around the room. "All the *antiques*. You've got it, Sergeant." He twitched Buchanan's list toward him on the mahogany side table, and jabbed at a name. "Mrs. Angela North. And Basil North—there's a poove's name; lucky for him he doesn't look it—for seconds. Trot along, Bill. And see if you can stir up the butler to bring us something to eat. There ought to be some hospitality going. I'm starving." His stomach made a loud sound in support of this statement.

Williams hesitated at the door. "Mrs. North first, or do you want to eat first?"

"Both, man, I can do both. Get along and tell Jeeves it's cheese and pickle I want, not caviar."

Left alone, Prior listened with pleasure to his stomach, and blew a smoke ring at the contemptuous cherubs.

He was at the window, smoking his cheroot to the stub, when Sergeant Williams showed in Angela North. As he turned, he grinned to see her waft a hand helplessly as if to make room in the air to breathe.

"Sit here, Mrs. North." While he waited he had hauled up a spindle-legged gilt chair from a desk in the corner of the little room, and dumped it a couple of feet away from the one he had placed for himself. Lady Roke had chosen to sit sideways on the arm of a small rose-splashed sofa opposite, and thereby managed to turn half from him and look down on him when he sat, literally as well as metaphorically. He wasn't having any more of that. This Angela North looked like no contest anyway. The only surprise was that such a faded little mouse could come out with her sort of story. He'd give her a bit of a fright and see how she stuck by it.

She sat as ordered, only putting the chair back a bit, and arranged the pleated mousy skirt carefully over her knees as if it were important to get it right, and without looking up. Lady Roke hadn't minded showing her legs, swinging an ankle, high heels, blue tights, and skirt rucked up a bit. What had made that fellow Roke marry this specimen ever? But that wasn't the question he had in mind.

"What made you wait to tell Lord Roke about your son? How old's the boy?"

"He is nineteen."

Susannah Stacey

Prior shot a final stream of smoke at the ceiling, exhaling almost in admiration, and stubbed the butt in the saucer. "Nineteen! For nineteen years you didn't tell him, so what made you wait till today?"

Angela North finally raised her eyes, having arranged the pleats to her satisfaction. The eyes were blue, but a pale blue, and the lashes fair. "I wasn't going to tell him. At all."

Yeah? In a pig's eye! "Not at all? So you chose today? When someone murders Lord Roke."

The eyes might be pale, but they could flash. "I hope you are not implying that was anything to do with it."

Animation gave a hint of what, twenty years or so ago, someone like Roke might have fancied.

"I'm here to inquire into what's fishy, Mrs.—North. And it seems fishy to me that if Lord Roke and you divorced, as I understand, because there were no children of the marriage," and Prior gave himself a pat on the back for avoiding *because you couldn't have children,* since she had proved she could, "then why are you claiming your son's the heir, not Lady Roke's?"

"Because he was conceived before I was divorced." Angela North spoke with precision, catching a pleat that had strayed from her arranging and folding it firmly back. "No, I didn't tell Benet then. He'd always had his jokes and his secrets, and this one was mine."

Prior had another go at grinding out the cheroot, which was smoldering, in the porcelain saucer as she watched. He was revising his impression of her as a mouse as she became more likely as a murderer.

"Your secret, eh? What made you give it away today?"

The door opened for a butler with a tray. On it was a large plate of sandwiches garnished with watercress, two mugs, a coffeepot, a steaming milk jug, and a sugar bowl. The butler put it carefully down on the mahogany table beside

92

Prior, pausing just long enough to allow him to remove Buchanan's list of the party. Then he picked up the saucer and said, "I will bring you an ashtray, sir." Turning his back on Prior, Knebworth bent discreetly to murmur to Mrs. North. "I shall bring coffee for you, madam. What sandwiches would you prefer?"

"I'll just have coffee, thank you. With milk and sugar."

"Thank you, madam."

Prior was not going to wait for her. He poured a steaming mug full, and attacked his sandwiches. Williams came diffidently to help himself. Through cheese and pickle Prior said, "You haven't told me yet, why today? You wait nineteen years, and the day you tell your ex he's a daddy, your son inherits. You sure you did tell him? Lady Roke's son says his father never sprung the glad news to *him*, yet he saw him after your little revelation."

Angela North took her time about replying. She watched him chew the sandwich in a way that made him self-conscious enough to be irritated. He thought about chewing with his mouth open, but decided it was beneath him.

"Of course," she said finally, in her soft voice, "you can believe what you like. After I was divorced, I went to Australia. Benet gave me a generous settlement—he was never mean—and there I married again. Almost immediately. Shane North."

Prior picked up his second sandwich. "What did he say to the baby boy? Or did you marry in time to pass it as his?"

The door opened just as she began to speak, and Knebworth, carrying coffee on a silver tray, came and placed it on a small table he set down next to Mrs. North. The coffee was in a delicate cup, Prior noted. Mugs were too coarse for genteel little mice. Knebworth, inclining himself courteously toward Mrs. North, passed from the room without a glance at Prior or Williams, a canceling operation Prior appreciated even while it irritated him.

She stirred and sipped her coffee before saying, "I told Shane before we married that I was going to have a child. Not that anyone needed telling by then. I never told him whose it was. He was a very good father to Baz."

"And you didn't have any more?"

"Shane knew already that he couldn't have children. I don't mind saying that, now he's dead. He was very happy I brought him a son." She smiled faintly and looked out of the window, making Prior feel uncomfortable without knowing why.

"And your son? What did he know of all this?"

"Nothing at all until today. As you saw."

Prior remembered the large young man's evident astonishment. Though he looked incapable of putting on an act, you could never be sure. The two of them could have rehearsed the thing for years, working it up for this chance.

"You wanted it to be a nice surprise that he was to be Lord Roke." Prior was not aware that he said the title as if it were a given name, with separate emphasis. The effect was to suggest that he doubted if it were real.

Angela made a quick dismissive gesture with her free hand and blinked rapidly. "But I've explained. I didn't *mean* or *want* him to become Lord Roke. I said to Benet: I didn't bring him here for that, I just wanted you to see him. It was Benet who told me Baz would have the title when he died. I said to him that I thought that as we'd divorced before Benet had the title, it didn't apply. Benet said Baz was conceived in wedlock and that made him the eldest son. It seemed to amuse him a lot."

Prior clanked his mug down on the tray.

"You said he was chuffed, that he preferred your son to

Lady Roke's. Hardly much chance to make the judgment, had he?"

Angela put her coffee cup down, very precisely and with only the slightest rattle. She laid her hands flat on her knees, pressing them down on the pleats. "I don't think I said exactly that. But he'd observed Baz as we were going around the house. Baz is a very good-looking boy. He has a sense of humor. I'm not sure that my story was a complete surprise to Benet . . . Baz is very like Benet as he was when I first knew him."

"And Lady Roke's son isn't?"

Angela did not so much shrug as slightly displace her shoulders. Prior gulped the last of the coffee, set the mug down, and thrust the tray away.

"And Roke mentioned the inheritance? That your boy's next in line?"

"I told him Baz wouldn't like it at all. It isn't his style, all this." Nevertheless, her glance around held, to Prior's mind, a certain complacency. "Benet said I should have thought of that before. Baz would have to inherit and that was that, there was nothing I could do about it."

You could, thought Prior, kill Roke and make it happen sooner. He said, "You done any archery?"

The question's crudity did not seem to throw her. She gave a brief smile and smoothed her skirt. "Oh yes. Benet's always been keen. He had a range and targets in the garden at Paisley House. I was rather good."

Doesn't she see what I'm getting at? Is she that stupid! Prior wondered. He decided to go straight in.

"So. You went to the gallery, took a bow, shot your ex-husband in the neck, left him there, came down the backstairs in time to see him stagger down the front ones; and you claimed you'd gone out to throw up because you'd seen Lawson dead."

She had turned spectacularly white. Her hands fisted and thumped her knees. "Of course I didn't! And if you'd seen Mr. Lawson hanging there upside down you'd have been sick yourself. I loved Benet. *Of course* I didn't kill him."

"You loved him!" Prior was incredulous. "You were divorced all that time; you hadn't seen him, according to you, for nineteen years!"

The hands banged her knees again. "What *difference* does that make? Don't you know *anything*? I let him divorce me *because* I loved him, because we both thought I couldn't give him what he wanted. I never stopped loving him."

Prior attacked. "Then why did you wait for nineteen years to tell him he'd got what he wanted?"

She turned her eyes on him, wide. Her face seemed to dissolve. She's going to cry, he thought. Her face became a white mask with open mouth and she began to scream.

"Get that WPC!" he shouted at Williams. The noise was shattering. If this was what she'd done when she saw Roke's body, no wonder Lady Roke hit her. But he daren't hit her without a police witness to his proper intentions. The screams dwindled; she sat trembling, sobbing, gasping.

The WPC came hurrying; struggling after her in the doorway were Williams, Unwin, and the young man Baz.

"Let him in, let him in!" Prior shouted as the policewoman bent over Angela. They let Baz go and he ran to his mother.

He roared at Prior, "What in hell did you say to her?"

Then he knelt by her, an arm around her, saying, "Ma. Ma, it's okay. C'mon," in a gentling tone.

The contrast did not escape Prior, who once more wondered about this pair's acting powers. The WPC was looking anxiously at her superior, as Angela North shuddered and wept in the circle of her arm. He nodded at the door, so she and Baz coaxed the woman to her feet. She said, "Come and lie down," and Baz seconded this, but to him Prior said, "Not you. I think I want to hear from you next."

"I'm looking after my mother first," said Baz.

"I'll do that," the WPC put in. "Don't worry. She'll be all right."

Angela North nodded dumbly, and with reluctance Baz dropped his arm and watched her go. He turned to Prior and glowered.

"Don't try giving *me* a hard time," he said.

Chapter

....

12

THE SPINDLY CHAIR LET OUT A GRUNT OF PROTEST AS BAZ SAT mistrustfully down on it. He still glowered at Prior with a belligerence that transformed a face meant for easy good nature. Prior took in the broad shoulders, the capable hands planted on the bleached denim knees. He could do with a few police recruits with that physique. Baz looked as if he could collar a man with each hand and ram their heads together—not an officially approved method of settling an affray, but an effective one. *Basil,* he remembered thinking, *a poove's name.* This type, if he was one, would be like the ones Prior had come across in a magazine story, a special battalion in an ancient army, that combed their long hair before a battle they all fought to the death in. He'd been surprised to read it. It contradicted his idea of gays as having no more chance in a battle than a bunch of flowers. He pointed a stubby finger at the scowling Baz.

"Your mother and this grudge against Lord Roke. What d'you know about it?"

"What grudge? I never even heard of Lord Roke before this trip."

"You didn't know your mother's first husband's name? Come *on*."

"Of course I knew. She was married to Benet Paisley. I didn't know until Nicholas Buchanan said, just now, that Paisley was Lord Roke's family name. He wasn't Lord Roke when my ma was married to him. It happened after."

"When did she find out he'd become Lord Roke?"

"How would I know?" His scowl had relaxed, as if his face was unable to hold it for long. "I just told you I didn't know a thing about it." He looked to Williams as if to collect a witness to Prior's loss of memory.

Prior tapped sharply on his chair arm. "So you really thought your father was your mother's second husband?" He made it sound an inexplicable piece of credulity on Baz's part.

"Shane North. He never told me different." His frown now was one of regret, and he was looking down while Prior got out his pack of cheroots and lit one. He may have been intending to keep Baz waiting for the next question, but the young man was evidently thinking of his stepfather still, and when Prior took the cheroot from his mouth and leaned forward and asked, "What did you think of your father?" he blinked, confused.

"Think of Dad? Oh, you mean my real father."

"Lord Roke. Did you talk to him?"

"A bit. Going around with the party. I thought he was a great guy—very funny, a real joker." He grinned suddenly.

"How did he like hearing you were his son?"

"He never knew. I wish he had, somehow."

"Your mother told him. What did you think was going on when he took her off into his study?"

A massive shrug from Baz. "He'd said he knew her when we first got off the bus and stood around. I thought, well, they must know each other from when she lived in England, that was all. We're staying with a friend of hers from then. She's been getting in touch with people she knew."

"You didn't go with her into the study?"

"I wasn't asked to. I was on a wander of my own. I mean, this place has plenty to look at." Baz glanced around the room, as his mother had done, but with only a frank interest. "I've never seen anywhere like this before."

Prior puffed on his cheroot and spoke around it. "Where were you when Lord Roke was killed?"

"Well, but when was that? I mean—"

Prior snorted and began to laugh; watched by Baz with innocent fascination, he pointed the cheroot. "Now don't get clever with me, laddie. You saw Roke come down the stairs with an arrow through his neck."

Baz gripped one arm, a protective gesture as if he had no wish to remember. "I did and I didn't. Nicholas was sheep-dogging us into the hall out of the rain—after Josh Lawson was killed, right—and Lord Roke was coming down the stairs, and soon as I saw him I really looked, just before he fell, and I thought it was one of his jokes, the best yet." The strong face changed. "If I'd known . . ."

He stopped. God, thought Prior, we're going to have tears. Him and his mother both, what a pair. Prior didn't normally mind if people he interviewed cried. He thought of it as a result of relentless interrogation and it often preceded, or accompanied, confession. This was different. Either the boy really hadn't known Roke was his father, or he and his mother were in for Olivier Awards. As he was closely observing Baz and debating the point, a side door opened and Lady Roke looked in.

"Just to say Knebworth's arranged lunch for everyone"— her glance fell on the tray at Prior's elbow—"who hasn't already had some." She smiled at Baz, who had sprung up, endangering the chair. "Just soup and sandwiches, I'm afraid. I hope you'll have some soup, Mr. Prior?"

"No thanks, Lady Roke. I'm busy." He turned to Baz, who had recovered himself, and said, "You can go, laddie, for the moment. Sergeant, I'll see Mr. Buchanan."

Prior's twitch at the reins of authority left him alone within half a minute.

Bone, feeling useless and trying not to be angry at it, wanted to be away from the group yet not to intrude on the family. There was in fact a general wish among the group to get out of the confined coffee room. As there was now bright sunshine outdoors, some of them ventured along the terrace, away from the room's windows and their associations, to the corner overlooking the formal garden. Keziah was putting out garden chairs that had been stacked under an ancient canvas cover. Bone stood in the front doorway, considering. Adrian Nash crossed the hall looking curiously elated, and went into the sitting room, where Guy's voice could be heard complaining. Bone headed for a painted bench that faced the house front beyond the drive. He dried a patch with a tissue and sat down.

He was drinking his mug of, by now, tepid soup, which was nevertheless real ham and green pea, when Grizel came toward him, bearing sandwiches. She was biting her lip to show mock guilt, and her eyes smiled.

"I had to escape," she said. "Oh, is it very wet? That tissue's no good! Can you get one out of this pocket? How intimate it is to have someone fish in one's trouser pocket

. . . Thank you, I'm sure that's drier. Guy's having an attack of acute egocentrics, and if I stayed I'd have smacked him. He's expecting Jane to arrange the universe differently for him. Then Adrian came in with a cat-got-the-canary face and said to Jane, 'I suppose you'll be moving out soon, what with the new Lord Roke and his mother,' and *Jane* said, 'I know who'll move out before I do,' and she swept out; and Guy started up a moan about Adrian, so I came away."

She sat down comfortably close. Bone was engaged in a relaxing contemplation of her profile when suddenly her eyes opened wide with shock and she exclaimed, "Dear heaven!"

He had heard a window in the house slide open and now, turning his head, he saw what Grizel had seen. Clothes were flying from the end window on the first floor which, after a moment, he worked out as Adrian's. Garments came hurtling out in clumps and singly: a spread-eagled shirt, flapping trousers, a camel-hair coat floating down in an attitude of despair, crumpling on the terrace parapet and toppling into the flowerbed below. A suede jacket with a matching cream silk lining emerged with some force, turned over, and descended on Sheila Simpson-Bates sitting amazed at a table below, muffling her. She sprang up and flung it off, in fright and a shower of soup, onto the wet flagstones, where Arnold Mabey, coming to her rescue, trampled it.

Socks, underwear, suits, more shirts, a blue denim and blond leather jacket appeared. A hairbrush hit a terrace urn with a ringing crack. Bone and Grizel had come to their feet but did not move; he was riveted and, he confessed silently, entertained. He could see Jane in the bedroom working in competent frenzy. The clothes still flew, the Simpson-Bates sisters, Arnold Mabey, and two others stumbled among the debris, fending off shirts, ties, and underpants in a flight toward the shelter of the porch.

The window slammed down.

Grizel started toward the house but Bone grasped her arm. "I don't think so," he said. Her questioning face began to reflect his suppressed, scarcely contained, amusement.

"But we can't—"

"Can't we? Here we are, a pair of busybodies by profession, and with for once no obligation at all to join in. What were you going to do? Pick up the clothes? They're Adrian's. Jane wouldn't thank you."

The bedroom window shot open violently. Adrian leaned out and looked down. The Simpson-Bateses were exclaiming together by the porch. He said, "My God!" and then, "My *God!*" and left the window.

Bone sat down. After a moment Grizel did too. She said, "It's dreadful, but it's as good as a play, isn't it?"

"Better."

They could hear reverberant feet on the stairs—Adrian had plainly ignored the police tapes—and he burst from the front door. Thrusting the amazed sisters aside he ran toward the wreck of his wardrobe and began to pick things up; his incredulous repetitions of *"My God!"* came to Bone and Grizel as he held up and surveyed shirts, suits, and waistcoats, rain-dabbled and muddy.

The window above the porch opened. Jane crossed her arms on the sill and leaned over to watch. The Simpson-Bateses had now advanced and were starting to pick things up. After a hesitation, Mabey followed.

Adrian suddenly discovered his suede jacket. He flung what he had so far amassed down across the table, regardless of the sandwiches, and picked up the jacket, turning it, his exclamations mounting the scale. He cried, "Who the hell got *soup* on it?"

"Well, you see, it came down—" Susan began.

He clasped the jacket to him and whirled on her. "You *bitch!*"

Bone was on his feet and starting forward when Arnold Mabey's stick jabbed Adrian in the chest, jerking him backward. Bone halted.

"That was quite uncalled for," Mabey said. "These ladies have been trying to help you."

"We don't know what's happened," Sheila said, "but believe me, we were only sorry for you."

"Sorry for me?" Adrian cried. "*Sorry* for me?"

He became, luckily, speechless. He stood for a moment, while Mabey held the stick at the ready for another prod, and then he swept up the clothes he had already gathered, sending the sandwiches and plates onto the flagstones, and stormed off indoors. From the window above the porch, Jane caught sight of Bone and Grizel, and raised a hand to them before she drew back and put the sash down. The show, for the moment at least, was over.

Bone and Grizel went back to their lunch. He accepted a cheese and pickle sandwich Grizel offered. They ate in silence for a while, observing the Simpson-Bateses picking up clothes and piling them on the parapet while talking to the others, and Arnold Mabey poking at a sock in a puddle. Grizel waved a hand at the scene.

"All that was great fun, but do you mind about being just audience? These goings-on are your country and you're an exile."

"It does feel odd, yes. I suppose I mind. But Prior's doing a good job, I suspect."

"Suppose you were him, wouldn't you ask you for a bit of trained help?"

"He is not going to ask for cooperation from a man he's got to call 'sir.'"

"Not a sympathetic type." Grizel eased her sandwich open to observe the disposition of pickle. "But then I can't expect all policemen to be as pretty as you."

"Pretty, and polite too. Now you're married to me I can

insist on proper accuracy. Close that sandwich, you're embarrassing it. Is Jane very upset?"

"Very. I believe she loved Roke. She seems cool but *that*"—Grizel nodded at the terrace—"shows how upset she is."

"I'll bet she longed to do such things to Adrian while Roke was alive. I wonder if Roke would have minded. He seems more likely to have laughed."

"M'm." Grizel finished her sandwich and threw a dry corner of crust onto the edge of the drive. A robin descended from nowhere to tussle with it. "I think she's angry with the whole situation. Not surprisingly. Losing her husband, her house, and her son's inheritance all at one go . . . it's enough to drive anyone into the bin."

"She believes Angela's story now." It was question-as-statement.

"You only have to look at Baz. And she told me she didn't think Angela was dumb enough to have come over here without the papers—birth certificate, for instance—that would bear out her story. What she can't understand is why Angela didn't tell Benet straight away when she knew she was pregnant, let alone when it was a son."

"I imagine Angela was angry too. Didn't Roke tell her he was marrying Jane because she was pregnant? Isn't that why the divorce got through so fast?"

Grizel pulled the shawl collar of her big scarlet cardigan closer around her throat as thunder once more muttered in the distance. "It's getting cold. Shall we go in?"

As Bone picked up his soup mug from the damp grass, she added, "Do you think Angela did it? Because she's still angry?"

Bone strolled beside her, taking the sandwich plate from her hand. Without looking at her he said, "Or Jane? There's no doubt that she's angry."

Chapter

· · · · · · · · · · · · · · · · · · · ·

13

PRIOR DID NOT FIND NICHOLAS BUCHANAN EASY TO MAKE ANY impression on. He had annoyed Prior from the start by bringing his sandwiches and wineglass in with him, and continuing his lunch as he answered. That he was pleasant meant to Prior that he was a creep, and that he spent his spare time bringing tour parties to other people's houses meant that he was a nosy creep. Fortified by this conviction, he tried to get Buchanan to admit that he knew of Angela North's desire to meet Roke. He was forced to give up that line after a bit in the face of continued, unruffled denial.

He turned to the question of Joshua Lawson and his fate. It could, after all, happen not to be merely a gruesome coincidence that he and Roke had died at much the same time.

"So you say you know nothing at all about Mrs. North?"

"Oh no. I knew she was a friend of Melissa Stone, who recommended her. Melissa's a very old friend of mine, a delightful person who's often been on these tours."

"Lawson had often been on them?"

"Once or twice. I wasn't keen."

"Why not?"

"Well . . . you see, he'd taken some unauthorized photographs on one tour. This is very naughty when everyone knows not to unless the owner says yes; and even then the photographs are not to be published. So I was keeping something of an eye."

"Was he popular?"

Buchanan raised his eyebrows and laughed. "Popular? If I didn't know his death was accidental I might well suppose someone had given him a shove. I did rather speculate on who."

Prior leaned forward. "Who's the most likely?"

Buchanan leaned back in automatic retreat. "No, I wasn't being serious."

"I am."

Buchanan blinked. Prior had a sudden and wholly unwelcome conviction that he was being found amusing. "No, really no one. Josh got across people. He was a loner and not a social asset. I was going to ensure that he didn't come on another tour ever. But no one would have murdered him. I assure you."

"Ah?" Prior said. "Thank you, Mr. Buchanan."

As Buchanan went out, Prior thought that he was not going to get a word that might involve tour members from *him*. He said, "Williams: who do you think we'll see next?"

The sergeant, with the air of one who knows he is going to get it wrong, suggested Bone. "He's a Super, sir. He will have noticed things."

"Will he? He can wait. I'll see him last."

"He was the one that lowered Lawson's body down."

Prior stared. "Was he now? Indeed?" After a moment he turned again to the tour list. "If you want the gossip, ask the ladies. I'll see these. The sisters." He stabbed his finger down on the name of Simpson-Bates.

They came around the door with anxious eyes, tall, thin, with pepper-and-salt hair; nicely dressed in forgettable good clothes. Prior was out of his chair at once, arranging their seating. He put them in the sofa, providing a cushion behind Sheila's long back, saying, "I'm afraid you ladies have had a couple of very nasty shocks."

Williams' regard of this was jaundiced. He knew Prior. Still, it was technique.

"I'm afraid we know nothing about Lord Roke, poor man. Is it true that nice young man Baz is his son?"

"That's for lawyers to say, eh? I wanted to ask you two ladies about something I'm sure you do know: Joshua Lawson."

"But we thought that was an accident."

"We have to concern ourselves with accidents as well."

"I suppose you do. Dreadful for you to have two things on your hands at the same time," Sheila said. Susan chimed in with "Very difficult. So confusing."

"You ladies can help me straighten things out." Prior sat in front of them in the rather higher desk chair, not close enough to make them feel crowded. They sat up, willing.

"Anything we can do, Chief Inspector—"

"Anything, of course."

"How did Lawson get on with other members of the party?"

They consulted each other with a glance.

"He wasn't very popular—"

"—He wasn't very polite."

"He was *rude*, Sheila! Rude to everyone."

"Rude to you ladies!"

"He was very scornful of the way we took snaps—"

"—We didn't like him before. We were very sorry to find he was on this tour."

"Nicholas—Mr. Buchanan, you know—asked us to keep a little eye open because he *would* take pictures in houses where we were asked not to."

"Did he actually quarrel with anyone?" Prior overrode the corroboration from Sheila. They consulted mutely with each other.

"We were saying yesterday, he seemed to have got across practically everybody."

"Anyone more than another?"

"There was an awful row with Mr. Spencer yesterday in one of the rooms at Haxley Manor—"

"—which shows you, because Mr. Spencer's really a peaceful gentle—"

"—It was the portraits. There were children's portraits—"

"—so sweet, in pastel."

"Mr. Lawson said, when we were admiring them, that people were better off without children."

"One of these children, in the portraits, had died. There were *two* dates written underneath, you know, so you could tell. Just last year—"

"We were so sorry for Mr. Kealey, poor man, he'd already lost his wife—"

"—she was buried in the chapel—"

"That's nothing to do with Mr. Prior, Sheila . . . Mr. Kealey wasn't in the room when this happened, luckily, because Mr. Lawson didn't leave it at that."

"He said a child dying was one less nuisance!"

"Mr. Spencer fairly flew at him!"

"We were quite frightened."

"Such a mild little man! He'd hardly said a word since we started."

"Took hold of him and shook him, as hard as he could."

"Really quite violently. But it was almost funny, he's so much smaller."

"He said: 'How *dare* you say such a thing!'"

"No, dear, I think it was, 'That's a *wicked* thing to say!'"

Prior put in, "Did you know why he was so upset?"

"Yes. It was so sad. Mr. Spencer had lost his own daughter—"

"—quite recently. He showed us her picture on the coach afterward, and he apologized—"

"—for bursting out like that."

"He'd come on the tour as a distraction—"

"—to get over it. It was so sad."

"Was he here having coffee with you this morning?"

"Was he, Sheila?"

They thought about it. Susan turned to Prior. "You see, Mr. Spencer's very quiet."

"—so very quiet, you don't notice him. I think he was there."

"So do I, but I don't remember him."

"Did Lawson quarrel with anyone else?"

"There wasn't really a *quarrel* with Mr. Bone—"

"—oh no, not a quarrel."

"What was it, then?" Prior edged forward.

"Mr. Bone stopped him photographing yesterday afternoon, it seems. He said absolutely awful things about him afterward."

"Who said?"

"Mr. Lawson. It was Mr. Lawson you asked us about," Sheila said, with slight reproof.

"It was really shocking."

"We didn't know Mr. Bone had been married before."

"Mrs. Bone is such a nice woman, and she wears—"

"—Mr. Prior doesn't want to know about Mrs. Bone's

clothes, dear . . . We didn't even know Mr. Bone was in the police. He's never mentioned it."

Prior leaned forward. "Talked about him being in the police, did he?"

"Not exactly. I mean that's how he got it hushed up."

"Susan, he mayn't have got it right. I don't think Mr. Lawson could be trusted."

"No, dear, but it's what Mr. Lawson actually said that Mr. Prior wants to know, and what he actually said was that Mr. Bone, whether it's true or not, and I really don't think I believe it—"

"Nor do I. He only drank a glass of beer at lunch yesterday."

"—killed his wife and baby in a car accident when he was drunk."

"—his *first* wife," Sheila said, to make it quite clear.

"And that was hushed up?"

"No, not that. What was hushed up was that *he* did it and he was drunk—"

"And it wasn't the other driver who was drunk at all but he went to jail and lost his license."

"I'm sure the police don't do things like that, but it was what Mr. Lawson said, he said there'd been a cover-up."

"Was Mr. Bone there when Lawson said all this?"

"When he told *us*, Mr. Bone wasn't there, nor was his wife. I was glad of that. Catherine—Mrs. Maitland—said she was sure it wasn't true. I don't know if someone told Mr. Bone afterward. We didn't. But Mrs. Maitland told Mrs. Bone."

"She gets on very well with her. I mean, so does everyone, but—"

Prior came to his feet. "Excellent! You've been very, very helpful. I'm sorry you've had such an upsetting day. And was there anyone else?"

"No. He was just unpleasant really in general."

Prior ushered them out himself. He turned triumphantly to Williams, and came back across the room rising on the balls of his feet, hands in pockets. "This case is turning out more interesting than I thought. Not just a dead lord but a bent copper. I'll see Mr. Superintendent Bone next, Sarge."

"Right, sir. If Lawson's death isn't an accident, can it have a connection with Roke's killing?" Williams was always chary of asking Prior a question. There was usually a put-down along with the answer.

"If it's not an accident, Sarge, then it's murder. If you're not as ready to investigate the death of a nasty little sneak snapshot as you are of a lord, what does that make you?"

Knowing better than to try justifying himself, Williams went for Superintendent Bone. He went himself, rather than sending the PC at the door, for bent or not, this was a Super they were dealing with.

He hadn't far to go. The wife, in green trousers and a big scarlet cardigan, was coming in at the front door; the Superintendent, in gray trousers and shirt and a multi-colored dark sweater, came after. The Super was gazing thoughtfully at the tape across the stairs, that young Nash had jumped when he came so furiously down; he did not look an appropriate subject for Prior to monkey with. He had fair hair with some gray in it, and severe gray eyes. It was a thin, uncompromising sort of face, that turned to Williams with sudden attention.

Mrs. Bone said, when Williams had delivered his message, that she would go and talk to Lady Roke again.

Bone prepared himself to give, in as impersonal a way as possible, his unbiased observation to the prickly Chief Inspector. As soon as Williams had shut the door, Prior on the hearth rug fired at him: "You were on the roof with Lawson. What were you doing there?"

"I'd gone up there to bring him down for coffee."

"What did you say to him?"

"Nothing. He wasn't there."

"Vanished into thin air, had he?"

"In effect, yes." Bone came forward. He said no more, but stood, with his hands in his pockets, waiting for Prior.

"Well, go on—sir. Tell me more about this conjuring trick."

"I had just turned to go back and look for Lawson in the house when I heard screaming below on the terrace; then I saw there was a rope over the parapet and I went to look down. I made out that a man was hanging by one ankle upside down about twenty feet or more below, apparently with his right foot caught in a loop of the fall from the builders' pulley."

"The fall?"

"The loose end of the rope. The people below were trying to reach him."

"How, in your opinion, had he got there?"

"It's possible that he caught his foot in the rope and lost his balance. There are recent scratch marks on the right-hand merlon that could have been caused by him as he went down. They could also have been caused by the builders."

"Could have been caused by the builders. Very useful, sir. Thank you. Did Lawson get on with the party in general?"

"Do you think this death is murder too, Chief Inspector?"

"I am sorry, sir," said Prior, and he grinned. "You'll recognize that you have to be treated as an ordinary member of the public in this matter."

The suggestion of lost rank had no effect on Bone. He said, "Lawson got on with practically no one."

"The exception being yourself, sir?"

"He was none too pleased when I stopped him photographing, yesterday afternoon."

"Was that your business, sir?"

Bone relied on his face to show nothing, but he recalled

Lawson making him feel officious. He said, "It was for the sake of all of us on the tour," which sounded like an excuse. "Buchanan undertakes that no one—"

"Yes, sir. We've heard that. And Lawson didn't come back to you for interfering, sir? He hadn't anything to say?"

"He too implied it was not my business."

"Was that all? Not saying nasty things behind your back?"

"If he did, no one told me."

"Really—sir?"

Williams was unsurprised that no one had cared to tell the Super Lawson's gossip. At the moment, a forbidding silence followed Prior's question, and Williams felt the power of it—an illustration of what he'd tried to use on suspects himself. Prior became restless.

"You mean you were the only person on the tour that didn't get to hear what Lawson was saying—about your drunk driving that killed your wife and child?"

The Superintendent didn't move or blink. His steady regard of Prior did not waver. Williams thought, awestruck: *any moment now he'll blow and Prior will be cinders.*

Prior said, quickly, "That's the story the Simpson-Bates sisters say he was spreading. He said the other driver got the blame and a jail sentence because the police look after their own. I mean, you and I know that kind of thing doesn't happen, don't we—sir?"

Bone swung and headed toward Williams and the door.

"Where are you going—sir?" Prior demanded, thrown.

"I believe this interview is over."

Williams found he had stood aside and opened the door.

Chapter

·····················

14

GRIZEL RAN JANE TO EARTH IN HER LITTLE SITTING ROOM AT THE back of the house, seated at her small Queen Anne desk and rummaging furiously in the drawers. She swung around as Grizel came in and said, *"Wasn't* that fun? I saw you had a good view. Cost him a fortune in dry cleaners' bills, I hope." Her eyes were glittering and her face flushed. Grizel might have thought she'd had a drink or several, but she was aware that throwing Adrian's clothes out of the window could well have produced instant euphoria. She sat on the peaches-and-cream brocade sofa while Jane turned back to the desk and wrestled with another drawer, crammed with papers that rose at once and spilled over its sides.

"You've lost something?"

"Not so much lost as simply not found. Benet's will.

Another of his jokes, you see. A sort of treasure hunt I think he'd envisaged."

"A treasure hunt?" Grizel was aware her responses lacked sparkle, but she could only take her cues from Jane; who now dropped a pile of papers on the floor, waved away Grizel's effort to retrieve them, and riffled through what was left in the drawer.

"He hid his will. Oh, he said he was going to. 'Provide a little excitement after my death' was how he put it. He couldn't know how much excitement *that* was going to provide all on its own."

Jane's hand halted a moment, then went on turning over papers. "He said it would amuse us to look for it." She stopped suddenly and said, more to the disarray before her than to Grizel, "Benet could be very cruel. I don't think he often knew how cruel." She pulled out another drawer with unnecessary force, sending a scatter of what looked like bills to join the spread on the floor. Glancing, Grizel saw the nearest was a receipt.

"But would he have hidden it in your own desk? Suppose you'd found it already, wouldn't that have spoiled his fun?" She could tell, however, that Jane's desk was a place where something was not likely to be found.

"It's quite his style. He might think I wouldn't dream of looking in my own desk." Jane's laugh balanced on the edge of hysteria. "I didn't live with Benet all these years without getting a kind of twist in my mind to match his."

"Can I help?"

"Oh, I don't know." Jane pushed the chair back, mashing papers on the carpet. "It's hopeless, somehow. Just as he planned."

Still facing the desk, she began to cry, bringing up her hands, making muffled sounds through her fingers that Grizel found dreadfully moving. She got up and put an arm around Jane's shoulders, feeling inadequate. There weren't words.

She remembered what Robert had said about Jane being angry. There was anger in this weeping. Something practical might be the best help.

"Won't he have lodged a copy with your lawyers? Surely it's too important a document to risk its not being found." Roke might be tricky and might be cruel, but *silly* she did not think he was. "Supposing it can't be found at all, then don't you, as the widow, get the house and so on?"

"That's exactly *it*." Jane's hands smacked the desk. "The house, this house, is entailed; it's like the title, so if her son is legitimately Benet's . . . But other things, like Paisley House, and all sorts of belongings like the collections . . . And he said more than once that things would go to 'my eldest son,' *because* it irked him that Guy didn't appreciate this place and was so self-conscious about the title . . . so you see, we *need* the will. Of course I'll get in touch with the solicitors in the morning, in case they do have a copy, but—" She swiveled around and raised a face on which blurred mascara gave her eyes the shadowed look of illness, and she seized Grizel's hand. "Would your husband help?"

"Of course." Though wills are not quite like murderers, Robert's sixth sense, like that of all good detectives, might be of service here, Grizel said to herself.

"You know, I don't believe this. Any of it. It's exactly how everyone says it is. *All the nightmares came to stay.* This morning Benet was alive, we made love, we talked about today. Now there's been everything. Angela and her son. And he's dead. Just so *quick*."

Grizel clasped Jane's painfully gripping hand. She thought: *I hope Robert doesn't really think Jane killed Roke.*

"M'lady." A discreet sound at the door heralded Knebworth, his eyes instantly changing direction from

Jane's tear-stained face to the littered desk and floor. "The vicar, m'lady. To see you. It appears he heard rumors in the village. My wife took the car to obtain more cheese." Knebworth seemed to imply that his wife's presence in the village had started suspicions at once. They probably never shopped on a Sunday. It was surprising a village shop opened on a Sunday at all. Grizel knew from experience at Adlingsden how village radar picked up news faster than any telephone. Probably, too, the police vehicles had to come through Winterford main street on their way to the castle.

Somehow she could not imagine the vicar as a usual visitor to Roke. It might be his first time here ever.

"The *vicar?*" Jane's emphasis strengthened this supposition. "Oh yes. Thank you, Knebworth. Give me a minute— and show him into the gold drawing room." Jane moved to a little rococo looking glass beside the desk, licked her third finger and passed it under each eye, studied the effect, and picked up a comb from the desk. Rain had started again outdoors, pattering on the window, darkening the little room whose apricot walls already made it cozy. Grizel went to the door saying, "I'll find Robert and ask him to look for what you wanted."

Jane gave her a bright, rather frantic smile and a nod. Knebworth held the door for Grizel, who, emerging, nearly bumped into a portly young man in a clerical collar who was staring all around this corner of the hall with a lively interest more suited to an estate agent than to a cleric importing sympathy. Knebworth regarded this with pursed mouth, and blocked him from surging forward into the sitting room.

He was at least *au fait* enough not to take Grizel for Lady Roke.

Grizel watched him ushered away, and saw Bone. "Robert! I was just coming to look for you."

Her pleasure at seeing her husband was tempered by

sudden doubt. He had been walking swiftly down the passage from the front hall and she was struck—almost stricken—by his face. She had seen him look bleak before. Work on a murder case does not produce ceaseless good humor. Now he looked frightening and, worse, his face hadn't changed when he saw her. He went on walking and she ran after, hearing the rain now descending in torrents, sluicing out of gutters onto the terrace flags and drumming high on the skylights over the stairwell as if it could purge the house of the horrors of the last few hours. Bone opened the door at the end of the passage and Grizel, pressing after, found they were in a garden room, tiled with terracotta, its low windows curtained in green and white check, furnished with wicker chairs and sofa with the same check cushions, and set about with big earthenware pots of ferns and palms. Something like a small tree had already reached the roof and, with nowhere to go, drooped dark foliage over their heads. The room was full of the melancholy splash of rain, which had even got in a little under the French doors.

"Robert, you look like the Day of Wrath."

He went to the windows, to stare out at a small courtyard obscured by rain, and answered her.

"Why didn't you tell me? Warn me what they were saying about the accident, that I was drunk and it was hushed up?"

It was not a tone of voice that she knew.

"What good would it have done to tell you? A stupid cruel thing like that. I thought it would only hurt." *And it has. Who's told him now? We've never talked of his wife—Charlotte's talked about her mother and the baby brother but he never has. You don't open up wounds to see if they're healing.*

"Who did you hear it from?" The voice was still hard. She might be under interrogation. He had not turned to face her. The room felt cold. Beyond the window, rain was cascading down onto the brick paving from some overloaded gutter.

"Lawson told the Maitlands, among others I think, and

Catherine told me. She said it was a ridiculous story, horrid and obviously untrue. It was spite, Robert, just spite because you stopped that obsessive camera of his."

"But how did he know?" Bone faced her and for one horrible moment she thought he meant it was true and that Lawson had somehow found out about a cover-up. "So far as I know I've never seen him before. The accident was four years ago. How did he hear of it?"

She came up to him, judging by the change in his voice that she could. "Didn't someone say that he sold his pictures to the papers sometimes? He probably saw some account and happened to remember your name. Perhaps he looks through files."

He put out a hand and she linked fingers with it. "I'm sorry. None of this is your fault." He smiled wryly and pulled on her hand, drawing her closer. "I'm not used to being protected. Everything's reversed. It's almost funny being a suspect, for a change."

"A suspect! Who—Prior suspects—what for?"

"Launching Lawson into space. After the cover-up of my misdeeds I naturally try to eradicate the source of knowledge about them. If it was true, I mean if I was like that, I suppose I might. Spite for spite, you could say."

"I can't contemplate your not being you," she said, and led him to one of the wicker sofas and made him sit beside her. "You know, Robert, you'll have to solve the whole case yourself—or both of them if poor awful Lawson didn't fall—if the Inspector is such a fool as that."

"He's not," Bone said.

"Whatever. Jane needs help too, and you're the one to help her."

"My help might not be to her advantage."

"You mean she might have shot the arrow herself? I *don't* believe she did. And it isn't just that."

While she explained about the will he picked at a loose

piece of wicker on the sofa arm and, as the rain began to slacken and more light came into the room, she thought his face had lost its pallor and its look of iron that had frightened her so. She had presented him with something to do. It might not be the case-solving he wanted, but still it interested him. When she had finished, he laughed.

"Shall we start under these cushions? Roke was a scamp, and insensitive to boot. Did he suppose it would cheer his widow up to have to find the will? I should have thought even he could see it would be adding trouble to pain. Perhaps he thought it would provide a counterirritant. But he didn't treat her well. From what I've seen and gathered, for all his undoubted charm he could be a bastard. If she did him in she wouldn't be the first murderer I've sympathized with."

Grizel for a moment faced a whole dreary experience of murder cases that had led her husband to know that someone like Jane, her friend, was a possible suspect. She thought, *he has to be cynical. I don't.* She leaned to kiss him but, having initiated the embrace, had to break out of it with quite some force.

"Snogging in the conservatory, Robert, is all very well; but I can't condone it when you've a job to be getting on with."

He smiled at her admonitory finger, and made a feint at biting it.

Before they left the garden room, she was gratified to see him solemnly lift the green and white check cushions and survey the wicker under them for a will.

Chapter
·····················
15

NICHOLAS BUCHANAN MET THEM AS THEY CAME INTO THE BACK hall.

"I was looking for you. With your usual genius you're exactly where I was looking. Colonel Makepeace left it absolutely open as to whether we turn up later in the afternoon; he said just to telephone when we knew. Said he'd been expecting us but it would make no difference to him at this stage; Lady Elizabeth had planned to give us tea and had made a mountain of scones this morning . . . I think he was rather thrilled to be the first to hear about poor Roke, actually."

Buchanan's face was for a moment demure. Bone had noticed, on the one or two tours he had managed, that owners of houses were intensely interested in other owners of houses. Buchanan provided not only a check for a pet charity but also discreet chat. Roke's bizarre death would set a good many phone wires humming.

"I told him we were all being *grilled* by the police and didn't think we could possibly make it." He paused. "No one feels very keen to go on, actually. Except the Webbs," and he gave them a wicked glance as he walked beside them toward the front of the house. "I'm afraid they feel they've been sold short for no very adequate reason . . . I didn't dare let on about Lady Elizabeth's scones." He paused, and went on in a different tone. "Frankly, when I think of how hard it was to get Lord Roke to agree to our coming; and this was to be the high spot of the tour . . . somehow I feel ridiculously responsible for things. Of course, I can't get out of the November tour I'm committed to, but I think all of us from this tour will be feeling rather haunted."

They were almost at the door of the dining room, which stood open on their left, and they heard, surprisingly, the voices of children. Then Jane called out, "Is that Mr. Buchanan?"

She appeared in the doorway and stretched a hand to Bone and Grizel as they prepared to pass on, "No, you too. I want you to meet my other boys."

She led them in, and explained in a low voice, "Jeremy and Hugo. John Morell ran them back and they arrived just now. I found they'd had nothing to eat since breakfast. When I rang, the Morells were just getting ready for lunch and they were sure that when the boys had heard about Benet they wouldn't want anything to eat, so they set off right away. But boys, no matter what's happened, can usually eat." She crossed the room toward a bay that hadn't been open when last they had seen the room, but had been rendered invisible by shutters incorporating the mural—so invisible that Bone was surprised to see it. The bay itself was painted to look like a stone balcony with urns of spiky palms either side. A small round table was laid, with a pitcher of orange juice and a big dish of sandwiches, and two boys looked up as their mother and the guests approached. The elder, introduced as Hugo, was perhaps thirteen and looked, with his slight build and flop of dark hair over one eye, rather like Jane and very like Guy. Jeremy at eleven or so already had sturdy shoulders promising future robustness; his fair hair and an oddly challenging expression were reminiscent of Roke and not unlike Baz. Seeing him, Grizel could not be surprised that Jane believed Roke to be Baz's father. They were silent as they shook hands, and subdued.

"It's impossible to take in what has happened yet," Jane said on their behalf.

"Yes, one doesn't believe it," Bone agreed. Prior had succeeded in rousing up his own memories, and his sheer incredulity, to begin with, about Petra's death.

Buchanan said, "A roomful of tourists doesn't help, Lady Roke, and I've every expectation of the police letting us go during the next half hour. I thought if I said goodbye now, then we needn't disturb you further."

"Oh, I'll come and say goodbye." Jane was decided. "Knebworth will tell me when you're ready to go. Of course I'll come."

"And there's the matter of the . . ." Buchanan reached into an inner pocket and half withdrew a checkbook.

"Oh. I'll . . . I don't think so, really . . . I'll come . . ."

Buchanan said to the boys, "It was very nice to see you," and went on his way, stopping only to look around once more and say, "It's a marvelous room."

"It is rather fun," Jane said vaguely. Buchanan was gone.

Jane took Grizel's hand urgently. "Have you asked Robert? I'm—I don't know where I am. Look, I'll go and say goodbye to the tour and—well—"

"I've asked Robert," Grizel said firmly, "and he'll look for it. Shall I come with you to say goodbye? Would you like moral support?"

"Yes. Yes, I should. You're always so good at knowing when someone needs backup."

Grizel put a hand on Bone's chest, and smiled at him briefly before she went, as if renewing contact. Jeremy had sat down again and got on with his sandwich. After a hesitation Hugo did the same.

"Have you had lunch, sir?" he asked Bone.

"Yes, thank you."

"What are you supposed to look for?" Jeremy inquired, to be squashed by his senior.

"Shut up, Tig. It's not your business."

"It is, I think," said Bone, pulling out a chair and sitting where he could look at the mural opposite. It gave an extraordinary feeling of spaciousness to the room. He remembered the small cell-like rooms of a Roman villa under the Capitoline hill, where frescoes of countryside opened the walls to deceived eyes, and must have made the little space more pleasant to live in. This mural was designed to bring the warmth of the Mediterranean to the dark side of an English house.

"When are we going to see this Baz?" Jeremy asked Hugo, who shrugged. "Is he really going to get Daddy's title, d'you think? What's Guy going to do?" Jeremy's voice was sharp with anxiety.

"Be pretty miffed. Wouldn't you?"

"Is he going to live here? Will he take the house and everything?"

"Oh, can it, Tig."

"But—"

Hugo jerked his head slightly at Bone, and Jeremy fell silent.

"I'm afraid that, though I'm a stranger, I do know something about it," Bone said to Hugo. "Your father played one of his jokes and hid his will. Your mother's asked me to help her find it."

Hugo may have wondered *Why you?* There was doubt in his face. He spoke in the lifeless tone of shock. "We can all look, I suppose."

Bone had achieved his object of providing a distraction. "Of course."

"I bet I know where it is," Jeremy said.

"You would." Hugo was crushing.

"No, really I do."

"Do you know this Mrs. North, sir?" Hugo made an effort at polite conversation, frowning under his swath of hair. He was very pale.

"I've met her, yes. She's a pleasant person. So is her son."

"Mother seems to be sure already that they're right." Jeremy took another sandwich. Hugo had taken a couple of bites of one. An absence of crumbs around it on the plate suggested it was his first. "Don't you think it's a bit iffy? I mean, them turning up like this?"

"Shut *up*, Tig."

"You don't think they—well—I mean." His voice dropped and he said awkwardly, "Did it?"

"Tig. Will you *can* it!"

Bone intervened, bearing down Jeremy's retort, "You said you knew where your father's will is."

"Yes. He told me he'd hidden this important thing, only it wasn't exactly hidden, I'd see it if I looked for it. Only *I* haven't seen it yet and I have looked, so it isn't that easy."

"But where'd he hidden it?" Hugo demanded.

"In my room."

"Mary Christmas," said Hugo.

* * *

The room was perhaps twenty feet square. Two windows overlooked the gardens to the distant low hills. These rooms at the top of the house were not tall like those below but had low ceilings and a less formal air.

There was, very likely, furniture in here but that did not at first make an impression. What did were the objects, small and middle-sized objects of various sorts and all colors. These objects were disposed on surfaces which resolved themselves into tables, shelves, and ledges; but also they hung from the ceiling. In the middle, a sagging bed under a chenille cover was strewn with amorphous furry things. Posters, among which the ones Bone could recognize were of Iron Maiden, Madonna, and Whitesnake, plastered the walls and the ceiling. Model planes and shadow puppets hung swiveling on the breeze from the quarter open window.

A trunk covered with a tartan rug was piled with shoes, sandals, chaplis, trainers, and Turkish slippers. They were all sizes, a collection, not a working supply. Next to this a tall whatnot, with five shelves diminishing upward in size, held model animals: an expensive blue-flowered kitten, an Indian elephant with howdah and small brilliantly clad riders, a moon rabbit of oxidized pottery gazing skyward; a glass dragon, a brass dragon, a green pottery kylin, a glass dachshund, a leather bear, a fur Pekinese . . .

Bone moved on. Jeremy said, "Sorry about the dust. No one but me's allowed to touch them and I haven't been here since the last hols."

An extensive bookshelf caught Bone's attention. He said, "I'm not bothered about dust. Did your father give you no idea as to what he'd hidden? I mean, say, the size of it?"

"Nup. Only what I said: 'You can see it if you look.'"

"Then it doesn't sound as if he put it inside the trunk, for instance."

"I don't know." Jeremy squeaked a trainer on the painted floorboards. "He could've. 'If you look' could mean *inside things.*"

Bone accordingly gave the books a once-over for extruding documents or paper, getting down on the floor for the lowest shelf. The floor was evidently permitted to be cleaned, he was thankful to find. "Then we may have to go through all these opening them up."

Jeremy whistled. "Hope not." He was feeling inside each of the shoes.

"But I rather think," Bone said, getting up, "that your father might have said, 'You can *find* it if you look' if he'd put it somewhere really out of sight."

"Well, yes, could be. That'd be better. With Daddy, though, you couldn't tell."

Bone moved on to a table full of model cars, vans, and trucks. Under it on the floor were toy cars, vans, and trucks, plastic and wooden. Bone appreciated the distinction. On the chest of drawers was a variegated group of model buildings, from a well-constructed cardboard castle to pottery village houses, and beyond the castle a homemade farm, card cut-out animals, trees and fences set in Plasticine holders; a duckpond, however, was of tin, its slightly raised surround painted with grass. A metal goose sat on it, with Plasticine goslings around her. On the end wall a puppet Evzone hung, moustached, his white skirt grayed and limp. Taped to one inert hand was an ouzo bottle.

The mantel shelf held small bottles of all colors, some chipped, from an iodine ribbed one to an opalescent little flask with dished sides and a tall neck. Above, a blown-up framed photograph of a pleasant neo-Palladian country house was hung.

"That's Paisley House," Jeremy said. "Daddy built it. I mean he had it built. I was born there." He had caught up with Bone's prowling, and he reached out and straightened the picture. "I didn't want to leave it and come here."

"Wasn't a castle more interesting?"

"Sort of; but it's freezing in winter; and there's so many rooms and it's miles to anywhere like down to the dining room; and the old part, the castle bit, it's spooky. And my room at home was all painted like a ship's deck with the sea all around and a treasure island in the distance. I really liked that room. The man came here and he did the dining room and we thought he'd do more but he'd become fashionable and we couldn't afford him. It's terribly expensive running this place. Daddy let Paisley House. I wonder if we could go back there. I mean if this person is going to have Roke."

"You'd like that?"

"I don't terribly like this place. I think only Daddy really likes—"

He stopped.

Bone, moving on toward the desk, said, "Life's difficult just now," in a carefully impersonal tone. "Things do sort themselves eventually." He did not say that Baz would, if he were Roke in fact, probably own Paisley House too.

Jeremy opened the desk (on top, pebbles of interesting shapes, a marble egg, a tiger's eye egg, and geodes) and with one adroit hand held back multifarious papers and magazines, a football shirt, a baseball cap, notebooks, a chocolate box holding, but only just, a score of felt-tips, and a pencil box in the shape of a fur monkey, very worn. He pulled out the flap supports and, after a pause in which they both surveyed this cornucopia, he said, "I hope it's not in here."

The breeze made a mobile rotate over Jeremy's head, and the picture above the fireplace rattled. Jeremy shut the window and went voyaging through the room to open the other one.

"Mother's been in. She's the one who opens that window; she says it gives a better through draft to air the room, but I've *told* her it makes that picture bang in the night. The wall's crooked, I think, since the chimneypot fell down."

"It didn't always rattle?" Bone moved to the fireplace and lifted one side of the picture to peer at the back.

An envelope was taped to the lower edge of the frame.

Chapter

....

16

BONE, HURRYING AFTER THE EXCITED JEREMY, FOUND THAT THE
front stairs had been freed from the police barriers. Jeremy,
who had no hang-ups about that part of the house—
perhaps no knowledge of where his father had died—
careered down to stand dancing beside his mother, in
conversation with Baz in the hall. By chance they were
under the portrait of the Roke ancestor whom Baz resembled, but it was the sight of Baz himself that stopped
Jeremy's impatient jig and made him soberly stare.

Still, he mutely held out the long envelope in front of
Jane, and she took it automatically as she talked. When Bone
came up she was saying, "Good, then we'll see you in an
hour or so."

Jeremy's tug at her sleeve made her put a hand on his

shoulder and give it a little shake to remind him of manners, but he was past that.

"Do open it, Mother. Open it. It was in my room."

She turned her attention to him, but only abstractedly, not taking in what he was saying.

"This is my youngest son, Jeremy. Tig, this is Basil Paisley."

Baz, disconcerted, almost corrected her, but halted, and held out his hand. He and Jeremy shook hands with mutual diffidence. Bone thought, they may each see the likeness. It must be a strange moment for them.

If it was, Jeremy did not dwell on it.

"Mother. Do open that. We *found* it. You know, where Daddy hid it."

Jane suddenly seemed to realize what had been said. "What! This? You found it?"

"In my room."

"I—Baz, excuse me, this is important. This may be the will Benet hid." She tore the envelope wide open and took out a folded bundle of paper. It was tied with that pink tape so oddly called "red." She slid the tape off and undid the bundle. Bone, with the incorrigible curiosity that had led him into his profession, watched over Jeremy's head.

"They're all blank! Oh, it's too bad. Another wretched joke . . . I'm sorry. Just take them, darling, and—"

"That one's got writing," Baz said. Jeremy, trying to fish it out, dropped the lot. He and Baz dived for it and came up with the written page between them. Baz surrendered it and Jeremy read:

*"The moving finger writes, and having writ,
It takes time off to poke among the shit.*

Oh, sorry; but it does *say*."

Jane took the paper. "It's Benet's writing," she said.

"It's a clue, it's a clue!"

Donald Spencer suddenly emerged from the room Prior was using on the other side of the hall and, without looking at anyone, crossed to the front door and went out. Bone was possibly the only one to notice him.

"Poke among the—" Jane looked at the paper helplessly. "What on earth—but I must say that's got Benet's signature on it."

"It hasn't," Jeremy objected, peering.

"A metaphor, Tig. Listen, darling: where was this?"

"Behind the Paisley picture in my room. Daddy said he'd hidden something, that I could see if I looked, in my room and if I found it I was to take it to him or if he was dead I was to show it to you. I know I've got that right because he made me say it over and over."

"When did he tell you this?" Bone asked. Jeremy started, having forgotten he was there, and turned.

"Ages ago. I mean really ages ago. Last year, I think."

"Could that be important?" Jane asked, puzzled.

"Habit," Bone said. "I'm sorry."

Sergeant Williams went along the far side of the hall to the morning room, just as the Simpson-Bates sisters came hurrying in from the porch and almost ran toward him. Bone heard their anxious account: Mr. Spencer had set off to walk home to the village, and he was very upset and didn't seem to have told anyone he was going and—

Sergeant Williams did not seem moved by this, merely remarking that he had Mr. Spencer's address and could see him at any time if it was necessary. He disappeared into the morning room, and the sisters, exclaiming that he had not understood, started on a beeline for Jane. Bone went to intercept them, and grasped that it was Mr. Spencer's state of mind that concerned them, not his apparent truancy. Bone recklessly promised to go down to the village next day and check on Spencer's well-being. He was prompted by both compassion for the man and, he inwardly confessed, a curiosity to know what had caused him to walk away so abruptly. He recalled his own response to Prior.

Everyone now began to emerge from the morning room, and Buchanan came toward Jane.

"We're being allowed to go. You're rid of us at last, Lady Roke . . ."

She went to meet him and, at the door, stood and shook hands with everyone going out, a task made even more difficult for her by the condolences most of them offered. Bone noticed how the Simpson-Bates sisters clasped Jane's hands, one each, longer than others did, with sympathetic murmurs antiphonally. Catherine Maitland, whose fine drawn face he had liked from the start, said little but struck, to judge from Jane's slight relaxing, precisely the right note. Maitland, following, seemed embarrassed, as though Roke's death was an error in taste much as his teases had been; Bone remembered Roke's genial hugging of Maitland outside the muniment room and the revelation that Maitland had worked for him in the past. Was it accidental that Maitland was on this tour? Had he, like Angela North, come on purpose to see Roke? And why? Had Prior heard about this previous association?

He did not see himself asking Prior if he had.

The Webbs by contrast gave a refreshing display of indifference. Bone supposed that, in the graveyard his fancy had selected as their home, another body would be neither here nor there. The only emotion they showed was a resentment at being robbed of the afternoon's visit. Mary Webb, extending a flaccid glove, said quite loudly, "Great pity" as though it were Jane's fault. As they wandered out into the porch, Mabey, backing off from Jane, fell over the bootscraper and collided with Mr. Webb, who tottered dangerously.

"Just what you did this morning, Lynda," Dr. Rose said,

but Lynda Rose shook her head as if he had said something tactless.

As Mabey and Webb were set upright, Bone thought: any minute now dem bones will disconnect from dem dry bones; he almost expected a clatter and a Hammer Films heap of dust on the ground. It was a relief to him not to corral his imagination as he always felt he must when he was at work.

Jane said to Baz, "We'll see you, then," and Bone realized for the first time that Angela was not there. She must still be lying down.

Finally Buchanan too was gone, and Jane stood on the gravel to wave the bus away. Jeremy had joined her. She came back with a strained face, making a smile, her arm across his shoulders. She glanced at the foot of the stairs where Roke had fallen, but resolutely kept her smile, patting Jeremy's sleeve with her fingers.

"Well, that's one step. One step at a time." She rubbed her face with the other hand and said, "I need tea. Just a cup of beautiful Assam tea and then—then we'd better discuss this clue of Benet's. Tig, go and ask Knebworth for tea in the little drawing room, and tell Marcus." As Jeremy ran off, she said to Bone, "I suppose that sooner or later it will properly come to me what's happened, but meanwhile I find myself thinking *Well, why don't we ask Benet what he meant?*"

Bone said in his deliberately detached tone, "That goes on for some time." It came to him that he probably had a wider experience of bereaved people than anyone else in the house, and he had seen most reactions. Jane gave him a sudden glance and nodded, wryly.

"Come and have some tea, Robert."

"I want just to have a word with Prior. Jane, are you sure you wouldn't rather have only the family here now?"

"Oh no. And it won't be just family. I didn't think Angela North should move, so I suggested to her son that he should bring their things here from the hotel. I feel it's only fair to Benet, and it's got to be sorted out; and I don't want it all done through lawyers. She says she has the copies of all the documents and things . . . I've got that to cope with. And anyway I can't *do* without Grizel. And you."

Bone heard the addition, and smiled. It was one of his grim smiles, and Jane gave a rather wild laugh.

"Until the unspeakable Adrian can be got to go," she said, "we're not *only family* anyway. And I really, truly will be glad of your company."

She went toward the small drawing room, where Guy could be heard, as the door opened, talking angrily.

Bone said to the PC at Prior's door as he crossed the hall, "Ask the Chief Inspector if he's free for the moment, will you?" and as the man went inside he stood waiting, listening to the house. Cold light filtered down from the skylight, sounds of crockery came faintly from the kitchen. A phone rang upstairs.

The PC came out and held the door open. Bone, mentally taking a deep slow breath, went in.

Chapter

············

17

PRIOR WAS IN THE DOMINANT, BACK-TO-THE-HEARTH POSI-
tion, although nothing could make him as tall as Bone. He
was smoking.

"Chief Inspector, I think I fell for your technique back
there. It's salutary and informative to be on the wrong end
of an interview—hasn't happened since I was in police
college."

Prior responded to this by a grin and a puff of smoke.
"Perhaps it should be put in revision courses, sir."

"Yes . . . I'm interested in the way you're conducting this
case. I've not seen anything both so close and from the
outside. It's a bizarre case enough." Bone had managed to
warm his voice. Two could play at technique.

"Bizarre! It's OTT."

"Can you tell me anything about your progress?"

Prior came forward, dabbed the cheroot toward Bone, and said, "I can tell you both cases have got suspects the way a dog has fleas."

"Of whom, in the Lawson case, I'm one."

Prior shoved up his bottom lip and nodded. "But in my personal judgment, sir, you hadn't heard Lawson's little rumor until I told it to you."

Bone shook his head. "No one passed it on to me. I don't know how current the story ever was."

"Well, say your own people heard it, they wouldn't care to tell you, would they, sir?" Prior was implying that the nasty little tale might indeed have been current around his home station. Bone wondered if Steve Locker, his own Chief Inspector, had heard it, or if it hadn't existed outside Lawson's fetid imaginings.

Prior glanced beyond Bone toward the door, and said, "Yes?"

"They're through upstairs, sir."

"Come on up with me, Superintendent?"

"I'd be interested." The invitation was, in its way, Prior's apology for his previous manner.

"Right." He turned to the sergeant and dropped his voice. "Where's the family?"

"Lady Roke's in the drawing room over there."

Prior turned his eyes up in a brief thanks-be-for-that, and it came to Bone that he found Lady Roke intimidating.

"How many drawing rooms has this house got?"

"Three," Bone said. "Downstairs, the rose and the small blue, upstairs the gold." He did not include Jane's little apricot sitting room.

"Christ." Prior led the way out, whipping suddenly back at the door to let Bone precede him. Bone, who, in the circumstances, had forgotten this etiquette, was very nearly wrong-footed.

They climbed the stairs. "The doc thinks Lord Roke was most likely semiconscious by the time he came down here."

"Lady Roke might like to know that—that he suffered less."

"She might." Prior's tone was a sharp reminder that Jane must be suspect.

Bone had not until now seen the gallery, because of Roke's refusal to show it before the tour came. It had a curious museum-like air because, once again, all illumination came from above through a long skylight of frosted glass, like a greenhouse cut off at the knees and inserted in the roof. This downward light showed the police packing up their own lamps and apparatus and carrying out a large plastic-wrapped parcel.

It showed also cabinets, cupboards along the wall, and the eerie presence of two suits of armor like the one Roke had worn; one stood at the far end, the other sat in a recess beyond a highly ornamented red lacquer cupboard.

"Apparently, Lord Roke sat in that"—the cheroot jabbed toward the plastic parcel on its way out of the open doors—"for some little while. Long enough for blood to get down the torso and seep onto the chair seat."

Bone pictured Roke, silent and dazed, sitting—as the other suit of armor was doing. Prior went on.

"That *could* account for Guy Paisley looking in here when he was searching for his father and not seeing him." They say the armor was always sat in that chair, on a metal framework. He could have seen what he was used to seeing and forgot Roke was wearing it—in his state of mind, and just a quick look. Prior went swiftly to the library door, opened it, and said to a WPC nearby, "Weatherby?"

"A fair-haired boy who said he was Jeremy Paisley went in there and took him away to have tea."

"Right." He shut the door. "It's possible to hear through this door; to an extent. Now I don't buy that Lady Roke and her eldest didn't know about the long-lost heir from down under. More than one of the tour lot saw Guy Paisley come into that coffee room and talk to Lady Roke very privately and in a hurry, and they both glanced at Baz North and then Lady R left. Well, they can play wide-eyed all they like, but *they knew*. And if necessary I'll get them to admit it."

Bone itched to look at the room's exhibits. He could see the lacquer cabinet, whose panels were alive with high-relief scenes in frames of gilded swirling decoration; but he kept his attention steadily on Prior, since the last thing he wanted was to cut off this almost genial, communicative mood. He nodded to show agreement.

"Then those who can't account for themselves at the vital time—"

The mortal time, thought Bone.

"—we have Guy Paisley; Lady Roke; Angela North; Donald Spencer; Dr. Rose; and those who were with someone else who might provide a suspect alibi: both Maitlands; Weatherby and Nash in the library there. And Lawson."

Bone's eyebrows rose. This pleased Prior, who rocked on his heels and grinned.

"Go through the motives. Young Paisley, he's been done out of an inheritance, and he and his father didn't get on—this could be the final straw. Lady Roke, ditto. Mrs. North, she'd like to see her son inherit straight off. Donald Spencer hasn't a motive against Roke that we know of, though he lives nearby and something could have brewed up; but equally, he lives nearby and could have got at Roke any day. However, he has a motive for tipping Lawson over the battlements, if he *was* tipped."

"Bit like a Chihuahua tipping a Great Dane."

Prior grinned at this. "But Lawson had his foot caught in a rope. A shove could have done more damage than you'd think, and the low parts of the battlements are just thigh level—dead right for an off-balance fall. He could have meant it, or only meant to shove him, and over he'd go."

Bone conceded this with a grave nod.

"The doctor was alone in the gardens and he has no motive we know of. Nor has Weatherby against Roke. That we know of. Adrian Nash is unlikely to kill off his meal ticket even if he was made fun of; like that trick in the pool with the alligator." Prior wagged his head. "Arnold Mabey told me about that. Sorry I didn't get to see it. Then the Maitlands have no motive; they're strangers."

Bone drew breath. "Then they didn't tell you. Roke knew Maitland all right. I don't know much about the connection but I think Maitland designed a house for him some time ago."

"Did it fall down?" Prior laughed. "You're going a bit far with that one, sir."

"But they weren't strangers."

"Right. Thanks for the information. Of course this is one for the books, this one. Most of our homicide cases are cut and dried. You're no doubt used to that." There was a complacent note here. Bone, his case load thus disparaged, wondered if Prior, whom he judged competent, had escaped higher promotion by a social skill at getting across people. "This one's got a lot more going for it. The labs and postmortems will have something to say." He jiggled keys and change in his pockets.

"You mentioned Lawson."

"Aha. That did surprise you." Prior leaned forward from the hips, peering into Bone's face, enjoying himself. "Ye-es. Well, Lawson was apparently recognized by Guy Paisley as the man that photographed a collection of Roke's that got stolen from the house they lived in some years back, and Paisley told his father. There may have been a confrontation. Lord Roke could have been killed then by Lawson, who rushes up to the roof to get away from the scene and to establish that he was photographing only up there; gets his foot in the rope and *whoosh*."

Prior's grin was ghoulish.

Bone responded to this irresistible picture with amusement, and for a moment he and Prior were in accord. He said, however, "I don't imagine Roke being off his guard with Lawson. The killer had to be able to take up a bow and arrow and shoot from quite close to, at the side."

Prior's hand came up. "Yes! You're thinking as I am, sir. The family. The commonest source."

Bone had gone to look at the rack of bows on the wall. He said, "These aren't strung, even."

Prior pointed. On the top of the display case lay a wicker quiver of arrows, fan-shaped, that spaced the arrows out so that they presented to the hand one by one. There was a gap in the row of them. The case had been dusted and prints lifted from it. Prior called to the WPC by the door, "Why did they miss this? It's got to go—you see, sir, the bow was strung all right. Laid down there and wiped off clean as a whistle, unless the labs can find traces prints couldn't raise."

"What traces are you expecting?"

"Ah. I'm looking at the ladies. Mrs. North's in a bad way, in shock, lying down. Reaction. That's one thing. The other is Lady Roke. Cool as cucumber, seeing off her guests, ordering tea, organizing . . . well in control, wouldn't you say? Now I've seen that before in widows. They cope with what has to be done, many of them—my own sister did it all, never broke down, marvelous. She told me, 'I did it like a zombie.' But that chucking the clothes out, all Nash's gear in the mud! That's emotion."

"So you're expecting—?"

"We won't get much that's conclusive from floor dust. Everyone's been in here; but from the bow, and the arrow perhaps, though I dare say other people handled that after he fell. Instinct to get it out, like. Did you notice anyone touch it, sir?"

Bone shook his head. It was impossible to be sure. He had moved on to look at a couple of swords on a wooden stand, their intricate metal ornaments gleaming. Above them on the wall were more hilt guards, flat rosettes pierced with the slit for the blade, chased and incised with patterns. *Weapons used to be works of art,* he thought, *when life was cheaper. Now we make more fuss about death, we even begin to recognize that war itself is a flawed method. And our weapons have only a functional and complicated ugliness. Though it may seem like beauty to some people.*

"Lots of stuff here, isn't there?" Prior said. His team had left, the WPC carrying away the quiver. They were alone in the gallery. "Pricey, I dare say. And he'd got his security." A new lit cheroot pointed at the glowing eye of an alarm system. "Pity he didn't have cameras."

"In this light?"

"Oh, very true." Prior came to lean over a display case beside Bone, and to look at lacquer boxes, small ones like cigarette cases, with cords attached, one with the small ivory of a netsuke on the cords' ends, and larger boxes patterned in gold or silver with waves, clouds, scenes, flowers. "Any idea what these'd be worth, now?"

"Thousands, probably."

"Amazing what people will give money for. I mean, there's workmanship there all right, but I wouldn't pay a thousand if I had it spare, for one of those."

The suit of armor at this end was, so far as Bone could judge, very like the one Roke had been wearing. It was on a seated armature, however, and imparted a strong sense of being inhabited. The breastplate and skirt pieces and neck guard were of fine plaited silk cord, row upon row, fastened down with braid at the ends, the braid stapled, as it were, with small metal plaques. The cord gleamed with lacquer. Bone wondered how much use it was against one of those deadly swords. Prior joined him.

"You fancy wearing one of this lot to fight in?"

"It looks more like parade ground armor." Bone was examining circumspectly the ferocious mask, like a black demon face, that was the visor. Above it the helmet swept up in a curious crest.

"Reckon they're for officers and the poor bloody infantry did the real fighting."

Bone had seen only one Japanese film, with his first wife years ago, *Seven Samurai*. It wasn't his impression that the officer class didn't fight; but his quite irrational instinct to contradict Prior's view was, luckily, suppressible.

"Mm-hm," he said.

Prior's square jaw was now jutting at a wall case of small carvings: two quails on millet stalks, not two inches high, in wood, with detailed feathers and thin bird feet and bright ebony eyes; a badger in a shawl, asleep; two laughing hairy little men, one with a broom and the other with a paper, in ivory . . . Bone thought, *I'll come back here for a good look. Charlotte would love these. I wonder if Jane would invite . . . but Jane might not be living here.* Baz, however amiable, was another matter. Baz might sell the lot, as Guy was reputed to want to. Baz might have to sell for inheritance tax.

Prior, bored, had taken himself off. A wraith of smoke hung on the air.

Bone looked around. He wondered if this collection was the work of Roke or of his uncle, or begun by the uncle and added to by his successor. In cases further along there was china, and at the far end that other brooding presence of armor.

He looked toward the gap where the absent carved chair

had been, twin to the one still here, by the shape of the shrouded object they had carried out—with a very wide seat, the back as low as the arms, carved with a formal resemblance to natural plant shapes. Bone pictured Roke sitting there, armed for his joke, the arrow through his neck, dazed and dying.

Chapter

· · · · · · · · · · · · · · · · · · · ·

18

WHEN NICHOLAS BUCHANAN HAD THANKED THE COACH DRIV-
er and handed him the party's gratuity (collected with
secretive chinking behind his back on the drive to the hotel),
the party disembarked. Buchanan received thanks from
everyone, although the Webbs tempered theirs with glances
of severe disapproval. Expecting that before they finally
departed they would ask for a refund for the missed part of
their tour, he hurried to the lounge to order a coffee and
sandwich before his drive home. He got into a last gossip
with others who had far to go and needed fortifying, while
the rest collected their luggage from Reception and exchanged desultory goodbyes in the lobby and in the car
park, each with the feeling that they could not possibly have
anticipated, when they left their cars on Friday, what they

would have witnessed before they drove away on this Sunday evening.

Arnold Mabey, affectionately embraced and cautioned to be careful by the sisters, got himself into a small red Austin, was just in time prevented from shutting his stick, souvenir of Roke Castle and an encounter with a cayman, in the door, and drove off; saluted on his emergence into the main road by an outrage of hooting from cars and a lorry whose paths he had serenely crossed.

The Webbs left in an ancient black Daimler whose likeness to a hearse would have pleased Bone, followed by the Roses in a green Volvo and the Maitlands in a silver BMW. The Simpson-Bateses, after a good chat over tea and buns, spent enough time rearranging their luggage to a proper balance in the boot of their Ford Escort, to find themselves saying a second goodbye to Nicholas Buchanan. A little restored after a strong coffee and a ham sandwich, he exchanged a final embrace and wave, and saw them off. Sheila nudged Susan just as they came to the gates, to make her glance at Baz loading luggage into a hire car. He was grave and preoccupied.

"That young man has a change in fortune," she remarked with satisfaction, and unwrapped two toffees and popped one in her own mouth and the other into her sister's, obediently opened, as they swung out toward the motorway. In the minds of both was the thought that they would be greatly sought after by their acquaintances in the coming weeks, for firsthand accounts of what would certainly be in the newspapers and might even appear on television. Both, watching the road and chewing, wore unconsciously a faint smile.

Donald Spencer, as the sisters had confided to Bone in their anxiety for his welfare, had much earlier walked straight home. He had not kept to the gravel of the drive that wound through the parkland, but taken a beeline across the grass, tramping over uneven ground as if on the bodies of enemies. He had reached the scrolled ironwork gates the driver had edged through that morning, and set off fast down the street as though drawn by a magnet. His sister had the kettle on for her tea, and was opening a packet of biscuits when she heard his key in the lock.

"You're early, Don," she called out pleased. "I didn't expect you till much later. Just in time for tea. Did you have a good time?"

A few minutes afterward, hearing no reply and bearing the tea tray into the sitting room, she saw that he had not.

He had sat down in the red cut-moquette armchair and was staring at the fire screen whose framed canvas hid the empty grate, at her embroidery of a very creditable Welsh dragon in red wool, as if he were seeing flames beyond it.

She was distressed. All the old signs back! She had so hoped that this weekend—out every day, seeing new things in the company of others—would get him out of himself, put him on the road to recovery.

She sat down, poured the tea, put his cup on the solid little stool by his chair, and popped one of his favorite chocolate digestives, on one of the celadon green plates, beside it.

"There, dear. You'll be tired. I expect you had a lot of walking to do; these old houses are so big. What was Roke Castle like, after all those times you and May used to wonder about—"

She could have bitten her tongue out. To have mentioned May! But it had broken Don's trance. He picked up his cup and began to stir the tea with his usual precise care. He glanced toward but not at her, his glasses flashing.

"She would have been disappointed. I didn't like it at all."

* * *

Arnold Mabey had no one waiting for him. He left the red Austin under the carport and bent to pull the heads off some dandelions in the cracks of the paving stones, sprung up in just two days. Then he picked up his bag, put his key in the door, and fell over the junk mail on the mat. With some difficulty, because he had his bag in one hand and still held his keys, he collected the fat packages and straightened up, sniffing the enclosed air of the little house with pleasure. They were always at him to leave, to go and live among other people in some "nice little flat" with a warden on call. Warden! Warder more like. "You'll be safer," they said. Safer! This was his house and he could do what he liked in and with it. He put down the mail he didn't want—there was only one letter and nothing, of course, from Canada from his daughter—and he ambled through into the kitchen to see what he could have for supper. An egg and baked beans on toast would do very well.

As he was taking the beans tin from the shelf he stopped suddenly and shook his head. Two people he had seen that day would never eat again. He put down the tin—he wished it hadn't occurred to him, quite put him off his supper.

He wandered to peer at his reflection in the little foxed mirror over the kitchen table. He brought up both forefingers, pointing them at either side of his neck.

"Wham!" whispered Arnold Mabey.

Catherine Maitland had telephoned her friend Anna from the hotel before they started home, to say there would be no need for her to go in and feed Wilbur at his usual time of six, as they would be back by then. Nothing was said in the car, but Catherine was startled that Ben swore when somebody cut in and slowed down ahead; something he hardly ever did. Of course he was on edge. She hoped no one had parked across the garage entrance again.

Everything had been going so well up to this afternoon. She had really thought that Ben had long ago got over what troubled him; had, as it were, buried the hatchet. If only she hadn't urged him to come! It was going to take a lot of Mogadon to obliterate that awful face staring up at them under the helmet as they leaned on the banister rail. He had fallen prone, but the women had of course turned him over, and he had seemed to stare . . .

Wilbur was waiting for them on the high wall. He came pacing along the bricks as they drove up—there was a space, thank God—with his tail lifting in greeting. Ben, as he went by carrying their bags, put up his face, and Wilbur generously stropped his orange cheek on Ben's pale one, knocking his glasses askew. When Ben stopped in the porch to put down the bags, straighten his spectacles, and get out his keys, Catherine thought he looked more wrought up than she'd seen him for years. It was, she supposed, yet another thing to blame Roke for. She envied Wilbur, who bustled before them into the kitchen, for he was anxious about nothing but the prompt appearance of his supper, served by the proper courtiers this time.

The Webbs had farther to travel than most of the tour party. Only a couple from Devon had farther to go, and they had booked to stay over at the hotel, but the journey did not trouble the Webbs. Mrs. Webb dozed with her head drooped, chin on chest, causing one man who drew alongside at traffic lights to wonder if the elderly driver had strapped in a corpse for passenger. A killer, he'd read, had done that with his victim only a year or so ago.

Mr. Webb drove as he always did, arms straight out in front of him, foot pressing evenly on the accelerator. He disliked having to brake. It annoyed him and he did not do it unless he was forced to, at the last moment. He did not like to use the indicator, judging for himself when he could overtake or resume the inside lane. He owed his life to the quick reactions of other drivers, and to some fate that had preserved him for so long for no immediately obvious purpose.

As they trundled up the steep cobbled high street of their North Country town, some hours after leaving the hotel, Mrs. Webb woke to the vibrations and began to tell her husband what she intended to say in her letter of complaint to Nicholas Buchanan that evening. Mr. Webb, grunting to show he was in agreement, slewed the Daimler suddenly along the curb at the top of the street, effectively blocking a woman in a Fiat who had trailed patiently in low gear after him for half a mile. He got out and slammed the car door, staring contemptuously at her as she got into reverse and started to try to edge past.

Mrs. Webb, leaving the bags to her husband, began to negotiate the steps up to their front door, pulling on the iron handrail with inflexible determination. Curtains twitched at the neighboring windows as this progress was watched and the statement made: They're back.

Like most of the others, they thought first of tea, and Mrs. Webb made her way to the kitchen and picked up the kettle. As the tap made its usual juddering whine, she went over in her mind the chief points of the letter, and looked, without seeing it, at the view from the window. It was, by day, green, peaceful, overshadowed by trees and now, in the autumn evening, the light from the kitchen window fell only on the nearest of the tombstones. It was nice to be home.

Dr. Rose lived almost as far away as the Webbs and was tired when he reached home. He was also hungry. The midday sandwiches were a long time ago, and he had felt hungry quite soon after them. He remembered that Lynda, saying how ravenous she was, had co-opted one of his. He hoped there would be a good dinner at home. He might be getting back earlier than expected, but at least he was expected back.

There was an excellent dinner: steak and mushroom pie, and plenty of mashed potato to soak up the rich gravy. As he ate, and began to feel at home and to relax, he could contemplate the day's ghastly events, as he had avoided doing on the way home. It was a pity he had been forced to reveal his profession, when he particularly wanted a weekend with no bother. He understood that the police might want him to confirm his statement on his observations of Lawson after they'd got him down on the flagstones and he'd tried resuscitation—although he'd known it was hopeless from the start. That worried him, but it was entirely possible it might never happen. The weekend until that incident had been marvelous, and he almost felt that what had happened over Lawson had brought him and Lynda closer in a way.

"Was it an interesting conference?" His wife cut another segment of the pie, knowing that John would certainly want a second helping.

The doctor held out his plate. "Oh, I don't know. The predictable bunch that one knows a bit too well. One or two good papers, though."

"Nice for you to get away from the dead and the dying, for a change." She heaped the potato, avoiding dumping it in the gravy as he so disliked. Handing the plate back, she thought he looked odd; but luckily she could not see inside his mind, which had instantly presented him with a vivid image of two faces: Josh Lawson's, suffused and suffocated, superimposed on Roke's, white in the shadow of that helmet, his neck so neatly skewered beneath.

Chapter

....

19

THEY HAD TEA IN THE SMALL BLUE DRAWING ROOM OVERLOOK-
ing the terrace, with autumn twilight misting the trees in the
parkland beyond. Bone drank his tea from a Coalport cup
without noticing, his mind engaged with possibilities. He
had observed that Jane's hand shook as she poured. Now, at
a sound of running footsteps in the hall she raised her head
and called, "Boys! Do you want tea?"

Jeremy appeared briefly, and was allowed by Jane to take
away a napkin filled with scones for himself and Hugo,
explaining, "We're busy, we're looking in all the loos.
Hoog's got the step-stool for getting on to look in the
cisterns." He ran out, absorbed in the occupation, and
reappeared to ask, "Can cesspits be got open?"

"*No*, darling. Do think. Daddy wouldn't have put a will in
a cesspit."

Jeremy turned the handle of the door, and swung from foot to foot. "Might have. Wrapped in plastic and stuff."

"We are not going to open any cesspit. Did you wash your hands before you came in here?"

Jeremy looked down at the bundled napkin. "No. Okay. We will. I'll see Hoog does." He ran out and they could hear his shoes thump into the distance and, from somewhere, a sound they had heard without noticing during the last half hour, the faint rush of a cistern emptying.

Jane sighed, a short soft breath, and looked around. "I'm glad they've found something to do. They're both more upset than they let on . . . more tea, Grizel?"

Grizel, presenting her cup, asked, "Is Angela North all right? Where is she?"

"Lying down in my room," Keziah said. "I looked in on her ten minutes ago and she was still fast asleep."

"It's shock," Jane said, "it'll be shock. Takes people different ways."

Bone heard Jane's nervous speed of speech and looked at her brilliant eyes, and wondered when she would crack and how. From his experience, she and Angela were demonstrating different ends of the spectrum. Of course, there was still the possibility that either of them could have killed Roke. That would provide an extra charge of adrenaline and a more pressing reason for some kind of collapse. He thought, *it's as well Grizel doesn't know what goes through my mind.*

Keziah was regarding Jane with her head on one side, her expressive face full of concern. "You should really try to get some rest, Jane."

Bone thought, *Charlotte should be here; if I'd been quick I'd have scored with that.* They had a long-established game, taken from advice given in every Hollywood B-movie or TV police series, to those who had just been saved from a car crash or attacked by a maniac; one could earn a point by urging the other to try to get some rest or, the other scoring cliché, "take it easy," when either was tired or off guard. If someone used the magic words, the scorer was the first to raise an unobtrusive finger and so catch the other's eye. It could be a heartless game, as now. Grizel, not yet initiated, shared Keziah's concern, but Jane flung herself back in her chair.

"No, I will *not* rest, Kizzy, it's the *last* thing I want. Rest, and start thinking! No thanks! Let's look for the will too, if you've finished tea. It's something to do and I'd like to know where I stand."

Guy had been silent, staring out of the window at the land which might not belong to him. Now he came out with a contribution.

"I think it's obvious that the shit is Adrian. Mother, did you look in the pockets when you chucked his things out of the window?"

"Oh no, Benet never . . ." but Jane's face made it evident that she would not put anything past Roke.

"Adrian would have produced it by now." Keziah shook her head, the great plait of shining dark hair swinging. "It'd be such a little triumph for him if Roke had left it with him."

"But suppose he doesn't know? As Jeremy didn't, about the clue?"

Grizel put a restraining hand on Jane's arm as she made to get up. "Jeremy did, Jane. His father had told him it was there somewhere. If Benet had given Adrian a hint like that, either he'd be crowing about it, or he'd have combed his room by now and found it."

"Perhaps that's just what he's doing." It alarmed Jane, though Bone did not see why. Guy, however, got to his feet.

"He'd open it and read it. And if he doesn't get what he thought he should, he might destroy it, the bastard—" Guy tried to shake off Jane's hand, but Keziah got hold of his other arm and they made him sit down again.

Bone saw no purpose in saying that destruction of a will was a criminal offense, although he felt perhaps he should suggest that solicitors or some such people would be bound to have a copy. He was wondering if Jane believed that Guy's temper had got the better of him already and fatally that day. Might she believe he could have killed his father? This was such a time of heightened emotions, which he saw usually as a detached officer of the police and not as a guest concerned for his wife's friend; he felt hampered by his lack of a definable role.

"I can't stand any more just now, darling." Jane pushed a hand through Guy's hair. She sat on his chair arm and looked at Bone. "Do you think, Robert, that we're being absurd? Does the clue mean anything or is it just another tease?"

Bone considered, aware of their attention on him, the professional. That, he thought, was absurd if anything was. "It seems to me that your husband didn't do things aimlessly. If he left a clue, it must mean what it says. All we have to do, and it's not a little, is to find out what that is. I do somehow doubt the obvious, the cesspit, interpretation."

Keziah had got the end of her plait between her palms, as though it gave her inspiration. "What about the library?"

"What on earth has that got to do with shit?" Guy demanded with impatient scorn.

"The dirty books. The illustrations, I mean. And so on. The erotica. That horrible collection of your father's. Why couldn't that be called shit?"

"It's an idea." Jane had brightened. "That's clever, Kizzy. And he might have told Marcus something, as he told Jeremy. Shall we go and look?"

Bone doubted whether, to Roke, the erotica would be equated with shit; but the rhyme might have had its appeal for him, and very likely he was aware how some might regard it. This idea was strengthened by Keziah, who made a face and said, "You can, if you like. If you can bear it. Benet showed me some once—a couple of them, just to see what I'd say, I suppose, and I threw one of them on the floor."

"What did he say?" Guy, no doubt thinking of the "rare books" aspect—the value—appeared slightly horrified.

"Oh, he laughed like a drain. But the thing—really, it just left my hands. I didn't intentionally throw it." Keziah switched the end of her plait, as an angry cat might switch its tail. "I told him it was a degradation of woman, and he said it degraded men as well and I should be pleased."

"Where *is* Marcus?" Jane looked around, as if she expected him to emerge from behind the sofa. "He usually comes for tea. Didn't Tig tell him we were having it in here?"

"He just doesn't want to come down." Keziah shook her head, echoing perhaps what she had seen Marcus do, for the movement was subtly unlike her own. "I went to see him, you know, checking if he was all right." Bone had a vision of the compassionate Keziah worrying about everyone in the house, even perhaps Adrian. He hoped Guy was ready, when they married, to share her concern with a great many other people. Into his mind jumped the wicked question: had she checked the alligator's health after its nasty shock of missing Adrian that morning? "Marcus was really fond of Benet."

"Yes. He and Benet got on very well. I don't know what he'll do now." Jane rubbed her forehead as if she would be rid of what was too difficult for her, as well as Marcus, to contemplate. Grizel glanced at Bone and said, "I'm sure he could get a job as a librarian anywhere. There will be people who'd be pleased to find someone with his sort of specialized knowledge."

Jane was beginning to reply when Guy got up abruptly. "Oh, let's all worry about Marcus, shall we? What *we* are to do without my father is more to the point." He glanced out of the window, at the crundle of gravel under a car, and then craned to look. "What the hell?" A car door slammed. "What the *hell* is that ghastly Aussie doing unloading luggage?"

Jane stood up too, anxious, propitiatory. "Don't create, Guy. I thought it best to invite him. We can't possibly send her home or to a hotel in that state."

Guy had whirled around to glare.

"You do realize *they* probably killed him!"

Bone made his voice casual, to damp down the hysteria crackling like an electric charge through the room.

"I'd say it was most unlikely. Besides, isn't it very sensible of your mother to invite them here where she can investigate their claims more closely?"

Guy's verbal reply was suppressed, but his eyes said very plainly: who are you to put your nose in? Jane, however, seconded Bone with relief. "There you are, darling. That's experienced advice."

Guy pulled away from her outstretched hand once more. "Don't expect me to talk to him, that's all. Anyone'd think you *want* him to take over. Just watch out he doesn't take the chance to murder me too if his mother hasn't got his birth certificate with the right date on it. I think I could have expected a bit of support from my own mother."

He stormed out of the room, a performance for which he had not quite got the presence; and Keziah, rolling her beautiful dark eyes at Jane in expressive apology, followed.

Jane stood, and Grizel came suddenly to her side. She leaned on Grizel's arm and her lip trembled.

"Have I been stupid, do you think? He's had such a terrible shock."

"I think you've done the wisest thing possible," said Bone firmly. "I'd like to talk to Mrs. North myself. It's not my business but there are a few questions I'd like to ask."

And God send, he apostrophized, *that there are better answers than the ones that spring to mind.*

Chapter

· · · · · · · · · · · · · · · ·

20

THE LIGHT FROM THE READING LAMP ON THE DESK IN THE library imparted a golden glow to the blond leather of the desk top. Bone had opened the door with his habitual quietness and Marcus had not apparently heard him.

He was poring over a book whose pale yellow pages, reflecting the lamp's golden glow, cast light up on his absorbed face. As Bone approached over the long stretch of faded Turkey carpet, Marcus apparently sensed a presence and, sitting bolt upright, slammed the book shut, exactly like a schoolboy caught with a naughty magazine. Then he half rose, peering over the lamp as Bone announced himself.

"Sorry I surprised you."

"Oh, Mr. Bone. Yes." He sat down again in the swivel chair, heavily as if his knees were weak. "A day of such shocks. Terrible day." He looked up at Bone, his face now in greenish shadow, his glasses glinting like tears. "Can I help you?"

"I'm hoping you can. It's about Lord Roke's will."

"Will? Oh no. Not my department and he never confided in me."

"Seems to have been a secretive man in general." Bone sat on the edge of the desk. Marcus immediately leaned both arms on the cover of the book before him. "No, I didn't really think he'd have told anyone where he'd put it, but there's a theory that it might be in the library."

Marcus laughed, a short nervous laugh, glancing around the big room with a glitter of gold-rimmed glasses. "Plenty to choose from. I mean, if he has . . . I've not got halfway yet with the catalog."

The rows of books seemed like presences in the room, turning secretive backs, defying any possible search.

"Lady Roke thinks that her husband may have hidden the will"—Bone did not quote the clue; it seemed tactless to imply that Marcus could be in charge of anything that could be termed *shit*—"in his collection of erotica."

Bone did not miss the sudden rigidity of Marcus, or his half-glance down at his folded arms.

"Oh. I suppose he might have, though I think I'd have seen it. I mean, I know the books very well." He stopped, and put a hand to his bow tie as if he had caught it trying to strangle him. "I mean, Lord Roke particularly told me to catalog that collection." The glasses signaled as he turned his face to Bone. "It amused him to think he was embarrassing me. Some of the collection, some of the books are very—"

He damaged the bow tie.

"I can imagine," Bone said, in a detached but not unsympathetic tone. "In my profession you come across some hair-raising things. You get used to most of them." Until now, he was reminded; he had seen men hanging but not upside down, and a crossbow murder a year or so ago had put the quarrel in the chest and not through the neck, nor had it the extra flourish of a victim in Japanese armor. "I expect it's the same with books. So you don't think it's among the erotica?"

"Not unless he put it there very recently. Well, he could have done that, of course. He was often in and out of the library." Marcus' tone suggested that this was not a comfortable state of affairs.

"You've been his librarian a long time?" Bone was conscious of framing his questions more circumspectly than he usually needed to do. He looked around at the shelves to take the pressure of his gaze from Marcus.

"Only since spring last year. Benet's been very kind."

Bone was constructing a question about how, if at all, these statements were related, but he was forestalled by the opening of the door from the landing and the advent of Adrian, who stood there surveying them. Even in the shadows he seemed to glow, the cream cashmere sweater enhancing the thick sweep of golden hair. After a moment calculated, Bone surmised, for maximum impact, he threw back the sweep of hair in a gesture of practiced charm.

"That's where you are."

By this, he was apparently looking for Bone, not for Marcus who, one might predict, was to be found in the library. Employing an accustomed technique, Bone did not ask why Adrian wanted to see him, but left it to him to explain.

This, Adrian was in no hurry to do. He sauntered to the desk and, by instinct drawn to the hidden, reached across and dragged the book from beneath Marcus' concealing arms.

"Ah-*ha! The Illustrated Petronius.*" He flicked over some pages, settled on one, and offered it to Bone to view. The drawing, as a design, was beautiful, an elegant inter-wreathing of limbs, in pen and ink, on the pale yellow ground that Bone had glimpsed before Marcus closed the book. What the three people whose limbs were there delineated were actually doing was not at once apparent because of the complicated detail, but it was neither woodwork nor embroidery. They might, of course, be trying to light a fire with two sticks. Adrian said, "They're good, aren't they? Worth a packet, Benet used to say. His uncle began the collection. There's his bookplate. And look at this for a frontispiece. But Benet didn't have the money to add much to it. He said."

Adrian lost interest suddenly, smacked the book shut, and pushed it back to Marcus. "Go on. Make the most of it. You'll soon be having to ask my permission to peek."

Marcus received the book as one might an injured baby, and squared its dust jacket carefully. He looked up over his glasses. "Your permission? Why?"

Adrian threw back his hair again. "Because they're mine. Benet said he'd leave them to me. Just you wait until his will's found."

Marcus was holding the Petronius to his chest and staring at Adrian. "*You* get the books! *You!*"

"Not all of them, dimwit, just the erotica. The books of particular interest. Benet said they were just my style."

He looked sidelong at Bone, as if hazarding what he would make of this, and Bone looked back, registering nothing. No doubt he was intended to imagine Adrian in some splendid entanglement, as illustrated, but he was certainly not going to waste his imagination on that. What did cross his mind was that Adrian might be rash in trusting Roke in anything, as Roke had shown so strong a disposition to tease him, whatever their relationship might have been. When—if—the will was found, Roke could well have left the erotica to the Archbishop of Canterbury and left Adrian a rubber duck.

"I don't believe it." Marcus still held Petronius to his bosom, and had risen. "Benet knew you didn't care for any books; he would never leave these to you."

"So who would he leave them to? Jane? She hates them. Guy? He'd sooner drool over catalogs of Harley-Davidsons. Benet liked things to be appropriate."

Marcus turned almost beseechingly toward Bone. "Do find the will. Do find it. I'm sure it's not true. They're worth a great deal of money." He put down the Petronius carefully on the desk and hurried to the shelves in question. "I'll look too."

Adrian stared. "What on earth makes you think he'd put it *there?*"

Marcus was busy taking out books and holding them up inverted, open, so that extraneous papers might fall out, replacing each book and moving on. "Mr. Bone said he might have done. I don't know why." He picked up the next book, too heavy and perhaps too fragile to upend, and began to leaf through it.

"Did he *tell* anyone he'd put it in the library?" Adrian demanded of Bone. Close to, it could be seen that his eyes were fringed with improbable lashes, either the unfair gift of Nature or a purchase from Boots but, either way, an adornment to elicit response. Bone's response, in spite of a prolonged training in impartiality, was dislike. He heard the coolness in his own voice.

"A clue's been found." Bone recited the couplet and watched the eyes widen.

"Shit? He probably meant—" Adrian caught himself in time. Without another word, he fled from the library. The door banged after him. Bone wondered if he, like Jane's younger sons, was about to search the lavatories. If so, he would find himself last in the queue.

"You know what I think?" Marcus replaced the volume he had been searching, with an air of relief. "I think Benet meant the old jakes. I'm sure there'd be room between the bricks."

"The old jakes?"

"The Tudor lavatories. Or pre-Tudor. They run down the side of the old part of the house, the castle side, like the shaft of a well, really. They were excavating them when I arrived last year, found all sorts of things. An archer's thumb ring, a little pair of child's slippers, a belt buckle, even a lock of hair. Benet had them put under glass in the muniment room. I expect Adrian's gone to see. The foot of the shaft is full of eroded bricks with gaps and hollows."

"Sounds promising." Bone privately thought *poke among the shit* was the process Marcus had described as going on when he first arrived here. If the results were under glass in the muniment room, might that be a good place to look? He felt a quickening of the pulse and a desire to abandon Marcus as abruptly as Adrian had done, to pelt off in pursuit of his idea. Absurd, that a hunt designed by a man now dead should engage such primitive instincts. If Roke, a derisive or quizzical ghost, were about the place, he must be relishing what he had caused.

"You know"—Marcus adjusted his spectacles with a forefinger on the bridge of his nose—"perhaps someone should keep an eye on him. On Adrian. If he were to find the will and open it, and it doesn't suit . . ."

Interesting that Marcus and Guy had the same estimate of Adrian's moral scruples. Bone wondered what was left at the bottom of the jakes, how one got down there, and whether it would yield anything to further investigation. Obviously if Roke had put his will there, it would have been during the last few months, or those clearing out the deposits would have had a chance to find it.

Marcus cleared his throat, and Bone realized that he himself was the person Marcus considered qualified to keep an eye on Adrian. Something about his profession evidently made people feel he ought to be where the trouble was, Sizing up the Situation, and no doubt Taking Charge.

"I'll go and see what's happening, certainly. Coming?" Marcus had drifted back to the shelves. "I'd be no use. No use at all. You know, you may be right about the erotica. I'll keep looking through until dinner, anyway." He took out a tiny book, possibly a postage stamp edition of the Kamasutra and, bringing it close to his glasses, began to flick through the pages. Bone wondered if his glasses ever steamed up. He could not very well anticipate finding a legal document in a book that size. What indeed was going to happen to Marcus now, a man so clearly happy in his work?

As Bone shut the library door, he had the feeling that Marcus was glad to see him go, even that he had been deliberately got rid of. Was it possible Marcus had a better idea of where the will was than he had let on?

Chapter

······················

21

BONE DESCENDED THE MAIN STAIR, WONDERING IF ANYONE IN the house who had seen Roke come down here for the last time only a few hours ago would ever tread the steps without remembering. Then, surprised, he realized how few actually had seen Roke come down which, of course, was the reason one of those missing could have been his killer. He was at the foot of the stairs when Jeremy emerged from the morning room where the tour party had taken coffee and been immured later.

"Is this yours, Mr. Bone?"

He held up a rolled gray plastic mac and a camera swinging by the cord of its carrying case. "It was under a chair in the morning room."

"Not mine." Bone approached and took the mac. It unrolled stickily and crackling to hang like the ghost of a coat. He saw something in one transparent pocket and fished it out, watched by Jeremy, craning. An envelope, stamped and torn open, had *Donald Spencer* on the front and an address in the village. Bone supposed that Spencer, leaving his house for the hotel and the tour bus when the post came on Saturday, had pushed his letter in the mac pocket. He put it back.

"It belongs to a man in the coach party that was here today. He lives in the village." He remembered the sisters' anxiety and his promise, and went on, "I think I'll take it to him. There's time before dinner." He took the loop of the proffered camera from Jeremy's fingers and smiled at him. "Any luck with the loos?"

"Not a sausage. Hoog fell off the steps and cracked his head on the wall. No secret panel slid open, though." He sighed dramatically. "Real life isn't nearly enough like Indiana Jones." His grin made Bone think of Roke, but he was pale and his hands made small tense movements. Joking was his method of managing shock, and for the moment it worked; Bone wondered how he would cope in the long run.

"Did you try the old Tudor loo? I think Adrian's gone there to look."

Jeremy's mouth had begun to droop; it picked up its corners once more. "Right! Hoog and I'll see if he finds it—wish we'd thought of that first." He turned and pelted off down the hall shouting, "Hoog! Quick! The jakes!"

Bone had secured a couple of watchdogs for Adrian. The jakes must be perfectly salubrious by now if Adrian had no objection to looking in there, he thought, as he went to tell Jane and Grizel where he was going.

Neither of them was in Jane's apricot sitting room. In the blue drawing room, Baz was sitting on the sofa with Keziah, who turned her dark head and smiled.

"Hallo—is my wife around?"

"She took some tea up to Ma," Baz said.

"Jane's telephoning relations and friends," Keziah put in. "Grizel's going to sit with her, I think. Guy—Guy's going off on his machine." Something in her voice suggested there had been words from Guy. Baz looked down, and was flushed. "He's very distressed."

"He must be," Bone said. Guy had evidently taken it out on Baz, who was innocently in the worst position possible.

"Yeah—I don't think I should be here. Maybe Ma and I will go back to the hotel when she's not feeling so crook."

"You seem to have a right to be here."

"Well—rights can be wrong," Baz said, half smiling.

"I'm going to the village to deliver this to one of the tour party. Would you tell Grizel? I don't think I'll be long." Bone did not feel he could get embroiled in the Roke inheritance. There could be little doubt that Baz was Roke's son, but the complications of dates of conception and birth were another matter.

As he set off he heard the dismal drone of a motorcycle engine across the parkland. He was glad of the opportunity to stretch his legs and get away from Roke Castle. He walked at a brisk pace down the gravel drive toward the distant wrought iron lacework of the gates, thinking that he could very well understand Donald Spencer's desire to escape. How much Prior's questions had contributed to this desire was something Bone would like to find out, and since Spencer had marched off abandoning mac and camera he must have felt driven.

As Bone walked, seeing the village lights in a cheerful cluster beyond, and smelling the acrid drift of someone's bonfire smoke in the October twilight, he reflected on the strange state of affairs he found himself in. All his instincts urged him to investigate the case, and he was forced to stand on the sidelines and watch this mysterious game in which the chief player, the murderer, was probably, like himself, under the variegated roofs of Roke Castle—more within his grasp than any other murderer he had hunted down.

A pigeon exploded from a tree by the drive and flapped heavily away to land in another, making the branch swing and dip wildly. Pigeons, thought Bone, seemed designed for more robust vegetation than life provided for them, few trees being up to their weight. Birds too had their problems —the pigeon balanced with energetic wings and tail—yet when one of them was shot at least no one had the responsibility of tracing whodunnit.

Spencer lived in the older part of the village, in a terrace of cottages whose doors opened onto a pavement. Tubular railings protected the outer edge of the pavement from parking cars and lorries; the houses were low to the street as if they crouched from the traffic the place had never been designed for. It was a village that had at least kept a post office, the board announcing its function nailed incongruously to clapboard across the front of a building put up when few people read or wrote.

Bone glanced in the window of a village shop as he waited to cross. A steady line of cars edged forward past a Land Rover parked nonchalantly a couple of feet from the curb. In the shop, beyond hands of bananas and piled oranges, the single tube of the safety light showed banks of shining glass cabinets. No doubt they held solid blocks of anything a villager could require from cod mornay to chicken tandoori. The Industrial Revolution had started a good many interesting changes in country life.

Beside the door of Spencer's cottage, a rose had been encouraged to root in a tiny square of earth left by the flagstones against the wall, and it had doggedly wreathed its way—with unobtrusive help of masonry staples—up against the brick to the overhanging tiles. Now at the end of October it held up a late brave rose, whose ragged petals defied petrol fumes and weather. Bone sniffed at it, catching the ghost of a scent, before he knocked on the blue, paint-blistered door. It had a diamond of leaded glass, ancestor of a thousand thousand suburban copies in the semis of ribbon developments.

The door opened and a woman stood there. She had a hand extended to draw Bone inside but she raised her eyes from their lower focus and dropped her hand.

"Oh—I'm sorry. I thought it was Don. He's forgotten his keys before now, you see."

"He forgot these, anyway." Bone, smiling, held out the rolled mac and the camera. "I'm Robert Bone. I was on the tour with him and he left these at Roke Castle, where I'm staying."

"Do come in. I'm Don's sister Dorothy, Dorothy Spencer. I'm afraid he's at the allotment. Would you rather go there? It's up past the church and then you turn—but he should be back, in fact, any minute now. It's getting dark." She glanced doubtfully out of the low window whose sill ran at thigh height in the little sitting room she had led him into from the cupboard of a hall. "Of course it's always lighter outdoors, but still . . ." She seemed unsure whether her brother might not work on in the dark, like some mole. "You'll have coffee? It's very kind of you to bother with his things."

Bone felt that coffee would give him an excuse for staying. He accepted, with the usual demur about its being a trouble, and he was invited to make himself comfortable while Dorothy Spencer went into the kitchen and put on the kettle.

He sat in an armchair covered in red moquette, and glanced around with his habitual curiosity, hearing the clinks and chinks from down the hall. A large Victorian mahogany cabinet took up a bullying amount of space, and paid for it by having its shelves filled, with plates at the back and every kind of ornament from paperweights to china pigs crammed in front, with photographs and miniatures propped among and against these. A small bookcase painted green held a row of heavily used paperbacks: Hillaby, *Travels to the Jade Sea*, Paul Theroux, Isabella Bird and other travelers; Tom Sharpe's *Wilt* and *Blott*; surprisingly, *Killing for Company*; and, awkwardly stacked, large glossy books on gardens and houses, while on the top stood more photographs. One in an oval brass frame was of Donald Spencer with his arm around his sister and a hand on the shoulder of a slender girl of about eighteen, staring from the picture as owlishly as Donald but without glasses. The family likeness was striking. Bone supposed the slender girl might be the daughter the Simpson-Bates sisters had mentioned, who had recently died. The girl's mother must be either divorced from Donald or dead, for Donald's support seemed to be his sister.

The walls showed the same anxiety to display. Pictures hung one above the other and Bone's eye was drawn toward a landscape, in a wood frame, of snow tinged with the orange of a setting sun. Through the snow, footprints led from the foreground toward a spindly wood of firs, raising the gravest suspicions as to what had trod so purposefully to lurk there.

Miss Spencer came in with the coffee now, a painted tray with two large mugs. One with pink pigs on she kept for herself; the other, decorated with poison-green shamrock, she arranged next to Bone upon a sturdy bamboo table which had to be wrestled from beneath another on which a parlor palm precariously trembled.

"I'm sure I don't know why Don isn't back yet. I suppose he's walking by the long way." She sat down in the wing chair opposite, arranging a limp cushion behind her back with the skill of custom. She held the mug up in both hands almost defensively. "He's upset, you see. This terrible thing at the Castle . . . Poor Lady Roke. Mrs. Whalley said Mrs. Knebworth said Lord Roke was killed on the stairs and fell dead all dressed in armor. It's upset Donald very badly. He's so . . ." She left the sentence to sink in the air between them, and tried to drink although the coffee was obviously too hot and she drew back her head quickly.

Her face was round, like her brother's, the eyes, too, round and a surprisingly bright pale blue under the arched lids. Her mouth was fuller than his, less primly closed, but her hair sat close to her head, ridged in old-fashioned gray waves like a plowed field under frost, as neat as his balding dome. She gave Bone a glance full of intelligence.

"What did happen? Were you there? The village is full of it, but who's got it right and who's pretending to know is another matter. Do the police know who murdered Lord Roke?"

Bone appreciated the bleak simplicity of this. "Did your brother talk about what happened?" He was interested in Spencer's viewpoint or, as significant, what he chose to tell his sister.

"Oh! I forgot the biscuits." She jumped up, nearly upsetting her mug, and hurried off to the kitchen again, leaving Bone wondering if she were giving herself time to consider her answer. Then he remembered: she didn't necessarily know he was police. In spite of Lawson's nasty story, not everyone might have heard; Spencer might not have realized it or not have passed it on. The usual caution of those he interviewed would not then apply.

"I hope you like those. They're Don's favorites, so they're what we tend to have." She took one herself, put a plate of them on his bamboo table, took up her mug, and sat down. "He didn't tell me much. Don *doesn't* tell me much. He doesn't say much at all, that's the trouble. He keeps everything bottled up and then there's an explosion." She turned up the pale blue eyes briefly, while Bone remembered Donald hanging onto Josh Lawson like a rat at the neck of a terrier.

"I understand there's been a tragedy in his life recently. Your niece?" Bone was glad that the question, which he needed to ask, did not have to be posed to Donald himself. Dorothy's eyes went at once to the photograph Bone had observed.

"May. Yes. Dear May . . . died; only a month ago. No, it's all but two months now. Time goes by so. I don't think Donald will ever get over it. She was such a clever girl. Very imaginative." Bone, handed the photograph to examine, gazed at the hollow-cheeked, slightly manic face in its nest of long wispy hair, and dead May stared, her round eyes accusing. Here was he, alive, and where was her imagination now?

"Don keeps her room," Dorothy's voice came in, "almost as a shrine, won't let me even dust it, as if my dusting could somehow dust something of her away." Bone had a fleeting thought of the tiny traces of hair and skin that Forensic found so illuminating at the scene of a crime; and also saw that imagination in this family was not May's alone. "I hope as time goes by . . ." She sighed and put down the coffee mug. "I suppose it's early days yet. I don't feel I'll get used to it myself." She glanced again at her watch. "If he's taken the long way home, he's probably dropped in at the pub. He has a few friends in the village, old friends, and they sit and drink and never bother him to talk."

She seemed to make up her mind of a sudden. "Come along, I'll show you. May painted some lovely pictures."

Bone followed her out of the room, speculating on whether May had painted the footprints in the snow. Perhaps seeing the daughter's room would give him some clue to her father's place in events. He had no sense that Donald Spencer was connected with Lawson's death, yet he had been missing at the vital time when both Lawson and Roke had been killed. Grief could drive people to extraordinary actions.

The stairs to the top floor were very steep, the carpet orange with brown splashes as though it had been subjected to a chocolate bomb. A picture on the stair wall, hanging a little askew, was a watercolor of a chinchilla kitten in difficulties with a quantity of blue ribbon. Bone decided that May was unlikely to be the artist of this piece of charm. Her style, by that psychotic stare in the photograph, might be more wolves than kittens.

May's room was the first off the tiny landing upstairs, and it was necessary for Bone to edge in past Dorothy to see it. May, too, had been the collecting sort. It was not unlike stepping inside the Victorian cabinet downstairs. There was much less room here than for Jeremy at the castle. What was it about the human instinct that led to this record of experience? Did Neanderthal man polish up trophies of mammoth bone and display them in the cave? His pictures on the walls were believed to have magical purposes, to bring good luck to the hunt; might there not also be an element of magic in these collections, an attempt to fix boundaries, to control life by talismans? May's collection had particular pathos since she was now as far beyond reach as any Neanderthal.

The walls were painted what decorators might call Sunshine Yellow. The effect, under the center light Dorothy had put on, was more sickly than brilliant, in the patches that showed between pictures, photographs, and posters. The largest poster was of the King himself, Elvis prancing in white satin hipster flares, charming a mike whose cord swung away from him like a cobra's tail; his belt studded, swagged with chains, sequins flashing on the white jacket above. This occupied most of the bed-foot wall, above the divan with the yellow candlewick cover just not matching the walls. Presumably May had gone to sleep and woken to the sight of the Presley pelvis.

Bone had been wondering for some time, and considering how to ask, what had carried May off at so early an age. Less than a hundred years ago he would scarcely have needed to ask, such was the wide choice of terminal illnesses village dwellers could incur, the likeliest being TB.

One shelf seemed to be home to a series of plastic rooms for a doll; the dust lay thick here as if May herself had deliberately neglected this childhood occupation but would not dismantle it. The top of a small chest of drawers was given over to mice—glass, pottery, painted stones, cloth— of all sizes. It was the walls, however, that attracted the eye.

"You see? These are all hers." Dorothy indicated, as if he might have missed them, the sheets of paper with their vivid blotches of color: purple, green, yellow, red, scribbled over with lines of ink as though a fussy scholar had tried to obliterate something disapproved of; and in a very different style, a series of Gothic pen-and-ink drawings of churchyards, dark gateways, crag-bound castles, figures in coffins, bats and mists and daggers, in a double row along the wall beside the bed.

"Very modern, aren't they? Some are abstracts, you see," she added, as if it were a term she had learned herself after an effort to make sense of the colored shapes, and she was passing it on helpfully to Bone.

"Was she a professional artist?" Bone was aware of the improbability of a girl of eighteen making money with either these abstracts or even the more macabre black and white, striking though they all were, when it was hard for the most experienced artists to make a living. The question was a clay pigeon. He wanted to find out about the situation rather than the girl, about why she chose to live in this cramped cottage in a small village, when adolescent instinct and the force expressed in these works would surely prompt her to break free. Again he wondered if the morbid outlook evident in the Gothic fantasies was premonitory. Perhaps illness had hampered her, keeping her within the scope of her family's care and support.

Dorothy was pressing firm a Blutacked corner of one painting that had started to leave the wall.

"No. She never had the chance, though that's what she wanted to do. She worked in Whalley's, over the way." Bone glanced across the street at the fascia board of the shop, still legible in the gathering dusk. "She wanted to go to art school but Don didn't like the idea of her alone in a strange town."

Bone, himself a father, could understand that well enough. Dorothy straightened one of the piles of magazines on the floor. Bone stepped over another pile to examine one of the paintings. The vibrant, dancing colors were barred over with those black furious lines. On the wall beyond this, over the bed, a photograph was taped, a flash photo but perfectly clear. The girl from the family group was dressed here as a fanciful bride, a cross between Miss Havisham—a dilapidated veil and one earring—and a witch, for she wore black flowers; she was showing her teeth in an odd way, and seemed to have got lipstick on her neck. The man, in whose arm she was embraced, wore evening dress, had fanciful blackened circumflex eyebrows and a pair of fangs, a genial vampire.

It was Roke.

Chapter

....

22

"Isn't that Lord Roke? Did May know him?"

Dorothy bent forward and peered beyond Bone's pointing finger.

"Oh—that was the famous party. She had such a lovely time then—she came home walking on air. I hadn't seen her so happy for a long time. It was fancy dress, you see. Lord Roke's idea for his son's eighteenth birthday. He held it up at the castle last year and invited all the village. Such a coincidence, her going dressed as Dracula's Bride and Lord Roke being got up as Dracula! Donald and I didn't go. I mean it wasn't quite our style, but a lot of people did. Probably most of the younger ones. And many old things like us."

Bone made the necessary deprecatory noises.

"Oh yes, we are . . . It was the first chance people had to see inside the castle. The last Lord Roke was a bit of a hermit."

Across the road an upstairs light clicked on above Whalley's, and Bone's eye was drawn to the window, where a blue glow of television showed and a blind was pulled down. The street was very quiet now, with something of the old Sunday evening feel to it. Solitary footsteps echoed. He was suddenly extremely anxious to get more out of Dorothy Spencer before her brother returned. That one glimpse of Roke with his arm around May's shoulders had altered the whole scenario. Donald's reaction, his walking out of the castle, might conceivably be that of a man who had killed, whether on the spur of the moment or on premeditation. The question was May's relationship with Roke; or, what her father thought it had been.

"Did she know Lord Roke at all?" It had to be asked again. Dorothy, despite the ban on dusting, had pulled a paper tissue from her sleeve and was wiping the top of a little table, taking up and setting down various glass animals on it. He thought fleetingly, that's what Donald didn't want. May was the last to touch them, she put them where they were. Now that's lost. Dorothy turned, surprised.

"Oh no. How would she do that? He never shopped locally, always drove straight through and rather fast, nearly did in old Mrs. Poole's cat once. No, May only saw him at that party. It'll be over a year ago now." She was holding a glass pig with a curly purple tail, which she now put down very carefully in its place next to a green glass crocodile, reminding Bone of Roke's alligator. "It so cheered her up, that party."

"When did she fall ill?" When time's short, you must be blunt. Donald could be here at any moment, having reached the limit of the time you can sit and not talk with people.

"Ill? Oh, she wasn't ever ill, not what you would call *ill*. Depressed, now. She was very depressed; after the police brought her home it was."

"The police?"

"They brought her back in a police car, which I think was dreadful, because naturally the village talked. I do think the police ought to think of things like that. A police car gives an impression. *You* know. Don was very angry."

"What had she done?"

"Nothing! She was sleepwalking. She'd always done a bit of sleepwalking, since she was a child. It was a lovely summer night and we never heard her go. She just went out, and I don't think she'd ever been that far before. Right into the grounds of Roke Castle, and up to the place itself and set their alarm off. Poor thing! It must have been a terrible shock, to have it go off suddenly, so loud and when she'd been asleep. They caught her running away, and she must have been dreaming about that party, you see, although she couldn't tell us anything, because she had the dress on"— Dorothy pointed the dusty tissue at the photograph—"and the veil they found by the castle." A little swath of dust fell from the tissue, and she bent to nip it up from the rug. "Don sits here reading her books and her letters—in that box there. She wrote a lot of letters that she never sent. Donald won't talk about them and he's never let me read them. He reads them over and over. I wish he wouldn't. It's not good for him."

So May had been up to the castle, dressed as a bride in her party gear, at dead of night, and been brought back by the police.

Bone reflected that May's father and aunt might well have been the last to know if the girl had in fact been seeing Roke. In his mind he saw the moonlit bride capering with Roke along the leads behind the battlements. Was Roke capable of an affair with a village shop assistant? Up to now, there seemed little that he was not capable of and, if he had seen it as a joke, it might well have appeal for him. Bone was pretty sure that Jane's married life had required a lot of tolerance from her; for Roke, amusement outranked many other considerations. Yet if an affair was going on, how had May come to set off the alarm system? Getting in and out of the castle should have been no problem, and Roke would surely have canceled the automatic police call.

The question about May's illness had not been answered, the question about her death had not been put, and he could hear, at last, a key in the front door lock below.

"What was the matter, that she died?" he asked quickly in a low voice. Dorothy had heard the key too and was thrusting him out of the room. He almost stumbled on the landing, but heard her hissing whisper.

"*She drowned herself.*" Then aloud, for the benefit of her brother in the hall below, shutting the front door and calling his sister's name, she directed, "Along there, on the left at the end."

Bone obeyed her, as she went downstairs, and found a small lavatory with a stained glass window, and a pile of women's magazines on the low windowsill. He stood a moment, thinking, and then pulled the chain. The plumbing obliged with a heartily noisy flush well deserving the name "Niagara" in raised letters on the cream cistern. He made his way downstairs toward the desultory talk in the sitting room.

She drowned herself. Bone did not imagine there was anything to be gained from talking to Donald Spencer but he did, with every fiber of his being, wonder what Prior had asked him and what conclusions Prior had drawn from his answers.

Although the name of Spencer would soon have conjured in the memory of local police the story of May's bridal midnight wanderings to the castle, Prior was unlikely to know of the connection Bone had discovered from Dorothy and from May's room. It occurred to him that although Roke might not have looked twice at a village shop assistant, the bizarre and Gothic ambience imported by the Bride of Dracula might well have appealed to his imagination.

Donald Spencer eyed Bone abstractedly as he took his leave. Dorothy made a point of thanking him rather markedly for bringing the mac and camera, and Donald, hastily joining in, was plainly avoiding explanation of how he came to forget them. Bone set off up the street, very much aware of the difficulty of having no authority to ask what he would like to know.

The walk back to the castle was longer than he would have liked it to be. He stopped at a curve in the drive to see a headlight moving aimlessly in the dusk half a mile beyond the bulk of the castle—Guy, from the sound intermittent on the evening wind, working off his emotions. As Bone came in sight of the castle frontage and its lit windows, he saw also someone walking up and down along the terrace, and made out in the dusk that the someone wore a hooded knitted coat. It pulled a hand from one deep pocket and impatiently brushed the hood back, showing pale short hair. He halloo'ed softly.

Grizel jumped the terrace steps and came running. He ran. They collided happily; her arms came around him. He took her head between his hands, and found her lips were cold. She drew her head back after the kiss and looked up into his face. In this light her eyes were gray.

"What were you up to, Robert?" she demanded; then she gave him a little shake. "You've found something."

"I should say I have. My wife. I've got the curious feeling I haven't seen you properly all day."

"Yes. It has rather been that sort of a day. It must be the same feeling that made me come out to wait for you: to get you to myself for a moment."

They lingered under the porch. Her lips were still cold, but only at first. Then she tucked her head under his ear and they stood enfolded comfortably. Inside the house, a voice called and then there was quiet.

"We must go in," she said.

"Yes."

"I've got to get into a dress for dinner."

"M'm. Where is everybody? Anything going on?"

She made a small snort he realized was a laugh. "The boys are in trouble. Adrian had climbed down into some sort of pit in the old castle and they pulled the ladder up. Jane was—well, she wanted to laugh, but she sent them to their rooms. She said to Kez and me that she was only sorry Mrs. Knebworth had heard Adrian yelling. She'd have been perfectly happy if he'd had to stay there all night."

"She can't wield any moral superiority after she chucked his clothes out. Why doesn't he go?"

"Because he's thick-skinned. He says he won't leave until it's proved that those books are his. Do you think Benet really left him something so very pricey? It could run into thousands."

"My opinion is that Benet was capable of practically anything so long as it amused him."

"Robert. Who do you think killed him?"

"I'd like to think Prior's right: that Josh Lawson did, and then tipped himself off the roof in his hurry to get away."

"But you don't think that."

"It's likely enough. It's satisfying. Let's hope it can be proved."

"Nothing else bears thinking about," she said, and shivered.

Dinner was delicious. The Knebworths might be trying, by the means at their disposal, to soothe and distract the family and their guests after the day's tragedy. Knebworth hovered solicitously by Jane in particular, offering food for which she patently had no appetite, and Bone felt correspondingly guilty at giving himself a generous helping of the crisp roast potatoes, the red cabbage with apple, to join the pheasant in its cream sauce on his plate. It consoled him that Grizel had done the same. For him, it might be put down to the callousness of a man used to dealing with sudden death. One other person ate with unaffected enjoyment, in spite of his recent captivity in a Tudor cesspit. He had come into the drawing room, helped himself to a drink, and glowered briefly at Jeremy and Hugo, who, also released from their rooms, sat side by side on the low tapestry bench before the hearth, drinking orange and tonic, and who had immediately dissolved into giggles with mutters of "poo," "give me air," and so on. Then, ignoring everyone, he had come to sit at his usual place at the table when Knebworth announced dinner. He had a plaster round his left thumb. Bone hoped he had had an interesting time searching in the crevices of the bricks, and he speculated that if an angel now interrupted with the Last Trump, Adrian would produce earplugs and get on with the pheasant.

As he ate, Bone raised his eyes to meet those of the painted figure of Roke, leaning along the balustrade and turned to look quizzically at them all. What was it he had said the night before—when the painter of the mural had offered to include the whole family? Roke had refused, remarking that the only person he could be sure of was himself. Ironic, it seemed now.

"Champagne, sir?" He allowed Knebworth to refill his glass, reflecting that Jane appeared anxious to imitate Roke's hospitality of the night before; or perhaps she felt champagne would help to smooth over the awkwardness of having Angela and Baz at table. Baz had been heartened by the example of Grizel and Bone to help himself as liberally, and was eating with subdued enjoyment, keeping a concerned eye on his mother. She had valiantly made up, but she looked pale. Her eyes were bright and, though she merely pretended to eat, she let Knebworth refill her glass several times.

Guy avoided looking at her and her son altogether, and pushed his food about. He seemed to disapprove of Jane's efforts at conversation, asking Angela about her impressions of change in England. Angela made brave efforts to reply. It was Keziah who watched Guy and showed concern. However, her concern was not for Guy alone.

"Did anyone feed Dundee?" Jane asked. "Guy, dear—"

"You know I hate the filthy creature, Mother. I'm not going to have anything to do with it."

"I will, Jane. I don't mind him."

"Bless you, Kizzy."

"I'll do it, Mother," Jeremy volunteered.

"You're going to bed, Tig. I'll come up and say goodnight. No, of *course* after pudding."

No one seemed to glance at the painted figure on the wall. It might be they were too used to it to remember it was there, and Baz had his back to it. The likeness was remarkable.

They ate brandied apricots in comparative silence.

As they were leaving the dining room, and the company showed a disposition to scatter, Jane captured Angela and Grizel and swept them off with her. Jeremy pounded upstairs to bed, Guy sloped off on his own. Hugo, after hesitating, diffidently asked Baz if he'd like to watch a video. "We've got all sorts. I mean pop promos or SF films and that. If you'd like." He and Baz climbed toward the boys' floor at the top, Adrian pursued Marcus to the library. Keziah had twitched Bone's sleeve and now said, "Will you help me with Dundee?"

"Of course." He did not find the creature prepossessing and in spite of her all-embracing compassion perhaps she did not either. She collected a plastic box from a pantry behind the kitchen, and led him to the pool through a service passage, stone flagged and whitewashed, that emerged under the sweep of stairs. They had to brush past ferns, a creeper that hung predatory fronds at head height, and some leaning grasses, and came out in the echoing space where Dundee could be heard splashing. His movements sent little shivers of water across the big pool's surface in response. They walked around to the cayman's enclosure.

Keziah put on a large rubber glove and opened the meat box.

"He's not pretty, poor thing." He came over, eyes and nostrils above the water, and opened his blunt jaws. Keziah lobbed a chunk in. He gulped, and gaped again. "It's cruel, isn't it?"

"Keeping him here?"

Her thick plait swung forward as she flung the meat, which was a dark, strong-smelling slab. She fingered the plait as she watched Dundee champ the piece into swallowing position.

"Not really. Benet couldn't get rid of him very well. He's captive-bred and would have to be trained to adapt to wild life. I don't know who would do that for caymans. No, I meant keeping him here alone. I said to Benet often that he ought to buy a mate."

"Don't you think breeding might be a problem? A continual supply of little caymans?"

She sighed, ruefully, and was silent; then gave Dundee the last of the meat, stripped off the glove and tucked it into the strap of the box, tossed her plait back over her shoulder, and said, as if she had come to a decision, "You took back Mr. Spencer's things to him. Did you know about his daughter?"

"I heard. Yes."

"She wasn't quite—quite right?" Keziah raised amber brown eyes for the first time. Bone had supposed there was a reason for her asking him to help with a chore she could do on her own, and thought it was perhaps merely that she disliked the animal. Her purpose was now emerging.

"That was the impression I got."

"She wrote to Benet. Several times. Rather weird letters."

"Weird." The word was a question.

"I helped him with his letters when I was here in the summer. I can use a word processor and type and so on, and he used to make big complaints and pretense rages about his correspondence, so I said I'd help. He laughed at May's letters, but not nastily. Really Benet had a lot of kindness. He showed me one of them, I don't know why. He never answered them. I'm not surprised, because she was obviously a bit peculiar."

Keziah looked at Dundee rolling underwater after a sinking gobbet of meat.

"Her letters *were* weird."

"Did he say anything about it?"

"He said, 'Silly girl,' in a not unkind sort of way, and threw the first letter I saw into the bin. I saw at least two other letters, sort of spaced, a few days or so between. She had funny handwriting. Disorganized."

"What sort of thing did she say, in the one you saw?"

She looked up again, frowning, then away. "The bit he showed me said *'I dream of the night you made me your bride.'*"

Chapter

....

23

As they went back through the foliage, and Keziah turned off the lights and shut the door, she was saying: "I don't know why I wanted to tell. I don't think that she . . . that Benet . . ."

"I wouldn't have thought so," said Bone. "Not that I knew him." Roke might in fact have higher standards of beauty—might prefer something, if one might say it of Dracula, a bit more toothsome.

"You must have to be good at estimating character in your job. When you arrived, when we first met, I thought you were just a policeman. But, well . . ."

The gold clasp at the end of her plait made a small tinsel noise as it swung to and fro across her tawny silk jacket.

Bone thought he had been flattered. He said, "Everybody's complicated."

What about the letters May didn't send? Dorothy had spoken of those Donald sat reading in his daughter's room. They might have been written to Roke, and supposing they were in the same vein, no matter what Keziah thought or what Bone's own estimate of Roke's taste, morals, and character might be, what would Donald Spencer think? Bone had his doubts about Roke. Spencer might have none.

Keziah put the meat box in the pantry sink, and ran water into it. She said, "Thank you" over her shoulder, with the small brief smile that means "over and out."

He was at the foot of the stairs when a door opened somewhere beyond the hall, and a burst of laughter emerged, laughter so helpless, so abandoned, that it made him smile too. The door shut, and Grizel's head gleamed as she came forward into the hall. She did not see him, but leant on the wall shaking. Bone hurried to her, suddenly alarmed until he realized she was overcome with laughter. She left the wall's support and lapsed into his arms.

"They're smashed, the pair of them—Jane and Angela." She hugged him, and he looked down into her face, her elegant cat face alert with energy. "I am too, a bit. They're exchanging stories about Benet, the sort that end *and you know there really was a frog in it.* I thought I'd leave them to it; they're getting on amazingly. They hardly noticed me go, I think. They're having a wake."

With an arm round each other, they started up the stairs. "No wonder Roke married them both," he said.

As they undressed, an occasional surge of laughter came up from Jane's sitting room somewhere below.

"I do hope they don't get horrendous hangovers," Grizel said, sitting on the bed and partly muffled by the dress she was pulling off over her head. Bone went to help her, but was only in time to kiss her emerging face.

"Don't worry about that. It'll be enough if they've found

common ground tonight." He submitted to having his tie pulled undone. "After what they saw today, they need to get drunk. I was glad of that champagne myself." He sat beside her to take his shoes off. "Two bodies in one day exceeds *my* ration."

"I don't suppose it comes Inspector Prior's way every week, either."

Bone glanced at her. She was looking astonishingly demure, even in a jade and moonstone necklace above a black lace bra. "You are reminding me, I take it, that they are not, technically speaking, my bodies."

She presented the back of her neck, with meekly bowed head, for the necklace to be undone. "I'm glad they're not your bodies, Robert. I've only known a few of your cases, and from the outside so far: if this is the inside of a case it's pretty dark and someone's gone off with the key."

Bone released the catch of the necklace after a moment of inept frustration, and let the warmed beads slide into her waiting hand. "I do see why the Japanese consider the back of the neck so erotic; it really is a shame I'm not a poem-writing bloke, I would spin a sonnet to it in a trice . . . This case is no darker than any other is at this stage. And there's usually a key, though whether I, or Prior, will find it is another matter. Let's not forget it isn't my business."

He was rather taken aback when Grizel turned on him with a green flash of eyes, the necklace bunched in her fist. "Of course it's your business! Jane's relying on you—everyone is."

"Not the murderer, I fancy."

"And who *do* you fancy for the murderer? Most of us were out gawping at poor Josh Lawson before Nicholas herded us in out of the rain. Does your visit to Donald Spencer mean he's on the list? He wasn't there with us then, I know."

"You don't mind if I take you back with me as sergeant?

Steve Locker could do with a little help." He watched as Grizel, having divested herself of the bra, settled the bootlace straps of a chestnut silk nightdress, known as The Trousseau, on her shoulders. "I'll just lead you into the interview room as you are and any suspect will break down on the spot."

"You've not answered my question. I hope you're not being evasive, Robert." Grizel picked up the necklace from the bed and went to lay it in the velvet nest of its little green jewel box on the dressing table. "Who do you think it is? As you haven't Locker here, use me to bounce your ideas off. After all, as you say yourself, it's not your case." She leant to peer into the glass, and then switched her gaze to his reflection so that Grizel in the glass regarded him. "Robert, you're not one of those who can't do two things at once, such as talk and undress."

Reproved, he stood up, and went to shed his clothes on one of the tub chairs. "Well. Without Prior's information on the whereabouts of everyone, it isn't so easy. I'd thought of Donald Spencer's attack on Lawson yesterday, when I went to his house, though there's no reason to think Lawson didn't simply trip and tumble. Then I find there's a connection with Roke."

"With Roke?" She paused in the bathroom doorway, one hand on the jamb of the door, looking, in The Trousseau's satiny sheath, like a girl from a thirties movie. "What?"

She disappeared into the bathroom.

"Through his daughter, a slightly unstable young woman with a crush on Roke. He doesn't seem to have responded, except—oh, there's an ambiguous bit in a letter she wrote that seems to suggest there had been some naughties, perhaps at a fancy-dress party here last year. The importance lies less in what did in fact happen as in what her father could have thought happened. You see, the poor girl drowned herself."

"Oh, Robert. Oh dear. Susan and Sheila said she'd died, but . . . oh, poor Mr. Spencer. He might have been brooding and revenged her?"

"He goes on the list, anyway." Bone came into the bathroom, to find Grizel, toothbrush in hand, contemplating the basin. "We do know he can be suddenly violent. Who's your favorite?"

"I know who Jane thinks: Adrian."

"The unfavorite favorite. It's perfectly true that one wants to think a dislikeable person's guilty—"

"Dislikeable? The man's *repellent*. Particularly as he is so very good-looking."

"But he has Marcus' word as an alibi. More cogent, I don't see someone so very money-conscious doing away with his meal ticket—did you see how he put away the dinner tonight?—as the saying goes, he may be an idiot but he's not a fool. And sadly, in my experience it can be the nice people who are just as capable of murder."

"I know. The only one I've been acquainted with, I was very sorry for; a sad person for whom life had just got intolerable. But who is there here? Jane herself? Angela wanting to make Baz into a lord? Guy furious because he'd found he wasn't going to become one? It does sound so, well, unlikely, Robert."

"Murder *is* unlikely. I'm not misled by meeting so much of it because it's my job. It *is* unlikely. Sometimes the reason someone kills is quite incredible, sometimes it's a reason anyone can understand. I've only once felt like it myself, so I suppose I'm lucky."

Grizel made a noise of sympathy, but she was brushing her teeth. Bone ran a finger softly round the top edge of The Trousseau across her shoulder blades, and she kicked back at his ankle and spat.

"Don't do that, Robert! I can't feel sexy while brushing my teeth. Will you have sense, man."

He laughed, and stood back. Rinsing her mouth, she spat again and reached for a towel. Then she pointed to the picture she had taken exception to, the martyrdom by flaying. "Just look what can happen to a man who makes inappropriate gestures."

"I'll try to keep it in mind. But I plead acute provocation."

She was not listening. "You know, we could take that picture down, now; and put it somewhere. I'd have done that before, since it's definitely no asset to the room, but I thought of Benet asking and teasing . . . he was such a curiously *powerful* man in that way. I'm sure he could make enemies simply by convincing people that his opinion was right, was important—och, you know what I'm saying."

"It's a bully's power," Bone said.

"I suppose he'd been doing that, browbeating or frightening or mocking, the person who . . ." She did not finish.

"I expect so. There's one thing that remains a puzzle to me." Bone followed her into the bedroom. "Marcus and Adrian in the library: a bow isn't silent, you know. It doesn't make a racket like a gun, but it does sound."

"Perhaps they were talking."

"I'd like to find out how much noise it would make. No one heard it. The Maitlands were upstairs, so was Guy. Jane had just come down. Angela was being sick in that cloakroom behind the hall, she says—"

A muffled but wild burst of laughter came from downstairs.

"They *are* going it," Grizel observed—"and Donald Spencer didn't appear till later. He told us he'd been exploring in the old castle and didn't know anything had happened."

Bone turned out the room lights, leaving only a bedside lamp, and got into bed. "I'll have to try out a bow," he said, "out of curiosity, to find out how loud—"

"M'm, you could do that tomorrow," she said. One of The Trousseau's gleaming brown straps slid off her shoulder.

Later, Grizel said sleepily into the dark, "I can't imagine, if Baz does inherit, what he'll do with all this." Waving her hand in a comprehensive sweep she hit Bone a glancing blow on the nose.

He rubbed it, and replied, "We know what he'll do if he follows Keziah's advice."

"What will that be?"

"Buy another alligator."

Chapter

. . . .

24

BREAKFAST HAD A POOR CONGREGATION. IT DIDN'T SURPRISE
Bone that Angela gave it a miss. The previous day with its
appalling shocks was enough to incapacitate, and no need
of a hangover to add to it. Jane herself, he felt, had come to
breakfast in her role of hostess only, to ensure that her
guests were being looked after; though anyone employing
the Knebworths need have no worries about the comfort
and welfare of anyone in the house. She was pale. The dark
gray sweater she wore was much the same color as the
shadows round her eyes. She did not seem hung over—
Jeremy's clashing of a dish cover produced no wince, she
managed a smile for Grizel, a greeting—but she did not
look well. As Knebworth hovered beside her with the
coffeepot, the door swung wide and Adrian entered. He

wore stonewashed jeans, cowboy boots of cream suede, and a huge jersey of azure cashmere that looked as if a summer sky had come to cuddle him. Any idea of mourning had evidently not visited his mind; nor did he greet anyone, but went straight to the sideboard and started helping himself to sausages and bacon.

Jane grimaced but turned to Grizel. "I hope you slept all right. Angela and I were a bit rowdy."

"Oh yes," Grizel hastened to reassure her, while Adrian came to sit down and demand coffee of Knebworth, who was already gliding toward him with the coffeepot. Bone thought he had caught Knebworth almost permitting himself an expression.

"We're in *The Times* this morning, I see," Jane said. "I'd rather not look at the other papers, I think."

"I'm afraid you may be besieged." Bone had been waiting for the opportunity to warn. "I'm only surprised there've been no reporters trying to get in yet."

"I kept the back doors and shutters locked this morning, m'lady." Knebworth might be of the old school, but he didn't need retraining.

"Guy not here?" Jane asked.

Keziah looked up from her toast. "He said he wasn't feeling very well, and didn't want any breakfast. He's out on the bike again, I think." Clearly, not feeling very well was a euphemism for not feeling very sociable. Bone couldn't imagine many physical conditions for which riding a Harley-Davidson over rough ground might be considered a cure.

"And Marcus? Has he breakfasted already?"

Keziah looked doubtful. "I don't know. I heard the phone ringing in the library."

"I don't believe Mr. Weatherby has come down yet, madam."

"Isn't it today he goes to see his father?" Adrian's

unexpected contribution drew everyone's attention to Dorian Gray eating sausages. "Well, isn't it? He goes every month." The fringed eyes met theirs.

"But he went about three weeks ago. Didn't he?" Jane addressed Keziah, swiftly abandoning Adrian. "And he always comes and says goodbye first. He's very polite." Bone heard this comment as loaded against Adrian, the guest Jane would be delighted to see leave with no need to say goodbye. Adrian shrugged gracefully.

"Didn't want to disturb?" he suggested, not as if it interested him.

"Everyone's upset. Perhaps he forgot." Keziah intended to soothe, as usual; but Jane, drinking her coffee black and bleak, was not soothed.

"It's just not like him, going off like that."

"Perhaps he hasn't gone off," Bone said. "Do you suppose he might have overslept?" He could picture the nervous Marcus gulping a sleeping pill as a way of escaping the nightmare that haunted them all—except possibly Adrian. Baz, at Keziah's left, was effacing himself as he ate a full breakfast. He scarcely looked up, and might well wish he were not there; and his feelings weren't evident.

Roke's place, at the head of the table opposite Jane, had been left blank by Knebworth when laying for breakfast. Bone remembered how genially and overpoweringly it had been filled yesterday.

"Would you like me to go and see if Mr. Weatherby has overslept, m'lady?"

"Oh, would you, Knebworth—"

"I'll go!" Jeremy, glad to be moving, sprang up. Hugo's place had already been cleared.

"See if his hairbrush is there. He'll have packed that if he's gone."

Jeremy hurtled from the room, and Jane added, "He might have taken a call in the library, saying his father was ill, and not wanted to wake anyone up. I remember something like that happened last year; but he left a note."

"There was no note with the morning paper, m'lady. Mr. Weatherby left it there on that occasion."

Jane took a piece of toast, broke it up, and began to nibble a piece, dry. "Poor Marcus."

Keziah turned to Bone and Grizel. "His father is in a home, you see. He has Parkinson's, rather acutely, and poor Marcus couldn't cope on his own. He's not been well himself for ages with this viral thing ME, and he'd lost his job because he kept having to go sick—"

"Benet thought being librarian here wouldn't be too much of a strain," Jane interrupted. "Benet was very kind like that." Her face crumpled suddenly and she crammed her table napkin against her mouth. Bone looked down hastily at his toast, feeling cowardly, wishing for words or a gesture that could convey sympathy without provoking more unhappiness. Grizel got up, put her arms around Jane, and, when she rose, went with her from the room.

Thundering footsteps overhead, then on the stairs, and Jeremy's voice ringingly proclaiming that yes, Marcus had taken his hairbrush, seemed to dispose of that problem. The footsteps halted, and Jeremy's lowered, awkward tone evinced that he had taken in his mother's state. He said that he and Hoog were starting their search again, then he tore off, and Knebworth shut the door. It was as well, Bone reflected, that they were taking their father's death in this way. Roke might have foreseen it in providing the puzzle, although he could not have imagined how violently traumatic his actual death would be. The full damage to their feelings would possibly not emerge for some time.

He was aware that Cha still missed her mother, and always would, no matter how lucky she and her father were in Grizel's care and comfort. There was no such thing as invisible mending on some wounds.

"Marmalade. If you please." Adrian's outstretched hand indicated that Baz was willfully withholding from him what he needed.

"Sorry." Baz thrust the glass dish across, knocking the spoon out of it onto the cloth.

"Oh *God!*" Adrian's tone, both exasperated and resigned, implied that this could be expected from someone like Baz. He reached for the spoon as Baz picked it up, so that his fingers closed on the bowl and received a generous layer of marmalade. Bone, refraining from applause, admired the way in which Baz too controlled what was still an obvious desire to laugh. His quiet and voiceless breakfasting had continued in a civilized way, stopping only when Jane broke down, resuming when she left. Knebworth had been assiduous in keeping him supplied with coffee and in offering more from the sideboard dishes, and Bone wondered if Baz's likeness to Roke inspired this tender care. That Knebworth might be considering the goodwill of a future owner of Roke, of the probable holder of the title in fact, Bone felt to be inconsistent with the butler's integrity as he had appreciated it so far. It was more of a surprise that Adrian was so uningratiating.

Grizel came in, picked up her coffee cup, and drank standing. "Jane's gone to her sitting room. She still has people to telephone, and the phone in her bedroom seems to be out of order."

"It is connected to the instrument in the hall lobby, which I took off the hook, madam. The press are ringing. They have been at the doors, too."

"I'll ask Jane if she'd like me to cope with that," Keziah said. Bone didn't doubt that she could do it. "What do you want to do today, Robert?"

"Oh . . . I'll scout about for the will again."

"Wanting another chance at the Rare Books section, without Marcus to cramp your style?" Adrian suggested.

Bone glanced at him and turned back to Keziah, only vaguely aware that Adrian had made an attempt at being rude.

"If I can be useful with the media or anything else, let me know."

"I wouldn't, Robert," Grizel said. "If they get hold of who you are and so on there'll be endless cracks about *Busman's Honeymoon*."

"Isn't there a book called that?" Bone said. "I'm sure I've seen it somewhere."

"A quite famous one, darling; Dorothy L. Sayers. Lord Peter Wimsey's honeymoon. Police procedure was very restful in those days sixty years ago."

"Are you going to be with Jane, Grizel?" Keziah asked.

"She told me she doesn't need nursemaiding, just would like to see me from time to time. She said why don't I look round the house—I missed some of the tour yesterday, what with news of my new nephew and helping with coffee. So I could do that." She sounded doubtful.

"I could show you," Baz said suddenly. "I went on the tour. You saw the alligator, didn't you?"

Adrian's chair grated back and he stood up, dashed down his napkin, and went out. Grizel covered her mouth, and her eyes above her hand were brilliant with amusement, so that Baz began to smile back.

"It's not his day," she said as the door shut with a defiant slam. "First Robert snubs him about the erotic books and then he's reminded of being rather inglorious in the swimming pool."

"I forgot that," Baz said, surprised, his grin widening.

"He never will. Do show me the bits I missed, Baz."

"Great. I'd love to." Baz had got eagerly to his feet and then paused, looking hesitant and embarrassed. His enthusiasm visibly dwindled, he thrust his hands in his pockets and glanced at Keziah. "I mean," he said, "I went on the tour, so I know that part."

Bone saw his anxiety to avoid any sign of proprietorship. Thanks to his eruption on the stage, it was likely that Keziah would not one day become Lady Roke. Bone, who had studied the scene, had his doubts as to whether becoming Lady Roke had ever been an ambition for her. He was not entirely sure she even wanted to become Mrs. Guy Paisley now. She smiled cordially at Baz.

"Benet did love it when people appreciated things about the place—and his ideas. You could show Grizel the roof, too. Or have you seen it?"

Bone recollected the clock's sonorous, deafening chime. Grizel laughed. "I wouldn't mind seeing it again."

"And remember the oubliette."

Bone was of the opinion that Roke had liked it even more when people did *not* appreciate his ideas. There had been much malice in that grin. Keziah, however, had made Baz feel better. He turned to Grizel with renewed energy. She said, "An oubliette? No, really? What fun!"

They went out while Bone was envisaging her remark in a balloon over the head of a manacled prisoner being prodded along a stone passageway by an enormous warder.

"Where are you going to look today? Do you know?" Keziah turned her head to speak to Bone as she began to put salt and pepper, the empty toast rack, and unused cutlery away in a cupboard hidden by the painted landscape.

"I thought of the muniment room. Marcus said that when the Tudor cesspits were cleared, Roke had the objects that were found put under glass there."

Keziah dimpled suddenly. "Oh, I see. Well, I hope you're right." She lost the dimples and added slowly, "Jane's had about all she can take. Benet couldn't know how badly this particular tease of his would operate."

A sudden banging on the front door, echoing through the hall outside, made her start.

"That sounds as if it may be the media," Bone said. "One recognizes their light touch."

She ran out into the hall, her plait, twined this morning with black silk cord, thudding on her back. Bone parted from her in the hall, running up the stairs while Knebworth paced to the door. As Bone reached the landing he heard Knebworth, valiantly backed by Keziah, refusing to disturb Lady Roke and refusing to answer any questions. As he opened the shining mahogany door to the muniment room, he saw flash reflected off all the surfaces round him like the lightning of yesterday's storm, accompanied by a shriek of rage from Keziah and followed by the reverberating slam of the front door. He hoped that Knebworth had got their toes.

The muniment room was a smaller version of the Japanese gallery, lit in the same way by a clerestory roof light of a similar style. There were also display cabinets here, including one long one down the middle covered in green baize, and along the left wall stood shallow-drawered collectors' cabinets and a map chest.

Bone drew breath and, to be methodical, started on his right.

A display cabinet held, as a card said, articles dug up in the grounds. A cursory glance convinced Bone that not only were they irrelevant to his quest but also that they were of stultifying boredom, being Roman nails and pieces of pottery, mold-encrusted metal and curled-up, cracked leather. Some had dates of discovery on their descriptive cards going well back into the eighteenth century, when presumably interest in these things was taken up by some Lord Roke.

There was a charter of some kind in the next case, with no explanation, in black illegible script and in Latin. Bone moved on. A typed notice on the next case warned him that

ON NO ACCOUNT should an attempt be made to open these SEALED cases with their CONTROLLED HUMIDITY. Bone did not think this notice stemmed from the most recent Roke era. Beneath the glass was a royal warrant. The case beyond held the items from the jakes.

A small leather shoe suggested that a child had lost one or thrown it down, and a card in small meticulously clear writing gave a suggested date of late sixteenth century. There were various coins, the earliest Norman, and a good deal of pottery, a small iridescent glass dish and a broken knife, a very large ring with the stone missing, labeled "Archer's thumb ring," a piece of cloth, a bit of ornamental corroded metal, "part of a brooch"; part of a purse; a hinge, corroded; a couple of links of stout chain joined to a broken arc of metal "thought to be part of a leg iron" . . . nothing that suggested a further clue. Bone mused on the items for a while, thought, *I'll come back to them,* and moved on to the center cases, lifting the protective baize and rolling it back.

Plans, drawings, and photographs of the castle occupied the space. Bone pored over these for any hint of an indication Roke might have put in as a hiding place for the will, but found nothing. The next case held the same sort of information about Paisley House, where Roke had lived before inheriting the castle, but far more detailed. There were newspaper cuttings, a page from *Country Life*, another from *House and Garden: Jeu d'Esprit, Benjamin Maitland's House for Benet Paisley.*

The house, in its basic, architect's drawing appearance, was a handsome neo-Georgian affair with one-story side wings. The photographs, however, showed otherwise.

It seemed that Roke had had the house painted.

Bone had come across painted houses in Austria, on his honeymoon with Petra—that took him back a while— houses with scrolls in elaborate curlicues around windows and doors, with Bible scenes and fairytale pictures spread all over the walls, like outdoor theater. This house was something else.

It could have been attacked by Chagall while suffering a bad migraine. Zigzags in azure decorated the wall to the left of the neo-Georgian porch, one column of which had been painted orange, the other stippled in pink spots. The wall to the right flaunted a shoal of green and yellow fish swimming across. If you looked again, the fish could be interpreted as a swarm of eyes, staring. Over the parapet topping the façade, clutching or drooping hands, outsize but quite realistic, had been painted. It was the uneasy concept of a madman—or a joker.

Bone speculated. Had Roke requested Maitland to provide a plan for these fantasies too, so furiously at odds with the dignified style of the house beneath? Then his eye was caught by a heading on one of the newspaper cuttings: *Architect Will Sue Client.* He bent to read.

The outer painting had by no means been commissioned. It had been done without Benjamin Maitland's knowledge and, unfortunately, just before *House and Garden* and *Country Life* had sent photographers for their features on it. Benet Paisley, however, had somehow neglected to explain that the decoration was not Maitland's design.

What Benet Paisley *did* say was that he was "surprised at the result" and both magazines had naturally deduced that he was also not pleased. From what he knew of Roke, Bone could well imagine how he had enjoyed the ensuing kerfuffle. Bone could also imagine what Maitland must have felt, no doubt happily anticipating articles on his first major work, which could establish him and attract patrons, opening the magazines to the full-color spread laid out here under glass. The effect had not been universally condemned: one rather minor journal hailed it as a triumph of Surrealism; but the general opinion was that the young architect was cocking a snook before he had the authority to do so. He was condemned for puerility, for an imbecile attempt to shock, for a blot on the landscape.

It had also blotted his copybook, for one writer warned any future clients of Mr. Maitland to expect egg on their faces and what looked like scrambled egg on their houses. Mr. Paisley was intending to have the whole front repainted.

Bone was sure Roke had thought the expense was worth it.

There were angry letters to the magazines in which Maitland explained that Paisley was responsible for the paint scheme, and next to them a long letter, evidently a draft of one sent by Benet, as there was a signature at the end. Bone wondered just why Maitland had come on the tour, and what he wanted in the muniment room. Roke had made it clear that he could find material there about Paisley House—that overfriendly embrace had seemed bullying at the time, even without hindsight. Had Maitland come to see if Roke still thought his brutal joke funny? Had he come to fuel his anger?

Bone bent to read Roke's letter. Benjamin Maitland had been among those missing from the group before Roke descended those stairs. He had come out, with his wife, to look over the balustrade on the landing when Roke's collapse had caused screaming. They had been, they said, here in the muniment room. Across the landing lay the gallery where Roke was shot. Bone recalled the police team taking the carved chair away, the chair where traces of his blood showed that Roke had sat before starting his last walk. How long had he sat there? Long enough for Maitland to cross the landing and return to his wife here before they heard the screams that had fetched them out? If Benjamin had been out of this room, Catherine must have known or suspected then.

Bone wanted, very strongly, to confront the Maitlands, to ask the questions that he doubted Prior would know to ask.

Prior ought to be told.

The door opened and Grizel came in. He went to meet her, shedding his preoccupation with an ease that surprised him; wondering that he had not so far become used to her face, that the brilliance of her eyes still struck him. She smelled of open air, and kissed him with her hands behind her.

"I'm filthy. That clock on the roof isn't any less loud at second hearing, and not much less of a shock either. I must wash—Jane's talking about elevenses in her sitting room."

Bone got her hands and pulled them around, turning the palms. "What have you been—"

"It's rust off the—"

Both of them stared.

"No, it isn't. This is blood."

Chapter
....
25

THE DETECTIVE AND THE BIOLOGIST LOOKED AT THE STREAKS OF brownish red on her two hands, the caking between her fingers.

"Where did you get this?" Bone heard his professional bark. From Grizel's quick glance he knew she had caught the note too. "Have you cut yourself?"

"I'd have cleaned it right away if I had, with that rust. I'm not an idiot." She surveyed her hands, frowning. "This must be what I took for rust. Baz and I were on hands and knees by the oubliette to look at the skeleton. He said to hang on to the grating because it tilted."

"Why is there dried blood on it?"

"A Roke joke? Like the skeleton?"

He still held her hands, examining them, as if of themselves they could tell him something. She withdrew them suddenly. "Robert, let's look. Baz said there was something odd about the skeleton."

He was at her heels as she darted from the room and headed down the stairs.

"Odd? What was odd?" He caught up with her and together they descended the lower flight, down which Roke had staggered only yesterday. Some things with bad associations you could destroy; a classical sweep of staircase you must live with.

Grizel was excited. The blond boyish hair was ruffled, her eyes danced when she looked around at him. Mysteries suited her. He was scarcely in need of further proof, however, that he had married the right woman.

"He said the skeleton's slipped—isn't how it was yesterday." She was ahead now, flitting across the black and white lozenges of the hall floor into the suddenly dark passage beyond, where the old castle began, abruptly reminding one of the difference by its stone flags underfoot, their uneven surface under the matting, heaved up by the ripples of Time's river. Now Time's river, thought Bone, pursuing the blond head in the gloom, that's done its job lately, bearing two of its sons away right here.

"Watch it!" he cried with sudden urgency. "The grating—"

"I know." Her tone reassured. He saw a light switch and flicked it down as she turned a corner ahead, and heard her say, "And Baz thought there'd been a bowl."

"There was," he said. She was on all fours peering down the grating, where he joined her. "Roke pretended it was the prisoner's last—Well, it's certainly gone. Baz is right, the arm's in a different position."

"Could they have been looking for the will down there?"

"That wouldn't account for this." Bone drew his hand along the iron bars and, feeling the incrustation, showed it.

Bone began: "It definitely came—"

"Sh!"

Bone sh'shd, and heard silence.

"I thought there was a sound down there."

"A rat?" They listened. He thought he heard slight movement. Fleetingly it occurred to him that Baz had taken on the Roke mantle and already installed a joke; then sanity reasserted itself, and prosaic thoughts of rats returned. It was the dried blood on his fingers, however, that drove him to utter a tentative "Hallo?" down the grating.

With the lights on, he could see that the floor of the oubliette sloped down out of sight. The skeleton, no longer reaching for the missing bowl, seemed to be hailing, its arm lying above its head.

He heard an answer. From the depth of the pit a faint sound, almost lost, reached them.

"Something's down there all right." He stretched flat on the matting and edged forward to peer into the dark. Grizel's hand clamped on his belt just as he felt the grill tilt under his arm.

"*Do* you mind, Robert? Bone among the bones would not be funny. What's down there, though? Is it a rat?"

He edged back. "I think Knebworth should know where that ladder is—the one the boys took away from Adrian. It'd be a good idea to have a look down there."

"What could it be?"

"I'm not thinking so much of *what*, more of *who*."

She jumped to her feet. "I'll get Knebworth and tell Jane."

"Leave Jane in peace until we know. The rat's still a probability."

When Knebworth came, however, it was with a rope, a stout length of line, and a piece of blanket.

"I'm sorry, sir, but the ladder's no use here. The roof of this passage is too low. When his lordship put the skeleton down, we found the ladder could not be maneuvered in. Finally we lowered Mr. Hugo."

"It had better be me," Grizel said. "I'm lightest. I don't think Mr. Knebworth and I could hold you, Robert."

"We'd better get help."

Suddenly an almost articulate sound came from below. Grizel, her face set, took the piece of blanket from Knebworth and wrapped it around her. Bone, loath to let her do it, supervised the round turn and two half-hitches of the rope, and he and Knebworth dragged the grating from its bed. The butler produced a torch from his pocket and gave it to Grizel. He took a bight of the rope around his body as anchor man, and watched her lie on the edge and swing her legs down. Bone braced himself with the rope. She lowered herself, giving him a sudden reassuring grin, and disappeared into the dark. He paid out rope slowly, from Knebworth's hand to his, feeling the strain of even her light weight on his arms, his shoulders. Then it eased.

"I'm down," her voice called hollowly. Bone knelt by the edge, blowing on his hands and flexing them, and peering to see the torchlight reflected on earth walls. She called again. "It's Marcus and he's hurt. I can't tell how badly. His head's been bleeding. He's very cold."

"I will telephone for an ambulance," said Knebworth, "and inform her ladyship and bring blankets."

Bone nodded. He saw the rope shift on the matting at his side as Grizel moved, and he put his hand on it and lay down again at full length. The oubliette began as a shaft and then opened up into a sloping cell, where the false skeleton seemed, now, an irrelevance in poor taste.

Grizel was talking to Marcus, to hearten him. The rope shifted under Bone's hand, connecting him with her. He could hear an inarticulate moaning in counterpoint, as if Marcus were trying to comfort both her and himself by making a noise, asserting his survival. The smell that rose from the pit was dark and overpoweringly ancient, the smell of soil disturbed that had slept for ages. Bone's mind busied itself. How did Marcus come to fall into an oubliette that the whole household knew about? If he were leaving the house, why was he using this out-of-the-way passage? Why not tell Jane in the normal way that he was going? Why not go after breakfast and by the front door? Was Marcus up to something? Could he be guilty? Or did he feel that he was letting Jane down by withdrawing moral support at this juncture— that it looked cowardly to leave so soon after the tragedy? Bone had formed the opinion that Marcus was a sensitive man, and vulnerable to criticism, not least from his conscience.

None of this explained how he came to be groaning at the bottom of this pit with his blood, apparently, on the grating. Had he hit his head on the grille that had tipped under his foot? Why, above all, had he trodden on it in the first place? Surely he would have had the light on?

It seemed he had meant to leave without explanation. What would Prior think of that? Marcus ought not to be on the move without notifying Prior. So far as Bone knew, Prior had not made an arrest; he must be hoping that his theory tying the two deaths together would satisfy his superiors. There was certainly an enormous convenience in the belief that Lawson had killed Roke and then gone up to the roof in a state of nervous exhilaration over what he had done; and being alarmed at something—a low flight; or perhaps a nightmare vision of Roke pursuing—had caught his foot in the loop of rope . . . or had leaned over to be "innocently" photographing. Prior probably thought it was Bone's approach that had triggered the fall. It might well be he would prefer to think Bone, the "bent copper," had physically pushed Lawson, but there was, and could be, no proof. Prior had very likely extracted his maximum enjoyment from hinting at the possibility.

Bone called to Grizel that it could not be long now until help arrived. She spoke cheerfully in return.

If I were a bent copper, thought Bone, *or a vindictive one, I could—and Prior may think I would—make life quite hard, in several ways, even for a Chief Inspector in another force. There are networks everywhere.*

He lifted the rope a little, and Grizel said, "Robert?"

"What's the air like down there?" He spoke mainly just to hear her.

"It must be fine. Marcus has been in it for some little while, and he's still breathing."

Knebworth came—advanced, rather, along the passage, bearing blankets like a holy offering. Bone told Grizel, and she appeared below. She had got the rope up under her arms, having evidently given the padding blanket to Marcus. Knebworth knelt, and dropped two gray camping blankets to her.

"The ambulance is on its way, madam. Will these be sufficient? This is for you, madam." He dropped a padded coat-lining. "I feared it might be cold down there."

"Thank you," she said. "It certainly is." She disappeared from view.

"I described the situation to the emergency service," Knebworth said, "in case they needed to bring special apparatus. I shall go and wait for them at the door, to lose no time."

He departed; now Jane and Keziah came hurrying, concerned, horrified, and puzzled. Jeremy arrived, and at once volunteered to go down and help. Keziah wanted to organize hot coffee for Grizel, who said she would rather wait; she continued to talk to Marcus, but Bone could hear no reply, either because Jeremy was restless and talkative or because Marcus was lapsing into unconsciousness.

Noise and tramping eventually heralded the ambulance team, one tall, dark with thick level eyebrows and an expression of bewilderment, the other short, sandy, belligerently staring under his eyebrows. Both were in gray denim trousers, trainers, white jackets. After a vague acknowledgement when Jane introduced herself, they went to view the shaft. Shorty, staring at the skeleton, said, "You called us a bit late for the gentleman in the altogether. Where's the injury?"

"He's at the bottom of the slope," Bone said. Shorty and Lofty bent to peer, exchanged a glance, and marched off, followed by Jeremy.

"Well!" Jane said. "That wasn't promising."

"You don't suppose they thought it was a hoax call," Keziah cried in alarm, "With the—"

"No, dear," Jane soothed, and both turned as the two men came back at a trot, laden with pieces of apparatus. Lofty asked Jane, "Could we perhaps knock an anchor point in this wall?"

"Do whatever you have to," Jane said. "Nothing matters but getting him out."

At the preparations for this, Bone called down, "Grizel, there's going to be a bit of noise. The ambulance crew are fixing an anchor point."

"Right," she called.

"My wife's down there looking after the injured man," he explained.

Lofty called down, "Cover your heads," but Shorty put a hand on his arm. "I best go down there, have a look at the stonework."

"Right oh."

Jeremy of a sudden ran off down the passage. Jane called after him to know what he was up to, but he had gone.

The men produced some tough white soft rope; Bone was interested to see Shorty make the same knot he had made. There were more strong hands to let him down than Grizel had had, which was as well. His stocky form disappeared below.

He talked to Grizel and looked, apparently, at Marcus. A

pencil light moved about. Shorty scratched at mortar. He came to the base of the opening.

"Eric. Give's a collar. And I'd like some boards down here if you're hammering. Some of this is going to powder down."

"Boards." Knebworth moved off at once, Keziah after him. Jeremy reappeared with an inspection light, a bulb in a cage of strong wire, on a long cable which he had plugged in somewhere. Without speaking, he knelt and fed the lamp down the hole. Shorty said, "Just the job. Ta," to the unknown supplier of this illumination, and went on inspecting. Jeremy stood up, himself aglow with satisfaction. Jane said, "Clever Tig. Was that from the garage?" and he nodded. She was standing with her palms pressed together, against the wall near the opening, while Lofty—Eric—picked at mortar where he meant to put his anchor.

Grizel's voice continued reassurances. Knebworth and Keziah returned with dusty deal boards, possibly shelves from some storeroom, stained with rusted ring marks. These were lowered to Shorty. Maneuvers took place in the cellarage. Lack of moans suggested that Marcus had received a painkiller. Bone felt cut off from the action, useless while Grizel conferred with Shorty.

"Right, I've got them protected. Go ahead, Eric."

Eric hammered a ring-headed spike into the wall by the oubliette. The noise slammed back from stone and brick. Jane covered her ears. The noise brought, peering around a corner, Mrs. Knebworth wearing a large white apron that showed up in the gloom, ghostlike; and Hugo and Baz, questioning. Bone wondered how many people had, in actual fact, died down here before it became a matter to make a joke of. Rattling on wood, debris down in the pit justified Shorty's safeguard, for which Bone was profoundly grateful.

Eric clipped a shackle to the anchor, put a rope through,

and tested it, leaning back. He looked around and picked up the arrangement of metal rods, straps, and plastic that was the stretcher, clipped it to the rope, warned Shorty, and let it down through the shaft. Shorty disengaged it and called, "The lady's coming up, Eric. You're wanted down here."

Grizel, hauled up on the rope by Baz and the boys, was received by her husband, covered in dust despite the boards' protection, cold of face and hands, with blood on her sleeve. She had got Marcus' travel bag.

Eric went down. There were subterraneous consultations and operations. Shorty called out to be hoisted, and then directed the careful and tricky lifting of Marcus, unconscious, his head supported by a rigid collar, his eyes shut, very white under the dust. Bone cleared everyone back to make room. He found Adrian unexpectedly at his shoulder, staring, with enough concern to make him for once quite likeable.

The ambulance had, at Knebworth's instructions, come to the kitchen entrance. It was already surrounded by the press, taking pictures and shouting questions—the opening of the back door set off a blaze of lightning. Shorty, with surprising authority—forestalling Bone, whose instinct had pushed him forward—asked for room and quiet. They fell back reluctantly, and a TV crew turned off their brilliant light. Jane drew out of sight at once, and spoke to her sons, but Jeremy was well in the forefront. Keziah had disappeared; she now turned up in an indigo duffel coat, and carrying Marcus' airline bag had a word with Jane and was into the ambulance as soon as Marcus was settled. As it drove away, Knebworth shut the door firmly against the clamor, bolted it, and said to Jane, "There have been persons on the terrace, m'lady. I have closed the ground floor shutters."

"That's good. Yes. And now I think we're all going to have a drink."

"Mother, how did Marcus get down there?"

"Heaven knows, darling."

"Mother—" Jane led the way back toward the hall. Bone stopped in the kitchen passage to wrap Grizel in his arms. She was still in the padded jacket and smelled of plaster dust and ancient stone, an oddly ecclesiastical smell. She stood making a good try at cracking Bone's ribs in a reciprocal hug.

When he let her go, she said, "Marcus was terribly anxious about something. He was trying to get at this in his jacket, and it had half come out of his inside pocket. I took it because it seemed to be worrying him, and said I would look after it, and that did seem to calm him down." She pulled from an inside pocket of the coat a small parcel which undid in her hand. The gilt, Art-Nouveau lettering on the cover of soft leather said *Les Fleurs du Mal*.

Chapter

....

26

"WHAT A BEAUTIFUL BOOK. NO WONDER HE DIDN'T WANT IT damaged." Grizel admired the cover and opened it. She stared. "Good grief. Are they really doing what I think they're doing or didn't I wash my mind this morning?"

"That, my child, is a sample of the erotica in question. Where we thought Roke might have hidden the will."

Grizel leafed over a few more pages and Bone liked her for not pretending she was not fascinated. "Amazing. Don't people think of unlikely things. You'd need rubber joints to manage some of them. And they don't have much to do with the poems." She made a face over one of them and shut the book suddenly. "No. I think I'd prefer traction."

"Are you two coming for a drink?" Jane's voice from the hall made them glance at each other over the book, and

Grizel called back, "Oh *yes*, but I must shower first. With you in ten minutes."

They went through the kitchen, where Mrs. Knebworth was washing a blender at the sink.

"Knebworth has taken the drinks to her ladyship's sitting room, madam. We've got all the shutters closed; you'd think those nasty news men would have more respect. And there are girls, too, I'm surprised. One of them took a picture just of me closing the shutters, they're that foolish." She had a face like an elderly mouse, with bright dark eyes in their nest of wrinkles. Bone refrained from uttering what instantly occurred to him: ground floor shutters would not prevent the use of a telephoto lens into upper windows, where the views might in any case be more interesting. In these days one could no longer be certain what editors might print. He would warn Jane.

He sat in the bathroom to glance at the book while Grizel showered. She said, "Don't get water on that book, Robert. Marcus would never forgive you."

"Nor would Adrian," he shouted back, going into the bedroom to eliminate a gap in the curtains against any prying lenses. Grizel, toweling herself, appeared in the doorway, her hair on end like a nestling's feathers.

"Adrian? Why Adrian?"

"He's sure Roke left him the naughty books."

Grizel dried the feathers, thoughtfully. "What was Marcus doing with that book?" She looked at it, lying in its wrappers on the bed. "He couldn't have been *stealing* it?"

Bone did not see why. "Unless to spite Adrian. How bad did he seem?" He watched the line of her back as she dried her feet.

"I couldn't tell. The ambulance men were terribly careful how they moved him. They put the neck collar on, and checked for fractures and so on. I'd just been lying behind him to try to keep him warm. Vance said—" She was getting into tights.

"Vance? The short round one?"

"Yes. I thought he'd be sure to laugh and make some ha-ha remark, but he only said, 'Couldn't have done better,' and as I was cuddled up to poor Marcus under the blankets it did offer a prize subject for—"

"How cold did you get?" he asked sharply.

"Oh, Robert, it wasn't too bad. It smelled tombish but it was only chilly, not damp. I felt so cut off from you, even though you weren't far away; as if I'd got into a bad dream. I was more than glad when they lowered the light."

She pulled a drawer open and stood, in jeans and bra, with a sweater in her hands. "Robert. What about Marcus? What was he doing? He had that little airline bag."

"Going to see his father. Perhaps his father likes the erotica and he was sneaking one out to him."

"What a kind idea." She threw the sweater over her head, scrabbled like a cat in a bag, and emerged. It was a Rusty Kate sweater in earthy tones of ochre, umber, sienna, and old rose. "Robert. You can't go down in that sweater either."

Bone inspected the dusty front elevation of his jersey and tried to brush it down.

"No. You're married now and your appearance reflects on *me*. A bachelor can look as he chooses. Take it off . . . What were you doing in the muniment room, by the way? Did you get any closer to the will?"

He sighed. "No. All I did was to find an infernally good reason for Benjamin Maitland to want to put an arrow through Roke."

She had been brushing her hair into order, and stopped and turned. "Oh dear. I do hope not. What was it?"

"Roke had a gift for it." He was grim.

"For—?" Grizel was leaning toward the dressing table glass, checking eyeliner.

"For making enemies. You'd think he had gone through life preparing a grand confusion of people with motives in case he ever got murdered." He watched Grizel put jade and silver studs, one of his wedding presents, in her ears, turning sideways with a supple twist of her back. "It's often totally obvious why someone gets murdered; here we have trouble finding out who got to be first in the queue."

"What did Roke do to Maitland? I thought he commissioned a house from him ages ago. Didn't he pay him?"

"Oh, I should think so. Money wasn't it. Do I have to?" This was addressed to a clean navy jersey fished from a drawer and held out to him so as to obscure Grizel entirely. He began to drag it over his head, continuing, as the neckband arrived for him to speak through, "No. It was another joke. Painted surreal pictures all over the façade, allowed it to be photographed and written up, without letting on it wasn't Maitland's idea. The poor man was devastated, to judge from a letter I was reading when you came in with blood on your hands."

"Meet Lady Macbeth." Grizel tucked in a corner of his shirt collar that had escaped from the jersey. "Typical of Benet; but surely one wouldn't kill because of that? Come on, Jane will be waiting." She made briskly for the door, saying over her shoulder, "I could kill for a drink, though. I think people must have died down that oubliette, Robert. There was a horrible feel to it."

Jane was, unexpectedly, listening to Adrian. Indeed he dominated the little room from the hearth; against the apricot walls his golden coloring showed well. Jane sat on the high-backed Regency sofa with a glass in her hand, and the silver tray with its bottles and glasses at her side on a little Pembroke table. Adrian was making animated gestures, and flinging back the swath of golden hair almost as if he could study the effect in the mirror behind him. Jane, thought Bone, was looking slightly stunned.

"Ah, there you are." Adrian sounded as if he, the host, had been waiting impatiently and they had committed the discourtesy of being late. It quite surprised Bone that he left it to Jane to offer drinks, but while she was pouring two gins and tonic, Adrian hitched one heel on the steel Matthew Boulton fender and went on, "I've been saying to Jane that we've got to talk things over. It's obvious we're not going to get any help from the police and it's also obvious something very fishy is going on here." He fixed Bone with his eye as though he expected a denial, a claim that falling from battlements was a natural hazard for photographers, that Roke had pranged himself with an arrow while playing silly buggers once too often. "I think someone meant to *murder* Marcus."

Jane had refilled her glass and was sinking it fast. She waved the glass in a negating gesture, swallowed, and said, "No really, Adrian, that's silly. Marcus wouldn't hurt a fly. Who would want to hurt him?"

Bone could have told her that victims were quite seldom selected for their power for general harm. Adrian wasn't impressed either. "There may be plenty of reasons we simply don't know about." He looked around at them all, working the unlikely lashes. It was probable that by now he was unaware of using these physical tricks of appeal. "What do we know about Marcus' private life?"

Jane snorted. "What do we know about anybody at all's private life? Surely you're not saying that somebody with a grudge against him sneaked into the house although all the alarms were set, and with the press on the doorsteps, and pushed him into the oubliette? What was he doing in that part of the house anyway? That's what I can't understand."

Adrian advanced and refreshed his whisky. Bone, who had taken one of the apple-green Osborne chairs, caught the look Jane directed at the bent golden head and thought that, were there another murder, he could guess its victim. Grizel, beside Jane, flickered her eyebrows at Bone with the rapidity of Groucho Marx, and he had to look down and bite his lip. It was hard to take Adrian seriously.

Once more Adrian stood with his back to the small fire. "Nobody seems to have thought"—his glance reproved Bone in particular, as one who might have made some professional effort in this direction—"nobody seems to have thought that Marcus knew all about the alarm and could have switched it off himself."

"Why on earth should he do that!" Jane's tone was contemptuous.

"Because he was going to meet someone, of course." Adrian drank, and favored them with a smile. "He was going through that part of the house because he didn't want people finding out."

If Marcus had by any chance intended to sell the book he had been carrying, it was interesting that Adrian should think of it. Possibly that gilt head was not as empty as it seemed. Bone said, "What do you think Marcus could have been concealing?"

Adrian enjoyed his audience. To mark his statement he tapped the side of his tumbler with a fingernail. He was, Bone noticed, still wearing the plaster on his left thumb, that spoiled perfection. "I think Marcus was concealing the fact that he was *stealing Benet's books.*"

"Nonsense," said Jane.

"What makes you think so?" Bone inquired. He did not look at Grizel, but wished strongly for telepathy to will her to silence.

"Simply because it costs an arm and a leg to keep people in these homes where his father is, and because he's the only person who knows what books there are and exactly how much they're likely to be worth."

"If this person was coming to meet him in the castle—if

he'd switched off the alarm for them—what was Marcus doing with a travel bag? If he was off to see his father, he could meet them anywhere else."

For a moment Adrian's eyes showed that his theory had not taken this into account. "Perhaps this was the most convenient place. I really can't tell."

"That still doesn't explain how he got down the oubliette. If this person put him down there, it would have to be someone who knew about it. How many people do?"

"Perhaps Marcus told them himself—warning them to be careful."

Bone contemplated this scenario in silence. The door opened and Guy poked his head around. He was wind-blown and, as usual, scowling. He announced, as one producing a surprise, "There's a pack of bloody vultures around both the doors and all the shutters are up. They took me for a courier or something. Shouting questions. I rode straight into the coach house and shut the doors. Where's Kez?"

"She went with Marcus to the hospital."

Guy came right in. "What did she do that for? I've been looking for her everywhere." It was another notch in his tally against the world. He did a double take. "Why the hospital? His father ill?"

"Marcus fell down the oubliette."

Guy stared. After a shocked second he said, "He can't have. Everyone knew it was dodgy. He's not such a fool." His amazement, in removing the habitual irritation, showed suddenly his likeness to Jane, and made him for that instant a good-looking young man. Jane was telling him how Hugo and Baz had taken a door off its hinges in the old pantries, and laid it over the grille. Bone's indefatigable brain was scanning possible reasons for Guy to have been Marcus' attacker; he could not interrogate, but he could do his best to eliminate the unlikely. Could Guy suspect tales of his father's books, perhaps, and in righteous rage . . . More sinister: suppose Guy and not Lawson to be Roke's murderer, and suppose him to think that Marcus could have heard, in the library next door, or even witnessed . . . But if Marcus had heard or witnessed anything, he had kept quiet about it so far.

"Would you like a drink, darling?" Jane asked her son.

It would not have been surprising if he did. Guy looked drawn. He glanced at the tray and then around the little room. His gaze halted on Adrian, ensconced before the fire.

"No, I'll go and change. When d'you think Kez will be back?"

"I don't know. She'll probably stay until he's conscious."

"Conscious? It was as bad as that?"

"Darling, it's about fifteen feet or more down that beastly hole."

"Poor old Marcus. God, that's rotten."

"She'll ring if there's any news."

"If I'm not around when she does, tell her I'll bring the car when she wants to come home." He turned to the door and added, "Perhaps I'll go anyway." With a final glance at Adrian he added, "Be better than here."

The door shut.

At lunch (a good vegetable soup, then cutlets with duchesse potatoes and small onions in a Béarnaise sauce, then cheese) Angela frailly appeared. She was pallid, and moved with the careful deliberation of one whose head feels made of glass. Guy, who had decided against the hospital, made an effort at civility, but ignored Baz. A pity, Bone thought, that Baz and Guy couldn't have a good booze-up together as their mothers had done. Jane and Angela were on cordial terms still, oddly enough considering their differences. If there had been less physical disparity between the young men, a good punch-up might have served the purpose just as well.

Bone went into the gallery after lunch, to try out a bow for sound. The natural wish of Prior's band to seal the gallery off had been frustrated because it was the only access to Guy's room and Keziah's.

The bow, he found, made a fairly ringing twang.

He took himself back to his task at the archives, thinking that he would get Grizel to listen from the library to another bow-twanging, to find out how well it could be heard.

Jane had told Grizel that she could cope with the telephone calls on her own instrument in the sitting room, which she had taken off the hook only while they had drinks and rested. The listed phone in the hall was still off the hook, and its extensions were therefore not available. Jane's line kept ringing with condolences and inquiries from her friends and Roke's. Bone could not avoid wondering how many of the latter might experience a secret relief at being subject to no more of his teases.

He knew, without needing to be told, that Grizel ached to help him in his search, and he admired her prompt cheerfulness in announcing that she intended to help Jane with answering the notes of condolence that local people had been putting through the door all day, braving the media siege. Bone had been surprised at the number of these on Knebworth's laden salver. It appeared that people were more anxious to communicate their sympathy than he had thought was fashionable. It was, he recollected, the first time he had ever been living with the victim's family after a murder.

Back in the muniment room, he stopped for a moment in the greenish light that sifted through the overhead panels of glass. He put his hands on the cool surface of the case that protected the objects from the Tudor cesspit, and he went over the clue again. There was shit, and there was metaphorical shit. Was there, in here, any shit that had hit the fan?

What sprang to mind was the eruption of rage and recrimination after Roke's trick on Maitland. Would that qualify? He moved to the case in the center, at the end, where the critiques and letters, the photographs and the drawings, were on display. It was hardly likely that a will could be disguised among all these. He had looked over the lot of them and thought he would have spotted anything extraneous. He began to study the letters for what he now thought would be a further clue rather than the thing itself. He reached, after a while, the letter he had been reading when Grizel came in with Marcus' blood on her hands, the draft letter from Roke justifying what had been done.

Roke took a high line in the letter, deprecating Maitland's distress, affecting astonishment that frivolity could be taken so seriously (Bone could see that theatrical astonishment on Roke's large handsome face), and suggesting that Maitland should have been entertained, even delighted that Roke had felt so at home with his creation as to decorate it further. Bone imagined Maitland reading all this; had he been in Maitland's shoes he might well have been reaching for the nearest sharp instrument. Yesterday morning Roke had, with that malicious embrace, that promise of showing these pages, rubbed Maitland's nose in it. There was something mocking even about the dashing signature, with its dislocated K and Greek E. A draft letter hardly needed a signature in any case.

But at the time when Maitland designed Paisley House for him, Roke had not yet been Roke; he was still Benet Paisley.

Bone came so close to the glass that his breath misted on

it. The signature occupied most of the lowest fold of the letter. It was not a fold, though, but a razor-thin cut ending the letter above the signature. There was a paper, signed by Roke, under the letter. It might belong to another letter. It might be extraneous. It might be a further clue. It might be the will.

Chapter

....

27

INSPECTOR PRIOR WAS ALSO MAKING HIS DISCOVERIES. ON THE strength of his work so far, he had obtained a search warrant for the flat of Joshua Lawson, deceased, and his team had found a number of promising items, some of them hidden, in its bachelor squalor. It had smelled, being shut up over a thunderous weekend, like an animal's lair, with a miasma of sour milk in the kitchenette, but it had yielded the packets of photographs in manila envelopes, labeled in scrawling ballpoint, that lay opened and spread before Prior on his desk.

"Look at this."

Sergeant Williams bent obediently to examine the print pushed across the desk by Prior's stubby nicotine-stained finger. "What do you make of that, hey?"

"An alarm control pad. A Safeteye." The sergeant read the name, distinct on the print. "Fishy."

"Stinks, my son." Prior plucked the empty envelope toward him and read the date on it, adding, "Bilberry Grange, taken in April. Last May they lost all their silver, remember? Alarm system all buggered up. They don't allow photography in the rooms either and it's not a private house. Guide in every room to watch no one snatches a snap or cuts a canvas from its frame."

"I reckon even guides have to go to the toilet, sir. He must've waited for his chance."

"And I reckon," said Prior sharply, "that guides can look out of the window from time to time. Wonderful view, if you get paid to watch it."

Williams pondered. "Do you think he set up the raid, sir?"

"Nah." Prior began to hit his pockets in search of cheroots. "He'd be the scout, nothing too ambitious, or too connected." He found, lighted, and spoke around his cheroot. "He's our man for that all right." He shuffled the envelopes about and threw one across in front of Williams. "Quite a hoarder. Take a good look at the date and name on that."

"Paisley House?" Williams tried to trace the echo in his mind, and Prior snorted smoke, a contemptuous dragon.

"Black mark, Sarge. Roke was Benet Paisley and Paisley House was where he lived before Roke Castle. Years ago. Read your notes, man. Guy Paisley—got it now?—told us he saw Lawson, who had a beard then and more hair, photographing his father's collection when he was a kid—"

"And he recognized him, and told his father, he said." Williams was too anxious to demonstrate his memory to notice he had interrupted, but he was in luck: Prior in triumph did not notice either. He tossed another envelope over, a white one with different writing.

"Take a look. Harry printed them for me off that reel in Lawson's hip pocket. Lucky for us he'd zipped it in, or it'd have pranged the flagstones when he took his dive. Must have just changed the film. His camera was wrecked with new film in it. Harry said he might have taken two or three, but they were all overexposed, black."

The sergeant picked up one of the prints.

"This looks like something, sir."

Prior shot his chair back, was on his feet, and twitched the print from Williams' hand. "That's what we're going to see about. Mrs. Doctor can do a bit of explaining, can't she?"

Mrs. Doctor, otherwise Mrs. Rose, was in. Prior was glad to hear it, and after he had shown his police card and asked to see her, he was invited into the hall. The woman who had answered the door was thin, severe, with dark wispy hair and the wrong shape of glasses, and wore a navy wool dress that made her complexion even more pallid. The pearl studs in her ears, and the choice of orange lipstick, combined to make her teeth look yellow when she smiled, hesitantly, at Prior and his sergeant.

"Don't you want the doctor? It's about the accident, isn't it?"

"Oh, we'd like to see the doctor, too, of course." Prior followed the navy dress, part of the shadows in the dark little hall. The stairs came almost to the front door as if to facilitate the doctor's plunge outside on a night call. A door to the left was propped open, by a flat black iron spaniel, onto a room smelling of pine disinfectant and wet macs, where seven or eight people sat on black plastic chairs, two of them listlessly thumbing through battered magazines, while a child with a swollen face and black eye sat on the stained carpet banging a ginger teddy bear monotonously on the floor. Prior did not need telling that "Doctor's in surgery" which the woman said as they passed.

They were ushered into a small room at the back, clearly a combined sitting and dining room, since a long table with a crochet cloth had to be avoided as they came in, jammed against the wall though it was, and with dining chairs pushed under it so that their tall slatted backs seemed to imprison the display vase of artificial flowers in its center. The vacant eye of a TV set stared from the corner, by the hearth filled with a monster electric fire in bronze and black. They were offered seats on a small chintz sofa facing the TV, while the woman perched on the front of the seat of a matching armchair, taking on her knee the workbasket that had sat there, smoothing over the piece of tapestry folded on top. She treated them to the teeth again.

"How can I help you, though? I didn't see the accident, you know. It was in the town center, and Doctor only happened to be passing. Lucky for the boy, of course. These motorists take no notice of cyclists." She settled back in the chair.

Prior stared at her. Then, suddenly, he grinned.

"Mrs. Rose." It was a neutral, noncommittal statement.

The woman smiled again. "Yes?" she said.

"I wonder if you can help to identify someone for us." Prior took out the white envelope, sorted through it, keeping it close to his chest, and presented a photograph to Mrs. Rose. She took it with a baffled air, still evidently puzzled by the police applying to her for help, but this expression vanished when she saw the picture.

"Lynda Colindale!" She tapped it. "My husband's secretary." She paused, and peered at it intently with pursed mouth. "Who *is* she with? I'm sure I know that face." She turned the print to and fro as if another angle might tell her who it was.

"She's your husband's secretary?" Prior had glanced at Williams. Mrs. Rose looked up.

"Oh, not *now*. Mrs. Beadle is his secretary *now*. Lynda

Colindale left in February." Her chin came up and she smiled primly. The change had been to her liking.

"The doctor didn't like her work?" Prior took back the print.

Mrs. Rose's ringed hands buckled the tapestry she had been smoothing. "Oh, her *work* I suppose was all right. I believe she was efficient. It was her character." She looked down her nose, frowning. The impression was that a bad smell had wafted into the room. "The doctor can't possibly employ someone people talk about in the town. It simply doesn't do."

Prior nodded. "Put it about a bit, did she?"

"I'd prefer not to discuss it." Mrs. Rose closed her lips tightly. Then she went on, nodding at the print in Prior's hand. "You can see from the photograph. Objectionable. I know I've seen that other person recently."

A child broke into howls in the next room, howls of justified rage that were muffled in the hall and cut off by the bang of the front door. Mrs. Rose said, "She had lots of unsuitable ideas. She wanted my husband to move his surgery out of the house; but it's *perfectly* convenient."

Prior regarded the tall rockery slope, hung with despondent ferns, outside the windows. Evidently Mrs. Rose didn't get claustrophobia. She leaned forward suddenly. "What's she been doing? Why do you want her identified?" Her face cleared as a pleasant answer occurred to her. "Something's happened to her? She isn't *dead?*"

Prior shook his head, grinning. "Police business, Mrs. Rose. Police business. When can we see the doctor?"

She hesitated. "Well. He's got a heavy surgery this morning—you saw. But as it's police business"—she did not say *and possibly incriminating Lynda Colindale*— "I'll tell Mrs. Beadle and I expect you can see him in between."

"Yes, Mrs. Rose. You do that. Say it's Inspector Prior." Prior's geniality seemed to cancel the imperative, but she stood up, replaced the workbasket firmly in the chair, and hurried out.

"Well now, Sarge," Prior said jovially, getting up, "I think you'll find that we're the doctor's next patients."

"Won't he come in here and talk, sir?"

"What, with wifey at the keyhole? Grow up, son." Prior moved confidently to the door and, before he had squeezed past the dining chairs, still endangering the vase of fabulous flowers, a large woman appeared, a woman with tight-curled gray hair and a brown-blotched complexion, flinging the door against the wall and grazing a chair back.

"Doctor will see you." Mrs. Beadle had been chosen for durability rather than seductive powers, no Lynda Colindale she. Her stare conveyed that she disapproved of their taking precedence over patients, but she led the way through the still crowded waiting room at a stately pace. Prior crushed a plastic car, that had got loose from the toy box for child patients, into the worn carpet, and kicked it under a chair. Faces all around were raised to study the two whose emergency put them ahead of the queue.

Dr. Rose was talking to his wife when they were ushered into the surgery; more accurately, listening to her. The room being too small for four people, Sergeant Williams had to stand on the threshold, blocking the view for patients craning to see what might be going on. Mrs. Beadle shut herself into a species of cupboard with her typewriter and telephone, and Prior held the surgery door open for Mrs. Rose with a gallantry she was forced to accept. The sergeant backed against a patient with a stick, which got between his feet and nearly felled him. He therefore entered the surgery at speed, saving himself by the door handle, and turned to shut it in a movement Chaplin might have approved. Boot-faced, he stood there while Prior took the patient's chair.

"You remember me, Dr. Rose?" Prior gave his grin.

Dr. Rose did not, patently, relish the memory. He shifted the folders in front of him, stacking them as if to form a barrier, and raised his eyes from them reluctantly, eyes with a curious expression that might be defiance.

"How can I help you? As you can see, I'm a very busy man and I can't afford much time. I'd have thought you had heard all I could contribute already."

"Well now." Prior extracted his envelope from the inner pocket again. "There are just one or two things you forgot to mention yesterday. Slipped your mind, I think, that Lynda Colindale's not your wife."

The doctor glanced at the door, as if checking that it was shut. He attempted dignity. "That was none of your business. That can't be what you are here about."

Prior did his conjuring trick among the photographs, this time fanning out four or five which he slid across the scuffed leather of the desk. "That's what we're here about. The holiday snaps Lawson took of you and the luscious Lynda."

"But it's not possible." The doctor stared at one print, of Lynda and himself with arms linked lovingly around the hips of a statue in the grounds of Roke Castle, a vast Roman wrestler who gazed down stony-eyed at this new form of ivy. The doctor's nervous hand pushed this clear of the print below where he and Lynda, in a closer embrace, were romantically framed against a bower of late, ragged roses. "Not possible. His camera"—he stopped, glanced up at Prior leaning forward, and went on—"someone said it had been broken in the fall—that the film was all exposed."

"*Did* they now? But you see we were lucky, he must just have changed the reel. That's the grounds of Roke Castle. I've seen the very spot. Isn't it?"

"Certainly. So, what is it you want to know?"

The telephone rang, a muffled hornet, in Mrs. Beadle's booth, and was picked up. Someone had a prolonged, juicy, bronchial fit of coughing in the waiting room. Prior let the doctor stew while he sorted through his pack for the trump.

"This. What can you say about this?"

It was a different man in the embrace, though the woman was the same. Lynda, hair falling free, bent back over Roke's arm, looking up under half-shut eyes into his face, her lips parted, while he bent over her in brooding anticipation. The darkness of a doorway threw the figures into strong relief. Only a background of dancers doing the tango could have made the involvement look innocent.

The doctor frowned instinctively; then he leaned back in his chair smiling.

"Oh, that was when Lynda tripped. Lord Roke had been doing his spiel at the start of the tour. He caught her."

"She tripped?" Prior, not concealing his disappointment, took the print from Rose's fingers and scanned it as if a trip should be visible.

"Yes. We were all crowding around, and Lynda got up on the step, then she moved back when Roke came forward and she caught her foot on the bootscraper. He was very quick, and stopped her from actually falling. I was on the other side," he added, as the natural catcher of his secretary. "If that's what you came about, you've wasted your journey. It's an amusing picture." He laid his fingertips along the edge of his desk, at arm's length, and added with a touch of mockery, "I assure you there was no involvement between Lynda and Lord Roke. I didn't plug him through the neck in ungovernable jealousy. Everyone laughed at that—you can see she and Lord Roke are hamming it up."

"Ah, well then," said Prior, "thank you for explaining. There's just another thing."

The doctor sat upright, his eyes once more wary.

"I wondered if you could tell me why Lawson took all these pictures of you and the lovely Lynda?"

"I've no idea. He took photographs all the time. I said to Benjamin Maitland that I wondered if Lawson ever looked at any object except through a viewfinder."

"I see. He took them like an obsession, you mean."

"Exactly."

"M'm." Prior regarded the prints that still lay before Rose. "Then why do you think those intimate shots are the only ones, in scores of snaps he took, that are of people?"

"How on earth do I know? I didn't even know Lawson."

"Never treated him as a patient?"

"No. I don't know where he lives, but certainly not near here."

"Did he know Miss Whats'ername—"

"Colindale."

"—wasn't in fact Mrs. Rose?"

"I don't see how he could have done, or that it was any of his business, or if I may say so, *yours*, if he did."

"But did he?"

Rose snapped, "I have no idea. It's immaterial."

"Is it? Is it now?" Prior's jaw was well forward. He said, "You were on this weekend with the lovely Lynda, not with the less love—the worthy Mrs. Rose. You knew Lawson had taken snaps of you and her; how pleased would Mrs. Rose be to see those snaps if Lawson sent them? How would it go locally if this weekend was known about? I'm saying it's not very immaterial that Lawson could have been onto you. Where were you when Lawson went over the battlements?"

Chapter

· · · · · · · · · · · · · · · · · · ·

28

BONE FOUND JANE IN HER APRICOT SITTING ROOM, ON THE
Regency sofa with the telephone on her knee, in a snowdrift
of the notes Knebworth had been conveying to her all
morning. He was bending over her now with his usual
courtliness, salver extended with another envelope.

When Bone came in, Grizel, sitting at the Queen Anne
desk with a welter of more papers before her, turned to give
him a brilliant smile of welcome. He thought: *this is
marriage—walk into a room and, straight away, you're linked into
someone else's mind.* He returned the smile, and heard
Knebworth speaking.

"—in the pocket of Mr. Nash's suede jacket, m'lady. He
gave me the jacket with the rest of his clothing which had
fallen on the terrace." Bone admired the way in which

Knebworth made it appear that the clothes had been afflicted by some entirely involuntary movement. "He wished me to take them to the dry-cleaners tomorrow when I go into Blastock for the shopping."

Typical of Adrian, thought Bone, *make use of the butler before you have to move on; and I suppose in this way Jane pays the cleaning bill.*

"So, m'lady, as I was preparing the garments for the cleaners, I emptied the pockets, and I came upon this, which I thought you should see."

Bone's surprise at Knebworth's referring a note in Adrian's possession to Jane vanished when she read the envelope and said, "It's addressed to Lord Roke."

Knebworth inclined his head in confirmation.

She turned the letter over, examining the sealed flap. "Is it a letter Mr. Nash wrote? I don't know the writing."

"I believe, m'lady, it may be a letter Mr. Nash forgot to give his lordship. Some weeks ago, it may even have been more"—Knebworth's voice became apologetic at the failure of human memory—"a gentleman came to the door. Before I could answer it," and Bone pictured Knebworth's measured pace across the hall, "Mr. Nash, who happened to be coming in, took the letter and said he would deliver it to his lordship." Knebworth paused. "I would have relieved Mr. Nash of the trouble but he was away up the stairs and I fear I was too slow."

Jane held the letter, still looking at it as if it were impossible to imagine opening an envelope intended for hands now lifeless. "Who brought it? Did you know him?"

"No, m'lady, not *know* him . . ." Clearly Knebworth had areas of deliberate social ignorance. "He lives locally and I have seen him from time to time in the village. He was here with the tour on Sunday. A Mr. Spencer."

"Oh, the poor man must have expected an answer." Jane's thumb, narrow, flexible, was under the flap and pulled it open. She took out the thin blue lined paper and read. Knebworth had withdrawn toward the door. Grizel half turned back, toward the letters she was writing, but suddenly looked at Bone, became aware of his acute attention, and stopped.

"Oh dear." Jane reread. "Oh dear. Robert, look at this."

As she was handing it to him, Knebworth got in his murmur of "Will that be all, m'lady?" and she nodded. The door shut. Bone could only admire such iron discretion in the face of what must, for Knebworth was human, be considerable curiosity.

Lord Roke,
  You are the cause of my daughter's death. Do not think you will not pay for it.

                                        Donald Spencer

Jane stretched her arm out for the letter and, taking it, swung it toward Grizel. "The poor man! Of course, he must be the father of that sad girl May Spencer who drowned herself. Why on earth should he pick on Benet, though? It's absurd. Of course, grief does odd things to people . . ."

She paused, as if pondering the consequences of her own grief, then picked up again. "I don't suppose Benet ever met the girl."

Bone said, "She came to the fancy-dress ball for Guy's birthday." As Jane looked up, bewildered at this display of knowledge, he added, "I've seen a photograph. Benet was Count Dracula, and it seems she happened to be dressed as the Bride of Dracula."

"Heavens, how pathetic. I didn't know that was May Spencer! But of course! I remember now. She turned up one night wandering on the terrace and set the alarms off. She must have tried to get in, I suppose." She turned to Grizel. "She was a touch simple-minded, I think. She was in her fancy dress, Benet said. He made a joke of it all—he passed it off as a joke, for the girl's sake. That she was doing it as a joke on him, I mean. He told me she wept like a fountain and clung to him like an octopus. I didn't go downstairs; I had my you-know-whats and a burglar alarm was the last thing I needed."

Bone thought: *and to be passed off as a joke was the last thing May Spencer needed.*

"Did she drown herself," Grizel asked, "because of *that?*" Jane spread her hands.

"The point is," Bone observed, "whether her father thought she did."

Jane's brown eyes, Grizel's brilliant green, fixed on him.

"I have to take the letter to Prior," he said.

"But what on earth could he think Benet did?" Jane demanded. "I mean, the normal thing, the drama, the village maiden thing. Seducing. Benet wouldn't. I remember that poor girl at the ball, got up in lace curtains. Oh, it's true Benet was unfaithful if he got an opportunity to be, but . . . I don't know how to put this . . . not village girls."

"No," said Bone, seeing again the waif in her bridal gear, tucked under Roke's jovial arm. Whoever took the snap had, probably on purpose, let the flash off straight at them, getting the red-eyed effect appropriate to their guise. "So I thought."

"As Robert said, it's what Donald Spencer thought that counts."

"Well, I'll take this to Prior. His team carried away all Roke's correspondence, I imagine? Yes. They'd have got this already if Adrian hadn't forgotten it. But I came to tell you," Bone launched on the subject he had been containing all this while, "that there's a paper in a case in the muniment room that will bear looking at."

Jane's eyes widened. "Oh! Do you think it *is?*"

"It's signed *Roke* when it should have been signed *Benet*

Paisley, and I think it may be lying underneath the letter it's supposed to be signing."

"In one of the cases?" Jane was on her feet. "Oh, where will the keys be? Benet's desk? The police won't have taken them, will they?"

"They weren't mentioned on that receipt you signed," Grizel said.

"Thank heaven I made you read it. I couldn't take it in."

"You look for them while I take this letter to Prior."

"Oh, I thought you'd—"

"Grizel will help you."

Jane paused, looking at the letter in Bone's hand. She said, "Oh God, I hope it wasn't . . . Sometimes I don't want it to be anybody at all; and then I'm so *angry* at whoever did it . . . I don't want to think. I'll look for the keys."

Bone drove off, causing a brief interest among the persistent press. He noticed that one cameraman had ensconced himself like a big hopeful bird in the Blasted Oak. Better remind Jane about bedroom curtains.

A threatening letter, even one as vague as the one he carried, needed to be taken seriously. It did not necessarily mean very much. Donald Spencer might be expecting divine retribution rather than promising his own. Bone was sorry for him, for those solitary vigils in his daughter's room; for his loss. He disliked having to turn the letter over to Prior, but he must. Spencer had been wandering about the place alone at the time of Roke's death.

Was it giving the letter unnecessary prominence to bring it himself?

The Bride of Dracula. A waif in lace curtains.

If the killer of Roke was Donald Spencer, what had become of Bone's theory that the same man had attacked Marcus? He had thought the murderer suspected Marcus of having heard, or even seen, what led up to the bowshot in the gallery. While Marcus just conceivably could have fallen into the oubliette by accident, he knew very well where it was, and its danger. Donald Spencer had as much chance to see that too, shown by Roke, but how could he possibly have made an assignation with Marcus? How could he have got into the castle otherwise? Only someone who knew about the alarm system could have switched off part of it to let someone in, or to go out.

Bone rather felt his theory had been shot down.

It left him with no guess as to why Marcus had been found in the oubliette with a head wound. Perhaps his own profession made Bone absurdly, risibly, suspicious: Marcus had mistaken where the grating was and had hit his head on the way down. Goodness knows there had been enough distracting things to upset anyone's mind. Josh Lawson had caught his foot and might have toppled off the roof with no help from any of those whose ill will he had industriously earned.

However, Roke had not shot himself through the neck.

Prior, to Bone's surprise, did not keep him waiting but came bustling out into the front office, scattering commands and generally showing busy, and ushered Bone to his room. His eyes were alert with inquiry.

Bone gave him the letter. The room was small, and rank with stale smoke, which had stained the yellow repp curtains a dingier yellow in streaks down the folds. Bone's chair, with a black wood frame, had a padded back and seat covered in a worn and greasy brown. There was room for a peeling radiator, two stacking chairs, another small desk, and some shelving full of box files. A window was open onto the car park, admitting an auxiliary smell of petrol fumes.

"How'd you get this?"

"Spencer brought it to the door and Nash said he would give it to Lord Roke. The butler Knebworth saw it happen, but only found the letter in Nash's coat pocket an hour or so ago."

"I'd have sent someone for it if you'd given me a ring."

This was gracious indeed. Bone said dryly, "I'm not muscling in. I came myself because of what I know of the story. Look at me as a private citizen if you like."

"I can't, y'see," said Prior, leaning back. A cheroot was burning to death in the ashtray. "You're not, any more than I am. But you know the story?" A discolored nail tapped the letter. "How was Roke 'responsible'"—his forefingers made quotation marks—"for the daughter's death? I'll tell you how much I know, for starters. Spencer had this daughter who was about ninety pence in the pound, right?"

Bone nodded. Few generalizations are entirely fair.

"Patrol car was directed to answer an alarm at the castle one August night last year. May Spencer had been straying across the park in fancy dress, and was taken home. Then a while ago she tried to take a walk across the river and found she wasn't Jesus. Now you tell me what Roke had to do with this."

Bone had been waiting for him to pick up the cheroot, and he did. Bone began. "May Spencer had a fixation on Lord Roke. It dated from a fancy-dress party a year ago last August. She kept a diary, and wrote letters to Roke that she didn't send, but which her father read after her death. I have no idea whether or not Roke seduced her, or whether Spencer thought he did, or whether it was all moonshine in May's head; but when she went to the castle and set off the alarm system, and the police came, Roke laughed it all off; and that seems to have contributed to her final depression."

Prior, predictably, put his finger on it. "Either way, Roke's responsible according to Spencer. So he gets himself into this touring party with the idea of saving God the trouble of a thunderbolt. I like it, Superintendent. I'll have a long word with Spencer. Other leads are now looking promising."

He leaned forward to mash the cheroot among other corpses of its kin, and opening a file, he extracted an envelope of photographs and showed one.

"Doctor and Mrs. Rose, taken by Lawson."

"Yes. We saw him take that one, I think. We were on the roof."

"Ye-es. I asked myself why this, and this one, were the only pictures—oh, and this—of human beings that Lawson took, when all the rest were of silver and valuables and security locks. I went to see the doctor today and his wife answered the door."

He grinned, and fished out another cheroot, lit it, took a deep drag, and said as he exhaled, "*Not* that one! An older model, obsolescent, you might say. Bit more aerodynamic: none of those bulges. That one on the tour is called Lynda Colindale, former secretary of Dr. Rose. I toddled off to see her; she hadn't got out of bed yet after her tiring weekend, but she wrapped herself in green satin and talked to us. Or she wouldn't, for a while. She had no *idea* why"—Prior's voice parodied an indignant female—"Lawson chose to take those snaps. No idea. Couldn't think. He could take what snaps he liked, couldn't he, just as she and the doctor could go off for a dirty weekend if they liked; it wasn't the first."

"My wife thought that Lynda Rose opened Lawson's camera on the terrace, deliberately."

Prior's grin almost caricatured itself.

"How Lawson came to know they weren't married, she won't say. She knows, but she won't say. The doctor's a better bet; he can be got at; but he has more reason than you to tip Lawson off the battlements. Right?"

"Frankly, I think Lawson's death was something of a relief to several people. According to that, Rose is definitely one of them."

"He was walking, he says, around the garden by himself

when Lawson left the roof in such a hurry. Y'know, all this bears out what I've always held: ordinary life is like a smooth, flat paving stone. Heave it up, and the underside's full of crawlies."

"I agree with you," Bone said. There was a slight pause while both of them experienced surprise at this. Then Prior leaned forward and jabbed the intercom.

"Yes, sir?" They always sounded like Donald Duck.

"I want someone picked up. Ask Whitehouse who's free."

"Sir."

Prior sat back vigorously, his chair protesting. "We'll talk to Mr. Spencer. You'd like to know what we get, sir?"

"I would."

Prior nodded, amiably. "Will do," he said.

Bone thought it counterproductive to give to this man his opinion that Spencer could not have killed Roke. It was only an opinion. He might misjudge the man; and it was Prior's case. He must question and, it could be hoped, eliminate Spencer. He was not one to appreciate either Bone's hunches or his scruples. Bone rose, saying only, "Have you heard about Marcus Weatherby?"

Prior's wide spatulate hand swiveled a memo on the desk. "Taken to hospital. Fell down some hole in the old castle. Right?"

"Yes . . . he was in a position, in the library, to have overheard events in the Japanese gallery outside. The bow would have made a noise."

Prior's grin was definitely indulgent. "So he was, sir. Well, if he says he was pushed when he comes around, we'll have to listen to him."

He came to his feet and rounded the desk. Bone decided to be amused at this unequivocal putting him in his place, and said, "So you will." He shook Prior's offered hand, and left.

On the way back, he wondered if Jane had found the keys;

if Marcus was conscious yet; he hoped Prior would not give Spencer a rough ride; his sister, Dorothy, would be very troubled—"helping the police with their inquiries" had taken on an accusatory sense these days.

I'm supposed to be on holiday, he thought. Whatever applied to Marcus—if he had been attacked because of what he could have heard—applied to Adrian, too. Adrian must be in danger.

My *brain's* on holiday, thought Bone.

Chapter

· · · · · · · · · · · · · · · · · · · ·

29

BONE'S HEADLIGHTS, AS HE TURNED INTO THE CASTLE'S LONG drive, picked out for a moment the crumbling stone eagles that peered haughtily on the gateposts. In the last couple of days, he reflected, they've had a stone eyeful: police cars, ambulances, the owner himself carried past for the last time. Any banshee foretelling misfortune would have contracted occupational sore throat by now. He traced this idea to reading to Charlotte, when she was small, a story of just such a banshee sipping a hot drink and complaining of overwork. How was Cha's holiday going? He hoped strongly that it was far less full of incident than his own.

Guy was propping his Harley-Davidson on its stand in the cobbled yard when Bone drew up. Guy kept on his helmet and turned a Darth Vader head to the press in the battery of flash. There were shouts of "Lord Roke!" and questions hurled at him. The title was, although they could not know it, infuriating. He put Keziah in front of him and shepherded her slight figure, in its duffle coat and helmet, to the door. He shouted savagely, "No comment." The dark rope of hair down her back affirmed their guess of this second figure being a woman, but cries of "Miss!" naturally fared no better. Bone got out, and was at Guy's heels. He turned at the door as if he were about to make a statement, and there was for a moment enough quiet for him to be heard. Dark gray lollipops were extended toward his face, a vast woolly caterpillar hung overhead.

Bone had been forced to make statements to the media in the past, to put up with challenges of "What are the police actually doing?" and "In fact you haven't got anywhere?" He was now anonymous, unaccountable.

"No comment," he said, and was through the door to a howl of frustration.

"How is Marcus?" he asked, in the kitchen lobby.

"They can't tell yet." Keziah's voice was strained, her eyes glittering, and she held her coat collar at her neck as though more than the wind had made her cold. "They're going to operate. He has a depressed skull fracture. He's in Alexander Fleming ward of the Blastock General. He's not out of the coma. I sat there and talked to him." Bone could imagine Keziah holding Marcus' hand, talking in her friendly soothing voice, watching his face; some people are born with a talent for music, some, like Keziah, with a talent for sympathy. "It was no good, though. And they told me I couldn't stay because I'm not a relation; it seems not to count that Marcus hasn't anyone but his father. And then Guy arrived and Jane rang—"

"My mother says the will's been found."

Jeremy shot out suddenly from the kitchen and hauled on Guy's arm. "Come *on*. Everyone's *waiting. Hurry.*"

It pleased Bone to be in time to hear the will. Natural curiosity, so strong in him, would have made him want to be there anyway, and he had also a proprietary feeling as he had taken some part in its finding. He followed Guy and Keziah, and saw Adrian run gracefully up the stairs before them, no doubt looking forward to triumph when everyone would have to acknowledge that the valuable books were his, and he could bear them off and remove himself from Roke forever. One person less likely to triumph was Guy, and Bone, treading up the stairs after them, saw Keziah link her fingers with his. If the will turned out as Bone thought it might, Guy was going to need as much sympathy as Marcus did, and Keziah would certainly supply it.

The gathering to hear the reading was quite a B-movie scene, lacking only the gray-haired wing-collared lawyer to look at everyone over his pince-nez. It took place in the big gold drawing room on the first floor. Bone had glanced around it before, when Roke took the party through on the way to the pool. There were gold brocade curtains, comfortably a little frayed, drawn across the glass doors that gave onto the conservatory and the steps down to the pool. Bone imagined he could hear a lonely splash from below, where Dundee perhaps wondered why he no longer saw the friendly grin of another alligator.

Long cream and amber rugs covered the narrow boards of parquet. Gilt picture- and looking-glass frames, and the gilding of tables, and the various golds of brocades on chairs and sofas, bore out the room's name. So did the gold leaf picking out the intricate plasterwork on the ceiling and the classical chimneypiece.

Jane stood by the fire, nervously turning the folded paper in her hands. There was a Knole sofa facing an ordinary one on either side of the fireplace, and several upholstered chairs had been brought to face the fire.

"Do, everybody, sit down."

Angela and an uneasy Baz were on the Knole settee.
Jeremy took his seat on a footstool almost hidden between
Jane's sofa and the fire; Jane beckoned Guy and Keziah to sit
beside her. Adrian seemed to be making for his favorite
place before the fire, but Jane pointed to a chair and said,
"There," and with a toss of the hair he took it. Grizel, Hugo,
and Bone sat on the other chairs. There was a pause.

"Can't we get on with it?" Adrian demanded.

"Not until everyone's here."

The door opened. Knebworth ushered Mrs. Knebworth
in, and she sat on a small lacquer settee by the door, while
he remained standing. Jane said, as if resuming an argu-
ment, "Are you sure you won't . . ." gesturing toward the
fireside group, and Knebworth replied, "If you please,
m'lady." When Jane sat down, he placed himself next to his
wife.

"Well then. I did get hold of Benet's solicitor on the
telephone, and he tells me he has no knowledge of any will,
that none has been lodged with him. And that this one must
be properly proved before it can be carried out. Benet told
me he had destroyed one he made before, and that the one
he'd hidden was the real one." She had been picking at pink
fastening tape, and now opened the folded sheets, bending
the signature flat where it had been turned back as a clue.
She read in a monotone.

*"This is the last will and testament of me, Benet Basil
Paisley—"*

Baz took a breath and turned to his mother.

"Baron Roke of Roke Castle . . . there's a lot about executors
and so on . . . I'll read what we want to know . . . It seems
to start . . . here." She resumed the monotone. *"I give and
bequeath free of all Capital Transfer and other Taxes the following
legacies: to my wife, Jane Rosalind—*well, it's about my share
as a widow. And he leaves Paisley House to me." She
sounded surprised and pleased.

"You'll have to boot out the tenants," Jeremy said. "Can we go back and live there?"

"Be quiet, Tig. *To my eldest son, Roke Castle its appurtenances . . .*" There was a little silence, Guy swallowed painfully, and Keziah's fingers folded more tightly around his.

"If that *is* me," Baz said into the silence, "it's not on. He meant Guy, and that's how it should be."

"Surely all that can be sorted out later," Adrian exclaimed dismissively.

"Yes, it will have to be," Jane said, and sighed.

Angela, who was pale and spoke tearfully, put in, "I told Benet we didn't come here for that."

"The gist of this part," Jane was reading on, "is that the collections here can be sold if the heir chooses. Then Hugo and Jeremy get legacies in trust, and there's one or two things that each of them gets that they were promised: Hugo gets the Purdey when he's old enough for a license, and Jeremy the ebony and ivory chess set. Keziah, he's left you the Meissen monkey band."

Keziah bit her lips and her eyes flooded. Guy, who sat slumped and looked devastated, turned his head toward her and said something in an undertone. She raised their entwined hands and kissed his fingers.

"*To Angela Mary North, my first wife*—he's put your address in Melbourne. He must have found that out."

Angela, bewildered, sat with open mouth.

"*—the pair of rococo looking glasses now in the gold drawing room which were brought from Paisley House.*"

Heads turned, following Jane's gaze, to look at the lilting golden curves of the frames. The glasses hung either side of a formal portrait of Roke himself, a likeness far less good than the trompe l'oeil figure in the dining room, but signed dashingly with a famous name. It conveyed no sense of Roke's presence.

"—and the Turkey carpet from the dining room of Paisley House, of which I hope she has happy memories."

Angela turned fiery red, and looked fixedly at her hands. Adrian was fidgeting.

"To my librarian, Marcus Arthur Wallace Weatherby, I leave my collection of curious books, since they will do him so much good. These comprise—"

"He said he was leaving them to me!" Adrian was on his feet. "He told me so. He said I was to have them. He definitely promised. What does he say he's leaving to *me*? What did he leave *me*?"

Jane's finger moved down the page. She turned it and looked at the last page of all.

"To Adrian Nash: his face is his fortune and I would not presume to add any gift to those which Nature has so bounteously bestowed on him."

Adrian, after a rigid moment, leaped across and snatched the pages. "It doesn't say that. You *bitch*; you've made that up—"

Guy had risen, and so had Baz opposite. Jane remarked, in quiet satisfaction as Adrian found the place, "It does say that. It says just that exactly."

Adrian read. He drew his hand back with the long pages half-rumpled, clearly aiming it at the fire, but Guy's hand clamped on his wrist. There was a moment of swaying struggle. Bone half rose, saying sharply, "It's a punishable offense to destroy a will." Adrian was distracted by this and Guy wrested the will from him.

Adrian was flushed a quite dangerous dark red. He looked up at Guy and further up at the looming Baz, whirled around, knocked his chair out of the way, and dashed for the door. Knebworth opened it for him.

"Now perhaps he'll at last take himself off," Jane said, leaning back in the sofa as Guy restored the crumpled pages to her hand. Baz, sitting down slowly, stared at the door as if he shared Bone's fear that Adrian was ripe to commit some damaging mischief. "Good riddance to bad rubbish."

Jane's cry made Mrs. Knebworth, her little bony hands clasped in her lap, nod emphatically until a touch from her husband, seated again, made her stop.

"Do you think he'll go now?" Hugo asked, and Jeremy, crouched on his stool, began to slap his hands on his knees to a chant of "Bye-bye Nash, bye-bye trash" until Jane tapped him on the head.

"That's enough. Well, he's got nothing to wait about for now, so we can certainly hope—"

"He'll go on waiting about if he thinks it'll drive us mad." Guy was still flushed with anger, and ignored Jane's signal to him to sit down. Bone thought him capable of inflicting real damage on Adrian if he came within reach again. He could hardly know that this tendency to be violent when angry kept him firmly on Bone's suspect list. Guy's father had been, after all, a dab hand at the art of annoying. "Anyway, you don't think he'll leave at this time of night?"

"Has he friends to go to?" Bone offered.

"Friends? Adrian got *friends*? Boyfriends, I suppose." Guy ignored another gesture from his mother. Jeremy and Hugo looked up at him with interest, Jeremy still drumming on his knees and silently mouthing his chant. "He'll have to organize someone to sponge off before he can go. I'd like to throw him out right off."

He stopped, because Jane had turned up her palms helplessly. He glanced at her, and she was looking at Baz, as it might be to say: only he has the right to throw anyone out of this house now.

It did nothing to settle Guy's temper. He strode across to stand before Baz and Angela, who drew in her feet nervously as though she feared to be kicked. Baz put a large hand protectively on hers, and answered Guy's stare with a slight frown suddenly reminiscent of their father.

These two half-brothers could hardly have been more different. The fragile, faded Angela had somehow produced the Michelangelo David of the blond curls and broad shoulders, while the dark, volatile Jane had triumphed over Roke's dominant genes to produce this slender gangling youth, all fire and discontent but without the physique to enforce his will. Bone wondered if Baz's likeness to Roke added a bitterness to Jane's situation.

"I suppose the people who've got to go is us." Guy's hands had fisted at his sides, "And you're the ones looking forward to throwing people out."

"You're not being fair." Baz had a surprising dignity, leaning back and apparently quite relaxed. "We didn't mean any of this to happen. Of course you don't go."

"I want to go myself!" Angela unexpectedly snatched her hand from under her son's and covered her eyes. Her other hand groped for the pocket of her blue cardigan and found a handkerchief. "I never wanted to get anything, never! I just wanted Benet to see—" Here she was overcome and began to sob, holding the handkerchief tightly against her open mouth as if trying to choke herself.

"Ma, no. It'll be all right." Baz got his arm around her, but Guy was only incensed.

"All right? All right? Of course it's all right for you! Coming here, the *eldest son,* changing everybody's lives, pushing us out of our home and—" he stopped, as effectively choked by his feelings as Angela by her handkerchief. He had moved back and was shifting from foot to foot like a boxer. Bone thought: dancing mad. Jane and Keziah were both on their feet, Jane moving to crouch by Angela, making reassuring murmurs, while Keziah clasped her hands around Guy's arm.

"Don't, Guy. It isn't like that. And Jane's not finished reading—"

Bone could have told her that the last thing Guy needed

now was to be soothed and coaxed. He ached to intervene. Guy turned on her savagely.

"It damn well is like that. You heard it. Are you too stupid to see it means he gets the lot?" His gesture swept at the room. "All this, everything."

"But he said; he doesn't—"

"D'you believe that?"

Baz said, "Hey, I'm—"

"Yes, I do believe that."

Guy's face was now a mask of pure rage. Bone had got up. Used to commanding, to being in charge of scenes and events, he wanted to intervene and could not. Very salutary, he thought.

Guy, with an indistinguishable word, seized Keziah's wrist and wrenched her hand from his arm. He hurled her back into the sofa and made for the door. Knebworth swiftly opened it, and shut it after him.

Bone wondered if this volcano had erupted for the first time or if this was an explosion secondary to one before. In his mind he saw Roke descending the stairs—as he had never in fact seen him—the arrow through his neck. If he had been able to speak, would he have accused his son?

Chapter

·····················

30

BONE RARELY FOUND IT HARD TO GET TO SLEEP. EVEN WHEN HIS mind was deeply engaged in the permutations of a case, his body would turn off when he turned out the lights. This had now and then contributed to solving a case by dredging up ideas in dreams for his waking mind to see the sense of, a process he never mentioned to his colleagues.

This night, though, he lay awake beside a sleeping Grizel, conscious that one among those, asleep or awake around him in this silent house, was most likely a murderer. He was unable to be sure who it was, without proof, and unable, for once, to do anything about it, officially or unofficially. It was useful experience, as so many unpleasant things are, to be a bystander and also, in a sense, personally involved.

Because Grizel was Jane's friend, he had landed in the midst of what he usually observed from outside, the recriminations and reticences, the tensions, the grief and shock, of the victim's family and friends. This should give him an advantage, reveal details which would illuminate the problem, but it wasn't so. Emotional steam clouded the air, made him confused and almost apprehensive. He was now concerned for people he hadn't known before this weekend. Deliberately he had not discussed the matter closely with Grizel, but he was sure she realized that either Jane or Guy could conceivably have killed Roke. Being fond of someone did not guarantee their moral strength. For that matter it was easy to see how anyone might kill Roke in the heat of humiliation or even the cooler blood of exasperation. As Bone shifted gingerly from one position to another, anxious not to wake Grizel, he grimaced at his surreal image of Roke, smiling sarcastically, twirling the arrow through his neck as a villain might twirl his moustachios. He remembered someone on the tour asking if the castle were haunted, and Roke's jovial surprise that such a question need be asked. Roke himself, now, was making a good job of it.

Bone tried to dismiss the phantom; turned once more, thinking that were he alone, by now he'd have sat up and started to read. If he were at home he could listen to the radio. The World Service had some good programs late at night, as he had found out in some weary months of recovery from his car crash. Cautiously, he extended his feet, seeking a cool place in the sheets without brushing against Grizel, who liked to lie prone and would recklessly strew her own feet anywhere in the bed.

Outside, an owl, coasting by the castle, saluted its battlements with a soft call. Cue in the clanking chains, thought Bone. If Roke's about he'll be getting almost as much fun out of being dead as he did out of life. Would he visit the murderer?

He tried his only form of sleeping pill: describing to

himself, in elaborate detail, one of the houses he had visited
in the past and particularly liked. He had reached the
carvings on the main staircase of Brae Top, Philip
Whitewick's masterpiece, when he drifted into sleep as
effortlessly as the returning owl drifted past the window.

Breakfast was even more subdued than dinner the night
before. Then, another superb meal from the Knebworth
cuisine had been eaten almost in silence, only Keziah doing
her best, with Grizel's support, to keep some sort of
conversation going. Jane had made an attempt to join in at
first, but Guy's empty place disturbed her; that Adrian was
also absent did not prove enough of a consolation, particularly when Knebworth gravely reported that Mr. Nash had
requested a tray in his room. Jane's ringing snort at this had
made Bone wonder what even more dramatic response
might have been elicited from Guy. Distant coughing roars
from the parkland, like some ranging frustrated leopard,
demonstrated that Guy was having a little trouble with the
machine. Bone, eating pork escalope in cream sauce and
thinking reverently of Mrs. Knebworth's bony but gifted
hands, had wished he had a chance to vent his frustration in
the same fashion. He had a wild vision of himself striding
out of the station and zooming through the streets of
Tunbridge Wells on some souped-up Honda. The Chief
Constable would appreciate that right enough.

Guy was not here at breakfast either. Possibly he wished
to avoid the sight of Baz and Angela, who had both been
brave and put in an appearance. Baz, looking hunky in a
navy sweater with green bands, had chosen a modest coffee
and toast but Knebworth, after a thoughtful moment, put
before him a plate with a selection from under the covers on
the sideboard: fried eggs, sausages, fried potato, and bacon.
Baz was not proof against this. After a token protest he set
to, only stealing concerned looks at his mother. Knebworth
had tried the same ploy with her, presenting a little

scrambled egg delicately escorted by sprigs of parsley on the blue and white breakfast china, and she toyed with it politely. She too wore navy, a long cardigan over a cream blouse with a string of pearls at the neck, as if in solidarity with her son, uniting against the hostile world of which they had suddenly come into possession. Navy imparted to her skin an eggshell pallor, bluish against the cream blouse, and she did not look well. She only spoke indistinguishable disclaimers in reply to Jane's kind inquiries. There was little to choose between their complexions. Roke's widows were showing their grief.

Keziah, who dressed habitually in layers, wore a purple wool waistcoat, sewn with little mirrors, over a crimson shirt over a dark polo neck, and glowed with vitality as much as Baz did—both of them subduing it—making Angela and Jane look not only of an older generation but also like cut flowers left to wilt. Keziah, coming in, had kissed Jane and Grizel, and seemed for a moment as if she were going to include Angela; even Baz glanced around hopefully.

Where was Adrian? Bone hoped Jane would ask Knebworth if a breakfast tray in bed had been demanded, but when Knebworth entered the room again it was to relay a telephone message.

"That was the hospital, m'lady." Everyone looked up. "Mr. Weatherby has recovered consciousness and has asked if he might see your ladyship."

Keziah clasped her hands together. "He's better. I knew he'd be better. Can I come with you, Jane?"

Knebworth gave a slight cough, as if in apology. "The person speaking for the hospital emphasized that Mr. Weatherby might have only one visitor. He is still very weak."

"Oh . . . but would you like me to drive you, Jane? I can wait outside."

Knebworth again coughed, to preface, "I shall be going

into town, m'lady, as usual, for the stores." He spoke with an interrogatory note. Jane looked up at him and smiled slightly.

"Oh, I think I'm fit to drive. Thank you, Knebworth. I can take the Peugeot. It'd be much easier than your waiting for me when I don't know how long I shall be. And Kizzy, it's sweet of you but I really shall be all right and it's better if you stay here." She did not explicitly say, Guy needs you more than Marcus does, but Keziah smiled, acquiesced, and finished her coffee.

"Would you like me along for company? I don't think anyone needs me here." Grizel shot a quelling green glare at Bone, sensing his inner protest. She looked even more than usually delectable this morning, in a black wool tunic over a white shirt with a little frill at the neck, giving her the air of something naughty out of a choir school.

Jane relaxed suddenly with a real smile. "Yes, that would be nice, if you don't mind sitting about, and if Robert really can spare you."

"Robert does not expect me to live in his pocket. He'll find things to do here."

Find the murderer, he thought. But though it might be far-fetched, it was impossible to preclude the idea of Jane herself as the one he had to find.

Angela suddenly spoke. "We can't go *on* living here, Jane. I'd like to go soon." She sounded as though she meant to spring up and dash through the park at once, but she was still arranging the scrambled egg decoratively on the blue and white plate, and had evidently not heard what was being discussed. Baz looked embarrassed, even anxious, and his quick look went to Keziah. Bone got the idea that Baz would be happy to stay on, and that Guy had perhaps even more problems than he knew.

"No, don't think about that just yet," Jane said with decision. "There will be plenty of time to talk and settle what we're all going to do when I come back. It needs talking about properly." She added with Machiavellian cunning, "Benet wouldn't have wanted you both to rush away, I know . . . I'll be back by lunchtime, but if anyone needs anything from town, Knebworth will add it to his list."

Knebworth confirmed this with an inclination of the head, and moved to open the door for Jane and Grizel, and followed them out. Knebworth's assumption that when he was present no one must open a door for themselves was, Bone supposed, the remnant of a system in which one rang for the footman to put coal on the fire. What would he do about taking Adrian's clothes to the cleaners? If Adrian intended to storm out today, he wouldn't want to come back to collect his clothes; he must plan to have Jane pay the bill; did he plan also for her to pay to have them sent after him? Had he left already? To storm out last night would have been more dramatic.

Bone, just in time preventing himself from stacking his plates, stood up. Keziah, pouring Angela more coffee, smiled at him warmly and said, "If you see Guy anywhere, do tell him breakfast is nearly over. Things won't be nice left too long on the hotplate."

Bone promised, and met in the hall Mrs. Knebworth, in brown and aproned like some Beatrix Potter mouse, wheeling the trolley that squealed over the marble en route for the breakfast room. Very likely, with her husband absent on the weekly shopping trip, she might well be on a tight schedule which Guy's lateness would disturb. Bone himself, rather than lingering over coffee, wanted to check on whether Guy was pursuing Adrian.

How to do this he was not quite sure. He knew where Adrian's room was. A knock on the door and an inquiry after Adrian's plans would be most likely to provoke a vituperative command to mind his own business. Adrian

would by now, as Guy had thought, have contacted someone who was prepared to put him up. His looks guaranteed
a queue willing to be conned for the privilege of Dorian
Gray's company. He must even have, when he chose to
exercise it, charm as well as looks, unless Roke had valued
him purely as tease material both for himself and as an
exasperation to others.

Bone, having climbed the beautiful sweep of stairs down
which Roke had staggered, was drawn to the Japanese
gallery once more, and opened the door and stared around.
He did not really expect to see the murderer revisiting the
scene of the crime, an action held by some authorities to be
an irresistible temptation. What he did see was surprising
enough. Hugo and Jeremy, early breakfasters, were
crouched by the door from gallery to library. They turned
their heads as he came in, simultaneously made a sound like
a dying cobra, and put fingers to lips. It was Hugo, by virtue
of seniority, who had the vantage point by the keyhole.

Bone knew at once what was happening and cursed
himself for not having thought of it before. He had shut the
gallery door softly and was advancing when Jeremy reached
past Hugo's head, turned the handle, and hurled the door
open, leaping past the crouched Hugo, who fell backwards,
and yelling, "Thief! Thief! Got you!" Hugo, scrambling up,
was after him, joining the cry with, "Thief! Those books
belong to Marcus!"

Bone, halfway to the door, hesitated between following
the boys or turning back to cut Adrian off on the landing, for
Adrian was running with an airline bag. By the time he had
decided to turn back, the rapid substratum of his thoughts
continued blame at not having foreseen what Adrian would
of course do; that he would see the books as morally—but
was that the word, given the nature of the books?—his.

On the landing the boys, hallooing with excitement,
hared across and into the gold drawing room. Bone sup-

posed Adrian must be making for the conservatory and the stairs to the pool, from which doors opened onto the garden and the drive. He must have some plan of escape. Had he a burden of books with him? Had the boys forced him to abandon them? Bone was already following them when he smelled burning. A billow of smoke came from the open library door onto the landing, as if in pursuit of the robber. Adrian had certainly had a plan. Bone turned back because he must.

The chase went on without him. Hugo caught the conservatory door that Adrian tried to slam in his face, but slipped on the wet stone. Jeremy hurtled down the sweep of stair after Adrian, shouting, "Stop him!"

Keziah had just brought the alligator's meat from the store. She had undone the latches of the railing, and straightened up at the noise, but before she could assess the situation Jeremy had caught up. He flung himself at Adrian shouting, "You *bloody* thief!" and Adrian, caught by the arm, turned with distorted face and flailed the airline bag around into Jeremy's ribs.

Jeremy lost balance, half-winded. His feet went from under him and he fell backwards with a great splash into Dundee's pool as Adrian reached the glass doors and was out on the drive.

Dundee, interested, slid into the water from his rock. Jeremy came up whooping for air, disoriented. He saw Hugo reaching for him and kicked out for the edge.

"Don't splash, idiot."

Keziah was flinging Dundee's ration to the back of the pool. It distracted him. He engulfed one gobbet and half turned toward another. Jeremy reached Hugo just as Dundee decided that the larger object in his pool was more worthwhile. Keziah scored a hit on the side of his jaw with a slab of lights and he slowed to snap it up. Hugo heaved Jeremy half out and dragged him onto the stone.

"Get after him!" Jeremy yelled ungratefully, as Dundee quested along below his dangling leg. Hugo rolled him to safety. A car started up at the far end of the terrace and Hugo shot out of the doors and was gone. Jeremy, on all fours on the margin, threw up.

Hugo saw Knebworth's usual transport being furiously backed with a scattering of gravel. He ran toward it without hope of catching up, staring with lethal rage at the blond head of the driver. In the distance Guy was sitting astride his machine aimlessly and Hugo stopped, drew breath, and yelled with all the force he could muster, "Guy! STOP him! STOP him!"

The ringing shout certainly reached Guy, who turned to look. He saw Hugo's pointing arm and Adrian at the wheel, and he revved up, turned in a tight arc, and picked up speed as Adrian wrenched the car around the corner and passed the kitchen door, with its posse of hopeful press and TV reporters on the yard bench. The car squealed around the next corner to the front of the house. Guy cut across the gravel and along the flags of the terrace, down the steps by the porch, across the fine turf of the lawn, and was alongside as Adrian swirled down the drive. The media, very pleased, joined Hugo in a skein that strung out as various states of fitness told on speed, a long-legged young woman well to the fore, heading across misty parkland.

Guy, living dangerously, had got ahead and was weaving, forcing Adrian to slow down. A curve in the drive offered a shortcut over the grass, bypassing Guy on his machine, toward the gates; Adrian swung the wheel. He had not taken into account that rough grass plays Wee Eppie Daidle on suspension and steering, and that Guy was perfectly at home on the stuff; nor, as he was jolted, and fought the wheel, and tried to avoid the passes of the roaring bike, did he sort out where he was being herded to. While hitting Guy would cause him no qualm at all, he had to consider the impact's effect on himself. The ground here was so rough that he was shaken about and could see only in disconnected snatches; moreover there was patchy mist. He saw Guy veer aside, accelerated to pass him, and ran his right headlight, wing, and offside front into the Blasted Oak.

There was an almighty reverberation overhead as the photographer from the *Blastock Gazette* shot from his perch and rebounded from the car roof.

Hugo, the long-legged woman, a legman from London, and Baz arrived simultaneously. They found a dazed photographer in the grass, already checking his camera's safety; Guy inquiringly peering in at Adrian, and Adrian inside fighting to open the car door. The rear hatch had sprung wide, and his clothes for the cleaner were mixed with gumboots and a burst bottle of windscreen fluid. He was now in panic, screaming, "Get me out! *Get me out!*"

Cameras whizzed as the media caught up. Baz wrestled with the nearside door, but it was locked.

"I'm hurt." Adrian's outrage at this discovery made him plaintive, but Guy, looking through the driver's window, suddenly roared, "Turn the ignition off, you bloody fool!"

Baz was climbing into the car through the boot, but Adrian seemed oblivious of it, still crying, "Get me out! Oh God, get me out! I'll tell you everything!"

"Turn the *ignition* off."

"Get me out—"

"Hoog, you get away. Get right back." Guy was wheeling the Harley out of range as he shouted. "Everybody stand clear. Get back."

The media spread out with apprehensive speed. Baz had reached Adrian and was manhandling him toward the passenger door as well as he could for the head restraints. Baz's long arm unlocked the door and Hugo pulled it open. As Baz scrambled back, Adrian fell out gasping, bleeding down the right leg, and staggered upright. Hugo ducked past him into the car, grabbed the airline bag, and was promptly slung six yards away by a raging Guy with, "Don't you ever do anything you're told?"

"I was getting—"

Guy propelled him back farther. With a vast, undignified WHOOMPF the car burst into flame. Above it, the Blasted Oak crackled and became a tower of fire.

Across the grass pounded wet Jeremy, fleet Keziah, Bone running strongly. There was a distant sound of a fire engine.

"My God, half my *clothes* were in there! And my bag!" Adrian, bent over, holding his knee, stared horrified at the blaze. He came upright and turned on Guy. "At least it isn't my car. What the hell were you playing at? You damn near killed me!"

Bone said, "We had best get back to the house and sort things out."

Adrian pointed to the bonfire and complained to Bone, "Half my clothes were in there. And I want to make a charge of dangerous driving."

Guy had set off to circle the fire and collect his machine. He stopped and gazed at Adrian. Hugo said, "Oh yes, and what about you, going to tell us 'everything'? Was it about this?" He was delighted with himself, holding the bag in his arms.

"We'll go back to the house," Bone said. His tone had such conviction that feet involuntarily moved. The party set off in loose formation, Adrian limping. The photographer from the tree, very pale, was also limping, and tenderly held his rump now and then. He was heard to say that his jacket had been in that tree. He turned for another picture.

"Poor old Blasted," said Jeremy.

The party from the house, under a barrage of questions, were silent, even Adrian, miraculously, not speaking. Keziah helped him along and he leaned on her, but she was grave and offered no condolences or promise of first aid. The boys, Guy now puttering beside them all, were full of suppressed questions. The media did not suppress, but were not answered. Bone wondered why Jeremy was wet, why Baz's knees and trainers were drenched in bluish fluid.

The fire engine had reached the gates. Bone said to Guy, "Would you go and tell them not to be sidetracked by the burning car? The library floor is the important thing."

"The library floor?" Guy looked at Bone, drew breath, and set off once more down the drive.

"The library floor?" the reporters took up the cue in vain.

Inside the house, with the door shut against the reluctant media, Babel broke out.

"Why the library floor?"

"Guy was fantastic!"

"I could have been killed!"

Bone looked at Adrian. He said, "You'd best be quiet." He went to the hall telephone. Prior's number had been written on the pad beside it and he dialed. When he got through to Prior he said his name; before he could speak Prior said, "Glad you called, Super. You'll be interested to hear we have a full confession to Roke's killing from Donald Spencer."

Chapter

. . . .

31

As Bone put the receiver down, he heard an outburst of voices from the blue drawing room, where the others had gone. He stood for a moment, absently looking at the telephone, so sleek in its cradle, hearing Prior's voice full of triumph. He hardly took in Jeremy, peeling off his soaked jersey, going upstairs, or the sounds of the firemen reaching the library by the backstairs. He ought to go up there and have a word with them . . . but it wasn't his business. He heard Mrs. Knebworth speaking to them, and a horrendous noise as old floorboards were wrenched up to check for smoldering beams underneath. It was not his business. He had no responsibility here.

Donald Spencer had confessed. Bone visualized the round, pale blue eyes behind the pebble lenses, focused on Prior while the questions were aimed at him to break him down. In any war of nerves Spencer would come without a shield. Time spent reading the letters of his drowned daughter, brooding over why she had died, was not going to render him proof to Prior's bludgeons and darts. Prior had used such tactics on Bone, a man of superior rank to him even if without local influence; he was not likely to spare anyone he had a decent chance of bullying without reprisal. Bone had very much disliked the necessity of taking Spencer's letter to Prior; it had brought this about.

Bone realized he was questioning the truth of Spencer's confession. His instinct was against it, even though he had not talked to Spencer himself; even though the letter to Roke contained a threat.

May in the photograph, the wispy girl with those same round blue eyes—she had incorporated Roke into her fantasy world as a lover. So might Donald cast him as villain in his own realm of imagination. Bone's instinct might well be at fault. He should not base an estimate on a photograph and a room, an aunt's story and a few paintings. Roke could have been the lover, even if only for one time on that make-believe night, of the pathetic May. Spencer might in fact have killed him. There was no knowing what the other letters had said. As always, it was what they had made Spencer believe that counted, and not the facts that now could never be known.

Thoughts are swift. Bone's musings had taken seconds. At this point the door of the blue drawing room was abruptly opened, and Adrian came out and was at once snatched back by one arm. The door slammed, making one of the portraits rattle on the wall, then was jerked open and emitted Guy. He marched across the hall and down toward the telephone, started at seeing Bone, and, perhaps to cover the start, announced, "I'm calling the police. I'm not letting that little shit get away with it." As he extended his hand toward the phone, the door opened yet again but, instead of Bone's subliminal vision of an undie-clad soubrette followed by a trouserless vicar followed by his battle-axe wife, there issued in just as rapid succession Adrian, Baz, and Keziah. At the same time, Knebworth emerged from the kitchen regions and came past Bone, but whatever he intended, his measured pace certainly proved too slow for him to open the front door for Adrian, who skillfully managed the feat for himself and tore out, Baz a close second, Keziah's plait all but horizontal as she followed. A wreath of fog and a half question from a surprised press-man lay on the air. Then Hugo floundered out.

Guy, with a wordless shout, dashed after them and, on cue, the phone rang.

Knebworth altered course but Bone had picked it up automatically, incapable of letting a telephone ring.

"Robert! You magicked yourself to the right place." Grizel's voice came warm and lively to his ear. "Jane asked me to ring. We're coming back. Just waiting to see the consultant, who's on his rounds. Marcus is under sedation now."

"How is he?"

"They're really pleased with him. He tried to talk. He's terribly weak, of course, but they think he's stabilized. He seemed to respond when Jane told him it was all right about the books, that they're his to do as he likes with. Poor soul, it was working on him. I believe he thought he was going to die with theft on his conscience."

There was noise from the firemen leaving the library and tramping down the backstairs, and also confused shouting outdoors, coming with the smell of mist. Knebworth stood holding the door and trying to see what was going on, unwilling to shut out the cold when the family was out there too.

"When he's had some sleep," Grizel said, "he may be

able to talk. We don't know. He's recovering in a room on his own off the main ward, being monitored."

"Can we expect you soon, then?"

"How nice that you sound so hopeful. Yes. *Soon.*" There was a kiss noise and she rang off. He felt invigorated.

As Adrian, flushed and twisting in the grasp of both Baz and Guy, made a reappearance, Bone came forward into the hall.

"I was about to ring the police, to get someone here to deal with this theft and fire raising," Bone said. "My wife rang first. Marcus is under sedation in a room on his own now; she and Jane can leave him and they're coming back."

"How is he?" Keziah pushed past and came forward.

Bone shook his head. "He tried to talk. It seems he's had something on his mind. They think he might be more collected this evening when he's had some sleep."

The Laocoön group of his audience stared at him. That Marcus was alive, perhaps even capable of talking, transcended the present squabble. Adrian stopped struggling for a moment, his golden hair in a swath over one eye, his cashmere sweater making an effort to settle in graceful folds where it had been grabbed at and hauled about.

Bone wondered if Adrian had hoped Marcus would die and the books by some magic become his. Adrian had as oblique a sense of reality as had Donald Spencer or his daughter. The books had been promised him once, so they were his. How many people could face life without a generous layer of comfortable self-justifying?

"You can't prosecute me." Adrian, still not having got his breath back, twisted to glare at Guy. "You don't own the books. You don't even have the right to give orders here." He spoke with viperish intensity, pushing his face at Guy. Guy, recoiling as though struck by venom, dropped Adrian's arm and, turning, flung open the front door and was out into the fog, through a hopeful blaze of flash, and out of sight. Baz let go of Adrian's other arm and stood looking down at him, contempt on his big handsome face, Michelangelo's David meeting the smell of Renaissance sewers.

"You're nothing but a rat. Nobody wants you. You get out of here."

Adrian threw his hair back vigorously and combed it with one hand. Bone noticed the raw red mark on his thumb. The blood on his ripped trouser leg also testified to the yet untended graze; it was a mark of Keziah's disapproval that Adrian's leg had not received the Florence Nightingale treatment.

"I certainly don't want to stay. This place is no fun without Roke."

It was a tribute from an unexpected quarter, an epitaph. Adrian, having delivered it, walked with some dignity, remembering belatedly to limp, out after Guy. The distant leopard-cough announced that Guy had taken to his usual solace.

"Should we have stopped him?" Baz asked. "I mean, theft and fire raising, you said."

"He pushed Jeremy into Dundee's pool. I don't think that he meant to," said Keziah, ever careful to be just, "but he didn't care."

Baz cocked his head. "Hope that's his own car this time."

Keziah said, "I hope we've seen the last of him."

Bone came to life. Had he been dreaming? He strode out of the door into the blank whiteness of fog, hearing a car go carefully down the drive. The media seemed to have drawn off, perhaps to find shelter, perhaps in pursuit of Adrian. He came back, making for the phone, saying as he went, "And Jane and Grizel are coming home. They won't be there."

The hospital number was on the ledge by the phone, in

Jane's handwriting. He prodded the numbers out. The ringing tone went on interminably, it seemed.

"Blastock General."

"This is the police. I am Detective Superintendent Robert Bone. I want the chief nursing officer." Bone used rank without regard to his local standing.

"I'll call him, sir. We're on emergency stand-by."

Bone said, "Emergency?" to a dead line. After a moment he was put through, and made his request for Marcus Weatherby to be kept isolated, without visitors.

"I'll do my best," said a Welsh voice. "This motorway pile-up has us on alert and I'm short-handed at the best of times. I'll see the ward sister's informed."

"It's a matter—"

"Leave it with me, sir. I must ask you to clear the line. You'll understand."

Bone put the receiver down. Keziah had come inquiringly up and he caught hold of her hand. "Quick. You must show me the way to the hospital. My car's in the stable yard."

She came, towed after him. "But if Marcus is under sedation, what's happening?"

Although firing questions, she was still obedient enough to run alongside and to get into his car as Bone slid behind the wheel and rammed the key into the ignition. *Lucky*, he thought as he set off, *that I didn't leave my car out on the gravel with the keys in, as Knebworth did. By now, it might be this car which concerned the insurance company.* The firemen and their pump were now dealing with that around the remains of the tree, seen suddenly in an open patch. The fog lay as in a Far Eastern picture, wreathed across the landscape, thick in the hollows, clear for long spaces.

Despite his sense of urgency, Bone forced himself to go slow through the gates, picturing the cold stare of the eagles above. As he looked either way before turning out, he imagined what a lick Adrian might have gone at through here if Guy hadn't cut him off. Perhaps he'd have fetched an eagle down on the bonnet, or with a little luck it would have emulated the photographer and, being weightier, have come through the roof and brained him.

These unworthy thoughts were interrupted by Keziah, leaning forward at his side, tensely pressing her hands together. "Take the left turn at the bottom here, it's quicker. I know the other one says Blastock, but it goes by the motorway."

"Where there's already been a pile-up." Bone took the village street and the left turn faster than he'd gone through a built-up area in years, faster than since his patrol car days when he'd chased after laddies not eager for police attention. There were moments of those times he didn't want to remember, one of them sharply brought back by Adrian's encounter with the tree, an image he'd had to avoid: the boy with blond hair not unlike Adrian's, on the run, on drugs, speeding from smashing up an old man to smashing up himself on a lamp standard. There'd been no Baz to get him out in time. Bone's partner had been driving. A patch of fog loomed white suddenly. He slowed, edging through it; sped on where the road was clearer; slowed again as whiteness loomed, watchful for side roads that could eject a howling motorbike.

He had not answered Keziah. She said, "It's Marcus, isn't it? Is he dying?"

Bone wrenched the wheel as, out of the fog, an elderly woman appeared on a bicycle with a Yorkshire terrier navigating from the front basket. She had turned out from a side lane with no apparent thought about other traffic. Keziah swayed toward him to the limit of her seat belt, and back as he regained his side of the road. In his rear mirror the woman disappeared at once, swallowed by fog.

"Yes, it's Marcus." Taking advantage of a clear patch,

Bone, calculating swiftly, pulled out and passed a huge truck toiling toward a hill where he would be stuck behind it. "If we're quick . . ."

Keziah leaned forward, working her own invisible accelerator. She shivered suddenly and Bone, realizing that he had snatched her from the house without time to get a coat, reached to turn up the heater. The trees loomed and vanished like tall ghosts, keeping the fog from the road though it was twined in their branches. They flung leaves petulantly against the windscreen.

"Guy . . . You don't think Guy did it, do you? He's been in such a state."

A red sports car grew large behind them, panted on their tail, swinging out and back, then regardless of possible fog on a descending turn ahead, pulled out. Bone, pumping the brake, prayed for nothing to be on its way up the hill as the red coupe scorched past. It cut in with barely time to avoid a van heaving up. To a prolonged burst from the van's horn, Bone answered Keziah, trying to soothe her; no need for her to get upset before she had to.

"Guy has every reason to be in a state. Whatever he felt about Roke, he was his father."

On consideration, not a good remark if Guy had put an arrow through him. Keziah was not soothed.

"You see, he thinks it's Jane—there's a T-junction ahead into a main road. Go right—Guy's so afraid his mother did it. He told me."

The junction was modern, with tall lights like flowers in the fog, strings of traffic crawling behind headlights from the right. Bone judged speeds and launched across, scolded by a white MG. Keziah let go of the grab bar and sat back.

"It's not as if he liked or wanted the castle. I don't think anyone but Benet was keen on it. He minds about Baz in a different way. Because he's so suddenly happened, I suppose. And he minds for Jane. I do wish Angela had come years ago, or not yet at all . . . But it's Marcus you're thinking of. Poor Marcus, it's such an inexplicable thing; do you think he'll know how he came to be down that horrible hole?"

"He may not. He may have traumatic amnesia."

"It's very odd, but when Benet was there it seemed quite natural to have an oubliette in the place, and an alligator, and the trick waterworks—"

"Trick *waterworks?*"

"You remember, Benet mentioned them at dinner. He said they were out of order, but I wouldn't be too sure. We come into the town by a roundabout. The third exit leads fairly straight to the hospital. It'll be on the left, a big white building, you can't miss it."

"Miss anything in this stuff."

"I should think it'll have all its lights on . . . You do know it *couldn't* be Jane. Not possibly. It must be someone on the tour who did it. I'm sure of it."

Her conviction, and Prior's telephone call, were in his mind as he swung into the hospital drive, and was held up by two pushchair-propelling women lingering to compare either their babies or their symptoms. They scuttled aside as he sounded the horn. Keziah was out of the car as soon as he parked.

Nurses in outdoor clothes were hurrying in. The place had a sense of urgent activity, voices echoing, controlled haste.

"Is this because of the motorway thing?" Keziah hurried ahead down aseptic corridors. "It wasn't like this earlier on."

"What's the ward?"

"The Alexander Fleming. Marcus was in there yesterday." Keziah trotted ahead, her plait swinging, looking Indian with her layers of clothes and floating chiffon and ornate complicated silver earrings, the gray rubber floor and cream walls a foil to her flying brilliance. Bone followed, with the cramp of aversion in his stomach at the well-remembered smell of disinfectant, the shadowless glare of strip lighting. In hospital they'd told him of Petra's death, of their child's death; they'd lied to him about Charlotte. Amazing now, when people were not left to die in their own beds but taken to hospital to die in brutally alien surroundings, that people didn't run screaming out of here pursued by resentful and bewildered spirits.

"It's this way." Keziah's word was borne out by a notice on the wall. A male nurse trundled a slumped old man past in a wheelchair, glancing at them without curiosity; their air of haste and purpose made it plain they had legitimate business here. Bone felt oppressed, as if he ran through sand. They would not reach Marcus in time.

"Here we are. Alexander Fleming. Marcus is in this—"

Bone saw the arrowed notice pointing to the left. As they approached it at a run, Adrian emerged. He was combing his hair back with one hand as he turned to walk away down the corridor, when he caught sight of them.

He was galvanized. He broke into a run, and Bone, shouting to Keziah, "Get a nurse! See to Marcus!" ran after him.

The corridor echoed to the drum of their feet. Adrian turned a corner so fast that he nearly fell, but he recovered, and Bone for a moment despaired of catching up; the nightmare effluvia of disinfectant and the underlying sourness it did not ever quite hide seemed to choke him, slow him down. At the intersection were notices: "Lifts," "Physio," "Emergency Exits," "X-rays," "Visitors' Toilets." A woman was coming out of the visitors' toilets farther down the corridor Adrian had turned into, putting something in her handbag.

"Jane!" Bone's voice rang in the space. "Stop him!"

Jane, startled, looked up as Adrian ran full tilt toward

her, swerving to avoid her intervention. A hospital porter appeared, trundling a trolley loaded with bottles and containers, rattling like a milk float as he made his way to the lifts. Jane seized the side of the trolley and as the porter struggled to regain control she slammed it across Adrian's path. He tried to dodge, but his own impetus was his undoing and carried him over the bows of the trolley, scattering bottles and making him whoop as the bar caught him in the wind. Still with the startled porter protesting and hanging on, Jane pulled it back. Adrian, his balance gone, staggered. She drove it hard at him again and sent him crashing into the wall, where she held him, rammed by the trolley and gasping with the blow to his back.

The porter still scolded. "What're you trying on? Who d'you think you are?"

"I'm a police officer." Bone had laid a firm hand on the trolley that corralled Adrian, who had recovered enough to try pushing it away. "This man is wanted on suspicion of theft and fire raising."

"*Fire raising?*" Jane cried.

"Police?" The porter, his small sharp face affronted, was not impressed. "You'll have to settle that with the CNO. I want the trolley. There's an *emergency* on, I'd have you know." He wrested the trolley to himself as Bone took Adrian by the arm; Jane whirled her handbag with menace.

"You bloody take your hands off me—I'll have you for assault." Adrian fought, with the violent energy of indignation.

"He's all right!" Keziah rounded the corner, running toward them, chiffon floating. "Marcus will be all right."

Adrian gave a convulsive, serpentine twist and Jane slung her handbag into his midriff. Keziah reached them, to cry as he bowed over, holding his diaphragm and crowing, "He tried to kill Marcus! Pulled out the tubes and things—but I got the nurse and he's all right again." Her fists were bunched, and she glared at Adrian's bent head with its hanging curtain of hair as he coughed and retched. "You murderer."

Grizel appeared from the stairs, carefully carrying two plastic cups. She stopped dead when she saw them, the coffee slopping simultaneously from each cup.

"What on earth—?"

The porter, with his thumb on the lift button, the trolley at the ready, called to her, "They're mad, the lot of them. Don't you have nothing to do with them." The lift doors parted; he wrenched the trolley in and turned it smartly to give them a parting glare as the doors closed on him. "Mad."

Grizel came up, wondering, carrying the cups as though she had forgotten what they were for, to be greeted by Keziah with, "He's a murderer! He tried to kill Marcus."

The screaming bray of an ambulance siren came nearer and stopped as it reached the hospital grounds. Adrian raised his head, face scarlet with rage and lack of breath, but he was still speechless when Bone, keeping his grip on the arm, pulled up Adrian's hand and showed the raw patch on his thumb.

"That's where the bowstring marked him. He may not have killed Marcus but it certainly looks as though he killed Benet. That's what happens to an archer who's not wearing a thumb guard."

Adrian came almost upright. He had regained his breath, and looked from one to another with astonishment; when he spoke, it was clear that his astonishment was not for the accusation of murder.

"He said I was *boring!* He said *I had become a bore!*"

Chapter

....

32

THE LIFT DOORS OPENED AND, ON CUE, TWO USEFULLY LARGE policemen stepped out; the porter's complaint of madmen and women in combat on the first floor, of the subversion of his trolley into a guided missile, had brought this response from men who had accompanied the ambulance. His complaint might have been disregarded, in face of the emergency, but for a call from the ward sister about an intruder who had tampered with a patient's drips. Marcus had suffered a setback but was not in acute danger.

Eventually Adrian was removed to the station. The others followed; they had to give statements about events at the hospital, and then the women went home. Grizel made a game effort to stay; she could, she said, shop for paperbacks and then sit in the café opposite the station—while Bone, after a private word with Prior, was then at his joyful invitation, silent observer of the interrogation of Adrian.

The session, duly taped, had been remarkable for Adrian's incredulity. Bone was strongly reminded of John McEnroe's classic address to the umpire at Wimbledon: "You cannot be serious!" Adrian seemed unable to conceive of any part of his behavior as culpable. The phenomenon was not new. Bone could remember a score of instances where a charge had been greeted with the equivalent of, "Well, I had to do it, didn't I?" Faced with the unthinkable option of their own suffering or loss, however minor, such people hadn't contemplated it for more than one disparaging moment. Someone else had paid.

Adrian's verbal writhings, his evasions and lies, did not upset Prior. With acute interest and dreadful good humor he persisted, caught up the lies, turned them right side out and presented Adrian with what he had been saying, and greeted the further excuses with every sign of enjoyment. A sergeant came from interviewing Marcus, but he was not yet able to give more than ambiguously vague answers. "It was not just the books . . . He was afraid of me in case the books weren't enough." The medical authorities had then over-ruled those of the law, and a PC had been marooned there to wait until Marcus could talk again. Bone was hoping for confirmation of what he had suggested to Prior before the interview with Adrian began.

Adrian's circumnavigations became so involved that Prior had sat back, grinning around his deadly cheroot, and let him talk. Somewhere in the thick of justification it appeared that while Marcus had had "a sort of thing" about Adrian, had "sort of fancied" him, Adrian, not being gay although people did tend to think, because of his looks, which after all he couldn't very well help because that's the way they were, had let Marcus know, nicely because gays were sensitive people and Adrian was a person who was naturally kind, that it was no go; Lord Roke had artistic values, which Adrian shared—Bone thought the only value Adrian was anxious to share was that of the erotic collection. Adrian now said that he did not think Marcus was spiteful although he had obviously got at Lord Roke to leave him the books when they'd been promised to Adrian.

"But," said Prior, his eyes blank, "didn't Lord Roke say he was bored with you?"

Adrian, negligently tilting his chair, used a puzzled frown, as of one not quite sure he had heard, while his lips moved and his gaze strayed, sorting rapidly through possibilities. Having started with incredulity, he reverted to it: "He didn't mean it, of course. That was just Benet for you."

With impenetrable belief in this, he contradicted the semi-admission he had made at the hospital, climbed on his high horse, and got ready for another gallop. It was at this point that Sergeant Williams came in with a message from the hospital: Marcus Weatherby had managed to say some more. The front feet of Adrian's chair hit the floor. He had to catch at the table edge to steady himself.

Mr. Weatherby was very distressed; he had been forced to provide a false alibi for Mr. Nash, who had found out that he had been secretly selling books belonging to Lord Roke and had used this to blackmail him. He had heard Mr. Nash and Lord Roke's voices next door in the gallery, though not what they said, and then a sound he later realized must have been the bow. He had been expecting Mr. Nash to tell Lord Roke about the books but instead, Mr. Nash had come in and said he would tell no one about the books if Mr. Weatherby would swear he'd never left the library.

Prior made a thumbs-up sign at Bone and, leaning forward, said, "Adrian Nugent Nash, you are charged with the murder of Lord Roke . . ."

* * *

Bone drove back to Roke Castle toward evening. He saw lights through the mist as he came along the drive. The remains of the car had been dislodged from the Blasted Oak, which no longer smoldered. At the porch, a lone reporter braving the chill and mist stood up and asked without much hope if Bone had any news. "What was it Nash was on about with his *I'll tell you everything?*"

"It could be that Chief Inspector Prior at Blastock may have some news," Bone said, and rang the bell.

Knebworth must have been fairly close to the door, for he opened it before Bone had a chance to deny more than once that he had anything to say. Bone stepped into the hall, and Jane came hurrying from the blue drawing room to welcome him, with Grizel at her heels. The sight of Grizel, her gleaming short bright hair, her cat face, her searching gaze, seemed to bring Bone into the present again, out of speculation, out of his professional world.

"Come into the warm and tell it all." Bone, his arm around his wife, let himself be drawn into the warmth. He could smell both the scent of her skin and the applewood fire burning on the hearth. It surprised him to find he was cold and tired.

"Yes," he said, turning to face Jane. "Prior's charged him with Benet's murder."

She shut her eyes for a moment. Then she said, "I always hoped it was him. I was just terrified that . . . one doesn't really know even one's own family. What made you think Adrian *did*?"

"Marcus and he gave each other alibis." If the case had been his all along, Bone thought, he would not have accepted Prior's neat theory of Lawson killing Roke and tumbling to his death thereafter; he would have inquired more closely into the convenience of Marcus and Adrian's shared alibi. "I guessed Adrian had already found out about

Marcus taking the books—probably to pay for his father's keep at that expensive nursing home—"

"He should have asked Benet! He would have helped, I know he would; but he could be so intimidating. I suppose Marcus didn't dare to talk. But why did Adrian suddenly want to kill him?"

"Adrian must have suspected he was going to scarper. Marcus wasn't the type to sustain a lie, and Adrian, who's razor-sharp about his own interests, must have been keeping a watch on him; and followed him on Sunday night and hit him on the head." Bone turned to Grizel. "That was the blood on the grating; it got there when he pushed him down the oubliette."

"Just a minute," Jane said. "There's Knebworth in the hall. I'm in need of Benet's panacea." She went swiftly to the door and called to Knebworth, and it was Grizel who pursued, "Why was Marcus there at all, though? He must have known the place was dangerous."

"I think he was heading for a door away from where anyone would hear the warning noise the alarm makes before it's turned off or blasts off. There's one at the garage door at the end of that passage beyond the oubliette. Marcus most likely meant to turn off the alarm, reset it, and go out without disturbing anyone."

Jane heard this as she came back. "He must have done that when he went off in a hurry last year. The time he left a note. It didn't occur to me."

Grizel was shaking Bone by the arm. "So you knew, when Marcus was attacked, that it had to be Adrian?"

"That's why I dragged Keziah off to the hospital in such a hurry when I couldn't be sure of Marcus' safety. Once Adrian knew he might talk, and he did know thanks to my saying so, and he knew that you two had left Marcus alone, or so we thought, in a room by himself . . . a gift."

He sank down on the sofa opposite the fire, still linked to Grizel, who moved with him as if she were a Siamese twin.

"Has Adrian admitted he did it?"

"Prior will put pressure on, I imagine. That's something he knows how to do."

"Yes, I suppose it can be left to Prior."

Bone had heard the implied superiority in his remark about Prior, and was glad she had missed it.

"That horrible little man." Jane perched herself on the arm of the other sofa, next to the fire. A relaxation about her showed how tense she had been in these last days. "He may be good at his job or he may not, but he is repellent. He asked me the rudest questions about Benet—things I can't see were necessary. I wanted to *kick* him." She gave a half-involuntary jerk of one long leg and her shoe came off. Bone smiled.

"That's precisely why he'll get places with Adrian. Rude remarks provoke our golden lad, if what he said is true."

"I can so well imagine Benet saying that to him. Adrian is a crashing bore. What I don't see is why Adrian should react like that all of a sudden. Benet *constantly* said things of that sort to absolutely everyone. Adrian was forever bridling at some dig or other." Jane looked into the fire. "I used to console myself with thinking that was why Benet insisted on having him to stay."

They word "insisted" gave Bone a picture of Roke and Jane arguing. If she had won, perhaps Roke would be alive now. He tightened his hold on Grizel's arm and said, "That's how I see it—as a reaction. He must have been angry with Benet over and over again, with no way of getting back at him. I imagine Benet would be impervious to anything Adrian could think up in the way of reply. And then—the insult about being boring. And perhaps he saw in it a coming dismissal from a cushy pad here. And unluckily the chance weapon was there."

Bone thought it possible Adrian had been playing with the bow while Benet talked, but that was not the vision he wanted to present to Jane. They were silent, looking into the fire, seeing that moment in the gallery they had not witnessed, seeing Roke putting on the armor for his joke, with no help from Adrian and turning, irked, to aim his own dart of scorn; Adrian, stung, letting fly the real arrow.

Knebworth opened the door and was there with champagne and the tall glasses. Grizel had said to Bone before this that Knebworth had Jeeves' trick of shimmering in. One became aware of him manifesting rather than entering. Bone had compared it to *Star Trek*. He and Grizel had become hilarious over the idea of Mrs. Knebworth beaming Knebworth up from a console in the kitchen, his molecules assembling where he was wanted.

Jane explained the usual champagne. "To celebrate Adrian's going. Knebworth, Mr. Nash has been arrested for the murder."

Knebworth inclined his head, with a very subtle change of expression. It was clearly not a butler's place to burst into triumphant cackles or a boogie of satisfaction; but Bone would have given something to hear how Knebworth would choose to break the news to Mrs. Knebworth.

"Shall I open the wine, m'lady?"

"Please. You know, Robert, when I think of Benet opening the champagne only—how long ago was it? Only Saturday! Only—three days?" She took the glass from the tray and shook her head as though to deny the possibility of time and event.

Three days and the world changes, thought Bone, watching her in sympathy. *It takes only a minute and you can't recognize your life.* It took only a couple of seconds, nearly five years ago, for that drunk young man to slam his truck into Bone's car. He recalled very clearly the incredulity he had constantly felt during the days in hospital, not so much the *Why me?*

people are said to feel, more a stunned conviction that what had happened couldn't have happened. Charlotte later said the same. Bone's loss of a wife and a baby son had brought him to doubt the existence not of God but of reality. Jane was going to continue waking up and wondering what was wrong for a long time to come, but Bone would not tell her that.

She had turned to Knebworth again. "Do you know where Mrs. North and her son are?"

"I will ascertain, m'lady."

"When you find them, would you ask them to join us here? And are *my* sons anywhere about?"

"I believe Mr. Guy is upstairs talking to Miss Barclay-Mayhew, m'lady, and Master Jeremy is having tea in the kitchen. Master Hugo is playing music in his room."

Knebworth, having geographically placed everyone except for Baz and Angela, set off with measured pace to track them down. Bone supposed that however keen they were to find out what had happened, they would be as anxious as ever not to intrude or to put themselves forward in any way. If Jane hadn't insisted they should stay, they would have dispersed with the rest of the tour.

He wondered very much what would happen about them. He had seen the hearty enjoyment Baz took in Roke's surprises here, and permitted himself a fantasy in which Baz, taking possession of what was rightly his, elaborated on his father's creation with a Gothic Disneyland. He would probably draw the line at skeletons in Japanese armor, a grotesque thought Bone himself instantly banished.

"When we arrived from the hospital this afternoon," Grizel said, "Baz was sitting on the stairs like an outsize waif."

"I believe he didn't want to go and sit in any of the rooms in case it seemed like—oh, like ownership." Jane swung her unshod foot, still looking into the fire. "That's something that has to be sorted out. He says he wants to go back to Australia. But the place is his. The title's his. He certainly was conceived before the divorce was absolute. When Angela and I were having our booze-up the other night, she showed me the papers. There's the date of birth on the certificate, well before Guy's; and a doctor's certificate that he was a full-term baby to the best of his judgment; and Benet's name as the father. And more convincing than absolutely anything is the look of him. Jeremy looks more his brother than Guy's. But Guy—oh, it's insuperable. Yet it has to be sorted out. Traditionally speaking I should clear out after"—she turned to look at them—"after the funeral. In a way I'd be glad to get back to Paisley House. But the tenants there—" She took a deep breath and added, "I don't know."

"You can't know anything at this stage," Grizel said with calm certainty. She had disentangled her arm from Bone's as if she felt the sight of their closeness might be painful for Jane. "Things do seem plainer with time."

Bone had a contradictory picture of Time, the great healer, putting down his scythe after a slashing blow, to fish out some ointment. After all, once it had been inconceivable that he himself should be sitting beside a second wife. As this crossed his mind, the second wife nipped his arm very sharply and said, "Robert could tell you that."

"Oh yes. Absolutely," said Bone at speed, and had started to frame some numbing cliché of life and its disaster-overcoming potential when the door was flung open and Guy rushed in. He looked wild, his dark hair partly on end and partly flopping over one eye, his shirt collar turned up at the side, and his scarlet sweater rucked into folds, suggestive of a one-man wrestling match.

"Is it true? What Kez says? Adrian killed Father?"

"Darling, it really looks like it. He's been arrested."

Guy had stood over his mother in fierce interrogation.

Now he sat down suddenly on the sofa beside her as though his legs had given way, and put his head in his hands. Keziah, who had followed him in, came up close and regarded him with infinite pity. Bone was astonished at his own cynicism to find he had thought she would have looked so over a wounded alligator. Jane, taking a mother's privilege, stroked the thick dark hair.

"It's all right, darling. At least we have one thing to celebrate: Adrian will never come back."

Guy raised his head and looked at the glass Jane was reaching to pour for him. He took it as though he could not work out its meaning or function.

"I didn't think it could be him because I wanted it to be." He looked around him and saw the others, aware of them for the first time. "He was such an obvious bastard." He examined the glass and tested it for content. "Well, thank God we know who it was and he's caught." He drank more deeply. "And I thought he wouldn't have had the guts either, you know?"

Bone knew. He knew too that with murder it could be less a case of not having the guts than of not having what the Bible called bowels. Adrian lacked not courage but feeling. His imagination had never engaged with the reality of anyone else's existence, so it was no moral problem to take a life. Bone had talked to murderers who had, genuinely, no idea what all the fuss was about, and to whom the word "conscience" was without sense. They saw no justice in being punished for what to them had been a simple necessity. *He wouldn't let me have the money, see . . . You understand I had no option . . .*

Guy was staring at Bone now. "Did *you* think he did it? You know about murders, I suppose."

"Robert got him." Grizel, cuddling her husband's arm again, spoke with a pride that startled and warmed him. Past tributes from Chief Constables had not given him such pleasure. "He chased him to the hospital—he thought we'd left, and, in fact, we had left Marcus alone. He and Jane trapped Adrian in a corridor. There was I coming along with the coffee and they'd got him pinned against a wall."

She made it sound quite a cheerful party; at the back of Bone's mind all that time had been the image of Adrian having somehow killed Marcus.

"Pour me more, darling. All around, in fact." As Guy got up to obey, Jane went on, "It's so appalling that a nasty sponging bit of *trash* like Adrian could kill Benet. And do you know why?" Jane's incredulity and indignation came to a head. "Because Benet told him he was boring. It's as if Benet had just realized what any of us could have told him weeks ago; I *had* told him, but he only laughed."

"But why the hospital? What was Adrian doing at the hospital?"

Keziah said, "He tried to kill Marcus." Guy was obviously only more bewildered. He began a question, but the diffident entrance of Angela and Baz made him shut his mouth firmly.

"Jane, Baz and I have been talking—"

"*Don't* talk about it. Not now." Jane had got up, to take Angela's arm and draw her forward into the enclave of sofas and chairs before the fire. "Sit here. And Baz. Benet would have been furious with me if I let you go like that." Her smile included Baz, who came a little awkwardly past Guy to sit where she pointed. "If I know anything about Benet, and I do, and so do you, he'd have wanted you to drink to the arrest of his murderer."

As the exclaiming and explaining broke out all over again, Bone sat down once more next to Grizel, nearly spilling what champagne he had left in his glass. He wondered if Prior, now he had got Adrian in his grasp, had let Donald Spencer go, or was the wretched man still in a cell somewhere, on ice in case Prior couldn't crack Adrian.

He was contemplating this, vaguely aware of another bottle being opened and his own glass being topped up, and then that glasses were being raised and a toast proposed by Jane. He raised his obediently as she spoke.

"To a happy future, wherever it leads us."

They drank, but Baz was inspired by the suggestion in her words to say his piece about clearing out again, under Guy's lowering stare.

"—because I don't want you to think for one minute that I want to take your home from you."

"Oh my God!" Guy was still standing, and now to emphasize his words he thudded one foot down hard on the rug. "When will you—all of you—get it into your heads that *I hate the place!*"

Chapter

······················

33

"I DON'T KNOW HOW HE CAN POSSIBLY HATE IT."

Grizel, a huge tartan rug coiled around her shoulders and muffling her face up to the mouth, hugged her arms against the cold and looked down from the battlements at the grounds of the castle spread beneath. It was a bright morning, but November had now arrived and, almost as if the change of month had an effect on the world, winter was plainly on its way. The brief storm on Sunday had stripped some trees, and the rest were deep in gold and russet. The melancholy shape of the Blasted Oak spread its charred boughs over blackened turf below. Bone, behind her, took her by the elbows and swung her slightly, to the right, to the left. She leaned on him.

"Oh, I don't know. He didn't grow up with it," he said. "Paisley House probably means more. The home of childhood's always more vivid than anywhere." Releasing her, he put a hand on the gritty stone and looked down at the terrace; abruptly recalling the sight of Josh Lawson hanging below, he straightened up, and perhaps the memory determined his choice of words as he said, "A place like this can seem a nightmare, in the way of responsibilities."

"Maintenance and so on." Grizel idly kicked at a dented bucket smeared with dried cement, abandoned in a corner beside a coil of frayed rope. "What happened to the workmen, do you know? The ones who left the gear?"

"I believe Jane put them off. She didn't like to have them clumping about here after what happened." Bone smiled involuntarily; the back of his wife's head emerging from the wrap resembled, more than usually, a day-old chick. "She'd never know, either, who was a genuine workman and who was a reporter who'd bribed his way in."

"*Death Wreaks Havoc at Roke.* What a shame the past tense of *wreak* isn't *wroke*; it'd have made their day."

"I thought *Death Takes a Bow* rather good."

Grizel shivered and Bone put an arm around her swathed shoulders. "You look like the Ilk of that Ilk in this wrap, Kinloch." It was a matter of some pleasure to him that her second name was Kinloch, and he saved it for private occasions. Hugging her reminded him they were nearing the end of their brief, eventful honeymoon.

"I was thinking of poor Benet. I believe I was beginning to like him; anyway, to see why Jane stuck with him for all those years in spite of everything."

"Such as Adrian and alligators."

"Adrian was fairly recent. But yes, if you take Adrian as representing a general range of afflictions . . . It was nice of Prior to ring and tell you he'd got a definite admission out of Adrian." Grizel, Bone's arm around her shoulders still, began to stroll slowly along the leads to the other end of the walk, to the view over the formal gardens. Beyond the hedges where they had seen Lawson creep up on Dr. Rose and his ex-secretary with camera poised, shone the target Roke had set up for archery, bright in the autumn sun as a giant eye.

"Prior was just slightly bragging. He didn't in so many words say I couldn't have broken Adrian down if it'd been my case, but his voice did. He's a clever man. It wouldn't surprise me if he'd flattered Adrian into it."

Grizel stopped and leaned against Bone, her head on his shoulder. "I can't imagine Adrian in prison. What will he do?"

"Refuse to believe in it, I suppose."

"But it won't go away even then."

"He'll find being kept by the State less amusing than being kept by Roke, but he'll discover his own ways of making it easier for himself. People of Adrian's sort—"

"Always land on their feet?" Grizel had tilted her head and the cat-green eyes took on extra light from the sky.

"I was going to say, they find a way of landing on somebody else's. Did you know you're looking particularly fetching today, Kinloch?"

After a few minutes, shrieking from somewhere in the grounds made them think they were observed and it broke up their embrace. Bone thought it unlike the manners of the Paisleys to comment on kissing, and he and Grizel, peering into the distance, perceived the cause of the shrieks to be the drenching of Baz.

Hugo and Jeremy, last heard to be offering Baz a conducted tour of the grounds after breakfast, and last seen departing, in scarlet and green jerseys among the hedges, either side of Baz in sober navy, were now capering and screaming with joy. Even Hugo, the more reserved and mature thirteen, stamped and bent and howled.

There was a long walk, paved along the center, between

hornbeam hedges, and the boys cavorted at either side on the grass, while Baz on the path was caught by two rows of jets from hidden pipes along the pathway. He too was yelling, and hitting the water at the boys; and he bent and deflected a jet full at Jeremy, changing his tune, then he left the path to rush at Hugo, and the water, evidently set off by his tread on the stones, died down and sank away. He hauled off his soaked jersey and flailed at Hugo with it, then leaped the path and wrung out the jersey over Jeremy, helpless with laughter on the other side. After that he seemed to examine the pipes and ask about them, and Hugo came to explain. Next moment he was grabbed by the arm and whirled onto the paving, and the obedient fountains sprang up all along. Baz joined him and began miming a shower, washing under his arms, scrubbing his head.

"Benet's sons for you," Bone said. *"They* knew the waterworks were perfectly in order." Grizel was laughing into her wrap, for the sight was irresistible. When the victim enjoyed himself as Baz did there was no one to be sorry for.

"D'you think he will stay on? Jane seems to want him to, now that Guy's set on his engineering course. I've a definite feeling that Baz is intrigued by the thought of being Lord Roke, not deadly embarrassed as Guy seems to be. Keziah told me Guy announced to his family years ago, when Benet inherited, that he would never use the title, which was a bit rough on her, I think." The boys now set off on a chase, to see some further object of interest or to get dry, involving more yelling.

"Perhaps Jane and Angela will stay here together. They seem to get on better than you'd ever expect. It must be that drink they had together. On the surface they don't seem to have a single thing in common."

"Except Benet."

They had turned and, by common consent, were making

for the door to the backstairs, when Grizel pointed. "What's that glinting?" She stooped, and came up with a small bronze-colored rosette. "Isn't it pretty? It's like a tiny chrysanthemum. I suppose it's off someone's shoe. Not Jane's style, but I suppose it could belong to someone on the tour. I think the lovely Lynda had shoes with something like this on." She held it out to Bone, who took it and was examining it when she picked it out of his hand. "Come on. I want my elevenses, and if you're going to drive you'd better get outside a biscuit or two so you won't be snapping my head off before we can find a pub for lunch . . . I'll show this to Jane, she might recognize it. Or, of course, it might belong to Keziah's Indian sandals."

Bone said nothing, but followed her docilely down the stairs. When they reached the first-floor landing, he took her hand and turned her toward the doors that faced one wing of the great double staircase descending to the front hall.

"Robert, what is it? We don't have to say goodbye to every room; particularly that one." He could feel her resistance, but she came with him all the same.

The gallery, even on that bright morning, was dim, the diffused light from above giving its strange, underwater effect to the objects around the walls, black lacquered armor shining like the carapaces of giant insects, helmets with crescent moons or dagger shapes mounted above the brow, or with huge curving horns rising on either side like Viking coal scuttles. The glass cases down the center shone, trapping the weapons displayed inside. Grizel stayed by the door because for her the room was haunted. She supposed her husband had learned to steel himself to such things.

Her eyes turned at once to the space under the bows and quivers, where a chair was missing, the chair Roke had sat in, the arrow through his neck, before he gathered the strength to stagger out and look for help. On the other side of the big display cabinet was a matching chair. As she glanced at it her heart seemed to stop beating, then to thunder. A figure in full armor, like that Roke had worn, sat there, gauntlets on knees and arms akimbo, staring ahead. A black ferocious mask below the helmet made the armor seem inhabited, but between mask and gorget a dark space did tell her nerves that the armor was empty, that the presence in that chair was created by an armature and not by bones or, worse, by spirit.

Her husband ducked down before this apparition. It looked like homage. He said, "See here."

Grizel took breath, and made herself walk forward. When she reached him, she saw he was looking at the leg armor. He said, "Let's see that object again." She found her hand had clenched on it so hard that its red imprint showed on her palm and middle finger. She gave it to him with her other hand.

"Look." He held it against a greave made of silk cords, laid tightly side by side and lacquered; the cord binding the edges was riveted in place by rosettes of bronze. They were the same size as Grizel's find, but trefoil shape.

"Oh. You think it came off armor."

"I think there could be a rosette missing from the armor Benet wore. It had this chrysanthemum pattern. Perhaps it's a family crest."

"But how did it get up there on the roof?"

Bone stood up. He linked fingers with her and drew her toward the far end of the gallery. "Guy told his father he'd recognized Josh Lawson; and he said that just after he'd told him, they saw a flash. It may have been lightning. It may have been Lawson using flash." Bone opened a door at the end. It gave onto a spiral stairway. "The turret stair. Up from the garden, where we saw Lawson and Rose and Lynda. Up to the roof."

He shut the door and took her back along the gallery, past the presence in armor on the chair, onto the landing.

"Roke was on the roof?"

"So it appears. Better not show that to Jane. She might realize it could have been Roke who helped Josh Lawson over the edge. Losing that jade collection rankled bitterly."

Chapter

34

ARNOLD MABEY'S KITCHEN SPORTED A CALENDAR, GIVEN HIM by a neighbor last Christmas. Knowing his fondness for visiting historic houses, she had chosen one with views of stately homes, and the November page had a photograph of Chatsworth in lurid color, against a cloudless cobalt-blue sky suggesting some kindly genie had transported it to the South Seas. The October page had a scarlet ring carefully inked round the date of the Buchanan tour's start. This month had another scarlet ring around a date in the third week, not now very far away.

Arnold Mabey sat stirring his tea and contemplating this mark of promise with satisfaction. He had got full value from the last tour, which combined the pleasure of seeing old friends with the drama of losing an old acquaintance. His was not a nature to bear malice, Josh Lawson's sneers had never upset him, and the events at Roke Castle had certainly been the highlights of the year. Neighbors who had done no more than pass the time of day for ages had been calling for a chat, or asked him in for coffee, after they'd seen the television news and heard he'd been there when it happened—for the calendar giver had not kept that knowledge to herself. He had very much enjoyed describing, over and over, what had occurred.

Beside that, he had spent a very pleasant week pasting newspaper cuttings about it into his Tour Scrapbook.

The toaster gave its metallic bark beside him and he juggled out its offering onto his plate and reached for the butter. He was really looking forward to this next trip. While the same excitements could not be hoped for, there was always something to be seen and investigated everywhere you went.

Nicholas Buchanan viewed the date in his diary with unusual pessimism. True there would be no Josh Lawson to keep an eye on, but Arnold Mabey would be there to poke his nose, and his stick, into everything, and there were always the Webbs. Then, although he would enjoy discussing the last tour with the Simpson-Bateses—discreetly, but it was always surprising how uproarious these hobnobbings could become—it hardly made for suitable dinner talk, nor, with the Frobishers and Mrs. Garnett new on the tour, did it serve as an advertisement for the future. He had only penciled in a few ideas for next year's tours, and begun negotiations with likely owners and those who had been willing, but not able, to accommodate a visit in the past. He had a dark vision of some owners saying: Buchanan? Kiss of Death *Buchanan?* No, thank you. It was all very fine for an owner to get a write-up in *Country Life* but making it to the front page of the *Sun* wearing an arrow through the neck

was best left to those with less demanding standards . . .
Then, a few tour people booked for this November had
canceled in spite of forfeiting deposits; rather as if Josh
Lawson, by falling off battlements, had demonstrated how
dangerous visiting old houses could be.

He picked up a letter that had arrived from Noel
Prestbury this morning, saying how sorry he was to cancel
their visit at such short notice but a family matter had
cropped up . . . he had to be out of the country that week
and there would be nobody to show them around Prestbury.
In a pig's eye! With this vulgar mental comment so like
Inspector Prior's, Buchanan folded the letter and wondered
when people would realize that Destiny was unlikely to
accompany him on future trips. His wife assured him that
people would forget, but his reply had been *"When?"* and he
was dead sure—uh-huh, he was very sure indeed—that he
himself never would.

Benjamin Maitland was quite glad he was not due to go;
Catherine and he had had quite enough excitement for the
year, although this was not what he said in his letter of
appreciation to Nicholas Buchanan; nor did he mention,
even to Catherine, that he was haunted by the entirely
irrational sense that his own ill will toward Roke had
somehow contributed to that bizarre death. Easy to mock
primitive feelings, but the less easy substrata of the mind
were not cool, educated, and urbane. One had much rather
not believe in the monsters of the Id.

It was lucky that nobody in the police had discovered that
past grudge against Roke, or he might have been numbered
among the suspects.

Donald Spencer, so conspicuously a suspect, knew nothing about the November tour and wouldn't have cared if
he'd known. The last tour had interested him only because

of the chance to see Roke Castle and its owner. In this, he
had been wholly satisfied. If Benjamin Maitland feared his
own ill will toward Roke might have helped to bring about
his death, Donald Spencer was totally confident that his
had. He had confessed to murdering the man who had
killed his daughter because of this very conviction. That he
could not recount any actual detail of how he had done it
was not important. In his mind he had killed the man. Now
the Inspector had said he was free, that someone else had
confessed. It did not matter so much whom God used to kill
that dreadful creature. He would not have minded prison.
One place was much like another now May was gone. Still,
Dorothy liked to have him back. Indeed she was quite
touching. Really he should think of her more, now they
were each all the other had. People in the village, too, had
come up and said kind things, giving him an impression
that they had been concerned about him, which was odd.

He thought he might go to the allotment. He hadn't
seriously worked on it since May died. He must tidy up, dig
it over, prepare the earth for spring sowing; put in the broad
beans. There were things to do before spring.

Lynda Colindale knew of the November tour but she had
never meant to go. John was hardly likely to be able to
invent another conference. At least the police hadn't come
again. She was fairly sure, as John was, that Lawson's snaps
were to be used to blackmail, and there'd been a moment or
two when she'd feared John, going to confront Lawson to
try to frighten him off, had pushed not just his luck but
Lawson as well; but she believed him when he said he
hadn't been able to find Lawson . . . She shuddered, remembering that swollen face—tried to lessen it by telling
herself flippantly that Lawson had managed the considerable feat of being uglier in death than in life. Somehow the
weekend had managed to put her off John. You couldn't

help associations. There were other pebbles on the beach, after all.

The Simpson-Bates sisters looked forward to the November tour with a pleasure as uncomplicated as Arnold Mabey's. It would be their fourth trip with Nicholas this year. They would see friends and have a lovely morbid gossip about what had happened last time around. They had described the happenings at Roke Castle to neighbors and acquaintances, in mutually corroborated detail and suitably hushed tones, over and again in the past few days; but really only those who had shared the experience could appreciate what it had felt like. Moreover, with Nicholas and one or two of the others, there could be a few enjoyable references in the worst possible taste, uproarious and apt to make them stared at in any hotel's bar lounge or coffee room. Their scrapbook, a combined diary and photo album, now contained a good many press cuttings too, out of a slightly different range of newspapers from Arnold Mabey's. Pride of place was given to their own photograph of Roke, smiling with menacing geniality under the Georgian portico and about to give his spiel about the house. Sheila Simpson-Bates said how lucky it was that she had been inspired to take her customary snap of Owner in Front of House *before* the tour instead of, as usually she did, after it.

The Webbs had no truck with ephemera such as photographs and scrapbooks. Their records, they would have said if anyone asked them, were in their heads, and their most vivid memory of the most recent tour was of missing the last house they were to have visited and not seeing all they had been promised of Roke Castle. Mrs. Webb had written her letter of complaint to Nicholas Buchanan but, in the opinion of them both, had received no very satisfactory reply. A mention of the unlikelihood of their missing anything more for that particular reason; a promise of an extra house on a tour next year; suggestions that the disgraceful occurrences at Roke Castle could be classified as Acts of God and that therefore their complaints could be redirected—all this was clothed in the utmost courtesy and humor, which Mrs. Webb thought ill-placed. They were not mollified. It is possible that as they sat, silent and drinking tea, with Buchanan's letter before them, the November sunlight golden but cool on the graveyard outside their windows, it came into both their minds that another year might find them out there rather than in here, and still short of their rightful visit.

The one member of the last tour with neither regret nor expectations was cremated the day Bone and Grizel left for Tunbridge Wells. Nicholas Buchanan had intended to go to the funeral, but business matters prevented him. The Simpson-Bateses discussed whether to go, until it was after all rather too late, and no one else thought of doing so, nor was one of his relations prepared to pay for a memorial stone for Joshua Lawson.

Chapter

. . . .

35

THERE WERE LONG BUT NOT UNCOMFORTABLE SILENCES ON THE journey from Winterford to Tunbridge Wells. Bone had been touched by Jane's farewell hug and her thanks for his help.

"I don't at all know what we'd have done if you hadn't been there. Thank God Grizel had the sense to marry you. I'm only sorry we gave you such a rotten 'honeymoon.' It would have been appalling if you'd only just been married."

She had, he thought, been on the verge of inviting them to come again and have a better time, when she remembered that it was not her place to ask. Baz had done his bit with a crippling handshake and the heartily expressed wish of seeing them again soon, which was perhaps the nearest *he* cared to get to an invitation for which neither he nor Jane felt able to assume responsibility.

Bone had been touched in a different way by Keziah's embrace, so enthusiastic that her plait, woven that day with purple ribbon and gold baubles, had caught him a bruising smack on the cheekbone. Still, this had earned him a healing kiss from both her and Grizel, so that he had offered to be damaged again.

Even Guy managed a smile as well as a handshake; he was noticeably more cheerful now that it had sunk in that he was free of the burden of inheriting Roke. Angela, too, was restored in looks. To have made a friend of Benet's second wife couldn't have been what she had expected, and Bone imagined they had a lot of reminiscences to catch up on together. Jane was going to need company, yet in the run of things Angela was the last person she could have looked for as a friend. Bone wondered what terms they would have been on if Roke had lived. He thought it would very likely have amused their husband to keep them provoked with each other.

They had been talking at breakfast of a nostalgic visit to Paisley House, to collect the rug Benet had left to Angela, and to discuss with the tenants the possibility of Jane's return.

"D'you think Jane really will go back to Paisley House?" Grizel, as often happened, was thinking his thoughts. Bone opened his mouth to answer and had a Rolo popped into it. He replied less than distinctly.

"They both might. Happy memories. I'm not sure how Baz can keep up the castle with inheritance tax swiping most of the income, but that is, I'm afraid, his problem. I know his stepfather was well off, but that kind of money's far to seek . . . I wonder what Keziah will do?"

"Depends whose son she marries. Baz seems to fancy Keziah and I have a definite suspicion she fancies him back. If Guy goes to Paisley House let's hope there's room for a wildlife park there."

Bone laughed suddenly as he saw what she was saying. "You mean if Baz stays at the castle the alligator would tip the scales. Quite a hefty tip; it's a sturdy animal."

"Please. The alliga*tors*. The mating pair."

The little girl in the car that now overtook them wished, as she caught a glimpse of the two in the front seats, that her parents, who had been squabbling with great concentration for the last hour, would laugh like that.

"I bet you haven't had as exciting a time as I had." Cha was sprawled in scarlet leggings and an enormous sweater the color of a new chestnut, stroking reluctant Ziggy while Grizel's cat, The Bruce, stropped one side of its head and then the other on her shoe. "We went to a hundred *châteaux*, Grue got off with a French boy, he looked like a rat but he was seriously sexy, and Miss Wallace got stung by a wasp *on her thigh* in the middle of the square in Rouen, and she hauled up her skirt in front of *tout le monde;* and Mrs. Garland got kissed by a boozy restaurateur, and I learned lots of French and I can order almost anything—" She gazed up at them triumphantly and Bone thought, *she doesn't have to grow up so fast, why can't she slow down?* Cha misread his expression and sat up abruptly. "Did it rain all the time? We had fantastic weather, tons hotter than here and everyone was wishing they'd brought more tee shirts. Grue wore shorts the whole time and I got so *bored* with cotton trousers." Charlotte's damaged leg had a gouged-out scar and a tracery of stitch marks. She would not show it among strangers.

Ziggy squeezed through her grasp like toothpaste from a tube and thumped to the floor, walking off with switching tail to express his opinion of those who went away leaving him to be fed by strangers and then expected cuddles when they got back.

The Bruce, in silent trade union solidarity, abandoned

Cha's feet and stalked off in the opposite direction. She watched them go.

"D'you think they got fed properly? They're so cross."

"You know how they like to play you up." Grizel began sorting out the biology folders she'd stashed in a cupboard recklessly before they left, and The Bruce came to get in her way. She pulled him out of the cupboard with cobweb on his whiskers. "Did you eat well?"

Cha turned up her eyes. "Yummy. Well, most of it. Grue says we'll empty the school tomorrow at assembly with our garlic fumes, with just the Mallet left choking on the platform." She drew herself up, Bone recognizing the straight spine of the headmistress, and then collapsed in hammed-up retching coughs that alarmed the cats.

"Didn't you finish your assignment?" Grizel had opened a folder and was surveying the last page. Her tone had been neutrally inquiring, but Cha's was defensive at once.

"I was going to. There just wasn't time with getting ready for the trip and everything, sorting clothes—"

"All right," Grizel said mildly. "This is not your wicked stepmother speaking. Do you want to have it now and do some before Monday? I've got several to finish correcting."

Cha flung up her arms. "Honestly! Work, work, work. Nobody'd think you'd been on a honeymoon. I thought you'd be having such a lovely romantic time and come back all sweet."

"There were interruptions," Bone said dryly, "but I was in very good company."

"Tell Cha what happened." Grizel spread folders on the floor and got down among them. The phone rang.

"It'll be Grue." Cha reached for the receiver, said, "Hello you. I'll go to the other phone—this place is littered with olds," and hurried upstairs. Bone, hearing her voice as she answered in his bedroom, put the receiver back.

He possessed himself of the week's pile of mail and of the

sofa, while Grizel lifted The Bruce off the page she was trying to assess. They heard Charlotte shrieking incredulity upstairs.

"There's quite a promising notice here from Molony." Bone made a dart of the estate agent's blurb and wafted it at Grizel, who put her hand on it and went on working; she sat up after a minute and was reading it when Cha came bounding down the stairs and marched accusingly into the room.

" 'Tell Cha what happened!' " she said. " 'Tell Cha'—you had a *murder* and you've been back half an hour and never said a *word!* How mean can you *get?*"

"Try me." Bone had injudiciously opened an envelope before realizing that it screamed on the outside: *OPEN WITHOUT DELAY—YOU MAY HAVE WON £150,000.* The actual letter, with a matched-in *Dear Mr. Bone,* asked if he wanted to give the Bone household the treat of seeing a luxury car outside the matched-in address. Bone thought it wouldn't be there long before it was towed away. "I'm so mean," he said, "that I'm not even applying for my free gift." He was about to junk the packet when it was twitched from his hand sharply by the youngest member of the Bone household, who had got down on one knee before him in a petitionary attitude. He wondered if the remarkably blond streaks in her hair were sun-bleached or of chemical origin, and whether Grizel could help him to find some earrings like the dangly ethnic ones Keziah wore, for Cha's imminent birthday.

His knees were being pounded.

"TELL! Grue said her mother said it was in all the papers, absolutely like a video nasty or something . . ." She stopped and looked back at Grizel. Her tone changed. "It was your friend's husband, though, wasn't it? It must have been really absolutely awful." From her altered expression as she turned back to her father, she had understood why their host's death had not been the excited topic of conversation from the moment they got home.

Grizel snapped a folder shut and picked up another. "We survived. I didn't know Benet myself before. We hadn't met before last Friday. It was Jane I was worried for. Your father kept his hand in by finding out who did it. Could someone make some tea?"

"But Grue said a Chief Inspector or someone made the arrest. You weren't in the papers at all. If Grue's mother hadn't known where you were going she wouldn't have known it was anything to do with you. Why did that Inspector get all the credit?" She had scrambled indignantly to her feet.

Bone pointed past her at the kitchen. "Etiquette. The local people make the arrest. But anyway I wanted to stay out of it."

Ziggy in the kitchen was making his feelings known by licking an empty saucer steadily across the floor until it clunked against the cooker.

"But it's not fair. I mean, it *isn't*. All right, Zig, I'm coming. You should have the credit. Why should you stay out of it?" Cha had gone into the kitchen. She called again, "It's not *fair*."

The Bruce trotted purposefully into the kitchen. Bone's eye met Grizel's as she looked up from her work. Perhaps she was thinking, as he was, of Lawson's death, conceivably at Roke's hands. Prior had said no word to Bone about any possible reversal of his original theory: that Lawson had killed Roke and then started like a guilty thing when surprised on the tower, and gone over. Prior had settled for the convenient probability of an accident. There had been no evidence to make the coroner doubt it.

"Some secrets are best kept."

"I'll remember that," Charlotte retorted, spooning catfood. "I'll remember that when I whip out a darling little surprise grandchild suddenly one day." She appeared in the doorway, beaming wickedly. "You'll have to grin and bear it, like me." Overcome by her wit, she rushed back into the kitchen and, laughing maniacally, helped Ziggy to clatter his saucer.

Bone gazed severely at his wife, who was laughing too. "The control of that object in the kitchen is what I married you for, you know."

"Yes, I know it. In fact, that was my real purpose in marrying you. But you must pull your weight as well, Robert. Idleness doesn't suit you at all. It's quite time you got back to work."

Bone found that this was exactly what he was looking forward to.